A KINGDOM RISES

Read the Crown of Three series

CROWN OF THREE

J. D. RINEHART

◆ BOOK THREE ◆

A KINGDOM RISES

ALADDIN

New York London Toronto Sydney New Delhi

If you purchased this book without a cover, you should be aware that this book is stolen property. It was reported as "unsold and destroyed" to the publisher, and neither the author nor the publisher has received any payment for this "stripped book."

This book is a work of fiction. Any references to historical events, real people, or real places are used fictitiously. Other names, characters, places, and events are products of the author's imagination, and any resemblance to actual events or places or persons, living or dead, is entirely coincidental.

ALADDIN
An imprint of Simon & Schuster Children's Publishing Division
1230 Avenue of the Americas, New York, New York 10020
First Aladdin paperback edition May 2018
Text copyright © 2017 by Working Partners Limited
Cover illustration copyright © 2017 by Iacopo Bruno
Also available in an Aladdin hardcover edition.
All rights reserved, including the right of reproduction in whole or in part in any form.
ALADDIN and related logo are registered trademarks of Simon & Schuster, Inc.
For information about special discounts for bulk purchases, please contact Simon & Schuster Special Sales at 1-866-506-1949 or business@simonandschuster.com.
The Simon & Schuster Speakers Bureau can bring authors to your live event. For more information or to book an event contact the Simon & Schuster Speakers Bureau at 1-866-248-3049 or visit our website at www.simonspeakers.com.
Book design by Laura Lyn DiSiena
The text of this book was set in Oneleigh Pro.
Manufactured in the United States of America 0418 OFF
2 4 6 8 10 9 7 5 3 1
The Library of Congress has cataloged the hardcover edition as follows:
Names: Rinehart, J. D., author.
Title: A kingdom rises / by J.D. Rinehart.
Description: First Aladdin hardcover edition. | New York : Aladdin, 2017. |
Series: Crown of three ; 3 | Summary: Just when Tarlan is about to give up on the prophecy that he is one of the triplets destined to bring peace to the land, he meets his long-lost brother, Gulph, and sister, Elodie, as well as their supporters, and they travel together to make a final stand against Lord Vicerin in an attempt to end the Thousand Year War and unite the realms.
Identifiers: LCCN 2016043474 (print) | LCCN 2017022091 (eBook) |
ISBN 9781481424516 (eBook) | ISBN 9781481424493 (hc)
Subjects: | CYAC: Triplets—Fiction. | Brothers and sisters—Fiction. |
Kings, queens, rulers, etc.—Fiction. | Prophecies—Fiction. |
War—Fiction. | Magic—Fiction. | Fantasy.
Classification: LCC PZ7.1.R57 (eBook) | LCC PZ7.1.R57 Ki 2017 (print) |
DDC [Fic]—dc23
LC record available at https://lccn.loc.gov/2016043474
ISBN 9781481424509 (pbk)

Special thanks to Graham Edwards

For R. K.

In Toronia, realm of three,

A tempest has long raged.

By power's potent siren call,

Weak men are enslaved.

Too much virtuous blood has spilt

In this accursed age.

When the stars increase by three

The kingdom shall be saved.

Beneath these fresh celestial lights,

Three new heirs will enter in.

They shall summon unknown power,

They shall kill the cursed king.

With three crowns they shall ascend,

And true peace, they will bring.

—*Gryndor, first wizard of Toronia*

PROLOGUE

Gryndor the wizard plucked a small pebble from the crystal bowl and spun it in his bony fingers. The pebble was smooth and milky white. In the bowl were thousands of other pebbles, each one a different shape and color.

My stones, Gryndor thought. *My magic.*

The bowl stood on a crystal table beneath the darkened window of Gryndor's tower. Outside, he could see red-and-black striped flags dancing on the night breeze, high above the magnificent sprawl of King Warryck's ruby palace. Surrounding the palace was the crystal realm of Celestis, the City of Stars. Its diamond roofs glistened under the moonlit sky, and its streets of sapphire shone like rivers. Surrounding the city were the defensive walls, higher this year than last.

Gryndor eyed them with worry. *If only we could keep the war at bay for one more season.*

Close by, his fellow wizards shifted impatiently.

"I am anxious to see what you would show us, Gryndor," said Hathka. His dark skin gleamed in the warm night air.

"And *I* am anxious to return to my work," grumbled Ravgar. Her face was as pale as Hathka's was dark, and her expression was even more sour than usual.

Gryndor stroked his thick, gray beard. Usually when he called Hathka and Ravgar to his tower, it was to share some new spell or to talk through whatever magical theory he'd been working on. But already those days seemed long gone.

"I too am anxious," he told them. He picked up his gnarled wooden staff. "Let me show you why."

Gryndor strode across the wide, circular chamber. His silver cloak swished dust from the floor. Hathka and Ravgar followed. As he walked, Gryndor's old bones creaked, and he was glad to have the staff to lean on.

A red spot marked the middle of the room, the only point of color on the white crystal. Bending stiffly, Gryndor placed the pebble he was holding on the spot, then straightened again.

"Old ocean bring stone," he chanted. "Stone bring magic. Magic bring truth. Truth bring enlightenment . . ."

He began to speak more rapidly, the words tumbling over each other. As he recited the spell, his mind flew back in time to his first days as an awakening wizard.

I walked along the Beach of the First Day, and the sea washed up the pebbles, and I gathered them up, and that was when I learned that every wizard's magic has its own unique song.

My song is stone.

"...stone roll wide, stone roll far. Stone show us one world, three realms. Show us true, stone. Show us true."

He broke off, gasping for breath. His body felt stiffer than ever, as if it too were made of stone. Hathka and Ravgar pressed close against him, one on each side, peering down at the little white pebble.

Except now the pebble was no longer small. It had grown enormous beyond measure. Or perhaps it was the three wizards who had shrunk.

Perhaps both these things are true, Gryndor mused as he gazed down at the world-sized stone, over which they now flew like birds.

Hathka laughed and spread his arms like wings.

"This is dangerous magic," grunted Ravgar. "What if we fall?"

"We will not fall."

Gryndor pointed with his staff. At the gesture, he and his companions began to sink toward the gigantic stone disc. Colored patterns appeared on the surface of the stone.

"It's a map of the kingdom!" cried Hathka.

"See Ritherlee," said Gryndor, pointing to a vast patch of grassland to their left.

"And there's Isur." Hathka indicated an equally large swath of dark forest ahead. "And there's Celestis! It's so bright."

Ravgar looked unimpressed. "Gryndor, we are all familiar with the three realms of Toronia. Your map is very clever, but do we really need—"

"Hush," said Gryndor. "Keep looking."

The closer they flew to the map, the more detail they saw. First towns, then individual buildings, finally people.

"Hundreds of them!" Hathka gasped. "No, thousands! And why are they . . . ?" His voice trailed away.

"You wonder why they are fighting?" said Gryndor.

The three wizards watched in silence as, far below them, battle raged. All across Toronia, ordinary people were fighting with farm tools and makeshift weapons against a common enemy: soldiers dressed in black and red.

"But that is the royal army," said Hathka in dismay. "Why is King Warryck fighting his own people?"

As Gryndor guided them closer to Ritherlee, it became clear that many of the fields were bare of grass. Thin figures trudged across the muddy plains, stooped and weary.

Hathka gave a cry of outrage. Ravgar's mouth set in a grim line.

"This too is King Warryck's work," said Gryndor. "He has

bled his people dry. No sooner do the crops of Ritherlee grow ripe than he takes them for the palace kitchens. While Warryck grows fat, his people starve."

Now they soared over Isur, where tiny people were felling trees and erecting sinister-looking towers.

"Hunting is forbidden for all but the king and his men. Those who defy the law are hanged. You think Isur is a realm of woodland? It has become a land of the gallows."

With a flick of his staff, Gryndor flew them to Celestis.

"As for the City of Stars," he went on, "nobody now can afford the taxes demanded by Warryck's collectors. The people of Celestis have nothing. All across Toronia, people have nothing. Is it any wonder there is rebellion?"

"I have spent too much time locked away with my studies," breathed Hathka. "I had not seen this suffering."

"The time for study is past," said Gryndor. "The time for action has come."

"Action?" said Ravgar. "Gryndor, we want to end these injustices. But we are wizards, not warriors."

"Nevertheless, we must act." Gryndor pointed at the columns of soldiers streaming out from the walls of Celestis. "More garrisons of the king's army, on their way to put down the rebels. Too many have already died. And this is just the start. Unless we act now, a full-blown war will come to Toronia."

Hathka looked horrified. "Surely it won't come to that. Even Warryck must see sense, sooner or later."

Gryndor suddenly clenched his fist. "What if I told you this war will last for a thousand years? What if I told you that death will not be measured in thousands, but millions?"

"How can you know that?" Hathka quavered.

"My stones," said Gryndor. "They have shown me all I need to know—that what we see now is nothing compared to what comes next. One thousand years of darkness. One thousand years of suffering. This is the future . . . unless we prevent it."

Ravgar's eyes narrowed with suspicion. "And what exactly are you suggesting we should do?"

"We must bring down the king!"

Gryndor waved his staff in a wide circle. The map fell away, the three realms of Toronia dwindling to mere specks as the magic collapsed, until once more the three wizards were standing in the topmost chamber of the crystal tower.

To Gryndor's surprise, Ravgar laughed. "Kill the king? A bold idea indeed! I for one would not be sorry to see that tyrant's head on a spike. I wish you luck with your quest."

But Hathka was shaking his head. "Gryndor . . . what of the prophecy? If we wait, won't the prophecy save Toronia from war?"

"Prophecy?" snapped Ravgar. "Pah! It is nothing but a tale for babes. Three children born to a king under the light of enchanted stars? Three children destined to save Toronia? Hathka, do you truly believe everything Gryndor tells you?"

Gryndor scooped up the milky-white pebble and dropped it in his pocket. *Even here a battle rages. If we wizards cannot live peacefully together, what hope is there for the rest of the kingdom?*

"The prophecy may be mine to tell," he said heavily, "but it is not of my making, as well you know, Ravgar. It is of the stars, as are we all in the end."

"If you think your prophecy will—"

"I do not think. I know. The prophecy has been made. But it will not come to pass yet, Ravgar. Not yet."

Returning to the window, Gryndor plunged his fingers into his collection of stones and swirled them around. The stones chimed against each other, ringing like bells.

"I cannot do this without you, my friends," he said, his voice low and earnest. "If I alone confront Warryck, I will fail. But he cannot stand against three wizards. No man can. Join with me, please, and together we can save Toronia."

Hathka gulped, seemed to consider this for a moment, then came over to the window. He seized Gryndor's hand. "I am yours to command, Gryndor."

Gryndor turned to Ravgar and raised his eyebrows. Ravgar frowned, her mouth compressed to a thin, white line.

"I have no faith in prophecies," she said at last. "But I do believe in justice. I will join you, Gryndor."

"When do we strike?" Hathka asked.

From outside, roars of laughter filled the night. The windows of the royal banqueting hall were brightly lit, the scent of smoke and roasted meat drifting on the air.

"The king is feasting," Gryndor said.

Realization dawned on Ravgar's pale face. "He will not be expecting a fight," she said slowly.

Gryndor nodded. "We may not have a better opportunity."

Now that the moment had come, his back felt as straight as it had when he was a young apprentice. His fingers flexed, eager for the fight.

"Let us strike now."

Snatching up their staffs, the three wizards raced for the door. Ravgar, ever competitive, lunged past them both and was first to close her fingers on the handle.

There was a hissing sound.

Gryndor stopped in his tracks, staring in shock at the spluttering strands of light that had suddenly appeared around the doorframe.

"Firedust!" he cried. He raised his staff.

Too late.

The door erupted into flame. A hot fist of air slammed into Gryndor and threw him backward. He landed hard, the breath flying from his lungs. White fire blazed furiously in the remains of the doorway. Inside its glow, Gryndor could just make out the twisted forms of two figures. Little remained of them but bones. Even as he watched, the brittle skeletons collapsed to ash.

Hathka and Ravgar were gone.

The floor was shaking. A crack raced up the crystal wall behind Gryndor. Dense, white smoke poured through it. A second crack opened in the floor, growing wider. The whole tower was ripping itself apart.

Gryndor struggled painfully to his feet, his heart filled with grief and dread. Warryck had done this, he was certain—he must have guessed Gryndor would strike, so had his chamber rigged with fire-dust to take him down. But did Warryck know what would happen when a wizard was killed?

Let alone two wizards?

The crack in the floor was widening into a chasm. Driving his aching bones into action, Gryndor leaped across it. In the doorway, the firedust continued to burn, white-hot. Behind him, the smoke was a thick, stinging fog.

Gryndor realized his hands were empty. He glanced back across the chasm. His eyes fell on a pile of wooden splinters.

My staff!

A tongue of fire belched from the doorway. Gryndor ducked beneath it and hobbled toward the window, his eyes fixed on the bowl of pebbles. Five steps short of his goal, he saw the tower tip sideways. The bowl flew from the sill, showering the pebbles across the tiles and into the huge crack in the floor.

My magic!

Another enormous crack split the entire tower in two. This time, what poured in was not smoke but starlight. Gryndor staggered toward it. Another tremendous concussion rocked the tower. Shards of crystal fell from the ceiling. Gryndor dodged two, but a third—a cruel diamond blade as tall as a man—sliced deep into his chest.

Howling against the pain, Gryndor pulled himself free and thrust himself through the crack. Emerging onto the open staircase that encircled the tower, he stopped again, horrified by what he saw. Fire had broken out across the whole of Celestis. The crystal streets were filled with people fighting, running, shrieking. On the roof of the palace, the flags burned.

But that wasn't the worst of it. The entire city had . . . *tipped*. For every building still standing, two had collapsed onto their sides. As Gryndor watched, the shining realm of Celestis broke into a patchwork of crystal pieces. It looked like a child's puzzle torn apart by its owner in a sudden fit of rage.

See what you have done, Warryck! By killing Hathka and Ravgar, you have killed Celestis, too!

The city tilted further. Gryndor clung to the crystal balustrade, ignoring the blood pumping from the wound in his chest, the agony that coursed through his whole body.

Below, the palace outbuildings had been reduced to a mess of broken crystal. People ran screaming through the ruins, only to be crushed by falling walls, or swallowed by fresh holes opening up beneath their feet.

Gryndor looked up.

His own humble tower was just one small part of a much greater structure: the Sky Tower, tallest in the realm. Alone in all the buildings of Celestis, it remained standing.

The staircase he was standing on led directly to it.

It's waiting for me.

Grimacing with pain, he staggered up the stairs. With every step he took up, he felt Celestis lurch down beneath him. All around the perimeter of the city, gigantic fingers of rock were rearing up. As Celestis fell, so the land was beginning to close over it.

As he continued his painful ascent, Gryndor wondered what Hathka and Ravgar were experiencing. Wizards could not enter the Realm of the Dead. Somewhere their disembodied spirits bored their way out of this world and into the next, leaving chaos and destruction in their wake.

He wondered where it was that they were going.

Soon I will not have to wonder. He pressed his trembling hand to the bloom of blood on his robe. *Soon I will be going there myself.*

But not before completing his final task.

Another bout of agonized climbing brought Gryndor to the very top of the Sky Tower. He wasted no more time with the spectacle of the collapsing city. Instead, he turned his attention to what he'd known was waiting for him.

The three crystal statues were huge—each one as big as ten men. Their snakelike bodies coiled in muscular knots of green emerald. Beneath each crystalline belly was tucked a pair of birdlike legs; from each back sprouted a pair of vast green wings. Gold-flecked eyes of dazzling red ruby glared from beneath angry reptilian brows.

The wyverns!

Gryndor dragged himself across the tower roof. In the light of the watching stars, the trail of blood he left was thick and dark.

Fingers shaking, he slipped his hand into the pocket of his robe. He drew out the pebble he'd dropped in there.

The last of my magic.

"Stone bring sky," he croaked, appalled at how weak his voice sounded. "Sky bring flight. Flight bring all to final right."

He tightened his fingers on the milky-white stone. The pebble shattered, driving splinters deep into his flesh. Gryndor paid them no heed. His attention was captured entirely by the wyverns.

As one, the three serpents uncoiled. Their crystal bodies flexed and creaked. Their wings extended like vast emerald sails, caught the air, and began to flap. Their clawed feet rose from their pedestals. Their jaws opened, revealing vicious ruby teeth. And they screeched.

As the birth-cries of the wyverns filled the sky, Gryndor fell onto his side. His work was done. All that remained was to die.

The realization made him desperately sad. Even worse was the knowledge that, with Celestis fallen, his worst fears would surely come to pass.

"One thousand years of darkness," he murmured. "One thousand years of suffering."

He gazed up at the wyverns as they soared against the stars.

Oh, he thought in wonder. *You are magnificent!*

His breath was ragged in his broken chest. Beneath him, the tower tottered as it began its final, fatal collapse. At least Melchior was safe, far away in his forest workshop, a young apprentice wizard dutifully learning all he was bound to learn as Gryndor's apprentice. The thought made Gryndor glad.

If only I had taught you the prophecy, Melchior. Will you ever learn of its existence? Will any of my books survive for you to find? When the prophecy stars finally shine out, and the three are born who will lead Toronia back into the light, will you know what to do?

Mustering the last of his strength, he shouted up to the circling wyverns, "Find a safe place in the world! Go there, and wait! If the prophecy should falter, then you will come to Toronia's aid! Then you will fly again!"

With a colossal, grinding roar, the Sky Tower pitched sideways. Gryndor looked on in horror as the nearest of the three wyverns was struck by a flying chunk of crystal. The creature's wing exploded into hundreds of glittering fragments. With a dreadful snapping sound, its neck broke in two.

Then, just like Celestis, the wyvern's lifeless body fell.

Gryndor was no longer in pain. All he felt now was despair, and that was much, much worse. The wyverns had been his last chance to protect the prophecy. Now they were dying before his eyes.

All is lost. The prophecy will fail. Toronia is doomed.

Then he fell into the abyss. Before the earth closed over him, Gryndor had one final opportunity to look up at the stars.

And the stars looked back.

ACT ONE

1,013 Years Later

CHAPTER 1

Tarlan slumped facedown on Theeta's back. His breath rasped in his smoke-scorched throat. His face was wet with tears.

Away, he thought. *It's time to go far, far away.*

He pulled himself to the downy hollow that lay between Theeta's warm neck and her huge, beating wings. After resting there for a moment, he stuck his head out into the open air and peered down.

Far below, the city of Idilliam burned. As Tarlan watched, the spindly tower rising from the ruins of Castle Tor crumbled and vanished into the smoke. Only moments earlier, he and Theeta had been swooping over the top of that very tower in an effort to save Gulph.

But we failed! My brother fell—and I never even got a chance to meet him!

Yet he hadn't fallen alone. As they'd flown past, Theeta had shoved the undead monster King Brutan into the flames too.

Brutan the tyrant, father to Tarlan, Gulph, and their sister, Elodie, was now just ash on the wind.

"We got justice, Theeta," Tarlan said through his tears. "Brutan killed Gulph, but he paid." He swallowed hard. "It isn't enough, though. It will never be enough."

Theeta remained silent.

"What was it all for?" Tarlan sat up, wiping angrily at his wet face. "The battle at Deep Poynt? All for nothing!"

"Star story," croaked Theeta. "Life light."

The thorrod's strange way of speaking frequently left Tarlan puzzled. Not this time.

"I don't care about the prophecy! I don't care about my so-called destiny. So what if some old legend says that Gulph, Elodie, and I are supposed to rule Toronia? Oh yes, our father's dead, like the prophecy said, but things are worse than ever. Gulph's dead! Elodie's turned traitor! As for me . . ."

He broke off.

I won't cry again! I won't!

"I'm done with humans. Just give me clean air, and a stream to drink from. That's all I had in Yalasti. I should have stayed there."

"Fly far," said Theeta.

"That's right, Theeta. Far away." Tarlan took in a deep breath, let it out slowly. "But there's one thing I have to do first."

Tugging gently at the ruff of golden feathers around Theeta's neck, Tarlan steered the thorrod away from the burning wreckage of Idilliam and back toward the green forest realm of Isur. Before long, they were circling over Deep Poynt.

As Theeta approached the slopes surrounding the fortified hilltop town, Tarlan's heart lurched. Where it wasn't scorched by fire, the battlefield was torn to mud. Tarlan saw that littering the ground, lying in pools of their own blood, were the bodies of bears and horses, tigrons and wolves. His loyal friends, who'd fought beside him. Who'd fought *for* him. All dead. He stifled a moan.

I had no right to lead them into battle, he berated himself. *What did it matter to those poor creatures who rules this land? Toronians, Galadronians . . . what's the difference?*

Turning his attention to the town itself, Tarlan watched as a group of men erected scaffolding around a jagged hole in the circular defensive wall. Once, this had been the gateway to Deep Poynt. Now the townsfolk were laboring to repair the considerable damage caused by the Galadronian war machines.

Directing the work was the Defender of Deep Poynt, a giant of a man with a bright thatch of red hair, known as The Hammer. Beside him stood a wizened old man in a grubby yellow robe. As Theeta's shadow passed over them, both men looked up.

Theeta opened her beak and screeched. The men repairing the town defenses clapped their hands to their ears. Even the animals lying wounded or wandering among the dead raised their heads to see what the commotion was.

Among them were two more thorrods.

"Nasheen!" Tarlan shouted. "Kitheen!"

The enormous birds lifted their wings and screeched back their greetings. A little of the weight lifted from Tarlan's heart.

My friends! My pack!

Theeta landed beside the thorrods and touched her beak to theirs, each in turn. As she was doing this, a blur of blue and white sprinted over the grass and leaped onto her back. Tarlan wrapped his arms round the young tigron's neck and allowed her to cover his face with hot, slobbering licks.

Filos purred. "I'm glad to see you, Tarlan!"

"Enough, Filos! You'll drown me!"

Filos tugged him to the ground, where Greythorn and Brock were waiting. Tarlan embraced the wolf and the bear in turn, taking care to be gentle with Greythorn's wounds.

"How's your sight?" Tarlan said, stroking the matted fur around the wolf's left eye. The eye itself was filmed over white.

"One eye does me well enough," Greythorn replied.

"Brock killed many enemies!" thundered the bear. He flexed two sets of massive claws in front of Tarlan's face. "Brock will fight whenever Tarlan commands!"

Tarlan pushed Brock's paws firmly away. "I won't be asking you to fight again, Brock. I won't be asking anything of you at all."

The big bear's brow contracted into shaggy confusion. "Brock does not understand."

Filos nuzzled his hand. "Tarlan? What's wrong?"

Tarlan ruffled the fur behind the tigron's pointed ears. "Nothing. Everything's going to be all right."

They were all looking at him expectantly: Filos and Greythorn, Brock and the thorrods. Behind them, a much larger group of animals and birds had begun to gather, the survivors of the animal army Tarlan had led against the invading Galadronians. His pack.

"Tarlan!"

A bony hand planted itself on Tarlan's shoulder and spun him round. Tarlan found himself face-to-face with the old man in the yellow robe.

"Melchior," he grunted. "I'm not staying."

The wizard frowned, multiplying the wrinkles on his age-worn face. He rubbed a bony hand through his matted white beard. "What do you mean, Tarlan?"

"Leave me alone!"

The frown became a look of concern. "What happened in Idilliam? Did you find Gulph?"

Tarlan pulled away. "I was too late! He died! Are you satisfied now?"

A ripple of growls moved through the watching crowd of animals. Melchior's eyes grew wide.

"Dead?" said the wizard, leaning heavily on his wooden staff. "Do you mean . . . ?"

"What do you think I mean? Gulph is dead. So your precious prophecy is dead too."

"What happened?"

Tarlan glared at him. "What does it matter?"

"Tell me."

"He fell into the fire. Is that enough for you? The whole city was burning and Gulph fell into it."

"But did you *see* him die?"

Tarlan shook his head. "I didn't need to. Nobody could have survived those flames. Nobody! Gulph is gone! And soon . . ."

Tarlan bit back the words. Turning his back on Melchior, he knelt before his pack.

"I'm sorry," he said, bringing his anger back under control. "I should never have asked you to fight for such a worthless cause. You're better off without me, all of you."

Both Greythorn and Filos stared at him in shock. Brock the bear shifted uncomfortably from one paw to the other. Nasheen and Kitheen lowered their heads. When Tarlan looked toward Theeta, she fixed him with her most piercing glare.

"You're free," he went on, the words choking in his throat. "All of you, free to go your own way. You don't have to follow me anymore."

Silence descended. Dampness from the grass soaked into Tarlan's worn leggings. He waited for them to reply. At the same time, he hoped they would say nothing.

"When you found me," said Greythorn at last, "I was a prisoner in Vicerin's castle. You released me." The gray wolf fixed Tarlan with his one good eye. "You freed me long ago, Tarlan. If I follow you now, it is because I choose to."

"You saved my life," said Filos. "Where you go, I go."

"You opened Brock's cage," rumbled the bear, looking lost.

From behind them—seemingly from across the entire battlefield—a discontented growl began to rise. The collective unhappiness of Tarlan's pack.

Exchanging an inscrutable thorrod glance, Nasheen and Kitheen stepped forward together. To Tarlan's surprise, it was the black-breasted Kitheen, normally so reluctant to speak, who voiced their thoughts.

"Stay, boy," cawed the giant bird. His eyes were dark and ferocious.

I can't, thought Tarlan, scrambling to his feet. *One moment longer and I won't be able to go through with this.*

He turned to Theeta, only to discover she'd flown silently to an empty spot on a nearby slope. From that distance she stared at him, her expression unreadable, her wings wide and poised for further flight.

"I'm sorry," he said to the others. "Good-bye."

His heart breaking, he turned his back on them and walked toward where Theeta was waiting. No sooner had he begun to move than Melchior was blocking his path.

"Tarlan, you're wrong." The wizard's voice was soft but strong. "The prophecy is not over. If you leave now—"

"I *am* leaving!" Tarlan tried to push past the wizard, but Melchior's hand seized his wrist. "Let me go! Didn't you hear me? Gulph's dead! Elodie's gone back to the Vicerins! It's over!"

"But don't you see? Gulph might still be alive. You and Gulph and Elodie are destined to rule Toronia. The prophecy says so, and the prophecy is powerful. More powerful than the fire you saw, more powerful than any of us can comprehend. Even an old wizard like me."

"Yes! Listen to the wizard!" boomed a new voice.

Over Melchior's shoulder, Tarlan saw The Hammer striding up. Behind the big man came a straggle of Deep Poynt townsfolk. Tarlan groaned. So much for leaving without a fuss.

"The prophecy brings hope," The Hammer continued. "Without hope, we are nothing."

"Then we're nothing," cried another voice from the crowd. "The boy's right. It's all been in vain."

More shouts rose up.

"What about the prophecy?"

"Forget the boy! We've a town to rebuild!"

"Listen to The Hammer!"

The voices blurred into meaningless chatter. Tarlan wrenched free from Melchior and ran to Theeta. He pressed his forehead against the huge, hooked beak of his closest friend.

"Tarlan go," Theeta croaked softly. "Theeta go."

You think you understand, Tarlan thought. *But you don't.*

"I'm sorry, Theeta. But I have to leave you, too. I'm . . . I'm not safe to be around."

"Theeta go," the thorrod repeated.

"No. Stay with the others. Look after them. They're going to need you."

Theeta swiveled her massive head to stare down the slope to where the other thorrods stood. The rest of Tarlan's pack pressed close against the flanks of the giant birds, looking confused and anxious. The people of Deep Poynt, including The Hammer, had fallen silent and were watching Tarlan with open curiosity. And why not? Had he not so long ago told them he was their king?

Melchior, the wizard who seemed always to know what to do, stood motionless, his wrinkled face drawn down into a mask of sadness.

Tarlan looked deep into Theeta's eyes.

You found me. He didn't trust himself to speak. If he opened his mouth, all that would come out would be the splintering sound of his own breaking heart. *You saved me when I was a*

25

baby, lost in the snow. You brought me to Mirith, the frost witch who was like a mother to me, when my own true mother was lost.

But you, Theeta . . . it was you who really brought me into the world.

He cupped his hand against the lethally sharp tip of Theeta's beak. The tiniest movement from the thorrod would have driven a hole through the middle of his palm. It was the ultimate display of trust.

"Good-bye, Theeta."

His feet dragging through the mud, Tarlan walked away.

For the first fifty paces, he had to pick through the ruts and scars of the battle-torn earth. Eventually the descending slope turned to rough pasture, and the going became easier. Ahead rose the waiting wall of the Isurian forest. All the way to the trees, Tarlan plodded with his head down, each footstep a dull echo of his thudding pulse. There were no thoughts in his head, just a thick roaring sound. He wasn't stepping out into the world, he was sinking into it, as a boy might sink into quicksand. The world would draw him down until it closed over his head. After that, all would be dark.

A faint rustling sound penetrated his daze. Blinking, he looked first around, then up. A shadow flitted over his head. Warm air wafted his face. Sunlight flashed, dazzling him.

Shielding his eyes, Tarlan watched in wonder as Theeta dropped from the sky to land an arm's length in front of him. Her golden feathers were ablaze. The sun reflected in the depths of her piercing black eyes.

"Tarlan go," the thorrod croaked. "Theeta go. We go."

"But—"

"No speak. We go."

The golden light filled Tarlan's head, driving away his powers of speech. No words, no thought. No people, no pack. Just him and Theeta.

Tarlan climbed onto her back. The thorrod kicked the ground with her huge talons. Her broad gold wings pumped the air once, twice, a hundred times. The world fell away. The high air was pure, like a cold mountain stream. Tarlan breathed it in and felt clean.

"Thorrod fly," said Theeta. "Fly far. Never stop."

It wasn't in the nature of thorrods to ask questions, but Theeta's slow circling told Tarlan she was waiting for instructions. He looked down at the forest, now a sun-dusted patchwork of green, then back over his shoulder toward the south, where his icy homeland of Yalasti lay.

Tarlan turned his attention north. He had no idea what lay in that direction. He'd never been there.

"That way, Theeta." The feel of his voice was amazing in his throat, as if he'd never spoken words before. "North, until the sun goes down. Then we'll stop to rest. After that, we'll go on."

"Never stop," said Theeta, powering ahead through the crisp, bright sky.

"That's right, my friend. We'll never stop."

CHAPTER 2

E lodie stared at the ghost's face. Everything else faded: the stone walls of her cell at the top of the White Tower, the blackness of the night beyond the barred window, Sylva and Cedric rising slowly to their feet beside her. And Samial, so often serious, grinning.

The ghost, who in life had gone by the name of Lady Darrand, said, "What is your command?"

An old expression came to Elodie, one that people used in Ritherlee whenever they felt nervous or excited: *I've got a moth in my stomach.* Except Elodie didn't have just one moth: she had hundreds.

"Freedom," she replied to the ghost of Lady Darrand. "That is my command. Freedom and victory!"

Her heart was racing. She knew—suddenly *knew* with a certainty that took her breath away—that her days of imprisonment were over.

That everything was about to change.

Lady Darrand rose to her feet. Her yellow robe fluttered against her shining armor. Sheathing her sword, she looked from Elodie to Sylva and Cedric, then fixed her gaze on Samial.

"You are like me," she said slowly. She half turned, indicating the line of phantoms who stood swaying behind her—the nobles of Ritherlee who, like her, had been slaughtered by Lord Vicerin mere days before. "You are . . . dead."

"But not forgotten, my lady," Samial replied, still grinning. "Elodie has seen to that. She saw me. She saw us all, our army. She led us in battle. . . ."

Samial broke off, glancing at Elodie as if for reassurance. She smiled at her phantom friend. *He's right*, she thought. *But what I've done here is different.*

And it was. The army that had risen from the Weeping Woods had come to Elodie of its own accord. But Lady Darrand and the Ritherlee nobles were here because she had summoned them.

At Elodie's feet lay a pile of possessions that had once belonged to these spirits, retrieved from the castle grounds by Samial: a gold necklace; a coin; a charred scrap of silk; Lady Darrand's ring. Somehow they had enabled Elodie to summon the spirits of their owners.

"Elodie," whispered Sylva. "We see them. Cedric and I—we see the ghosts and hear them too. How can that be?"

Elodie smiled. "You can? I think I must be getting stronger."

Lady Darrand held up her sword, running her fingers down the flat of its blade. Behind her, an old man dressed in a fine gold tunic was looking around Elodie's cell. Many of the other ghosts were doing likewise.

"Freedom and victory," said Lady Darrand. Her voice was strong, yet oddly distant, as if she were calling from the other side of a canyon. "Tell me more."

Elodie pressed her lips together. Where to begin?

"I've been a prisoner my whole life," she said at last. "I grew up thinking Lord Vicerin was my protector. But he was lying. He promised me that one day I would be queen, but now I know that he was using me. I might have become queen in name, but he was the one who would rule."

"Oh, Elodie," said Cedric, hanging his head. "Sylva and I can never forgive our father for what he did to you."

"From daughter to puppet," Lady Darrand mused. "From puppet to prisoner. How do you come to be here in this cell, Elodie?"

It was a relief to tell the story. For weeks Elodie had been playing a part, pretending to be on Vicerin's side when in truth she'd been searching for a way to free Fessan. When Vicerin had realized this, he'd had her imprisoned. Now, after all the lies, it was wonderful to be speaking the truth.

"Months ago, I was taken from Castle Vicerin by Trident. They wanted me to be their leader. Trident is—"

"The rebel army dedicated to seeing the prophecy fulfilled, I know. I supported them, sent them weapons and food when they needed." Lady Darrand's eyes widened. "What are you saying, Elodie?"

Elodie took a deep breath. "Lord Vicerin was right about one thing: I will be queen. The prophecy says so."

Murmuring broke out along the line of ghosts. As one, they knelt before Elodie.

"A triplet of the prophecy," said Lady Darrand in wonder. "So, have you found your siblings yet, Elodie, one of three?"

"One of them. He was with me when Trident attacked Idilliam. Then, when Lord Vicerin captured Fessan—he was the leader of Trident—I came back here to try to save him. But . . ."

"But what, my dear?"

"Vicerin had Fessan executed. Then he forced me to marry him, so he could take my throne." She waved a hand at the ridiculous gold wedding dress, with its trail of ribbons. "I'm his prisoner again. But now that you're here, I will be free."

Fire flashed outside the tower window. Orange flames flickered in the night sky.

Samial ran to the bars. "Fighting," he reported. "The elk-men are attacking the Vicerins. Many Vicerin soldiers lie dead in the courtyard. There are flames in the West Tower."

Elodie told Cedric and Sylva what he'd said.

"The elk-men?" said Cedric, joining Samial at the window. "Do you mean the Helkrags?"

"Those who murdered us?" put in the ghost in the gold tunic.

"Yes," said Elodie. "But I don't understand. I thought they'd joined forces with Vicerin."

"I doubt it," said Cedric. "From what I heard, the Helkrags are loyal to no man. The only thing they care about is getting paid."

"Our father *paid* them to kill people?" Sylva sounded both faint and shocked.

"What did he pay?" Lady Darrand's voice was cold and harsh. "What was the price of our lives?"

The rest of the ghosts had bunched around her. Several had drawn swords and daggers. All looked furious.

"Children," put in Samial. "Vicerin keeps children prisoner. He was going to give them to the elk-men as slaves."

"How do you know?" said Elodie.

"I overheard two of the castle guards talking. You overhear a lot when you are invisible."

"Remember the children we freed?" asked Elodie. She, Cedric, and Sylva had led them from the cells and into the care of Captain Leom, a grizzled ranger who took them to safety—where, Elodie didn't know. "The children were the price," she said in disgust. "The Helkrags must have turned on him when Vicerin couldn't make the payment."

A rising ball of flame turned the night sky briefly yellow. Screams floated up, rapidly followed by the rumble of collapsing masonry. Everyone clustered at the window, human and ghost alike. All except Elodie. She knew what battles looked like; she had no need to see this one. But it did offer the perfect diversion for their escape.

She quickly gathered up the belongings she'd used to summon the ghosts. She stuffed them into the pocket of her mud-stained wedding dress where she kept the arrowhead that belonged to Samial, and kept him able to walk the world of the living. She hoped the other things would let the noble ghosts stay too.

"Listen to me!" All faces turned to hers. Elodie focused on Lady Darrand's. "You asked for my command."

"And you gave it," Lady Darrand replied. "Freedom and victory, as I recall."

"Yes. But not just for me." Elodie took a step toward them. "This is what we're going to do. We're going to get out of this cell. Then we're going to recover the jewels. . . ."

"Jewels?" said Cedric.

"Green jewels." Elodie fought back impatience. The time for talk was over. The time for action had come. "One each for me and my brothers. They're important—I don't know why, they just are. Vicerin stole two of them."

"Then they must be returned," said Lady Darrand.

"Oh, they will be!"

"And when we've got the jewels?" said Sylva.

"We raise an army and march on Idilliam. We find my brothers. Together we take the crown. I will be queen! My brothers will be kings! The prophecy will be fulfilled! *That's* what I mean by freedom and victory. Not just for me. Not just for you. For the whole of Toronia!"

Elodie stopped, breathless. To her amazement, most of the ghosts had dropped to one knee again and bowed their heads. As she watched, Lady Darrand and Samial followed suit.

Boots echoed on the stairs outside. A man coughed, and then Elodie heard the sound of a key in a lock. She whirled in time to see the door swing open. Four burly guards, dressed in scuffed armor and blue Vicerin sashes, marched in. One—a stocky man whose red face was beaded with sweat—held up a collection of jangling chains and spiked manacles.

"You're to come with us," he snapped. "Away from the fighting. Lord Vicerin says . . ."

His voice trailed away. His eyes, and those of his three companions, were staring not at Elodie but at what lay beyond her.

Elodie crossed her arms. "You were about to say something about Lord Vicerin?" She felt something soft brush her shoulders as the ghosts of the Ritherlee nobles strode past her and, with their phantom swords raised, bore down on the guards.

The red-faced guard squealed. Spinning on his heels, he dropped the chains and blundered past his comrades, who took one look at the roomful of ghosts and followed fast behind him.

"All of you, follow me!" Elodie called, running after them.

She descended the stairs in a breathless blur, holding up the hem of the wedding dress so as not to trip on the ribbons. Behind her came Sylva, Cedric, Samial, and the ghostly nobles. After three complete turns, the spiral staircase brought them to a narrow hall, beyond which a gaping doorway opened onto a scene of utter chaos.

On the far side of the open yard lay the remains of the White Tower's smaller neighbor, the West Tower. The squat stone structure was now just a pile of rubble within which the smashed remains of wooden beams were blazing.

In and around the ruins, hundreds of soldiers were fighting hand-to-hand: the Vicerins with their shining breastplates and blue sashes, the barbarian Helkrags with their battered leather armor and tooth-covered furs. Everywhere, the air rang as Vicerin swords met Helkrag axes.

"The Northern Regiment!" Cedric cried over the noise of the battle. "Father's called for reinforcements!"

Looking in the direction he was pointing, Elodie spied a squad of Vicerin horsemen plowing a steady course through the confusion. The horses were huge and shaggy; the men on their backs wore heavy armor and silver spiked helmets.

"I can see him," said Sylva. "Look, in the middle of them."

Elodie took in a sharp breath. There he was: Lord Vicerin, the man she'd once called father.

Except you're not a man, she thought grimly. *You're a monster.*

Vicerin's horse was bigger even than those of the Northern Regiment—a massive white charger with a thick, plaited mane. His polished armor caught the light of the nearby flames, and the huge blue feathers rising from his helmet fluttered in the hot, gusting wind.

"Our lord looks quite the hero," said Lady Darrand archly.

"If a hero stays safe behind five rows of mounted knights," Cedric muttered.

Elodie watched as Vicerin waved his sword and shouted his orders—mostly threats, warning his soldiers what would happen to them if they failed to defeat the enemy.

"I've never seen the Northern Regiment called back to the castle before," she said.

"They're not the only ones," Cedric replied. "There, beyond the flames—do you see the flags of the Expeditionary Force? It looks like he's called back every regiment. The whole army is here in Castle Vicerin."

"He is desperate," said Lady Darrand.

"And weak," said Elodie.

All eyes turned to her.

"Weak?" said Sylva. She tossed her head toward the battle. "I've never seen so many soldiers."

"He's weak," Elodie repeated. "He's brought all his soldiers to the same place. That makes them vulnerable." She shook her head. "Doesn't he know anything about basic military tactics?"

"That man is a pampered, powdered fool," said Lady Darrand. "Elodie—I see a gap, there. Run through it. I will keep the Vicerins at bay to your right."

The old man in the gold tunic touched his sword to his forehead. "And I will deal with the Helkrags to your left," he said.

"Thank you," said Elodie. "I'm sorry—I don't know your name."

"Lord Winterborne. My estate lies in the western plains, close to the sea. And I am yours to command."

"Do you think you can see us safely to the outer wall?"

Lord Winterborne bowed low. "It will be our pleasure, Your Highness."

Sweeping their swords like scythes through grass, the small band of ghosts split in two, then proceeded to cut their way through the fighting. Elodie and the others hurried through the gap they opened up. With grim satisfaction Elodie observed the looks of surprise and horror on the faces of the Vicerin and Helkrag soldiers as phantom blades descended on them out of the firelit night.

As she ran, she heard voices. Very faint. Very old. Very weak. Voices that reached her despite the clash and roar of the battle.

The voices of the dead.

They were coming from the walls of the castle that loomed overhead, huge and ancient.

Can I summon them, too? she wondered.

Turning a corner, they found themselves in a small herb garden. High ivy-covered walls shielded them from the battle. The sweet aromas of sage and parsley were welcome after the stench of blood and smoke. Through a narrow door on the far side of the garden came a faint red glow that wasn't fire, but the light of the coming dawn.

The long night was nearly over.

"Someone is here," said Winterborne. He raised his voice. "Come out!"

Peering past the ghost's shoulder, Elodie watched as two dim figures materialized out of the gloom.

More ghosts?

Then the figures became solid—not ghosts at all, but living people whom Elodie recognized.

"Frida!" she cried, darting forward to embrace the black-robed witch who had tried to cure Lady Vicerin of her husband's poison. Frida had clearly been hiding here with her son. The little boy clung to his mother's arm, his eyes wide.

Frida touched a hand to Elodie's cheek. "You're safe," she said. "Thank the stars."

"But what about you two?" said Elodie. "If Vicerin finds you . . ."

"I have ways of keeping us unseen."

The wind gusted, bringing with it the smell of smoke—and the murmur of ghostly voices. The voices were stronger now, echoing all around the garden.

Frida peered closely at Elodie. "You hear them, don't you?"

Elodie nodded.

"It is the song of the past. The song of the dead. It is rooted in this castle. Rooted in this land."

Elodie seized Frida's hands. "Help me, Frida. I know they can fight for me. But . . . I don't know how to summon them."

"If you call them, they will come."

"But how? I know I can summon ghosts—a whole army, if I need to." She released Frida and ran a hand through her short hair in frustration. "But I need something to hold. Possessions. Clothing. Anything. Unless I can touch something, I can't . . ."

"Things are not important, my dear. Your power is within you."

"But how do I . . . ?"

"Go to them. Be near to them. Find the place where they lie, and speak to them there. They will hear you. And they will rise."

The witch led Elodie to the narrow door in the garden wall. She pointed past the knotted ivy at a distant hill topped with a thin straggle of trees.

"Beyond there is a place," Frida said. "You will know it when you see it. They call it the Forgotten Graveyard."

As Elodie looked toward it, the morning sun broke through, casting the hilltop with gold. For a moment the trees seemed alight with flame. The warmth bathed Elodie's face and she narrowed her eyes against its fierce glare.

I'm coming, she told the dead who lay there. *You will be forgotten no longer.*

She turned back to the others.

"I will call the dead of Castle Vicerin," she proclaimed. "Today they become my army. Today they rise!"

CHAPTER 3

Two days of steady flying brought Tarlan and Theeta to the foothills of a vast mountain range. Idilliam was far behind them, Isur even farther. In the distant south lay Ritherlee and beyond that the icy land of Yalasti, which Tarlan had once called home. Tarlan thought of Yalasti now, as Theeta's broad wings lifted them higher into air that grew increasingly thin. The mountains ahead were gigantic, capped with snow. Their slopes were steep, their peaks jagged; they looked altogether more threatening than the mountains of his old home.

I can't ever go back, he thought. *Yalasti's just a graveyard now.*

Grief washed over him as he remembered Mirith's dying face, the icy gaze in the frost witch's eyes. And poor Seethan, the oldest thorrod in the flock, butchered by Helkrags before Tarlan's outraged eyes. Death upon death.

Clenching his teeth against a sudden blast of cold air, Tarlan patted Theeta's neck.

"What do you think, Theeta? No castles here. No sign of humans at all. Just you and me, and all the game we can hunt."

"New home."

"Exactly."

The wind gusted again. Something gritty stung Tarlan's face; he shook his head and blinked it away. He opened his mouth to speak, and another gust filled his mouth with more grit. He spat it away and wiped his lips. When he brought his hand down, he saw that it wasn't grit at all.

It was sand.

"Air hot," Theeta remarked. The wind tossed her this way and that, and she had to fight to keep flying level.

She was right. As the gusts continued to batter them, Tarlan realized he was sweating.

"What's going on?" he shouted over the rising howl of the wind. "We didn't cross any deserts."

A column of sand reared up before them, spinning wildly. It looked like a gigantic yellow snake spiraling into the sky. Its tail was rooted in the ground, far below; its head was lost in the clouds.

"Storm sand!" cried Theeta, weaving instinctively around the whirlwind.

Two more snakes surged upward, blocking their path. Hot

sand clogged Tarlan's throat, making it hard to breathe. His eyes streamed.

"Go back!" Theeta cawed, her voice even more of a rasp than usual.

"No! I won't turn back! Go on!"

Theeta's wings faltered. For a moment Tarlan thought the storm had beaten her. Then he saw he was wrong.

Theeta was hesitating.

She's never ignored my command. Not once. So why . . . ?

Before he could complete the thought, the giant thorrod surged forward with her wings pumping, veering first left, then right, powering her way between the snaking columns of sand. Whatever doubt she'd had seemed to have passed.

But why is there sand in the mountains? he thought, clinging on as Theeta swerved through it. *Is this some kind of magic?*

Could it be Melchior, come to stop him?

He peered through the stinging sand, trying to see down to the ground. But it was hopeless. Besides, this didn't feel like the kind of spell Melchior would cast.

His magic is all about numbers.

Sweat was trickling into his eyes. He flicked it away. The air was warm.

Sand. Heat.

A thought came to him. Sometimes, when he was forging a

bond with a new group of animals, the same sensation of sandy heat washed over him.

What did it mean? Was it something to do with the prophecy? Was there someone down there with the same powers as him? Magic that came from the desert?

But Tarlan was no wizard. And already he'd lost interest in where the sandstorm had come from. Whoever had conjured it, they came from the world of people. The world he'd turned his back on.

"Keep going, Theeta," he muttered, spitting out another mouthful of sand. "Don't look back."

Theeta flew on, her great black eyes pinched against the storm, her golden wings thumping through the treacherous updrafts. Tarlan buried his face in her feathers and clung on.

Eventually the sky began to clear. The wind subsided and the air grew colder. As they emerged out of the sandstorm's veil, the mountains melted back into view.

"We made it!" Tarlan clapped the side of Theeta's neck, then looked back over his shoulder. The sky was quite empty. When he looked down, he saw only a featureless plain of snow. No storm. No sand.

Did that really happen?

The closer they drew to the mountains, the more the land seemed to swell beneath them. As the sun fell toward the western horizon, Theeta began sinking toward the icy slopes that were rising to meet them.

"We can go a little farther," said Tarlan, tugging at her neck ruff.

Theeta didn't reply. Instead, she tilted her wings and flew in a wide, descending circle, bringing them in to land beneath the shelter of a rocky crag. The weatherworn knuckle of black stone loomed over them, like the finger of a giant who'd been frozen while trying to break free from the snow.

"What are you doing?" Tarlan tugged again. "We still have daylight. I want to go on."

"No farther," Theeta replied.

Tarlan was astonished. Theeta had never challenged him like this before. What was wrong with her?

"Are you tired, Theeta? Is that it?" He looked around uncertainly at the icy wasteland. "Well, I suppose that rock gives us a bit of shelter. . . ."

"Not tired."

"Then why did you . . . ?"

"Wrong way."

"This isn't the wrong way. We've been flying north all the time, like we decided."

"Tarlan decided."

"All right, like *I* decided. But we're still—"

"Tarlan wrong."

That silenced him. Sliding from Theeta's back, he crunched through the snow to stand before her. She glared down at him, her eyes as black as the rock that towered over them both.

"Why am I wrong?" he said quietly.

She regarded him for a long time, as motionless as a statue.

"Wrong place," she said at last.

"What's wrong with it?"

Theeta clacked her beak together and tossed her head, a sure sign of her frustration. "Wrong future. Wrong past. Wrong now. Place wrong. Tarlan wrong." She paused, then added, "Not . . . *des-tin-y.*"

Tarlan knew what she was trying to tell him. He was sick of hearing it.

"Everyone keeps telling me what to do!" he snapped. "I can't stand it. This is *my* life. *My* choice. And I choose to be here, whether you like it or not!"

"Not like. Not want."

"Well, I didn't want you to come in the first place! Remember?"

"Want go."

"Then go! I'm not stopping you!"

Tarlan stalked across the snowfield, kicking aside great flurries of snow. Behind him, the black stone stood in sharp silhouette against a sky turning swiftly purple. As the sun disappeared behind the mountains, the first stars winked into view. The brightest of them were the three stars that had been looking down on Tarlan ever since he'd first left Yalasti.

The prophecy stars.

Except one was not as bright as before.

Tarlan stood in the snow, gazing up into the twilight. Two of the prophecy stars—one green, one red—shone just as brilliantly as ever. But the third star, the one tinged with gold, had faded almost to invisibility. Somehow worse, its light was stuttering, like a candle flame about to be extinguished.

One star for each of the three, Tarlan thought sadly. *Now Gulph is dead—his star is dying too.*

A voice cawed softly in his ear.

"Theeta go."

Tarlan's throat tightened. His eyes stung.

"Theeta help." Her voice sounded more distant. The words were accompanied by the rustling beat of Theeta's wings, growing gradually fainter. Tarlan didn't turn to look, only stared at the black stone.

She's leaving me.

"Theeta help. Find change. Tarlan broken. Theeta mend . . ."

The thorrod's voice dwindled as she climbed into the twilight sky. When he could hear it no longer, Tarlan at last looked up. Theeta was a tiny speck of gold crawling over a field of indigo, flying high enough to catch the last rays of the sun.

For a brief moment, her wings burned brighter even than the prophecy stars.

Then she turned, and Theeta's light went out.

Tarlan walked through the night, his tattered black cloak wrapped tightly around him. His face grew stiff in the biting cold, and his chest felt tight and hard. His teeth chattered constantly. His hands and feet were completely numb. That was fine. Feeling numb was better than feeling lonely and full of grief. Tarlan wondered if he'd feel those things in the morning, when the sun returned and his body thawed.

The moon rose, painting silver shadows across the rolling plains of snow. As Tarlan moved steadily upslope, he passed more black crags jutting from the ground, until a forest of dark stone surrounded him.

He stopped and turned a full circle.

Which way is north?

He looked up at the sky. Thick clouds had rolled in, destroying any chance of navigating by the stars.

I'm lost.

Cold wind blasted against his frozen face. Snow began to fall.

Pulling his black cloak around his shivering body, Tarlan stumbled on through the towering fingers of rock. The numbness ebbed from his body. Tingling pain replaced it. Every footstep was torture. He rubbed his hands against each other, terrified his fingers would snap like icicles.

Just when he thought the blizzard could get no worse, it doubled in strength. The wind was a hammer, battering him from all directions, first knocking him back on his heels, then slamming him forward. It hurled snow at him from every side, now piling it up on the back of his neck, now ramming it into his mouth and trying to choke him. The storm howled, and as Tarlan staggered on, he howled along with it.

Strange thoughts flew through his mind like frozen leaves whipped up by the wind.

I howl like a wolf!

I fly like a thorrod!

I am not who I was!

For a time, he believed this was not a blizzard but a sandstorm. He was not cold but hot. His arms were melting, his legs were melting. He was on fire, and the fire was inside his head.

Bright! It's so bright! I'm burning!

He squinted against its glare.

Take it away! Take it all away!

The light stubbornly remained. Tarlan's legs stopped moving of their own accord, leaving him tottering knee-deep in powdery snow. The air was still and clear. He could hear nothing but the ragged sound of his own breath as it clawed its way through his ice-scorched throat.

He forced his frozen eyelids to peel themselves apart.

Is that the sun?

It was. Low in the east, an orange glow sent bright tendrils of light climbing into a sky wiped clean. Not fire after all. A new day.

I'm still alive.

Sometime during the night, he'd left the forest of rocks behind. Only a single tower of stone remained: a black spire thrusting up from the snow and leaning toward the dawn. It was thin, not so much a finger as a claw.

There's something on top of it!

Tarlan took three plodding steps forward, then stopped again, exhausted. Had the thing on the spire just twitched?

Not one thing. Two!

Or was that just his blurred vision betraying him?

Tarlan wiped his eyes with the back of his hand. He could definitely see two creatures perched at the tip of the giant stone claw. They were hunched over, making it impossible to determine their shape. Were those wings?

"Theeta?" he croaked. "Nasheen?"

Neither of the creatures moved. Tarlan took three more faltering steps and something flashed in the shifting orange light of the rising sun. Teeth? Talons? Impossible to say.

YOU ARE NOT READY.

Tarlan staggered. The voice had pierced his head like . . . *like a tooth, or a talon* . . . and its strength had almost knocked him over.

He waited, staring at the things perched on the rocky spire, daring one of them to move. Daring one of them to speak.

Nothing happened. Tarlan sank to his knees in the snow. The sun burned through the distant clouds, painting him with its fire. The sudden warmth was shocking. His vision blurred again. His ears roared.

"Ready for what?" he cried.

No movement. No reply.

Tarlan thought he heard someone calling his name. His eyes closed and he fell into a blackness that wasn't the night.

CHAPTER 4

E lodie led the way up the shallow slope to the copse, the shadow of a meandering hedge keeping them hidden from anyone who might have been watching from the castle. By the time they reached the trees, the sound of battle had faded. In its place Elodie could hear a low buzzing. She wondered what it was.

"More fires have broken out," said Cedric, turning back to face the castle. "I wonder who's winning."

Elodie didn't bother to look. If the Vicerins wiped out the Helkrags—or the other way around—that was fine by her; it would make her job easier. Either way, the outcome of that particular battle was out of her control.

But here . . .

. . . *here is something I can control. I hope.*

Beyond the narrow belt of trees, the ground dropped away. At the bottom of a shallow, rocky slope lay an enormous field of thick grass dotted with scrubby bushes. In the low dawn light, the long shadows cast by these bushes looked like scratches drawn across the land by huge unseen claws. Something like a heat-haze seemed to ripple over the grass, despite the coolness of the early morning air.

The buzzing noise grew louder.

"So this is the Forgotten Graveyard," said Elodie.

"They are here," said Samial. There was a dreamy look on his face. "The dead. They have been waiting, I think."

"Waiting for what?" said Sylva.

Elodie bit her lip. "Waiting for me."

She began to climb down the slope. After a couple of steps, she hesitated, overwhelmed by what she was about to attempt. At once, Lady Darrand was at her side. Behind the phantom woman, perched easily on the rough boulders, was the rest of Elodie's small band of ghostly allies.

"We are with you, Elodie," Lady Darrand said.

"We have nothing to fear from those who haunt this place," added Lord Winterborne.

Reassured, Elodie descended the rest of the way, then stepped out onto the grass. Her feet sank instantly into the ground, all the way up to her ankles. She threw out her arms, fighting for balance. The wet soil belched, spewing up bubbles of foul-smelling gas.

"Ugh!" exclaimed Sylva. "What's that awful smell?"

Elodie tried to take another step, but the swampy earth sucked at her legs, dragging her deeper. Now she was up to her knees.

"Help me!" she cried.

Samial was there in an instant. He grabbed her outstretched wrist . . . but to Elodie's shock, his ghostly fingers passed straight through her flesh.

"Samial!" she gasped. "Why—"

A hundred giant insects descended on her, then a hundred more. The swarm buzzed around Elodie's head like a living tornado. Their glassy bodies made them hard to see; it was as if the air itself had come to life. Some detached part of her understood that these bugs had caused the rippling she'd seen from the trees. The rest of her just wanted to scream.

"Here, Elodie!"

It was Cedric. With one foot planted firmly on a grassy mound, he reached down and seized Elodie with his one remaining arm. Sylva took her other hand, and together they pulled. Gradually she began to emerge from the slime. She felt something like an oily rope tighten briefly around her right ankle before relaxing and slithering away.

With a horrible sucking sound, her legs popped free of the ooze. She fell backward, landing on her back and elbows.

"Are you all right?" said Sylva. Behind her, Samial was wide-eyed, clearly distressed.

"I'm fine!" Elodie replied. "Don't worry."

But she was shaking. If Cedric and Sylva hadn't been there, she would have drowned, swallowed by the mud, and the prophecy with it. . . .

She pushed her fears aside and got to her feet. Taking care to keep to the higher, drier ground, she made her way onto the grassy hillock. There was a brooding presence here. She could sense it. Something powerful. Something waiting.

Lady Darrand joined her. "Can you do it? This place feels different from anything I've known. It feels . . . treacherous."

Elodie tossed her hair out of her face. "I think so. I hope so. Up until now, I've always needed objects—like your ring, Lady Darrand. But if Frida's right, I don't need anything now. Just myself."

She took a deep breath and fixed her gaze on a nearby swarm of insects. The rippling wings made her think of hot summer days. It almost looked like . . .

. . . *like heat over a desert.*

How could she know that? She'd never seen a desert.

But I've felt this before. I feel this way whenever . . . whenever I use magic.

The heat began to build in her. It began at her feet and flowed up through her, scorching her body, her arms, her head. Hot wind blew through her. Her mouth grew dry. Sand grated between her teeth.

She planted her feet wide and stretched out her arms. The morning sun turned the grass to gold. The insects were diamonds dancing in its light; Elodie could pick out every single one of them, each spinning in its own private waltz. The swamp yawned, opening itself to her all-seeing eyes. She saw the grass, and below the grass she saw the mud, and below the mud she saw . . .

. . . *the dead.*

They were there, just as she'd known they were. Ten thousand men and women, the fallen enemies of Lord Vicerin, buried here and forgotten . . . but forgotten no more.

Desert light glinted from shovels and pitchforks, swords and pieces of armor. Heat shone in their unblinking eyes. The dead were motionless, held down by the weight of the mud, and the slow, slow passing of years.

"Rise up!" Elodie cried. She raised her arms, as if by lifting them she could lift these waiting warriors. "Come back to this world!"

No movement. Nothing at all. Yet somehow she knew they were stirring.

"Wake up! The time has come! I am here!"

Something rushed toward her: all the insects in the swamp, swept up in a sudden wave of scintillating light. The air filled up with their wings. The air *was* their wings. Everything was buzzing: the swamp, the insects, Elodie herself . . .

"What . . . ?" she began.

It was all she managed to say before the insects vanished and she was falling. Above her or below her, a million stars sprang into view. Their heat was unbearable. The heat intensified, then seemed to burst, leaving in its place an iciness that was beyond cold, a whiteness that was also black, a sense that she could see everything there was to see . . . and yet see nothing at all.

The emptiness swallowed her up.

CHAPTER 5

G ulph floated in silence.

I'm dead, he thought.

His body rolled, first to the left, then the right.

But I have no body. I must be a ghost, or else I've passed over into the Realm of the Dead.

Something washed over him—a cold wave.

Perhaps I'm not dead yet, he thought. *Perhaps I'm still falling.*

Gulph kept his eyes stubbornly closed as vivid memories returned.

On top of the tower . . . flames all around . . . Brutan!

As the city of Idilliam had burned around him, he'd been faced with a ghastly choice: allow his undead father to turn him into a rotting, walking corpse . . . or jump into the chasm separating Idilliam from the forest realm of Isur.

Gulph had jumped.

Better to be dead than one of Brutan's skeleton slaves! he told himself. *Better to rob him of victory! Better to be dead than undead!*

Except he wasn't dead.

Was he?

Slowly Gulph opened his eyes.

Hazy gray light washed over him. Rising into the light was a wall, impossibly high.

No, that's not a wall. It's a cliff.

Something splashed across his face. Water?

Gulph realized he was soaked from head to toe. His body rolled again; this time he thrust out his arms for balance. His elbows dug into something soft and crumbly. When he kicked out, his heels met the same yielding substance. Still on his back, he scrabbled his way awkwardly out of the shallow water in which he'd been floating.

Once he was on dry land, Gulph flopped back and stared up at the cliff wall towering above him. Thick haze obscured its heights.

His head lolled to the side. He watched the rippling water as it flowed slowly through a narrow channel in the damp ground. Gulph clambered to his knees and crawled to the river's edge. He cupped his hands and scooped up a little of the water.

It was silver.

And he finally understood what had happened to him.

He was in the lost realm of Celestis. His leap into the chasm hadn't been to his death; he'd landed in the river that ran beneath Idilliam.

All very well, but the impact should have killed him.

He stared at the shining liquid, remembering the last time he'd been submerged in it. When he and his friends had fallen into the lake in the center of Celestis, the silver water had healed the cuts and scratches he'd suffered during his descent.

It must have healed me again, he thought in wonder. *However badly hurt I was when I landed, the water fixed me.* Then Gulph remembered something else about the silver water of Celestis. Scrambling to his feet, he moved hurriedly away from the river until his back was pressed against the cliff. He'd already had one encounter with the bakaliss, a gigantic red serpent that prowled beneath the waves, and only narrowly escaped with his life. He had no desire to make its acquaintance again.

The air tasted bitter. When he looked up, he saw that what he'd thought was haze obscuring the top of the cliff was actually smoke. It came rushing back—how he'd climbed the chasm wall and set the city on fire to destroy Brutan once and for all. He shuddered as he recalled standing on top of the tower, surrounded by flames. He remembered the terrible heat, the stifling smoke. His undead father bearing down on him.

What he couldn't remember was what had happened to Brutan. *He must have burned. There was nowhere for him to go.*

But Gulph couldn't be sure.

He flexed his back. Crooked as it was, it occasionally troubled him with aches. Now it was racked with pain. As he rubbed his hands over his shoulders, a terrible thought came to him.

My backpack! It's gone!

Gulph waded through the shallows, frantically turning over crystal rocks until, to his great relief, he found the tightly wrapped bundle lodged between two chunks of diamond. He snatched it up and checked the large pocket on the side. His fingers settled immediately on the cold, hard curves of the gold crown of Toronia. Like him, it had survived. Otherwise, the bundle was empty. The fireworks he'd used to burn Idilliam were used up, and at some point the food and water he'd packed must have fallen out.

As soon as he made this discovery, Gulph's stomach rumbled.

How long is it since I fell? he wondered. *I could have been floating for days!*

When he'd begun his climb up the near-vertical cliff, the people of Celestis had been preparing for the invasion of Brutan's undead army. Could the undead have set off before Gulph started the fire? Could they even now be in the tunnels beneath the city, safe from the flames, making their way to attack the underground realm?

It was horribly possible. Ossilius and his friends would be waiting in Kalia's house, desperate for news of his mission. Gulph had to warn them. . . .

Keeping his distance from the water, Gulph set off at a loping run. At first he managed a brisk, determined pace. His wet clothes dried rapidly in the warm air. He felt strong. But soon he began to tire. The ache in his back spread throughout his whole body, and his pace dropped to a stagger. At one point, a coughing fit stopped him in his tracks. When he moved his hands from his mouth, he saw he'd coughed up specks of black ash.

I must have breathed in a lot of smoke up there.

He stumbled on until at last he reached an opening in the cliff wall between two massive crystal pillars. Through it lay the way back into Celestis.

Exhausted, Gulph leaned against the base of the nearest pillar. Each time he took a breath, he felt a sharp pain in his ribs. He slumped to the ground. He couldn't go any farther.

"Gulph!" The woman's voice was faint. Where was it coming from?

"Is it him?" A man's voice.

On his hands and knees, Gulph dragged himself through the gap. Compared to the brightness of the chasm, the interior of Celestis looked as dark as night. Who was talking? He couldn't see anyone.

A slender gray figure solidified out of the gloom: a cloaked woman, running to meet him. She dropped to her knees beside Gulph and gathered him in her arms.

"Gulph," she sobbed, covering his thin cheeks with kisses. "Gulph, it's me. It's your mother."

The woman's hood fell back to reveal a pale face marked with burn scars. Gulph stared at her, stunned. Like everyone in Celestis, his mother had been put under a spell by its ruler, Lady Redina, which had made her forget everything—even her own children.

His hand trembling, Gulph brushed a lock of hair away from Kalia's scarred face. Her hair was red-gold, just like his own.

"You . . . you remember me?"

"I remember *everything*!"

Gulph gazed deep into her bright green eyes. He could feel himself grinning. *She knows me! At last, she knows me!*

"And now that I've found you," his mother said, her eyes shining, "I'm never losing you again."

A second figure strode up—the man who'd called out. He was gray-haired and dressed in a tattered soldier's uniform.

"Gulph!" he exclaimed. "I cannot tell you how good it is to see you!"

"Captain Ossilius!" Gulph clasped the hand of his old friend. "Did you do this? Did you . . . ?"

Ossilius grinned. "Just as you asked, Gulph. Your mother put up quite a fight when I held her under the surface of the lake! Didn't you, Kalia? But I managed for long enough that the magic could heal her memory."

"Lady Redina has a lot to answer for!" Kalia said bitterly. "She poisoned me, as she has poisoned every other person in Celestis."

"She's done something to the wine," Gulph said, remembering how he'd snatched it from Ossilius's hands.

"It's not just that," said Kalia. "She gives orders that make no sense, yet people obey her. She is cruel, yet people love her. She does not wield power like a sovereign. She casts it like a spell."

"A spell?"

Kalia nodded gravely. "I believe that Lady Redina is a witch, like me."

"Not like you!"

"Perhaps not, but she is a witch all the same. How else could she have remained in power for so long? But her magic is of a kind I have never encountered before."

Ossilius nodded. "And she's furious with you, Gulph."

"With me? Why?"

"The undead have reached Celestis," Ossilius said.

What was left of Gulph's strength drained from his tired body. He sagged against the pillar. Ossilius slipped an arm around Gulph's shoulders before he fell.

"I knew it. I was too late. It was all for nothing," Gulph said, gazing past him into the hidden depths of Celestis. "How bad is it?"

"It's already over. No, we won!" Ossilius said hastily when he caught Gulph's horrified expression. "There were not many of them. No more than a hundred, I should say." With his free hand, he drew his crystal sword from the scabbard he wore. "Your mother's blades made short work of them."

"Those who wielded them were brave," added Kalia modestly. She was searching her robes for something and brought out a small vial of dark liquid. "One drop on your tongue, Gulph." She smiled. "I see how your body aches. Before you do anything else, do as your mother says."

Gulph opened his mouth. The potion was cool and sweet. Three breaths after the liquid went down his throat, the pain in his back began to ease.

"Now," Kalia went on, "are you ready to tell us what happened up there?"

Gulph eased himself away from Ossilius's arm and straightened his twisted back as best he could. "I'll tell you on the way."

"On the way?" said Ossilius. "Where are we going?"

"Where do you think? To see Lady Redina."

Kalia shook her head. "That is not a good idea. She is dangerous. We know that now, my son."

She calls me son!

Gulph couldn't get over it. He hoped he never would.

"You should lie low for a while," Ossilius agreed. "We can hide you."

Gulph pulled the crown from his pack. Its gold contours

glimmered in the smoke-soft light. "Not as long as I'm carrying this. I can't rule Toronia if I'm skulking in the shadows. And I can't turn my back on my enemies. Lady Redina must pay for what she's done. I'm finished with hiding."

Gulph stepped between the pillars and into the darkness. Captain Ossilius and his mother followed.

"The climb seemed to take forever," he began, rolling his shoulders in their sockets and enjoying the warmth of the potion's magic working through his body. "When I got to the top, at first I thought Idilliam was deserted. Then I saw them."

"The undead?" Kalia asked.

"Yes. The undead. That's when I started to set the fires. . . ."

By the time Gulph came to the end of his tale, they'd reached the other side of the narrow strip of crystal that spanned the lake. Ahead, at the top of a narrow, emerald-colored lane, stood the grand and glittering house where Lady Redina lived. The high cavern roof hung over it like a sullen purple shroud.

"You robbed Brutan of his victory when you jumped," said Ossilius. "That took great courage."

"I didn't have a choice," Gulph replied. "None of it really turned out how I'd planned."

"Nothing ever does," Ossilius said. "But thanks to you, Brutan is gone, and the undead are destroyed."

"The city's destroyed too."

Ossilius squeezed his shoulder. "Cities can be rebuilt."

Kalia held a hand to the pink scar covering the side of her face. Her eyes were troubled. "You faced the monster who tried to kill you, and your brother and sister. The monster who tried to burn me alive at the stake—and who would have succeeded if not for Melchior's magic. Oh, Gulph, I am so sorry you had Brutan for a father!"

"None of it was your fault," said Gulph.

"Brutan is gone at last," Ossilius soothed. "Do not distress yourself."

"I am glad to be distressed!" Kalia cried. "Lady Redina's magic has poisoned my mind for too many years! Every memory is precious to me now, even the bad ones." Her voice softened. When she smiled, Gulph could almost forget the scar was there. "And especially the good ones. The memories with you in them."

A warm breeze carried a woman's voice to them, powerful and commanding. It was coming from the house.

"Lady Redina," said Ossilius, his hand dropping to the hilt of his sword. "Has she not yet finished with her victory speech?"

"It sounds like she's giving quite a performance," said Gulph. "Let's see what we can add to it."

Several hundred people had gathered in the ornate crystal garden surrounding the house. Lady Redina herself was standing on a platform of pure ruby, addressing the crowd. She wore a flowing red dress the same vibrant color as the shining platform, so that she seemed almost to grow from it. She looked even taller than Gulph remembered. Her milky skin seemed to glow in the perpetual Celestian twilight.

"Marcus and the others are there," whispered Ossilius, pointing out a knot of people huddled beneath a diamond sculpture of a knight on horseback. "There is Hetty, do you see? And the little girl."

"Jessamyn. Yes, I see them."

Gulph recognized the three companions who had fled with them to Celestis through the tunnels beneath Idilliam. But what really gladdened his heart was the sight of those who stood with them: his old friends, the Tangletree Players. Noddy and Dorry were gazing respectfully up at Lady Redina, their hats in their hands. Sidebottom John was shifting uncomfortably, tugging at a loose thread on his smock.

Gulph turned to Ossilius. "Did you . . . ?"

"Dunk John in the lake?" The former Captain of the Guard was smiling. "Yes. His memory has returned, just like your mother's. I asked him not to tell the others, though. I wish I could have restored them, too, but I couldn't risk Lady Redina getting suspicious."

Gulph nodded, but he was only half listening. Among the knot of players, he'd spotted a gentle face framed with short curls: Pip, Gulph's oldest friend. She was watching Lady Redina too—and like the rest of the crowd, her upturned face was dull and blank. Only Sidebottom John wasn't in a state of complete belief and trust.

Gulph no longer felt exhausted. His mother's medicine had worked miracles, but it was more than that. Despite all his trials, he felt strong. Despite carrying no weapons, he felt invincible.

The crown of Toronia is the only weapon I need, he thought, relishing the weight of the gold on his back.

"Lady Redina has been making speeches here for far too long," he said. "I think it's time somebody shut her up."

The closer they drew to the ruby platform, the louder Lady Redina's voice became.

". . . the battle was swift and sure, and the undead invaders have been brought down. Yet we cannot rest. The enemies of Celestis are plotting against us still. We must be ceaseless in our vigilance, and guard these precious shores against the endless danger . . ."

Faces turned as Gulph pushed his way to the front of the crowd, Ossilius at his right shoulder, Kalia at his left. Gasps of recognition went up, and then people began to cry out:

"The crippled stranger—he's come back!"

"None who leave Celestis may return!"

"He must be punished!"

Ignoring them, Gulph shouted, "You say there's danger here in

Celestis, Lady Redina? Well, I happen to agree with you!"

At the sight of him, Lady Redina recoiled. Her red dress flowed around her in sinuous folds. Her pale face contorted with rage.

"You!" she cried.

"The danger is *you*, Lady Redina," Gulph went on. "*You're* the enemy. If anyone needs bringing down, it's you!"

The cries from the crowd turned to jeers and shouts of anger. Lady Redina's lips writhed and her eyes bulged. "Guards! Seize this deformed creature and take it away!"

On the far side of the platform, two uniformed men began making their way toward him. Gulph became aware of the furious expressions on the faces of the people around him. A woman standing nearby waved her fist, while the man beside her actually drew his sword. Gulph wondered if this had been such a good idea after all.

"You are doing well, my son," his mother murmured from just behind him. "Stay strong."

"Leave the guards to me," said Ossilius, hurrying past Gulph with his crystal sword drawn.

"Banished!" Lady Redina was screaming. She paced back and forth along the platform, wringing her hands. "Exiled! This miserable creature was sent from these shores and yet he has the audacity to return!"

This isn't anger, Gulph thought, astonished by the depth of her reaction. *This is utter fury. What's happening here?*

"You!" Lady Redina stabbed a trembling finger toward Kalia. "The earth-charmed witch! You pleaded for this freak and his wretched friends when they arrived here from Idilliam, and I was foolish enough to listen!" Her eyes swiveled back to Gulph. "I will not overlook your treason a second time. You defied my exile once, and I was foolish enough to grant you mercy. Now you have defied me twice. Now you will taste my wrath!"

"Gulph!" Pip's thin voice drifted across the crowd. "Be careful!"

He shot a glance in her direction. She was trying to get to him, but Noddy and Willum were holding her in check.

"Keep back, Pip!" he shouted. "Stay out of danger!"

By now Ossilius had intercepted the guards. The Celestians drew their swords and began to circle him warily. A gap opened up in the crowd around them.

"Idilliam is destroyed," Gulph announced. This raised a gasp from the audience. "I set fires. I burned it to the ground. The undead are gone, all of them, turned to ash. There's no danger from above. There's no reason for you to hide underground anymore."

The crowd's anger seemed to have abated a little. Many of the nearby people were looking at him with interest. On several faces he saw something that might have been hope.

"It's true," he went on. "You're free! Don't you see that?

You don't have to live like this anymore." He pointed at Lady Redina. "And you don't have to listen to her."

Now the crowd was muttering. For every person who looked angry, twice as many were regarding Lady Redina with confusion, or even suspicion. Something was moving here, Gulph realized—not a physical movement but something else. Something was changing.

"She's been poisoning you!" He advanced so that his chest was pressed against the platform. Somewhere in the distance, he heard crystal blades chiming as Captain Ossilius began trading blows with the guards. "All these years she's been holding you down. But you don't have to stand for it anymore!"

Lady Redina advanced to the edge of the platform, planting the sharp toes of her crystal shoes right in front of Gulph's face. She glared down at him. Her fists were bunched. Her cheeks blazed like torches, as red as her dress. She looked impossibly tall, impossibly slender, almost as if she were . . .

. . . *growing?*

Gulph dismissed the thought. He would not be intimidated by her. The tide was turning, he could feel it.

"How dare you!" Lady Redina's voice, low and menacing, pierced the air like a spear. All around, the crystal sculptures of the ornamental garden rang like bells. The sound of clashing swords stopped abruptly. All eyes were fixed on the woman in the red dress.

"How dare you!" she repeated. "*I* rule Celestis! *I* say what will be, and what will not be! Nobody speaks to my people like that!"

Was her voice growing deeper? Gulph could feel something pulsing out from inside Lady Redina, a growing force that was trying to push him away, yet at the same time seemed to be drawing him in.

I'm sensing her thoughts, he realized. It felt familiar, and in a rush he realized why—it was exactly like when he'd first found Sidebottom John in Celestis, when Gulph had entered John's mind. . . .

"Nobody speaks to *me* like that!" Lady Redina was ranting. Her voice was thick, somehow full of splinters. Not a woman's voice at all. "Least of all a broken, twisted, tiresome little grub like you!"

Without thinking, Gulph summoned the feelings that had now become so familiar to him: the peculiar sensation of dry heat, of coarse sand in his mouth. The taste of his own magic. If he chose, he could use these feelings to turn himself invisible. Or . . . Lady Redina's twisted face filled his vision. The crowd melted away. Everything dissolved except her face, and what lay behind it. Gulph rushed toward her, even though his feet remained firmly planted on the ground, and suddenly . . .

. . . there are bodies, and there is blood. The bodies float and the blood spreads in a vast red cloud, because both are trapped in silver water.

The bodies are struggling—people screaming, trapped and trying to break free. But something is keeping them in the water, circling beneath the waves, making a whirlpool and sucking them down.

The something is red.

It bursts from the lake, rearing up like a striking snake. It has coils and claws and a huge unspeakable head, and the head has a face.

It is the face of Lady Redina . . .

. . . Gulph broke the connection. Gasping, he staggered away from the platform. His feet tangled together, and he would have fallen if Kalia hadn't caught him.

"Gulph," she said, her voice trembling. "What did you see?"

He gaped up at Lady Redina, glowering down at him from the platform. She looked . . . normal. Not bigger, as he'd imagined. Not monstrous. Tall and imposing, to be sure, but a woman all the same.

Except you're not! I know exactly what you are!

"Bring more guards!" Lady Redina screamed. "There are traitors in our midst!"

A door opened in the side of the house, spilling a dozen armed men into the garden.

"There's something I have to do," Gulph said to Kalia, trying to ignore the oncoming guardsmen. "I think you should probably stand back."

Bunching his fists, Gulph banished his thoughts, his doubts, his fears. Magic was a physical thing, he knew that now, an act not of the mind but the body. Magic was like running or swimming or climbing or leaping. Like turning somersaults before a crowd.

Come on, Gulph. Time for another performance.

He tensed his shoulders and summoned the hot desert wind. It came at once, filling him up until it gushed from the pores of his skin. Tears poured from his eyes. Thunder boomed in his ears. Once again he sprang free from his body. This time he took the wind with him.

An eye blink later, he was inside Lady Redina again. Not in her mind this time, but in her muscles. The sandstorm drove through her physical body, gusting through her veins, howling inside her heart, pushing at every fiber of her being, pushing, pushing . . .

Change! Gulph thought. *Show everyone what you really are!*

Hot magic spun him round, swept him up, and carried him back. He collapsed into himself again, his arms and legs accepting his return like well-worn clothes. He staggered, giddy and breathless. Sweat was spilling down his face. He spat sand.

All around him, people were screaming.

Gulph looked up.

Lady Redina was growing, and this time it was no illusion. Her body swelled beneath her bright red dress, expanding until it seemed certain the fabric would burst. But it didn't. Instead, the dress grew thick scales that slid one across the other, multiplying with dizzying speed. At the same time, her neck stretched and thickened. Her head elongated, her lower jaw extending to become a snout. Her eyes grew enormous, losing their color and adopting the flat white gaze of a corpse.

I knew it! Gulph was caught between triumph and terror. *I knew it!*

On the platform, the thing that had once been Lady Redina spun rapidly around. As it turned, its arms and legs dwindled. By the time it was facing Gulph again, they'd vanished completely. What remained was a mass of squirming coils.

Kalia grabbed Gulph's arm. "Now I see!" she said hoarsely.

Red scales flashed in the Celestian twilight. A forest of orange quills burst from the creature's back. It reared up, glaring balefully down with those inhuman eyes as it towered over the crowd. Below those eyes, two pairs of gills pulsed with a slow, hypnotic rhythm.

The jaws opened to reveal teeth like knives.

"This is what she really is!" Gulph yelled to the crowd. "Lady Redina is the bakaliss!"

CHAPTER 6

"Tarlan? Are you awake?"

Something like a feather tickled Tarlan's cheek. He brushed it aside and turned over. His head ached.

"Leave me alone, Theeta," he mumbled. "Let me sleep."

"Tarlan?"

The tickling came again. Tarlan groaned. Bleary-eyed, he heaved himself up on his elbows.

"Theeta—I told you to . . ."

He stopped. What he'd thought was a feather was in fact a thick bearskin covering his body; its bristly folds must have fallen across his face while he'd slept. But who had put it there?

He sat up, and saw that he was in some kind of cave. Stalactites hung from the gray stone ceiling like stone icicles; ancient carvings decorated the walls; a small fire flickered orange, sending a thin column of smoke up toward a smoke hole set high in the far corner.

Mirith? he thought, stunned by how similar this place was to the Yalasti cave that had once been his home.

"At last," said the voice. "I was beginning to think you would sleep forever, Tarlan."

Not Mirith. Not Theeta. Then who?

Turning his head, Tarlan saw a weatherworn man in his middle years sitting comfortably on a knuckle of rock. He was big—perhaps even as big as the bear that had given up its pelt to keep Tarlan warm.

"Who are you? How do you know my name?"

The man's leathery face rearranged itself into a smile. His eyes were kind. "I know you don't recognize me, Tarlan. We met just hours after you were born. Thirteen long years have passed since. The circumstances then were . . . difficult."

Tarlan stared at him. "Thirteen years?"

"Thirteen years ago I took you to Yalasti, where I meant to keep you from King Brutan's murderous reach. But our time together was brief. It ended when a band of Helkrags scented my trail. I had no choice but to leave you near a thorrod nest and trust that they wouldn't let you come to harm. The elk-hunters held me captive for years. It was torture, not because I was a prisoner, but because I did not know if you had survived." The man's gaze bored deep into Tarlan's eyes. "I did not know if I had kept my promise."

Tarlan tried to respond, but found he had no voice.

"And then, years later, I saw a thorrod flying over the snowfields with a boy riding on its back. A boy who looked perhaps twelve or thirteen years old. A boy with the same red-gold hair as the baby I'd left, and wearing a black cloak. The cloak in which I'd wrapped him all those years before." His smile broadened. "It was you, Tarlan."

"Captain Leom!" said Tarlan as understanding finally dawned.

"And so we come full circle," Leom replied. "At last I fulfill my promise and take you back from the snow."

A knot of wood exploded in the fire. Sparks flew. The rock walls seemed to move in the dancing light, as if the cave were breathing.

Tarlan stared at Leom, dumbstruck. He should thank this man, he supposed, for saving him not once but twice. But he couldn't find the words. Nor could he quite believe that chance had brought them together again after all these years. No sooner had he decided to abandon the world of humans than he stumbled over a man whose fate was tied up inextricably with his own.

Is there no escaping these people?

"Here." Leom dipped a ladle into a pot that was warming near the fire. He poured sweet-smelling broth into a rough metal bowl, which he handed to Tarlan. "Eat this. You must be starving."

At the smell of the hot food Tarlan's mouth filled with saliva. He seized the dish and held it up to his lips.

"Here," Leom repeated, this time holding up a spoon.

Tarlan grabbed the spoon and started shoveling the broth into his mouth. Hot and spicy, it ran down his throat like a stream of fire. His stomach growled its appreciation. When he'd finished, he set the dish down on the bearskin and gave a loud, appreciative belch.

"Would you like more?"

"No." Tarlan shrugged off the bearskin. "I think it's time I was going."

Captain Leom looked puzzled. "So soon? You ought to rest, Tarlan. At least stay until you've eaten your fill."

Tarlan eyed the pot hungrily. He could certainly manage another bowlful. But a second helping might lead to a third, after which he would begin to feel sleepy, and then . . .

"I can't stay," he said abruptly.

He got up, tightened the collar of his black cloak, and slipped past the fire to the cave entrance. Just before ducking through the low archway of rock, he glanced back.

"Thank you," he said.

"For what?"

"For rescuing me. Both times. But I travel alone now."

Tarlan stepped out into what he'd thought would be the darkness of night. But instead of the open air, he emerged into the warmth of another cave. This one was much bigger than the first, and its curved walls were dotted with many tunnel entrances. Crackling torches hung in mounts on the walls. Flames painted the gray rock with orange light.

He stared, stunned, at the people hurrying to and fro in the tunnels. Conversation buzzed. All were wrapped in thick furs, and most had their hands full. Some carried waterskins, others firewood. One thickset man bore the carcass of a deer on his back.

Tarlan couldn't believe it. He was desperate to be in the wilderness, the land stretched out before him, the endless sky overhead, nothing to worry about but traveling ever onward. . . . Instead he felt trapped. He could feel something like panic rising in his chest.

"Where have you brought me?" he demanded.

"You are in the Fortress of the Flown," said Leom, joining him at the cave threshold.

"Well, I don't want to be here. Where's the way out?"

Captain Leom didn't answer. He was looking thoughtfully at Tarlan.

"Please, Leom! Show me the way out. I'm not meant to be here."

"Perhaps not," Leom said slowly. "Come. It's this way."

Leom set off down the nearest passage. Tarlan hurried after him. The tunnel was low, and he frequently had to crouch to avoid banging his head on the rocky ceiling. Every few breaths he had to dodge sideways as someone pushed past on some unknown errand. At one point, a small pack of short-furred dogs scurried past, yipping at each other's heels. Busy as all the people appeared to be, they walked with their heads down and their shoulders slumped. Tarlan often found it hard to interpret human expressions, but one thing was clear: the people of the Fortress of the Flown were unhappy.

The tunnel delivered them into a vast cavern with craggy walls rising up to a high black ceiling. When Tarlan looked again, he saw that it wasn't a ceiling at all but the night sky. He took deep breaths of the outdoor air, snowflakes clinging to his face. This wasn't a cavern; it was actually a rocky bowl cut deep into the mountain landscape.

Tunnels led away from the open-roofed chamber in all directions. It reminded Tarlan of the town squares he'd seen in various human settlements, and like many such places, this one was filled with people—some standing at its edges, many more squatting on the piles of boulders that covered the chamber floor. Despite the size of the crowd, there was hardly any sound. Even the packs of dogs, curled up beside the many small fires, were silent.

Tarlan looked around uneasily. Misery hung in the air. "Who are these people?"

"They are the Flown," Leom told him. "People have been gathering here ever since the war began, a thousand years ago. Some here are their descendants. Many more have only recently arrived." Leom gestured to a group of shabby-looking men and women in one corner of the square. "They fled from Idilliam before the bridge fell." He nodded toward a group of men in uniform. "Deserters from Nynus's army. We also have wanderers who fell foul of Brutan, and fled his clutches. Even farmers from Ritherlee have made their way here, after being brought to ruin by Lord Vicerin's cruel taxes."

Leom spread his arms wide to take in the entire chamber.

"Refugees all. Wretched folk with nowhere to go. Nowhere but the Fortress of the Flown."

Tarlan scanned the crowd. There were children here, he saw. Toddlers clinging to their mothers' knees, babies staring blankly into the night. Nearby, two boys huddled miserably together, returning Tarlan's gaze. They looked identical; Tarlan supposed they were twins. The hands of both were badly burned.

Don't think about them, he told himself. *This has nothing to do with you.*

"The first tunnels were cut here at the start of the Thousand Year War," Leom went on. "Since then, the Fortress has continued to grow. It appears on no maps; ask anyone about it and they will deny its existence. Yet exist it does—a secret haven to which the lost make their way, and where they find the safety they seek."

"But they look so sad."

"They want to go home," said Leom simply. "Life here is hard. Food is scarce in the mountains, and the winters are long and harsh. But as long as war rages in Toronia, they have nowhere else to go." He hesitated. "Like you."

Tarlan glared at him. "I'm not like them! I didn't run away."

Leom nodded. The small, calm smile on his face was infuriating.

"I played my part!" Tarlan continued. "I fought. I won a battle! I just . . . I just suddenly realized how pointless it all was."

"Sometimes we have no choice but to run away."

"But that's what I'm trying to tell you! I *didn't* run away, I chose to leave! I didn't . . ."

Tarlan broke off. His chest was heaving. The dull ache in his head had turned to a sharp, insistent pain.

This is the trouble with humans! They make everything so complicated!

"I didn't run away," he repeated.

"I never said you did," Leom replied.

Tarlan spun away, feeling the heat of anger rising in his cheeks.

If only Theeta were here. She'd carry me out of this place.

Or would she? Hadn't she abandoned him too?

Wrong future. Wrong past. Wrong now. Place wrong. Tarlan wrong.

He pinched his eyes shut. Theeta had never said such a thing before. He thought about Melchior, how the wizard had pleaded with him to stay. He thought about Filos and Greythorn and Brock.

He realized that the heat in his cheeks wasn't anger at all.

It was shame.

"You said you'd show me the way out," he said dully.

"It's across the square," said Leom. "But, Tarlan, where will you go?"

"I don't know. I just know I don't belong here."

"There is nothing out there."

Tarlan rounded on him. "Are you going to show me or not?"

"This way."

He followed Leom as he trudged through the crowds of people

to a narrow passage on the other side of the square. All the way there, Tarlan kept his eyes averted from the curious gazes of the inhabitants of the Fortress of the Flown.

The passage was short and dark. At the far end was a stout wooden door.

"Here," said Leom, lifting aside the heavy bar of timber that had been dropped across the frame. "This door will take you out onto the mountainside, not far from where I found you. From there you can . . . go wherever you please."

"There were stones," said Tarlan. "Standing stones, like claws sticking out of the ground. Are they far?"

"The Snowspires? They are just a short walk downslope, but the way is treacherous. Why do you want to go there?"

"What's that got—" Tarlan began angrily, then cut himself short. Leom had done so much for him, not just here in the mountains, but back in Yalasti, all those years ago. He'd kept his promise to show Tarlan the way out.

No, it wasn't Leom who Tarlan was angry with. He was angry with himself.

"I saw something," he said, "on top of one of the spires. Thorrods. I think they were my friends."

Leom rubbed his grizzled chin. "Thorrods, you say. Are you sure?"

"Yes. I mean, I think so."

"How many did you see?"

"I'm not sure. Two, I think."

"And you wish to see them again?"

"Yes. I have to. If only to say good-bye."

Leom nodded. He grasped the latch and pulled open the door. Outside, snow-covered slopes rose steeply toward a line of jagged mountains gnawing at the night sky. Bitter wind blasted their faces and rocked Tarlan back on his heels.

"As I said," Leom shouted over the howl of the gale, "the way is treacherous! I will lead you."

"Thank you," Tarlan replied. "I can find my own way after that. It's like I said . . ."

"I know. You travel alone."

They stepped out into the snow. The door slammed shut behind them. The night air was filled with freezing splinters of ice.

Tarlan welcomed the cold seeping into his bones, the frost already forming on his clothes and hair. But being back outdoors didn't bring the relief he'd hoped for. He felt strangely empty.

"What you find may not be what you expect," Leom said with the trace of a smile.

"What? What do you mean?"

"When we get there, you will see. Come."

Leom plodded down the slope, sinking almost up to his knees in the deep, drifted snow.

Tarlan watched him for a moment, puzzled. Then he followed.

CHAPTER 7

The bakaliss lunged at Gulph. He threw himself across the crystal platform, leaving the giant serpent's teeth to snap shut on empty air. Cheated of its prize, the bakaliss threw back its head and roared.

All around Gulph, people were screaming. Those nearest the bakaliss took to their heels and ran. Soon the panic had engulfed the crowd and hundreds of Celestians began to flee.

To Gulph's relief, Pip and Sidebottom John had ushered the rest of his friends toward the shelter of the house. Ossilius and Kalia had their swords raised to fend off the approaching guards, but at the sight of their mistress's transformation, the Celestian soldiers had taken to their heels.

Scales scraped on the crystal ground. Having recovered from its lunge, the bakaliss was now sliding toward Gulph. He tried to move his feet, but they were rooted to the platform. He was transfixed by the empty gaze of the bakaliss's huge, blank eyes.

It's the legend! Terror was welling up inside him. *The king went under the mountain to slay the bakaliss. But the bakaliss ate him instead!*

"Gulph!" shouted Kalia. "Look out!"

Gulph snapped awake, reminding himself that this was no story. It was time for him to face reality. It was time for him to fight.

"You might have won in the legend!" he yelled through his fear. "But you're not going to win today!"

The bakaliss thrust its gaping jaws forward with blinding speed. Gulph jumped straight up, somersaulting over its snout and off the platform. He landed beside Kalia, who brandished the blade of her crystal sword at the onrushing monster.

"Run, Gulph!" she shouted.

"Never!" he replied.

The bakaliss lunged off the platform, and suddenly Captain Ossilius was there, slicing at the serpent's exposed throat. The bakaliss retreated, hissing and spitting. Hot yellow saliva splashed across Gulph's face. He wiped it away in disgust and fumbled for his sword, then remembered it wasn't there. He'd left it in Idilliam, thrust into his undead father.

Moving with astonishing speed, the bakaliss circled behind Kalia and Ossilius. The orange quills sprouting from its neck rattled along the hard ground. Its tail whipped against a pair of crystal statues, which fell and shattered. It plowed through what was left of the crowd, knocking people aside. But its eyes were fixed on Gulph.

It's only interested in me!

Kalia struck out again. This time her blade hit home, burying itself in one of the monster's muscular coils. With a yell of triumph, she jerked it free. Scarlet blood jetted into the air, and Gulph's hopes rose. But then the creature's huge scales closed over the wound, sealing it shut. Recovering from her swing, Kalia stood utterly exposed, easy prey for the oncoming beast.

Ossilius ran immediately to her side, but the bakaliss ignored them both and continued its advance on Gulph.

"Get everyone to safety!" Gulph screamed. "I know what to do!"

He backed away from the oncoming monster, preparing to summon his powers of invisibility. They'd helped him before, when he'd faced the bakaliss in the lake.

But before he could manage it, the bakaliss was on him again. It whipped its spiked tail around, clearly intending to sweep Gulph's legs from under him. Marshaling all his strength, he executed a perfect back flip that took him out of reach of the spikes . . . and toward the bakaliss's jaws. Acting on pure instinct, Gulph ducked and rolled. Ruby teeth crashed together, slicing through the straps of his pack.

He hit the ground on his shoulder, rolled again, and came up in a crouch. His pack had ripped open, spilling something gold and glittering onto the crystal ground.

The bakaliss reared up to strike again . . . then stopped. It glared down at the crown. Gulph saw the circlet of gold reflected in the monster's soulless eyes.

"So now we're even, Lady Redina!" he shouted. "I know what you really are—and *you* know who I really am!"

The bakaliss screeched. Steaming spittle dripped from its mouth and splattered around the spot where Gulph lay.

A small hand grabbed his. "Gulph! This way, quickly!"

It was Pip, pushing her way through the forest of the bakaliss's quills. She looked terrified.

"No, Pip! Go back!" he told her. "Get to safety!"

She shook her head. "You'll need this."

Pip was pushing something into his hand. A crystal sword.

He grinned at her. As she scrambled away, he struck at the nearest segment of the giant serpent. The bakaliss avoided his blow with ease. He lashed out again, only to find the belly of the beast descending toward him. He held his sword straight up—maybe the vile thing would impale itself!

The bakaliss's tail smashed into his shins. His legs flew from under him and he crashed onto his chest. All the air exploded from his lungs. Gasping, he rolled over to see a pair of enormous crimson jaws descending toward him.

From somewhere far away he heard Kalia shriek, "Gulph!" and then the monster's huge teeth were on him, under him, gathering him up and lifting him off the ground. He tried to wriggle free, but the jaws of the bakaliss had closed around him like a vise. He tried to wield his sword, but both his arms were clamped to his side. He tried to scream, but the bakaliss's jaws were crushing his chest.

It's going to bite me in half!

But it didn't. Holding Gulph high in the air, the bakaliss paused. For a brief moment all was still. Gulph dangled in its jaws. Above him hung the rich purple canopy of the cavern roof, alive with its starlike gems.

Then the view rotated, and Gulph found himself staring down at the horrified, upturned faces of Kalia and Ossilius, of Pip and Noddy and the rest of the Tangletree Players.

Still holding Gulph aloft, the bakaliss slithered out of the garden. The twin racks of gigantic teeth continued to hold him tight, but they didn't bite down. He heard the scrape and rattle of scale and quill as he was carried at high speed. Ahead lay a rippling silver sheet: the Celestial Lake. It expanded until it filled Gulph's vision.

It's going to drown me!

Without hesitation, the bakaliss plunged into the lake. There was no time for Gulph to take a breath. Water crashed into his mouth, up his nose, into his eyes and ears. He screamed into the cold silver liquid, his cries transforming into a tortured stream of bubbles.

The deeper they went, the more the pressure mounted in Gulph's ears. Water streamed past his face. He fought against the cage of teeth, but they held fast. His lungs tightened, began to throb.

I can't hold out much longer. I've got to take a breath.

If he did, it would be his last.

Just when Gulph thought his lungs would burst, the bakaliss made a gut-wrenching turn before erupting from the lake once more. Opening his mouth, Gulph dragged hot, stale air into his aching lungs.

Blinking furiously, he saw that they'd emerged not into open air, but into a huge cave filled with rippling green light. Behind them was the flooded tunnel they'd just come through. Ahead, a series of ancient stone steps climbed to a large platform covered with broken skeletons. Skulls grinned at him from amid piles of bones.

Human skulls.

This is where it feeds!

On the tail of that horrifying thought came another.

This is where the bakaliss will eat the king!

Surrounding the platform entirely with its scaly coils, the bakaliss threw Gulph onto the topmost step. His fall was broken by a heap of bones, which scattered like pebbles down the stone staircase.

Sprawled on the step, Gulph saw that the walls of the cave were studded with gems. Emeralds, like the green jewel hanging against his chest on its chain of gold. They filled the cavern with a rich green glow. He scrambled up and saw something else—on the platform were three thrones with high backs and ornate arms. One looked as if it were made of emerald, the next ruby, and the third gold.

The throne room of Toronia! But why is it buried down here?

The bakaliss reared over him again with its jaws agape. The sight of it filled Gulph with terror. He shoved all thoughts of thrones and jewels from his mind and summoned the feeling that was now so familiar to him.

Sand! I'm surrounded by hot desert sand and you can't see me. Do you hear? You can't see me at all!

Heat seared him. He became the heat. The moist air of the cavern turned dry. A tremor ran through his body, from the crown of his head to the tips of his toes.

He held his breath.

The bakaliss froze. Its head weaved first to the left, then to the right. Gulph finally dared to look down at his body.

His magic had worked. He was invisible.

Towering over him, the bakaliss roared in frustration.

As long as it can't see me, I still have a chance.

Keeping tight hold of the crystal sword that Pip had handed to him, he summoned all his waning energy and sprinted up the slope toward the three thrones. Bones shattered beneath his feet as he ran. Following the sound, the red-scaled serpent dropped its head to ground level and slithered after him.

Gulph reached the thrones barely a breath before the bakaliss. No sooner had he crawled beneath them than the bakaliss's tail whipped in and hooked him out again. He fell into a mountain of skulls, which scattered like the playthings of some evil monster's child. Quickly he scrambled away, knowing their movement would give away his position.

There's no way out of this place! he thought, desperately casting his eyes around the chamber. All he could see were the gem-covered walls and the single waterlogged tunnel through which they'd entered.

I'll never be able to swim back. I'd drown before I got even halfway.

He might be invisible. But he was also trapped.

Hot breath scalded his face. The head of the bakaliss floated before him, its enormous jaws split in a cruel and heartless grin. Red scales shimmered in the eerie green light of the underwater cave. The bakaliss sniffed, then swiveled its head until its gaze was locked on the empty space where Gulph was standing.

It can smell me!

The bakaliss reared over him. Above its massive head glittered the jewel-encrusted ceiling, and for a moment Gulph imagined that it was a sky filled with stars.

The prophecy of the three, he thought. *The legend of the king. Maybe they both need to come true. . . .*

The bakaliss's jaws opened like the gates of doom, but a strange calm had descended over Gulph.

Taking a deep, deliberate breath, Gulph allowed his magic to drain away until he was standing before the bakaliss, visible and revealed. Sliding the sword through his belt, he held out his hands, palms up.

"All right!" he shouted. "All right! Let's make the story true! Come for me, Redina, or whatever your name is! Come and eat the king!"

Red coils squirmed into knots. Sharp quills cut through heaps of polished bones. Jaws parted.

Gulph leaped . . . between its teeth.

The jaws of the bakaliss slammed shut . . . behind him.

He landed on something soft and slimy.

Its tongue!

Tucking his arms against his body, Gulph performed a forward roll that sent him tumbling headlong into the squirming tunnel that was the monster's throat. Wads of moist flesh pulsed against his body as he slid deeper and deeper into its gullet. It was utterly dark. The smell was unspeakable. He was surrounded by echoing gurgling sounds, beneath which he could hear a deep, regular thump.

Something wet slapped his face. He twisted, resisting the urge to throw up. The darkness was dreadful, the sense of being trapped overwhelming.

Just when he thought he could stand it no more, the tube of flesh down which he'd been sliding opened out into a larger cavity. He splashed into a pool of thick, glutinous liquid. Bubbles popped in the darkness, releasing a stench that was ten times as bad as anything he'd experienced so far. Sticky lumps bobbed just below the surface. He didn't like to think about what they might be. Hard things grated beneath him—more bones, probably.

The thumping sound was coming from right behind his head.

"The bakaliss has eaten the king!" he shouted into the darkness. He wondered if the monster could hear the voice coming from its own stomach. "The legend is fulfilled."

Thump! Thump! Thump!

He took the sword from his belt and raised it up out of the slimy liquid.

The old tales say that's where the story ends, he thought. His arm felt strong. His sword felt light. His whole body seemed to thrum with power. *But I say the story goes on!*

He plunged the crystal sword into the bakaliss's stomach wall. The lining ripped like silk. A flood of sticky juices poured over him. Using both hands, he drew a great slash through the flesh and forced his way through it. Strange blobby things thrust against him. He carved them into pieces and headed toward the thumping sound.

From somewhere that seemed both nearby and very far away, he could hear screaming.

Thump! Thump! Thump!

The sound was almost unbearably loud. He could sense its source in the darkness before him: a hot, vibrating globe hanging like a huge, dark fruit and pumping, pumping, pumping.

Gulph raised his sword, and with a single blow sliced the baka-liss's heart in two.

Blood boiled out. It was like standing inside a volcano. Head down, Gulph pushed through it, hacking and slashing, hacking and slashing, wanting to scream but not wanting to open his mouth, not wanting to swallow the awful . . .

Hot flesh peeled apart, and suddenly Gulph was breathing clean, cold air again. He slid into the brightness, his sword swinging through empty air. His feet skidded on a raft of bones. Steaming fluid bubbled around him.

He stopped, panting for breath.

Behind him, something huge fell to the ground with a sickening, wet thud. Accompanying the thud was a deep, rumbling crash.

Gulph opened his eyes.

He was standing in a lake of blood. Torn scales jutted from the dark liquid like the hulls of broken boats. Gulph was covered from head to toe in blood and slime.

Slowly he turned around. Behind him rose a mountain of red coils sparkling beneath an aura of purple light. Orange quills sagged like dead branches. A pair of pale eyes seemed to glare at him for a long, long moment before rolling back into their sockets and turning black.

The bakaliss was dead.

Gulph coughed, and the cough started a fit of spluttering. Retching, he staggered free of the trail of blood and gore he'd released from the monster's guts. To his relief the crown was nestled nearby amid a pile of broken bones, covered in gore but in one piece. He snatched it up.

Then he simply stood for a moment, breathing hard, the crown clasped to his chest.

Feeling steadier, he stowed the crown safely in his backpack and made for the flooded tunnel. At least there he would be able to wash himself clean. . . .

He stopped as something struck him.

The light. It isn't green anymore.

The cave's emerald glow was now cut through by beams of purple. They were coming from the other side of the bakaliss's corpse. Circling around it, stepping between gore and pools of blood, Gulph saw a gigantic crack in the cave wall. The monster must have smashed it open in its death throes.

Through the crack, he could see the familiar twilight of Celestis.

In a daze, Gulph stumbled out of the throne room and onto the shore of the Celestial Lake. Without hesitation, he plunged into the silver water, ducking himself repeatedly under and scrubbing himself and the crown of Toronia clean.

He felt relieved, and wondered if he should feel more. But he was exhausted beyond anything he'd ever experienced. Perhaps the feeling of triumph would come later.

Crossing the lake seemed to take forever. Gulph swam slowly, not just because his battered body protested against every stroke, but because his thoughts were hopelessly tangled together. If he took his time, perhaps the knots would work themselves out before he reached the other shore.

He remembered his younger years, tagging along with the Tangletree Players as they'd traveled across the realms from one village to the next. He'd been small for his age, a weakling with a bent back who earned his keep by carrying around the money pouch at the end of each performance. The people who put coins in the pouch used to laugh at him.

With Pip's help, he'd discovered a talent for tumbling and become an acrobat. Audiences still laughed at him, but it was when he did something funny. When he did something amazing, they applauded.

And now . . . now he was a bakaliss slayer; one of the prophecy three; a survivor of prison, war, and a leap from the tower of Castle Tor; a future king who still carried the crown of Toronia on his back.

What would those crowds say about him now?

Around him, Celestis was silent but for the gentle lapping of the water as he swam.

He tipped back his head to gaze at the crystal ceiling. The gems shone like stars.

Applause doesn't matter, he thought. *The only thing that matters is who you are inside, and what you choose to do with your life.*

Smiling to himself, he struck out once more across the lake. His body still ached terribly, and the muscles in his crooked back were horribly cramped, but for the first time that day—in a long time, in fact—his mind was at peace.

Exhausted, Gulph crawled out of the shallows onto a wide beach of smooth blue sapphire. He flopped down onto his front, utterly spent.

Movement flickered at the corner of his vision. A figure, darting around the beach, peering into the silver lake as if it were looking for someone.

"Over here!" Gulph managed to shout, his voice wet and rasping.

The figure ran toward him with great loping strides, his head thrown back over his shoulder. Now Gulph recognized him. It was Sidebottom John.

"John!" Gulph called weakly. "John, I . . ."

"It be him!" John yelled delightedly. "Gulph's a-livin' and a-breathin'!"

By the time John reached him, the rest of the Tangletree Players were running toward him from all over the beach.

"Oh, Gulph, you were so brave!"

"Just as we was giving up hope of finding you!"

A pair of arms gathered him up. It was Pip.

"Gulph!" she sobbed, her voice joyful despite the tears. "Thank the stars. I thought you were dead!"

"Let go!" Gulph laughed. "I'm filthy!"

"I don't care! I'm never going to let you go again!"

But she did—reluctantly. Stepping back, she wiped the tears from her face and said, "Can you tell us what happened?"

Gulph took the hand Pip held toward him and got to his feet.

"I can," he replied. "But . . . I think I need to tell everyone."

With Pip supporting him on one side, and John on the other, he led them from the beach to the garden where Lady Redina's true identity had been revealed. Pip helped him clamber up onto the platform where, not long before, Lady Redina had turned into a monster. He stood there, swaying a little. Most of the Celestians had fled when Lady Redina had transformed into the bakaliss, but they were returning now. Before long the garden was full again. As he gazed out over the crowd, it struck Gulph that the Celestians looked different somehow—wide-eyed and full of wonder.

Lady Redina's magic died with her, Gulph realized. *They've woken up at last.*

Ossilius was there too. When Gulph caught his eye, he dropped to one knee. Beside Ossilius stood Kalia, his mother, her scarred face full of love, her eyes bright with tears.

I'm back, Mother, he thought. *I'm back and the prophecy still lives.*

"The bakaliss is dead!" he cried. "Lady Redina is dead! You're free! All of you—free!"

The crowd roared.

"Now tell them," Ossilius called up. "Tell them who you really are."

"My name is Gulph!" For the first time in his life, Gulph felt as if he were standing up straight. "I was born under the light of the prophecy stars. I am one of three triplets destined to rule Toronia. Today I have brought peace to Celestis. Tomorrow I will bring peace to the whole kingdom!"

Another roar, this one ten times as loud. Now people were

pouring into the garden from all directions, curious to see what the commotion was.

Gulph took out the crown from his pack. He held it up for a moment, gold and glittering.

The crowd fell silent.

He raised his arms and settled the crown on his head.

The crowd gasped.

"I have freed Idilliam from the tyranny of Brutan!" Gulph proclaimed. "I have freed Celestis from the tyranny of Lady Redina! Now the rest of the kingdom deserves the same! Will you help me bring freedom to Toronia?"

"Yes!" The roar of the crowd echoed like thunder through the crystal cavern. Gulph saw that Kalia and Pip were weeping. Even Ossilius was wiping at his cheeks. Gulph grinned, and as he waved his hands in triumph, another sound joined the massed voices of the people of Celestis.

It was the sound of applause.

CHAPTER 8

Elodie woke into darkness and silence.

Am I blind? she wondered, holding her hands up in front of her face and seeing nothing at all. *Deaf too?*

She heard a shriek, faint and very far away. Not deaf, then. She rubbed her eyes. A pale glow fluttered at the edges of her vision, like the wings of a bird.

Or an insect. She shuddered, remembering the swarms of giant bugs that had filled the swamp.

But she was no longer in the swamp, was she?

The glow intensified. Now she saw blurred shapes floating all around her, dark clouds moving against a sullen gray sky. Her vision sharpened, and she saw that they weren't clouds after all but slabs of rock. They drifted, weightless, as if the flagstones from Castle Vicerin's courtyard had been torn free and given permission to fly.

Only each slab was as big as the castle itself.

Elodie saw she was sitting near the edge of her own floating slab. It was much smaller than the rest—about the size of the Vicerin banqueting table. Her wedding dress was gone. In its place was the same green tunic she'd worn when she'd ridden at the head of Trident's army. Her hand crept to her throat and closed around the precious green gem that Lord Vicerin had stolen from her shortly after that hateful wedding.

She shivered, thinking she was cold, then realized she wasn't cold at all. She wasn't warm, either. There was no temperature here at all, no breath of wind . . . just an empty nothingness.

The stone lurched beneath her. Her stomach lurched in sympathy. The view changed as the platform circled slowly round to face a neighboring slab. At the same time, Elodie heard the scream again; this time she saw who had made it.

On the nearby slab stood a woman wearing crude leather wraps. She was tearing at her hair and wailing at the blank gray sky. Her face was twisted in anguish. Behind her on the slab were hundreds more people, some crying out, some wandering aimlessly. Many simply crouched with their heads down. Their bodies moved like mist, not exactly transparent but hardly solid.

Elodie's eyes continued to adjust to the peculiar flat light of this unearthly place. All the slabs were occupied except hers. On some, the people wore fine clothes like those she'd been used to seeing around Castle Vicerin. Other slabs bore people in garments Elodie knew dated from earlier ages—even from before the Thousand Year War. They crowded the floating slabs, the helpless passengers of a fleet of bizarre stone ships, adrift in an ocean of colorless air.

They all looked like ghosts.

But they're not ghosts, Elodie realized. *Ghosts haunt the real world.*

Her heart clenched in her chest. Her own slab bumped against its neighbor, and her stomach lurched again.

She knew where she was.

This is the Realm of the Dead!

Suddenly she understood why so many people were screaming. She could feel her own scream bubbling up inside her throat. If she released it, the sound would tear her apart.

I can't be dead! I can't be!

The edges of the two slabs ground against each other. The noise they made was thin and lifeless, like the memory of sound.

All these people were dead. This was their resting place for eternity . . . except they weren't at rest. Elodie's guts were crawling.

I'm not dead! I don't belong here!

A tall man moved slowly through the crowd. He wore armor and carried a lance. For a moment, Elodie was convinced it was Sir Jaken, leader of the ghost army she'd raised.

Then the man turned his face toward her, and she saw that it wasn't Sir Jaken at all. It was just another dead soul.

Nevertheless, there would be people she knew here.

Fessan. Poor Palenie. My mother . . .

Panic seized her. Was this dreadful place really where the dead spent eternity? It was too much to take in, too much to bear.

The woman nearby uttered a low, desperate moan. It was an awful sound, the cry an animal might make when caught in a trap.

Horrified, Elodie clamped her hands to her mouth. The woman was only a stone's throw away on the great slab, just starting to drift away from Elodie. Her face was pleading. Many of the wraithlike people looked downcast, or even distraught. But a few were staring at Elodie with open curiosity.

There must be thousands in this place, she thought. *No, millions. All miserable, all trapped.*

Elodie lowered her hands. The panic ebbed a little.

This isn't right. These people are supposed to be at peace.

She was certain that something had gone terribly wrong here.

"I'm going to help you," she said.

The ranks of the dead stared at her. She got to her feet, took several paces back, then gathered all her strength and sprinted forward. At the slab's edge she jumped into the clear gray air, her arms flailing. She felt oddly weightless, almost as if she could fly. Clearing the gap with ease, she landed with a gentle thump on the bigger slab nearby.

When she stood, she saw that the little crowd of dead people was gathering around her.

"The light has returned," said a young man with a thin, transparent beard.

"The other brought the darkness," said an old woman, addressing Elodie directly. The furs she wore would have been thick and heavy in the living world; here they looked like wrappings of mist. "Now you bring the light."

Elodie was aware of a faint golden radiance in the air. Looking down, she saw that her whole body had begun to glow. Pale fire pulsed from her arms, her legs, her hands. When she moved, the fire left thin trails of light filled with firefly-like sparkles.

"What do you mean?" she said. "What 'other'?"

"He came," said the young man. He spread his translucent arms. "He did this."

"Who came?"

"King Brutan!" cried the woman whose screams had first attracted Elodie's attention. She tore at her hair. "Brutan! Brutan! Brutan!"

The man settled his arm around her shoulders and whispered in her ear. Slowly she calmed down.

Meanwhile, Elodie was reeling.

My father? He's here?

The last time she'd seen King Brutan had been during the Battle of the Bridge, when she'd led the Trident army in their doomed attempt to storm Idilliam. With a shudder, she remembered the dreadful sight of his living corpse striding through the ranks of his undead army, the rotting flesh hanging from his bones, the awful red light burning from the empty eye sockets of his skull. . . .

"He was here before," the old woman went on. "Just for a short time. Then a strange wind carried him away."

Elodie's brow creased as she tried to puzzle it out. "He was killed," she told them. "But then he rose from the grave."

The dead moaned.

"Someone must have killed him again," said the old woman. "Now he has come back and turned all to darkness."

Elodie clenched her fists. The gold fire flashed around them. *Gulph killed Father before*, she thought. *Now I will finish him for good.*

"Where is he?" she demanded.

"At the Shadow Cage," said the old woman at once.

"The Shadow Cage? What's that?"

"Brutan conjured it from the darkness he brought. The Shadow Cage is his domain, and it is growing all the time."

"He holds prisoners there," added the young man. "Those who stood against him in the living world."

Like Fessan, Elodie thought. *And my mother.*

"He tortures them," the young man went on. "Their screams are . . ." His voice broke.

Elodie could feel her pulse throbbing at her temple. A red mist wavered in the corners of her vision. She knew the sensation only too well—it was the rage she'd once experienced during battle. The anger felt clean and good, but she fought against it all the same. It would be useful—perhaps very soon. But not quite yet.

"I'm going to set them free!" she announced. "Who will show me the way?"

The watching people exchanged uncertain glances, but said nothing.

"Surely one of you knows where this Shadow Cage is?"

"We know," said the man. "And you are brave. But your quest is doomed. The Shadow Cage is guarded by a terrible monster. Nobody can get near it."

"I'm not afraid of monsters."

The old woman took a step forward. At the same time, the rest of the crowd seemed to melt back into the grayness. For the briefest of moments, it seemed to Elodie that only the two of them were present.

"You remind me of another I knew," said the old woman. "I will take you."

Elodie became aware of the crowd of the dead again, and of the faint gasps rippling among them. Ignoring the shocked expressions on the faces of her companions, the old woman beckoned. "Come."

She led Elodie to the opposite side of the gigantic slab. Another island of stone was floating nearby.

The woman leaped into space. Her misty furs billowed around her like wings, and she flew to a soft landing on the other slab. Remembering the curious weightlessness she'd felt earlier, Elodie steeled herself and leaped after her. She soared onto the slab with ease.

"You have magic, child," said the old woman as they hurried across the cracked surface of the stone. "That's good. You will need it."

Elodie looked at her glowing skin. "You mean this light?"

"You have that and more, I can tell. You see, I had magic myself once, when I was living. But not here. No frost, you see?"

Elodie frowned. There was something about the old woman's voice that sounded familiar—an accent she'd heard before.

"So, my dear, tell me about Tarlan," her new companion went on. "Is he safe? How is he coping with all those humans?"

Elodie halted. She stared at the woman dumbfounded.

"How do you . . . ?" she began, then closed her mouth. She didn't have to ask; she'd worked it out. "Mirith! You're Mirith!"

The old woman smiled. "Well done. But you have me at a disadvantage. You know my name, but I do not know yours."

"Elodie. I'm—"

"Tarlan's sister. I know. You carry his same strength, and you carry it with beauty and grace. Now, please, tell me how he is."

Elodie couldn't help smiling. Even in the Realm of the Dead, there were friends to be found.

"He's all right," she said as they continued along the slab. "At least, he was when I last saw him. He has, well, a pack. Of animals. There's Theeta, she's a thorrod. And a tigron called Filos, and Greythorn the wolf . . ."

Mirith's ghostly face was bright with pride. "Did he ever find Melchior?"

"Yes! Yes, he did! Melchior helped us. Tarlan went away with him on a mission—that's the last time I saw him. But I think"—she pressed her hand to her heart—"I'm sure he must still be all right. I think I'd know if he wasn't."

"My boy," Mirith said. Her voice was choked. "My lost-and-found boy."

"How did you know I was his sister?"

"He is one of the three who will rule over the three realms of Toronia—including the Realm of the Dead." Mirith pointed to Elodie's hands. "The light shows that this realm is yours, Elodie. You illuminate it like no other."

Elodie frowned. "The Realm of the Dead? I always thought . . . well, the prophecy talks about the crown of three, and there are really only three realms, aren't there? I always thought I'd rule over Ritherlee, and my brothers would take Idilliam and Isur."

"Oh, my dear. What makes a realm? Is it fields and trees? Castles and cities? Or is it something more?"

"I don't know. I suppose I've never really thought about it."

Mirith smiled. "You sound so like your brother—and look like him too, with those dark eyes and hair of red and gold. As soon as I saw you, I knew exactly who you were."

Picking up the pace, Mirith led Elodie to the edge of the slab they were on, and across the gap to the next. Sparks streamed out behind Elodie like the tail of a comet.

"Now," Mirith said as they ran toward the next jumping point, "tell me how you come to be here."

Elodie frowned again. "Back home—I mean, in the real world—I can see ghosts. I can summon them. That's what I was trying to do: summon a whole army of ghosts to fight against Lord Vicerin. He's trying to take the throne."

"What happened? Did something stop you from calling your army?"

"Yes. I think so. I could feel them—I was trying to pull them toward me. But something pulled back."

Mirith was nodding. "It was Brutan, or rather Brutan's magic. His heart was ever dark. Now it is beyond even darkness. He died, was raised, and died again. His return has poisoned the realm, and trapped the dead in this dreadful emptiness. None can leave to wander the mortal world."

"Twice dead isn't enough for that monster," Elodie said. "I'll bring him down, I swear it. I'll bring him down and free you all." She was trailing flames, but inside she felt only cold determination.

"Then there'll be nothing to stop my ghost army from rising."

Without warning, Mirith came to a halt. Elodie ran on for a few paces, then stopped herself.

"What's the matter?" she asked.

"We are here."

Elodie looked around. The slab they were standing on was deserted. The gray air surrounding it was filled with hundreds of smaller slabs, each one turning slowly end over end.

"I don't see . . . ," she began.

The swarm of slabs drifted apart, gradually revealing what looked to Elodie like a vast cloud of black smoke hanging in the sky. The cloud wavered in and out of focus, but its shape was unmistakable.

"A castle," she breathed.

"The Shadow Cage," said Mirith.

A fat strand of smoke rose from the edge of the slab they were standing on, extending all the way up to the Cage. It looked a little like a staircase, but as they approached, Elodie saw that it was writhing slowly, like a huge, sleepy snake.

"It will hold our weight," said Mirith, stepping onto the first smoky step. "But we must be quick."

As fear mounted inside her, Elodie felt a great urge to turn and run.

I won't stop now. I won't!

As they neared the yawning entrance to the castle of smoke,

tortured sobs shook the air like broken bells. The sounds made Elodie's spine jangle. She pressed her hands to her ears.

"It's awful!" she said. "What's he doing to them?"

"Tormenting them. The dead can feel pain, you know. Hurt them enough and their spirits will dissolve, and be gone forever. Brutan calls it the Shadow Cage, but it is really just one big torture chamber."

Anger shot through Elodie. "He'll harm no one again," she said grimly. "I'll make sure of it."

Something moved inside the entrance. There was no gate, just a gaping mouth filled with black shadows. Elodie's hand dropped instinctively to her side . . . but she carried no sword in this realm.

"What is . . . ?" she began.

A huge green shape burst out of the darkness. For a moment Elodie could make no sense of it: The thing seemed to boil in the air, a shrieking, chaotic whirlwind. Then, with a metallic snapping sound, its movements settled enough for her to make out its form.

The creature looked a little like a serpent, a little like a bird. Powerful wings kept its scaly green coils clear of the smoke. Cruel claws slashed the sooty air. Red eyes glared malevolently down at them. Like all the inhabitants of the Realm of the Dead, its body was translucent.

Elodie's hand went to her throat.

Green. Like my jewel.

"The wyvern!" cried Mirith. "It guards the Shadow Cage. Stay back."

The wyvern lunged, jaws gaping. Ruby-colored teeth snapped shut directly in front of Elodie's face. Screaming, she leaped backward, teetering on the edge of the smoky stairs and almost toppling into the emptiness beyond.

"Let me distract it!" Mirith called from the other side of the staircase. "You run past!"

The frost witch raised her arms and waved.

"Here!" she shouted. "Over here!"

The wyvern's head swung round. As it did so, Elodie spotted something clamped around its scaly neck.

A collar?

Flapping its mighty wings with ominous slowness, the wyvern advanced on Mirith. Something trailed behind it, something attached to the collar.

A chain. This thing isn't a guardian. It's a prisoner!

"Stop!" Elodie shouted to the creature. "Forget about her! Come to me!"

"Elodie! What are you doing?"

"It's all right!"

Elodie's heart pounded as the wyvern approached. Her mouth was dry. She could see everything with such clarity that it was almost painful to look.

You're no different from the others. You died, and now you're trapped here. Just one more ghost in a realm of ghosts.

As the monster bore down on her, its ruby fangs dripping some unspeakable poison, she found herself thinking of her brother.

Do you feel this terrified, Tarlan, when you're facing some new beast, hoping to tame it into your pack?

Now the wyvern was hovering directly above her. Its claws flexed toward her body. Its red eyes glared down. She saw that they were flecked with gold.

Green scales. Just like my jewel. Red-gold eyes, like my hair.

She'd never met a creature like the wyvern before, yet it seemed so familiar.

"Don't be scared," she said. "I'm here to help."

She was vaguely aware of Mirith throwing up her arms in horror. But Elodie kept her gaze fixed on the wyvern as it lowered its head slowly toward her. She could feel the pulse of its breath on her face, neither hot nor cold but simply *there*. She could see every crack on every scale. Even though she could see partially through the wyvern, it seemed more solid than anything she'd ever encountered before.

It's like crystal.

"Elodie!" Mirith screamed.

Elodie closed her eyes.

Something touched her forehead. She stifled a scream. There was a gentle thud. The air stilled.

She opened her eyes. The wyvern stood before her with its wings folded. The tip of its muzzle was pressed against her head.

"I can help you," Elodie murmured. "We want the same thing."

A noise came from deep in the creature's throat: a booming rumble that sounded like tiny bursts of thunder.

It's purring.

The pressure left Elodie's forehead as the wyvern lowered its muzzle to the stairs. This brought the collar within easy reach. The message was clear, but no matter how hard Elodie tugged at the welded seams of the neck-ring, it refused to budge.

"It's no good," she said, staring disgustedly at the gold fire encircling her hands. "I'm not strong enough."

"You are wrong." Mirith walked up. "Look at you, Elodie. You're ready for battle."

Elodie glanced down at her Trident uniform.

This is how I think of myself now. As a warrior. Is that why these clothes appeared when I arrived here? Did I conjure them up?

Perhaps there were other things she could conjure.

She lowered her left hand, but kept her right hand raised. She imagined it full of sand instead of fire. Her fingers continued to glow, but now when she flexed them, they felt hot and dry. From somewhere far away a wind was blowing.

Her stomach jolted, as if something inside her had locked into place. The fire spat sparks from her hand, only now each spark was a grain of golden sand. The heat became a delicious throbbing that ran from her fingers all the way up her arm to her shoulder.

There was something in her hand.

It was a sword.

The sword was made of light. It felt as weightless as the wind and as heavy as the world. As she raised the sword, it pulsed. It hummed. So did she.

"Sand and fire!" she shouted.

She brought the sword of light down on the wyvern's collar. The collar shattered, not breaking into pieces but dissolving into dust.

With a guttural shriek, the wyvern spread its glassy green wings and hurled itself into the air. The chain fell loose onto the shifting surface of the stairs. Still shrieking, the serpent turned loop after loop, clearly overjoyed to be rid of its shackles.

"One prisoner freed!" cried Elodie. "Now for the rest!"

She ran up the final few steps to the castle entrance. The heavy shadows from which Brutan's guardian had emerged had condensed into a smoky portcullis. The thick bars of this immense gate wriggled like a nest of snakes. The way was blocked.

Not to me!

Elodie raised her sword and brought it down.

CHAPTER 9

A re we nearly there?" said Jessamyn.

Gulph squeezed the little girl's hand. "Not much farther now."

He paused, looking up the granite corridor that would lead them to Idilliam. Then he looked back, down the crystal tunnel they'd just climbed. It was like standing at the junction between two worlds.

By the light of a thousand burning torches, he saw a straggling line of refugees dwindling far back into the darkness.

All the people of Celestis, he thought in wonder. *And they're following me.*

He thought back to how he'd stood before them after defeating the bakaliss, and how quickly he'd gained their trust. With Lady Redina dead, the people of the lost underground realm had emerged from a kind of daze. Hungry for news of the world above, they'd listened in fascination as Gulph had told them about what was happening in Toronia.

"I'm going back," he'd concluded. "There's still a lot of work to be done. Will you help me?"

Quiet though the crowd had been as he'd told his tale, their gratitude to Gulph for killing the bakaliss had converted into willing support for his cause.

"Yes!" they'd roared as one.

Things had moved quickly after that. Ossilius and Marcus—the two former soldiers—had organized groups of people to gather supplies for the journey. Gulph had stowed the crown of Toronia back into his pack, which Pip had loaded up with food and water.

"Remember when we were just a couple of wandering acrobats, Pip?" Gulph had said. "A lot's changed since then."

"You haven't changed, Gulph." She'd given him a quick kiss on his cheek, then shrunk back blushing.

"I suppose you haven't either. You'll probably sneak half your stuff into my pack when I'm not looking, and *still* complain that yours is too heavy."

"When did I ever do that?" Pip had innocently blinked her big brown eyes.

"Just about every day we were on the road."

She'd shouldered her pack with a grin. "Looks like we're going on the road again."

Oh, Pip, Gulph thought now, glancing at his friend as she walked through the tunnels at his side. *Whatever happens on this journey, I'm glad you're with me.*

To begin with, the tunnel walls had been pure crystal—a corridor of rich blue sapphire, a stretch of yellow topaz, around the next corner a seam of dazzling emerald. Now they made their way through the tunnels of cold gray granite that lay directly beneath Idilliam.

"These tunnels were scary," remembered Jessamyn, clinging on to Gulph's hand. "That bad man Slater got squished."

"Yes, he did," Gulph said. "But we didn't, did we?"

They made good progress, stopping occasionally for rest breaks but for the most part forging ahead. Gulph was keen to get to the surface as soon as possible. It seemed that the people of Celestis were too.

Kalia joined him at the head of the column. She'd been moving among the Celestians, taking care of minor injuries as people cracked their heads against the low ceilings or scraped their arms on the jagged walls.

"Is everything all right back there?" Gulph asked.

"They are hungry to see the light," his mother said. "As am I. It's so long since I saw Idilliam. Tell me about your time there, Gulph. Ossilius tells me the first time he saw you, you were performing for your father and Queen Magritt."

So Gulph handed Jessamyn to Pip's care and told Kalia everything, beginning with the capture of the Tangletree Players as prisoners of war, and his imprisonment with Prince Nynus, his half brother, in the Vault of Heaven.

"Nynus was always such a playful child," Kalia said as Gulph told her about the plot the prince and his mother, Queen Magritt, concocted to kill Brutan. "It's sad that he turned out to be so cruel."

Gulph thought back to the pale, strange boy he'd first met in the Black Cell. He remembered how much he'd liked him. "Magritt was the cruel one, really. Poor Nynus was just . . . broken."

He stopped, suddenly aghast.

"What is it?" said Kalia.

"The bridge! How could I have forgotten?"

"What about the bridge?"

"Nynus had it torn down. Even if we get to Idilliam, we'll be stuck there. There's no way across the chasm." He wanted to shake himself. "We'll have swapped one prison for another!"

"Is everything all right, Gulph?" said Ossilius, catching up to them. "Why have you stopped?"

But when Gulph explained that there was no way for them to reach the rest of Toronia, Kalia and Ossilius smiled.

"I don't know what's so funny," Gulph protested. "I can't just stay stuck in Idilliam. What about Elodie and Tarlan? I've got to find them. How am I going to—"

"Hush," said Kalia, patting his arm.

"Listen to me, Gulph," said Ossilius. "Destiny has brought you this far, has it not?"

"I suppose so."

"And when destiny has deserted you?"

"I . . . I suppose I've carried on anyway."

"Precisely."

"Listen to Ossilius," said Kalia. "And have faith, my son. Your determination has carried you when all else has fallen aside. It will carry you further yet."

"And destiny?"

Kalia's smile widened. "Oh, I am sure there is still a little more of *that* waiting around the corner."

At last they reached the storeroom inside the postern gate—the dark chamber from which Gulph and his companions had made their first descent into the underground labyrinth. Except now it was anything but dark.

"The door's still open," said Gulph, stepping from the tunnel into the storeroom and shielding his eyes from the daylight pouring in. "Last time I was here, I couldn't close it." He shook his head in frustration. "That's how Brutan's soldiers found their way to Celestis."

"It couldn't be helped, Gulph," said Ossilius. "Come."

After so long underground, the daylight beyond the doorway was dazzling. Gulph blundered into its glare, his eyes streaming. Behind him, many of the Celestians cried out in shock, and even pain. He could only imagine how bright it must seem to these people, who'd spent their whole lives underground.

Gradually his vision cleared. The area immediately around the postern gate was a wasteland, littered with rubble and charred bodies. Ruined buildings slumped, their shattered walls black with soot. Beyond them rose the city's outer wall. Once straight and proud, it was now as jagged as a jaw full of broken teeth. Clouds of ash hung low in the sky, sliced by beams of smoky sunlight.

And yet it seemed peaceful.

"They're gone," said Gulph in dawning wonder. "Brutan's army. The undead. All gone."

Yet with his relief came something else: a nagging sense of impatience.

We have to move faster!

In the open space that lay between the city gate and the end of the broken bridge, Gulph called a halt. They'd brought thousands of people up from Celestis, people who had set out with bravery and resolve, but who were now looking increasingly uncertain. In the bright sun, their skin was pale and unhealthy, their eyes were squinted half-shut, and most looked more than tired after the long climb. They looked ready to drop.

Gulph stepped up onto a low wall. "There's enough food for everyone, and the injured will be looked after," he announced. There were no cheers, but an audible sigh of relief washed through the crowd. "I wish I could take you farther. There's a forest on the other side of the chasm. Plenty to eat, plenty of places to shelter, but . . ."

He indicated the broken bridge. The gap in the middle said everything that needed to be said. It also sent a spike of frustration through him that there was no way across.

He called Pip over. "We've brought plenty of food up with us," he said. "Could you get some tables set up in that ruined guard-house? The Tangletree Players are good at entertaining a crowd. Let's see if they can feed one."

Pip nodded. "I'll get Hetty and Jessamyn to help."

"Good idea." As Pip trotted away, Gulph turned to the Celestians.

"I can see that some of you have bruises and scrapes from our journey. Show them to my mother—she'll help you."

Kalia was already setting up the small cauldron she'd been carrying. Within moments, she was sprinkling herbs into a sweet-smelling potion. As the steam began to rise, a line of Celestians formed before her. The others were heading for the broken-down guardhouse, where Pip and Hetty were directing the rest of Gulph's friends in the task of laying out food on rows of trestle tables.

"What will you do now, Gulph?" asked Captain Ossilius.

"Well," Gulph replied, "once everybody's fed, I suppose we need to think about where we're all going to sleep tonight."

"No. I asked what will *you* do?"

Gulph sighed. "I don't know. I just know I've got to find Tarlan and Elodie. . . . I have to find a way over the chasm. But I can't see how."

Together they walked to the chasm's edge. The deck of the bridge extended only a short distance out into empty space before ending in a ragged stump. Far beyond it, the opposite deck stretched all the way to the forest on the other side.

Between the two halves yawned a gap as wide as the Isurian River.

"It can be rebuilt," said Ossilius. "There are plenty of timbers lying around. And plenty of people willing to help you, Gulph. It would take time, but—"

"But that's just it. I don't have time. The other two need me now."

"How do you know that, Gulph?"

"I just know."

Gulph could feel the impatience swirling through him, a hot, dry sensation that reminded him of the way he felt when he used his powers.

Invisibility won't help me here. Mind reading's no use. What I need is to be able to fly!

"What is that?"

The voice belonged to his mother. She'd arrived so silently that Gulph hadn't even heard her approach.

"How are the injured people doing?" he asked.

"They are doing well. Hetty is tending to my cauldron." She seized Gulph's hand. "But never mind that. Look, there's something you need to see."

"What is it?"

Kalia raised his hand. She extended his finger, sighting along it and making it point at the sky.

"There," she said.

For a long time Gulph saw nothing. Then, gradually, a tiny dot appeared against the thin blue haze.

How good must your eyes be, Mother?

"Yes, I see it! But what is it?"

Kalia said nothing, merely waited as the dot became a speck, and the speck became a growing blur of motion.

"Is it a bird?" said Gulph. "If it is, it's a big one."

"It's a thorrod!" said Ossilius in wonder.

The blur was now a golden dart with beating wings. Its shadow sped across the pointing finger of the bridge's far end, vanished momentarily as the giant bird crossed the gap, then reappeared on their side.

Gulph stared in wonder at this titan of the sky, his breath taken by its beauty, its majesty.

I've seen you before! he realized with a start.

"On the battlefield!" he cried. "It was there. It flew in and saved me. Tarlan was riding it!"

Beside him, he heard Kalia's breath catch in her throat.

The gigantic bird touched down just a few strides in front of him. This time, the thorrod's back was bare.

Ignoring Ossilius and Kalia, the thorrod hopped up to Gulph and lowered its head. Its beak shone as bright as the Toronian crown; its gold feathers ruffled in the wind blowing up from the chasm. Its black eyes were deep, like pools of night.

It gave a single cry—a harsh, rasping croak—then sank farther toward the ground, offering its back to Gulph.

"If it could talk, it would be telling you to climb on," Ossilius said.

Kalia's grip tightened on Gulph's hand. "If this bird belongs to Tarlan, why is he not riding it now?"

Gulph couldn't tear his eyes away from the thorrod's intense, liquid gaze.

"I don't know," he said. "But I don't think this bird is the sort of creature that 'belongs' to anyone."

He ran his fingers through the ruff of coarse feathers that

sprouted between the thorrod's wings. Pressing his hand against its neck, he felt the sure, steady throb of its pulse.

"You could carry me away right now, couldn't you?" he whispered. The thorrod looked back at him, making no sound.

"A thorrod!" came an excited cry from behind him. It was Pip, running over, her face flushed. "I never thought I'd see one up close! It's so gorgeous!" Hardly pausing for breath, she went on, "So are you leaving us, Gulph?"

He stared at her. How could he leave Pip, or Ossilius, or his mother? Or any of those who'd pledged their support to him? How could he fly away and leave them in this burned-out shell of a city?

And yet, somewhere on the other side of the chasm, were Elodie and Tarlan. Destiny was waiting.

"I . . . I don't know," he said truthfully.

Pip rolled her eyes. "This is the thorrod your brother was riding on, isn't it?"

"Yes, but . . ."

"But nothing. He needs you. It's obvious."

"Pip is right," said Ossilius. "Besides, whatever battle is to come—perhaps the final battle for Toronia—I believe it must surely happen here. Remember the throne room you told us of? *This* is the place, Gulph. It doesn't matter if you call it Idilliam or Celestis—*this* is the heart of Toronia. You will return to us here. Because here is where it all began . . . and where everything will end."

"Destiny has brought you here," said Kalia. "Now you must bring your brother and sister here too."

Ossilius jerked his head toward the people of Celestis. "They may look like travel-worn wanderers, but by the time you return"— he gave Gulph a winning smile that made him look thirty years younger—"I will have made an army of them!"

Overwhelmed by his friend's loyalty, Gulph hugged him.

"You've done so much for me, Ossilius. Can you believe all we've gone through since that day you dragged me off to the Vault of Heaven?"

"I knew then that you were special, Gulph."

Gulph turned his attention to his oldest friend. "As for you, Pip, you seem pretty keen to get rid of me."

"Can't wait to see the back of you." Her eyes brimmed with tears. Unable to hold herself back anymore, she threw her arms round him. "Be safe," she said, her voice choked.

"I'll try." He smiled. Ending the embrace, he turned to Kalia. "I wish I didn't have to leave you again. We've only just . . ."

"I know," said Kalia, seizing his hand, "but Tarlan's thorrod must be here for a reason. You don't want to leave me, and I don't want to leave you. The solution is simple."

"It is?"

"Of course. I'm coming with you!"

His heart overflowing, Gulph helped his mother onto the

thorrod's back, then climbed up himself. It felt strange to be sitting astride the giant bird, yet curiously like coming home.

Tarlan sits here, he marveled, stroking the thorrod's sleek golden feathers. *My brother.*

"Come back safe!" shouted Pip as the thorrod spread its enormous wings and lifted slowly into the air.

"We'll be waiting!" called Ossilius.

They raised their hands in salute. Gulph waved back; Kalia, seated behind him with one arm around his waist, waved too. The thorrod wheeled, and the air rushed past them, and before Gulph knew it, they were flying over the chasm, over the forest, out into the wider world.

Where are you taking us? he thought, wishing he could speak the thorrod's language.

But of course he knew the answer.

You're taking us to Tarlan!

CHAPTER 10

Tarlan followed Captain Leom down the steep mountain slope. To his relief, the cold wind that had assailed them when they'd emerged from the Fortress of the Flown had quickly died away.

The snow was deep, making the going hard. At first, the drifts came up to their knees; as they descended, the snow thinned and became patchy, revealing a narrow, rocky path.

"Take care," said Leom as they rounded a large boulder. "There are fissures."

"Fishes?" Tarlan had never heard the word before.

"You'll see." The burly man's breath seemed to glow as it condensed in the air. Glancing east, Tarlan saw the sky blushing with the pale pink of dawn. Above them, the clouds were thinning. Light was coming. It was going to be a beautiful day.

As soon as they'd passed the boulder, Tarlan understood what fissures were. Ahead lay a sloping field of ice-covered rock, broken in a hundred or more places by wide, wandering cracks. The nearest of these fissures was only a few paces away; Tarlan stepped cautiously up to the edge and peered into its depths. He saw nothing but blackness.

"As I said," remarked Leom, "care is required."

As the sky lightened around them, they made their way down the slope, leaping across each of the cracks in turn. Tarlan was amazed by Leom's agility.

"Did you spend a lot of time in Yalasti?" Tarlan gasped, pausing for breath at the lip of an especially wide fissure.

"It was my home once," Leom replied. "Ice and snow are my friends."

Tarlan nodded. Despite his pledge to abandon humans and seek the wilderness, he couldn't help liking this gruff man.

"Mine too."

Tarlan leaped the chasm, only to find his way blocked by Leom's hulking fur-clad form.

"What's the matter? Why have you stopped?"

"See here." Leom crouched and tapped the ice. "What do you make of this?"

Tarlan peered uncertainly. "I don't see anything . . . Oh, is that a footprint?"

Leom's wrinkled fingers traced the outline of a boot. "Kalldrags have passed, and recently."

"Kalldrags?"

"Wandering hunters. Like the Helkrags of Yalasti, only twice as savage."

The sun's disc peeped over the horizon and struck them with its rays. Long shadows fled from their feet across the field of fissures. Tarlan looked anxiously around, suddenly aware of how exposed they were.

"We must find another route," said Leom. "This way—quickly!"

Trotting nimbly across the ice, he led Tarlan into a jumble of boulders that had fallen from a nearby slope. Protected by the shadows of the gigantic stones, Tarlan began to feel safe again.

"I'd never have seen that footprint," he remarked as he followed Leom through the rocky maze.

"I learned to track in Yalasti, but it was in the city realm that I trained to become an Eye of Idilliam."

"Eye of Idilliam? What's that?"

"An agent of the king. It was our task to travel the kingdom and keep the peace—and impose the law. It was an important job, and I was proud to do it, until . . ." Leom puffed out another cloud of white vapor.

"Until what?"

"Until King Brutan ordered us to start killing babies."

Tarlan felt sick. "The prophecy."

Leom nodded. "Brutan knew what had been foreseen—that three would come to kill him and take the throne. When the prophecy stars appeared in the sky, he feared the arrival of these triplets. So he ordered the death of all newborns in the land."

"Couldn't you have refused?"

"Brutan gave us two choices: either wipe out the triplets, or be executed ourselves."

"What did you do?" Tarlan wasn't sure he wanted to hear the answer.

"I found a third option."

"Which was?"

"Disobey the king and go into exile forever."

By now, they'd completed their journey through the maze. Below them, a vast white plain sparkled in the low dawn light. Black spires of rock jutted from deep drifts of snow. Tarlan's heart clenched as he recognized the place where he'd seen the thorrods. Then it sank as he realized he was about to say good-bye to the man who had twice saved his life, and who in another time and place might have become his friend.

Perhaps even something close to a father.

"Brutan's plan worked, in a way," Tarlan said glumly. "The triplets are no more."

"What do you mean?"

"Gulph is dead. Elodie's turned traitor. And I'm—"

"What? What did you say?" Leom grabbed Tarlan's shoulders urgently.

"Gulph is—"

"Tarlan, I am sorry about your brother. That is awful news—awful for us all. But what did you say about Elodie?"

"She's gone over to the enemy. She joined the Vicerins and—"

"No!" The sun caught Leom's eyes, making them blaze. "I *saw* Elodie. I was with her. She freed the children who were prisoners in Lord Vicerin's dungeon. She put them in my care, and I brought them here. She's no traitor! She allowed herself to be caught to save her friend—was his name Fossa?"

"Fessan." Tarlan reeled. There was a roaring in his ears. His stomach was trying to fold itself in half.

Not a traitor!

"Fessan—yes, that was it. Your sister is very brave, Tarlan. She took terrible risks. I fear she may now be Vicerin's prisoner herself."

Tarlan barely heard what Leom was saying. His thoughts were a storm. He saw the world around him in sudden, blinding clarity: the coarse black of the boulders, the dazzling white of the snowfield, and the crisp pink of the dawn sky.

All this time I've been thinking she betrayed Trident, handed them over to Vicerin. All this time I've been wrong!

"Theeta knew," Tarlan murmured.

"What did you say?"

"Nothing. I've made a terrible mistake." He gazed at the rocky spires reaching up out of the snow. "And it's time to start putting it right."

The thorrods are here. They'll take me back. Back to Elodie. Back to the fight!

He ran out across the snow toward the nearest spire. He didn't care about fissures. He didn't care about Kalldrags. He just wanted to make up for his mistakes, rejoin his pack, fly again . . .

"Theeta!" he shouted. "Theeta, I'm coming!"

Halfway across the snowfield he stopped. The rocky spire lay directly ahead, its glossy surface gleaming in the sunlight. Perched at its tip were the two birdlike shapes he'd seen the previous day.

Except they weren't birds.

"What?" Tarlan sank to his knees in the snow. "I don't understand."

The things on the spire looked like snakes with wings, sculpted from green crystal. Their eyes were huge red orbs flecked with gold. They weren't creatures at all.

They were statues.

The disappointment was overwhelming. Yet, even as he stifled a cry, Tarlan's hand crept to the empty place at his throat.

Green, like my jewel.

"I said you would be surprised," said Leom, catching up with him. "They are wyverns."

"Wyverns?"

"Only two remain, alas. Once there were three. But that was long ago, in the days of Gryndor."

Tarlan's dismay was turning slowly to fascination. He could hear something—it sounded like a distant drumbeat, very slow, very deep. A war drum, marking out the rhythm of some long-gone battle.

Not one drum. Two.

"I can hear their hearts," he said suddenly.

Just for a moment, he imagined himself not out in the snow but inside the crystal skins of these strange, sculpted wyverns. Their heartbeats were loud, like thunder.

Inside a serpent. Seeking its heart. Why does that make me think of Gulph?

He shook the thought away.

"Some say they are dead," said Leom. He was studying Tarlan closely. "Others believe they are only sleeping."

As if in a dream, Tarlan stepped forward through the snow. The sun struck the green crystal coils of the two wyverns, piercing their glassy bodies and fracturing into ten thousand glowing shards of light. Tarlan clenched his fists, the ragged nails biting deep into the beds of his palms.

You chose a cold place to sleep. Let's try warming things up.

Again he tried to place himself inside the wyverns, this time seeking not their hearts but their minds. But their crystalline forms seemed to repel him. He kicked the snow in frustration. The night wind had sculpted its surface into a sea of rolling waves.

Like sand dunes.

Tarlan closed his eyes. He felt the meager warmth of the dawn on the back of his neck.

Then in a rush the feelings flooded through him, so strange, yet so familiar. His palms tingled as his fists filled up with sand. The sand burned, jetting hot pain up his arms. His whole body was on fire. He opened his eyes and the fire leaped out of him and struck the black spire of rock, a gush of invisible heat that wrapped itself once, twice, three times around the wyverns, then poured into them, filling them, melting them. Tarlan swayed as the fire sucked all the energy from his body. His vision dimmed; his legs began to shake.

I can't keep this up!

He staggered, nearly fell, and then gathered his resolve. His magic allowed him to speak to animals, but it did more than that— it gave him the power of command.

This is like trying to command a pair of rocks.

"Tarlan!" exclaimed Captain Leom. "What is happening to you?"

Peering down through half-closed eyelids, Tarlan saw twin trails of golden sand gushing from between his fingers. The sand began to pile up on either side of him. Where it touched the snow, the snow hissed and gave off clouds of steam.

Command them!

Tarlan threw back his head and yelled, "FLY!"

The instant this single word left his mouth, the fire fled from his body. His fingers jerked apart, clutching at empty air. He gasped for breath.

"What . . . ?" Leom began.

From the top of the spire came a tremendous cracking sound, followed immediately by another. To Tarlan it sounded like a pair of lightning strikes. The wings of the wyverns ripped apart, spraying sunlight. Their claws detached from the spire; their bodies uncoiled.

They opened their jaws and shrieked.

Their red-gold eyes fixed on Tarlan. Beating their green crystal wings with slow, deliberate menace, the wyverns flew down toward him.

Tarlan spread his arms. "Come to me!" he cried.

"They are doing that already," observed Leom.

Tarlan ignored him. "Come to me! Speak with me!"

One of the wyverns had a notch in its left wing. It swooped in low, doubling its speed in the blink of an eye. Snow exploded in its wake. Its blazing eyes grew large with incredible speed. Its jaws gaped, revealing shiny ruby teeth.

Tarlan stood his ground.

I hear your hearts! I hear your minds! Come to me! Obey my command!

The wyverns' thoughts were cold and distant, hard and ancient: *We have slept. Now we wake. You are here, but you are not yet ready.*

Tarlan threw up his hands, palms flat to the sky.

"STOP!"

The leading wyvern punched the air with its wings, coming to an almost instantaneous halt directly in front of Tarlan and Leom. It slammed down into the white ground, red claws plunging deep. A barrage of snow cascaded over Tarlan's feet. A moment later the second wyvern landed beside it.

Tarlan stared at the wyverns. They stared back, twin crystal serpents, each twice the size of a thorrod, their bodies crackling with ice and blazing with sunlight.

"You have come," said the wyvern with the notch in its wing.

Leom clapped his hands to his ears. Tarlan wondered what he was hearing.

"We have been waiting," said the second.

"Waiting for the longest time."

"Now our wait is over."

"But yours must begin."

Tarlan blinked. Their voices were deep, rich and hypnotic. "Begin? What do you mean?"

"Now it is your turn to wait. The time is almost upon you. But you are not yet ready."

"Ready? Ready for what?"

The two wyverns spread their wings and took off once more. Snow cascading from their claws, they circled once, then struck out toward the mountain. Soon they'd vanished behind a crag of ice-covered rock.

Tarlan gazed dismally at the empty sky. He felt cold, drained of energy.

"It didn't work," he said. "I've failed."

Leom's gray eyebrows went up. "Failed? Do you call that failure? My boy, you have woken two beasts that have lain dormant for hundreds of years. Perhaps a thousand. You have set them free." He grinned through his beard. "Something tells me your fate is bound up with theirs."

Leom's words were warming. Tarlan kicked the snow from his boots and stretched the kinks from his spine. The morning sun bathed his face.

"What do I do now?" he said.

"Only you know the answer to that question." Leom's grin widened. "And I believe you *do* know. Am I right?"

The Fortress of the Flown was in pandemonium. Most of its population had gathered in the central chamber, where many were anxiously scanning the morning sky, bright above the open roof. Following Leom toward the middle of the arena, Tarlan overheard fragments from countless anxious conversations:

". . . flying beasts—what were they?"

". . . if the Kalldrags have found us . . ."

". . . it's a bad omen, I tell you . . ."

Many hands clutched at Leom. One young woman dropped to her knees in front of him.

"What's to become of us?" she pleaded, wringing her hands. "Where in all Toronia can we be safe?"

Leom whispered to Tarlan, "They need someone to reassure them."

"Well, aren't you their leader?"

Leom's eyes bored into his. "I was once."

"Well, if you're not anymore, then who . . . ?" Tarlan broke off as he realized what Leom meant.

"Tarlan, I think the time has come to tell them who you really are."

Tarlan gazed up at the sky. The clouds had departed, and the pink of the dawn was melting into clear blue. Directly overhead, the prophecy stars shone, bright despite the day.

Tarlan gaped.

Three. Three stars. One red, one green, one gold.

All as bright as one another!

His eyes fixed on the gold star. Gulph's star.

Is he alive? Is Gulph really alive?

Filled with hope, he returned his attention to Captain Leom.

"I think you're right!" he said.

He sprang onto a high platform of rock in the middle of the chamber. The faces looking up at him were fearful but also curious. He remembered that none of them knew who he was.

"My name is Tarlan. And I . . ." He faltered, began again. "The flying creatures you saw just now were wyverns. They've been asleep for a long time. Now they're awake. . . ." He paused. "I'm the one who woke them up."

Far back in the crowd, a man laughed. Tarlan felt a flush of annoyance.

A woman called out: "How could you do such a thing?"

Tarlan thought for a moment.

"When I was born, it was thirteen years ago," he explained. "My father was King Brutan. Gulph and Elodie and me—they're my brother and sister . . ." The words seemed to tangle in his mouth; would he ever be any good at talking to people like this? "We were born beneath the light of the prophecy stars." He swallowed. "I am one of three."

The man at the back laughed again, but many in the crowd gasped. Tarlan wished he could read their expressions better— were they hopeful or suspicious? It was so hard to tell with humans.

"A son of the stars," said the woman. "Can you set us free?"

"That's why I'm here," he said. The words were coming more easily now. "Prophecies are one thing. Sometimes even I don't believe in them. But you all want to go home, live peaceful lives. I think I can help you. But it will be hard. If you want your freedom, you'll have to fight for it. Are you ready for that?"

A small chorus of "ayes" echoed across the chamber. Several people cheered. But just as many remained silent. Tarlan was frustrated but not surprised. He was just a scruffy boy blown in on the wind. Why should they believe anything he said?

As if reading Tarlan's thoughts, Leom stepped up onto the rock beside him.

"You all know me," he said. "I guided many of you to the Fortress of the Flown. Will you hear me now?"

Another chorus of "ayes," this one much louder.

"Tarlan *is* who he says he is. I know this because when he was a babe, the wizard Melchior entrusted him to my care. I was the one who carried him to safety. Now he is grown, or nearly so. Hear him. Believe him." Leom paused, then concluded, "Follow him."

Something like a wave moved through the crowd. A certain tension seemed to leave the chamber, leaving the audience bright-eyed and expectant. Yet even now, Tarlan could see knots of people huddled in whispered conversation, clearly unwilling to pledge allegiance to a stranger.

"I told you I woke the wyverns," he said, taking a sudden step forward. "And that's the truth. But I can do more than that—I can command *any* animal, large or small."

"Prove it!" shouted the skeptical man at the back.

Tarlan smiled. "All right!"

He raised his fists and summoned the familiar magical heat. At the same time, he sent his thoughts flying out to the small packs of dogs scattered throughout the chamber. He found their minds at once; they shone like beacons, alert, obedient, eager to please.

After the wyverns, it was child's play.

"Come to me!" he shouted. This was purely for effect— the actual command he sent was as silent and invisible as the desert wind.

For a moment, there was no reaction. Then people were jumping aside, looking comically down at their feet, as countless bundles of fur raced in from their various dens toward the stone platform on which Tarlan stood. High-pitched yips and yowls echoed round the chamber. Then a wave of small bodies surged up onto the platform, the little dogs clambering over one another in an effort to be first to reach their new master.

"We're glad you came," cried one of the dogs.

"All these humans do is sit around," yapped another. "We want a proper walk!"

"Easy, easy!" Tarlan laughed. One dog climbed on the back of its neighbor and launched itself at Tarlan's face. In midair, it extended its tongue and gave him a wet, slobbering lick on the nose.

The crowd erupted into laughter.

"Down," Tarlan said, sending out calming thoughts to the mountain of dogs. They settled at once, planting themselves at his feet with their muzzles raised attentively and their tails beating the ground in excitement.

"A few days ago, I turned my back on destiny," Tarlan told the crowd. "That's how I ended up here. But since I've been here, I've learned something. However far you run, fate always catches you in the end."

He scanned the sea of upturned faces, confident at last that they believed what he had to say.

"So here's my question," he went on. "Are *you* going to keep running? Or are you going to follow me and fight for what is yours?"

The crowd roared. The dogs at Tarlan's feet lifted their muzzles to the sky and howled. Tarlan tossed back his long red-gold hair and howled too.

Above him, still brilliant in the morning sky, the three prophecy stars blazed.

The sun was barely halfway to noon when Tarlan and Leom stood once more at the end of the exit passage. Tarlan now wore a mantle of heavy fur over his tattered black cloak, and on his back he carried a large pack filled with food and water.

"Are you sure you want to go alone?" Leom asked. "The people are ready to follow you. Your speech inspired them"—he shook his head—"like nothing I have ever seen before."

"I'm sure," said Tarlan firmly. Though he had no definite plan, of this he was certain. "An army marches slowly, and I've got to get to Elodie as quickly as I can." He hesitated. "You could come with me."

Leom raised a grizzled eyebrow. "Me? Why?"

Tarlan shuffled his feet awkwardly in the snow. "I don't know. You could help me watch out for Kalldrags. Keep me on the path."

"You do not need me for that, Tarlan. You can look after yourself."

Hiding his disappointment, Tarlan tried to tell himself that Leom was just a man he'd stumbled over in the wilderness.

But he was much more than that.

"Besides," Leom went on, "you need someone to turn this rabble into a real fighting force."

Tarlan looked at him, taken aback. "Really?"

Leom clapped Tarlan's shoulder. "Go and do what you must do. The next time we meet, your army will be waiting."

Tarlan grinned his gratitude. "I believe you."

Slapping his back a second time, Leom sent him on his way down the slope toward the narrow path that would lead him back to Toronia. Tarlan looked back over his shoulder once to see him hunched against the wind, his hand raised in salute. Then the rocks closed around him and he was alone once more.

I'm not alone as long as they're shining, he thought, gazing up at the prophecy stars. They were burning so brightly now that he suspected even the full midday sun wouldn't be enough to banish them from the heavens.

Three stars. Gulph's alive—he must be!

He reached the crest of a high ridge and found himself looking over the rolling foothills of the Icy Wastes. Far ahead, the land flattened into a vast rocky plain. The horizon was shrouded by low gray cloud. Beyond it lay the three realms of Isur, Idilliam, and Ritherlee.

Toronia.

His destiny.

Something moved in the sky.

The wyverns?

Tarlan narrowed his eyes against the blue glare. He saw wings beating out a slow, steady rhythm. Large wings. The high sun flashed on their golden tips.

Gold!

Tarlan started running down the slope. His face stretched wide in a joyful smile. He waved his arms. He laughed.

"Theeta! Theeta—I'm here!"

CHAPTER 11

Elodie swung her sword of light at the portcullis. The glowing blade sliced effortlessly through the barrier. Lines of smoke twisted skyward like black silk scarves and vanished.

Swinging her sword back and forth, Elodie advanced one ferocious step at a time. The red mist of battle rage hovered at the edges of her vision. Gradually she understood what had given the Shadow Cage its name. This was no castle, but a dense mesh of black bars crisscrossing through space, close enough together that the whole structure seemed solid—at least until someone took it apart.

With each stroke of Elodie's blazing sword, another set of bars flew aside. Between each row, dozens of prisoners were huddled, ragged robes hanging limply from their thin, translucent bodies.

As she cut her way past them, their gray, downcast faces lit up with hope.

"Run!" Elodie cried. "There's someone outside who will help you!"

Glancing back over her shoulder, she saw that Mirith was already beckoning to the first wave of escapees. As soon as they reached her, the frost witch had them line up on the smoky staircase, making room for more to emerge.

There was no sign of the wyvern.

Turning back, Elodie brandished her sword again . . . then stopped.

Right in front of her, behind the nearest set of bars, stood a man. He was tall, dressed in green. Despite the scar running down the side of his face, he was handsome.

Beside the man was a girl just a few years older than Elodie. Her hair was red, her face alight with joy.

The red mist faded. Elodie's lungs felt flat, her limbs weak. The sword hung limp in her hands.

"Fessan," she whispered, staring at the man. She turned tear-filled eyes to the girl. "Palenie."

"Well, what are you waiting for?" said Palenie, smiling. Palenie, Elodie's friend from her earliest days in Trident. Palenie, who'd taught her how to fight. Palenie, who'd believed in her even though she'd been such a spoiled brat.

Palenie, who had been murdered in Elodie's place.

Elodie touched the tip of her sword to the bars that lay between them. The smoke disintegrated.

Palenie threw her arms around Elodie. Her touch was strangely soft, strangely cold, and entirely welcome. Elodie returned the embrace. The urge to cry was overwhelming. She didn't fight it.

"You can't be here!" Palenie was sobbing. "You can't be dead!"

"I'm not . . . ," Elodie began.

"If you're dead, the prophecy's dead!"

"She is not dead," said Fessan in wonder. "Are you, Elodie?"

Stepping back, Palenie looked her friend up and down, her jaw sagging open.

"You're glowing, Elodie! How are you doing that?"

"My powers, I think." Elodie smiled through her tears. *Trust Palenie to get straight to the point!* "I'm sorry. Both of you—I'm so sorry I couldn't save you."

"You just did," Fessan replied softly.

Elodie wiped her cheeks with the heel of her hand.

Her heart was full, her head was spinning. Now that she'd found Fessan and Palenie, all she wanted to do was grab their hands and lead them far, far away. But she still had a job to do.

"You're not safe yet," she said. "I've got to defeat Brutan first."

She started swinging her sword again. Left, right, left, right, deeper into the Shadow Cage. Each stroke cut a swath through the forest of smoke, releasing another cluster of prisoners.

"You've been practicing," said Palenie proudly.

"Go outside," Elodie gasped. She hadn't realized her friends were following her. "There's a woman. A witch. Her name is Mirith. She'll—"

"We are coming with you," said Fessan. "Whether you like it or not."

Elodie regarded them both. Her throat was tight.

"I like it," she said.

As they penetrated deeper into the Shadow Cage, the bars of smoke drew closer together. They were following a sort of spiral, Elodie realized, the bars tightening gradually toward a knot of blackness at the very center of the prison. Soon only a few layers of smoke lay between her sword and this dark core. One after the other she cut them aside, and the last remaining prisoners made good their escape.

Fessan circled the floating ball of tangled shadows. "The heart of the Shadow Cage," he said. To Elodie, it looked like a nest woven by some huge, unimaginable bird.

"Who's inside it?" wondered Palenie.

Elodie licked her lips. The glowing sword suddenly felt very heavy. So did the jewel around her neck. The golden fire, covering her body like a second skin, flickered fiercely.

"Kalia?" she called, her voice quavering. "Mother? Are you in there?"

There was no reply. Yet Elodie was sure she was right. Her mother had lied to Brutan, entrusting her three babies to the care of Melchior rather than let him murder them. And Brutan had killed her for her treachery. Where else would her mother be now, if not in the darkest corner of the prison he'd built for his dead enemies?

"We are with you, Elodie," said Fessan. "Whoever—or whatever—may lie within."

Elodie drew back her sword, preparing to make the almighty swing she would surely need to breach this final obstacle. Then she stopped herself. The battle rage had faded from her vision. She didn't need it anymore, she realized. Here, in the Realm of the Dead, all she needed was the magic she'd brought.

All she needed was herself.

With trembling hands, she brought the sword gently forward until the edge of its blade kissed the wall of black smoke.

The smoke tore itself apart. There was a faint popping sound, and then the last remaining piece of the Shadow Cage evaporated like morning mist. Nothing of Brutan's prison remained now but the floor—a swirling gray blanket of fog that lapped against Elodie's feet.

Three people stood before them: a heavy-set man with a close-cropped beard, a tall woman with a haughty expression, and a skinny boy perhaps the same age as Palenie. All wore splendid robes. All wore simple silver crowns. All had the same wavering, soft-edged look as the rest of the dead.

Elodie didn't recognize a single one of them. But of one thing she was certain.

My mother is not here.

The boy stumbled forward and embraced Elodie clumsily. She was too shocked to fend him off.

"Thank you!" he cried. "You freed us! Thank you! Thank you!"

His face was thin and his hair was long and matted. His eyes rolled wildly in their sockets.

"Nynus!" Fessan exclaimed. "It's Prince Nynus! I recognize him from when I was at court with my father." He pointed at the two adults. "Queen Magritt. And King Morlon. I remember them all!"

Freeing herself from Nynus's clinging hands, Elodie studied the people she'd released. She knew the names, but there the familiarity ended. It was like meeting characters from a story she'd heard as a child.

Morlon, my father's brother, who he murdered to take the crown.

Magritt, my father's queen.

Nynus, her son. My half brother.

As Nynus retreated, biting his nails, Magritt curled her lip and glared.

"Who," said Magritt in a slow, deliberate tone, "are you?"

Her dim wraith's eyes flashed with sudden gold—a reflection of Elodie's glowing skin of light.

"My name is Elodie. I am sister to Tarlan, sister to Gulph"—at the sound of Gulph's name, Magritt flinched—"and I am one of three. I come here from Toronia to right the wrongs my father has done."

Morlon dropped to one knee. To Elodie's astonishment, he removed his silver crown and bowed his head.

"I have been here too many years," he whispered. His voice was like soft wind through reeds. He lifted his eyes to Elodie's. "And I know my brother will be coming for you. You must leave us. Leave us and run."

Hiding behind his mother's translucent skirts, Nynus wailed, "Don't let the sword-girl get me! I didn't mean to hurt Gulph. I don't want to be punished!"

Elodie pointed her sword at the cowering boy. At once Nynus fell silent. Magritt's face was stony, showing neither fear of Elodie nor concern for her son.

"You took the crown when it wasn't yours," Elodie said. "You killed Melchior's apprentice, Limmoni. You destroyed the bridge, and sent hundreds plunging to their deaths. You *should* be punished." She took a deep breath. "But that's not why I'm here. I promised to free the dead from Brutan's tyranny. *All* of them. That includes you. Now follow me!"

With Morlon, Magritt, and Nynus trailing behind, Elodie and her friends retraced their steps through the Shadow Cage ... except there *was* no cage. Thanks to Elodie, the spiral of shadowy cells had been utterly destroyed. All that remained was an undulating blanket of fog through which they ran all the way to the smoky staircase.

"Hurry," said Palenie. "Remember what Morlon said—Brutan will be coming."

As they approached the freed prisoners thronging the stairs, the wyvern swooped low over Elodie's head. Its shrieks cut through her like blades of ice.

Something like a wave moved through the fog, then another. Elodie stopped. Not noticing, Fessan and Palenie ran on, urging the three former prisoners ahead of them. The fog rippled again. Strings of gray vapor lapped around Elodie's knees.

She turned.

The strands of fog were knitting together. Fingers of mist rose up and closed around each other, making a kind of ghostly fist as big as a man. Elodie watched with mounting dread as the fist *became* a man—a hulking bear of a figure with heavy arms and a thick beard. Red robes hung from his massive shoulders. On his head he wore a gold crown.

The man was Brutan. Her father. Twice dead, now standing before her, no longer the rotting corpse she'd seen during the Battle of the Bridge, but the vivid lifelike soul of an actual man.

Elodie's whole body was shaking. She tried to tell herself that this hideous, death-defying monster was not really her father . . . except she knew that Brutan had been a monster in life as well. Now here he was, standing before her eyes for the very first time, the beast that had killed her mother.

"Who dares to challenge my rule?" Brutan bellowed. From the scabbard hanging at his waist he drew an enormous broadsword. Its blade was the same flat gray as the fog.

The wyvern looped over Elodie's head again, filling the echoless air with its shrieks.

"I am Elodie!" she cried, raising her own sword. It was as bright as Brutan's was dull. "Your daughter!"

Brutan took a startled step backward.

"Daughter?" he spat. "Yes, you do look like your mother. How fitting, for I will kill you, too."

Growling deep in his throat, he displayed his teeth in what might have been a grin or a grimace. The fog clung to him as he advanced, as if reluctant to let him go. In some way she didn't understand, Elodie realized her father *was* the fog.

That's how he was able to take over every corner of the Realm of the Dead. He's everywhere!

"Elodie!" Fessan called. "Wait—I'm coming!"

"Stay back!" Elodie shouted over her shoulder. "All of you, stay back!"

"We can help!" cried Palenie.

"No, you can't!"

Nobody here has the power to resist Brutan. The dead can't defeat him.

She tightened her grip on the hilt of her sword.

But I'm not dead!

Brutan took three more paces toward her. The fog spread behind him like a comet's tail.

"One of my three," he boomed. "I remember the first—the scrawny cripple. He poisoned me, but that was not enough to keep me down."

"Don't talk about my brother like that!"

"I remember the agony of dying, *daughter*. But what I prefer to remember is the moment I rose again. To be undead is to be free! Invincible!"

"If you're so invincible, what are you doing here?"

Brutan's face darkened with fury. "Your brother—your other brother, the filthy one who rides that bird—cast me into the fire! I knew agony again, a thousand times worse than the first time!"

Elodie's mind was racing. Tarlan had killed him again?

Grinning, Brutan spread his arms. "My treacherous son thought I was gone. Yet here I am still!"

He reached into the fog that was swirling around his feet. When his hand came up, it was holding something that looked like a club made of gray smoke. The smoke became solid—or as close to solid as anything was in this nebulous realm—and Elodie saw that it was a gigantic mace, with a long shaft and a huge spiked ball at the end.

With his broadsword in one hand and the mace in the other, Brutan rushed toward her.

Hands shaking, Elodie continued to hold out her own sword. It looked puny against the brutal weapons of her father.

But it's made of light, and his are only shadows!

Yet she was afraid.

Already Brutan was on her, lunging with his sword. Elodie sidestepped and the blade missed her waist by a whisker. In the same instant, he swung the mace round in a wide arc, aiming the cruel spiked ball at her head.

Elodie twisted and ducked. Off-balance, she fell to her knees in the fog. The misty vapor sucked at her, trying to pull her down.

He's everywhere, she thought in revulsion, and scrambled to her feet again.

"Your brothers could not defeat me!" Brutan roared. "And neither can you!"

The mace came round again. This time Elodie avoided it with ease. It was a terrifying weapon but slow. All she had to do was keep moving. But she was already gasping for breath.

How long can I keep this up?

"Twice killed!" Brutan growled, circling her now as he looked for an opening. "And still not enough. What makes you think you can do better?"

Elodie turned slowly, tracking him with her glowing sword held out at arm's length. Something was scratching at her mind, something Mirith had said. What was it?

"Hurt them enough and their spirits will be gone forever."

Mirith had been talking about Brutan torturing his prisoners. But her words had held a hidden truth.

The dead could be destroyed.

Of course, so could the living.

"Enough of this play!" Brutan thundered. "Now fight!"

He swung his sword. Elodie brought up her own blade in time to parry the blow. The two weapons locked with a dull clanging sound, and then the mace was coming down again. Elodie whirled, lifting her sword over her head in time to block what would otherwise have been a killing blow. Brutan grunted as she slipped beneath his arm and spun to face him again, breathless and alert.

"Take care, Elodie!" Fessan shouted from where he was watching on the staircase.

"Remember what I taught you!" Palenie cried.

The crystal serpent shrieked.

Then came Mirith's voice. It sounded very close.

"Remember the prophecy!"

Brutan feinted with the mace, then came in low with his sword.

Anticipating his move, Elodie wasn't fooled. She swiped his sword aside with her own, her shining blade eclipsing his shadowy weapon with its brightness. Again they parted, and the circling resumed.

I can keep him at bay. But can I defeat him?

Yet again Brutan struck out with the mace. This latest attack took Elodie by surprise, and she found herself tottering backward toward the staircase, but not before she'd whipped her sword round and straight through Brutan's wrist, sending his hand and the sword it carried flying away.

Howling, Brutan continued running with his mace held high, smoke spewing from the stump of his arm.

"Look out, Elodie!" Fessan and Palenie shouted in unison.

Gasping for breath, Elodie dodged aside. Brutan barreled past her and slammed straight into Mirith, who was standing at the very front of the watching crowd. Wrapping his crippled arm around her neck, he lifted her clean off the ground. He whirled to face Elodie, the frost witch held in front of him like a shield.

"Now!" he bellowed. "Strike me if you dare!"

Elodie passed her sword anxiously from her right hand to her left, then back again. Brutan leered and clamped his forearm more tightly around Mirith's throat. Smoke continued to spurt from the stump where his hand had been.

I can't kill him without killing her!

"Do what you must do!" Mirith croaked, forcing the words

out through her crushed windpipe. "Forget about me!"

"You heard her!" roared Brutan. He ran toward Elodie, Mirith dangling like a doll in his grip. The mace tore streamers of gray vapor from the fog-shrouded ground.

At the last moment, Elodie sidestepped. As Brutan lumbered past, she brought her sword round, praying that her aim was true.

It was.

Instead of striking Mirith, the shining blade sliced into Brutan's thigh. Gold sparks flew, and the shadows surrounding her father's body seemed to flinch momentarily. With an agonized roar, Brutan flung out his arms, dropping Mirith even as he recovered his balance.

"You dare to strike me?" he thundered. "You dare?!"

Off-balance herself, Elodie darted aside, narrowly avoiding a potentially lethal blow from Brutan's mace. But her feet slipped from under her—or maybe it was the fog tripping her up—and she sprawled backward. Her sword flew from her grasp. The instant it left her hand, its light went out. It fell into the mist and was gone.

Gripping the mace tightly, Brutan loomed over her. The fog condensed around him, a cloak of shadows as dark as her own skin of fire was bright.

"Elodie!" screamed Palenie.

Her scream broke off. The silence was immediately filled by a shriek from above.

The wyvern!

It dropped out of the sky like a stone. An avalanche of green crystal coils fell upon Brutan, knocking the mace out of his grasp and hurling him forward. He landed on his knees right in front of Elodie, a look of utter shock on his broad, bearded face. Their eyes met.

"Now, Elodie!" Mirith cried, picking herself up from where she'd fallen. "The jewel! The prophecy!"

Green crystal flashed as the wyvern encircled Elodie and Brutan with its coils. It bared its ruby teeth and hissed but kept its distance.

I have done what I can, it seemed to be saying. *Now it is up to you.*

Snarling, Brutan drew a long knife from beneath his smoke-rimmed robes.

Green crystal! Elodie thought.

Her hand went to her throat.

Finally she understood.

"They shall kill the cursed king," she said. They faced each other, both on their knees, father and daughter, while the fog of the dead boiled around them. "That's what the prophecy says. Not he. Not she. But *they.*"

Brutan's face contorted with rage. He no longer looked like a man, nor even a bear. He looked like a monster from Elodie's darkest nightmares.

"You died twice," Elodie went on. Her body blazed with golden fire. "First Gulph killed you. Then Tarlan. Now I'm here."

"Not for long!" Brutan screamed. He drew back the knife.

"Three deaths! That's what the prophecy means!"

She closed her shining fingers around the green jewel that was hanging around her neck. She tugged. The chain snapped. The jewel was cold, its tip sharp.

"Three deaths for the crown of three!"

Elodie plunged the jewel into her father's chest.

The shadows shrouding Brutan vanished. His cloak of fog evaporated. Suddenly exposed, he looked oddly small.

"What . . . ?" he croaked. He pressed his one remaining hand to his chest.

Brutan collapsed onto his side. His skin turned gray. So did his once-magnificent robes. Something was flying from him—a breath or a shadow, Elodie couldn't tell. The grayness folded over him, softened him. He grew smaller still. The remains of the fog drew him down, reducing him to a rag of a man. Then the rag disappeared, and only the mist remained, thinning until it was barely visible, almost gone . . . and then vanished.

He's dead. Really dead.

The wyvern's coils parted to reveal Elodie's friends. She saw broad smiles and heard applause. All the crowd was clapping and cheering. The faces of the dead were filled with joy. As Elodie staggered toward them, many sank to their knees and bowed their heads.

"All hail!" cried someone, and the others took up the chant. "All hail! All hail!"

Elodie stumbled, almost falling before Fessan and Palenie managed to steady her. As soon as she was standing again, they too fell to their knees. Behind them, Mirith did likewise.

"No," said Elodie, "you don't have to . . ."

"Yes, we do," Fessan replied.

Bowing its massive head, the wyvern let out a long series of guttural rumbles. It was purring again.

The fog cleared, revealing Elodie's sword. Fighting back tears, she picked it up off the ground.

"Command us!" someone called. "Whatever you ask of us, we will answer!"

Elodie hefted the sword. She felt both exhausted and wholly alive.

"Soon!" she shouted. "I will have something to ask of you very soon. If I call you forth, will you fight for me?"

"YES!" thundered the gathered dead.

"You are our queen," said Fessan when the tumult had died down. "We will do anything for you."

"You have destroyed Brutan forever," Mirith added. Her eyes shone.

Elodie could hardly believe it. "Where will you all go, now that he's gone?"

"Go?" said Palenie. "Why would we go anywhere?"

Elodie looked around. With the Shadow Cage gone, all that remained were the steps and the floating slabs. All remained gray in the Realm of the Dead.

"It's just so dark here," she said.

"Yes, indeed." Mirith smiled warmly. "Which is why we need a little light."

Understanding at last, Elodie held up her sword. Its golden light flared, brighter than the sun, drawing gasps from the crowd.

Squinting through half-closed eyelids, Elodie watched in wonder as the light expanded outward. The sword's glow swelled, turning the slabs to vast floating shards of multicolored crystal. They were as dazzling as the original stones had been dull.

The light continued to spread. Elodie began to see flower-filled meadows, high towers connected by soaring walkways, rivers of silver, and fountains of gold. The sky turned a dazzling turquoise, the color of no sky she had ever seen before. It was beautiful.

"Peace has returned to the Realm of the Dead," said Mirith. She was fading. Everything was fading. "For that we thank you, Queen Elodie. May the shadow never return."

Elodie reached out her hand to touch Mirith's, but saw that her own flesh was turning transparent too.

"Elodie?" called Palenie, seemingly from very far away. Her voice was like a thread floating in the air. "Do you have to go?"

Elodie wanted to respond, but the words choked in her throat.

By the time she could speak, the Realm of the Dead had disappeared behind a veil of golden light. Wind picked her up, carrying her high and then letting her fall, fall, fall. . . .

Darkness. The only movement was something brushing against her face—a strand of her own hair. It was only dark because her eyes were closed.

She heard voices. Something was sticking into her back. She was lying on something prickly. A pile of sticks? The air was damp, filled with a faintly noxious smell.

The swamp! I'm back!

She tried to move. Exhausted from her duel with Brutan, she felt every muscle in her body protesting. She gave up. Even opening her eyes was too much effort.

She concentrated on the voices instead.

". . . gathered here together," someone was saying. Cedric? Sylva? She was so woozy she couldn't even tell if it was a man or a woman.

"We will never forget the sadness of this day," the voice went on. It sounded familiar.

Horribly familiar.

"This is the day we bid farewell to our queen. Such a sadness, to see a life snuffed out so young."

Lord Vicerin!

The realization split her heart like a dagger. What was he doing here in the swamp?

"Such a sadness," Vicerin repeated, "that we must stand here today to mourn the passing of our dear Elodie, whom once I was proud to treat as my daughter, and whom I now must remember as my poor, lost queen."

Shocked into action, Elodie opened her eyes. She wasn't in the swamp at all, but lying on a great mound of branches in a smoke-blackened courtyard. Foul-smelling steam rose on all sides, the aftermath of the fires that had been set around the castle, and which were now extinguished. A small group of people were gathered nearby. Lord Vicerin stood at their head.

But Elodie had no time for her sworn enemy. She was more concerned by the man standing beside her. The man who was lowering a blazing torch toward the branches on which she lay.

It's a funeral pyre!

The torch touched the branches beneath her head, and flames erupted all around her.

ACT TWO

CHAPTER 12

The flames licked against Elodie's skin. A horrid stench drifted past her nostrils—her own hair, starting to singe. Filled with sudden terror, she sprang to her feet and leaped off the pyre. She landed awkwardly, but Samial was there, reaching out to steady her fall.

"Elodie, are you . . . ?" he began.

His voice was immediately drowned as screams echoed round the courtyard. The mourners who'd gathered for Elodie's funeral were backing away, their faces drawn down in fear.

Smoke billowed past Elodie's face. She looked wildly around. Clouds of steam were rising from the damped-down ruins of burning buildings, while beyond the courtyard walls the sounds of battle continued, even louder than they had been when Elodie and her friends had left the castle. Fire spurted from most of the windows in the twin south towers.

Castle Vicerin was overrun.

Soft footsteps were padding toward Elodie. Whirling, she saw Lord Vicerin bearing down on her. His skin had lost its usual coating of powder, and looked pink and pockmarked. His teeth were bared. To Elodie's satisfaction, she saw that his nose, which she'd kicked and broken during Fessan's execution, was crooked.

"Back, foul spawn of the swamp!" Vicerin shouted. He held up his shield, cowering behind it as he continued to advance.

More screams rose up from the crowd. Faces curled up in fear. Several onlookers backed away.

"Go back to the land of death!" Lord Vicerin yelled. But once he was close to Elodie, he dropped his voice to a whisper. "Your magic tricks don't scare me, treacherous girl. You will burn today. And I will keep your crown."

Elodie saw that he was indeed wearing a crown—a delicate silver circlet studded with tiny diamonds—and equally ornate armor she'd only seen him wear on ceremonial occasions. Blue sashes swung from the breastplate. The polished metal gleamed in the firelight.

But what really caught Elodie's attention was the pair of jewels swinging on gold chains around Lord Vicerin's neck.

Green jewels.

Mine! And Tarlan's!

Vicerin's armored boots squelched in the muddy ground as he

turned to the astonished onlookers. The flames crackled louder, taking hold of the pyre's inner core. Elodie could feel the heat baking the side of her face.

"Undead!" shrieked Vicerin. "This is not Elodie, but some malevolent demon returned from the Realm of the Dead! It must be burned! Guards!"

Four uniformed men barged through the crowd. To Elodie's dismay, one of them was Stown.

Three of the guards fanned out, leaving Stown to march straight up to Elodie, the tip of his sword aimed at her throat.

"I have seen the undead," he murmured. "You don't look like one of them to me—which will make burning you all the sweeter."

He forced her toward the pyre. The heat flared against her back. Smoke wrapped around her, as if eager to pull her in.

Burned to death! This is how my mother died. Am I to go the same way?

The muddy ribbons of her tattered wedding dress caught at her feet. She tugged angrily at the folds of the ridiculous garment. The silky material felt heavy, as if there were something caught inside....

There is something inside!

Her heart hammering, Elodie plunged her hand into the pocket hidden inside the skirt. She fumbled briefly, and then her fingers folded around a small cluster of objects beside Samial's arrowhead: a coin, a scrap of silk, a necklace, a ring.

"Why are you smiling, little girl?" growled Stown.

Elodie tightened her grip on the talismans.

Sand and heat rushed through her, that warm, gritty magic that still felt so peculiar. Stown felt it too—she saw it in his sudden stumble, his look of confusion.

"Come to me!" she shouted. "Stand by me now!"

Figures stepped out of the flames. At first they seemed made of fire, then their bodies darkened, became like smoke. They glided out into the courtyard with phantom swords drawn. A dozen vengeful ghosts. The murdered nobles of Ritherlee.

The crowd retreated with a chorus of shrieks and wails.

"It's Lady Darrand!" cried one of the courtiers, dropping to his knees in the mud.

"And there's Lord Winterborne!" The woman who'd sobbed this was tearing at her hair. "But he's dead! They're all dead!"

The panic spread to the guards, who broke and ran.

Stown stood frozen to the spot.

"If you don't drop your sword," Elodie told him, "my friends will kill you." Then she added, "My dead friends."

Stown held her gaze for a moment, then dropped his sword and blundered past Vicerin, who was himself edging slowly away from the spot where Elodie was standing.

"She is a witch!" Vicerin shouted, his voice wavering.

Elodie strode away from the pyre. "Is it witch? Or is it

undead demon? You really should make up your mind."

Lady Darrand slipped up to her. Her stare was fixed on Lord Vicerin. Her ghostly armor seemed to soak up the light from the fire and hold it, so that she glowed from within. Vicerin gaped at her shimmering form, his mouth flapping like a stranded fish.

"Would you like me to take care of him?" Lady Darrand asked Elodie, drawing her sword.

"Just don't let him get away," Elodie answered.

With a fierce grin, Lady Darrand advanced.

Even as the rest of the ghostly nobles cornered the fleeing guards, a small group of Vicerin officers rushed into the courtyard.

"Turn and face them, you cowards," one of the officers cried.

Their faces white with terror, the guards turned. At once ghostly swords began to slice the air with an eerie swishing sound. Trembling and pale, most of the Vicerin troops stood unresisting as the phantom blades cut them down.

"My horse! My horse!"

The shouts came from Lord Vicerin. Retreating, he'd managed to reach the long row of stables at the end of the courtyard. There, a pair of terrified grooms held a sleek white stallion.

The jewels!

Picking up her skirts, Elodie raced after him. Lady Darrand ran with her, but as they neared the stables, a wooden gate exploded into a shower of splinters. Smoke gushed through the opening, followed by five Helkrags mounted on armored elks. The men's faces were hidden beneath their tooth-lined fur hoods, and their leather armor was barbed with cruel iron hooks.

"Run on, Elodie!" Lady Darrand cried. "I will try to hold them!"

Lady Darrand slashed at the forelegs of the nearest elk. The bones snapped like twigs and the huge beast hit the ground, throwing its rider and bellowing in pain.

Elodie ran on. Already grooms were hoisting Lord Vicerin into the saddle. A single slap on the horse's flank sent it galloping toward a narrow gate half-hidden between two of the stable blocks.

I won't let you get away!

Vicerin had just reached the gate when a horseman appeared out of the smoke.

". . . not much time . . . ," Elodie heard him shout to Vicerin. ". . . soon be upon us . . ."

She strained her ears to hear more, but the words were lost in the uproar. Having heard the message, Vicerin angrily spurred his stallion through the gate.

What did that man tell him? she wondered. Whatever it was, it had been urgent enough to convince Vicerin to abandon the battle.

Elodie sped in pursuit, but she slipped and fell headlong into the mud. She tried to stand, only to find a length of rope had tangled round her ankles. She yanked at it, watching in desperation as Lord Vicerin and the other horseman disappeared.

"Elodie!" Samial reached down, helping her untangle the rope. Tired and bedraggled, Elodie heaved herself to her feet. Her mud-caked dress felt as if it weighed more than she did. She scanned the courtyard.

The funeral pyre was well and truly ablaze, flames belching thick smoke high into the morning sky. Only one of the elk-hunters lay dead—the one felled by Lady Darrand. The others were circling, their axes finding fresh victims with every stroke.

"It's time to go," Elodie said. A dreadful thought stopped her cold. "But, Samial, where are Sylva and Cedric?"

Samial's brow furrowed. "We thought you were dead," he said apologetically. "You fell in the swamp. They got you out, but your body was cold. The rest of the ghosts had vanished. I couldn't do anything." He held up his smoke-thin hands helplessly. "Then Vicerin came with his men. They brought you here."

"Where are Sylva and Cedric?" Elodie repeated. Her throat felt tight.

Samial shook his head in sorrow. "Vicerin had them locked up. They are in the castle. Somewhere."

Elodie's mouth set in a grim line. "Then we will free them."

Lady Darrand ran up to them. "Vicerin got away," she said. "I'm sorry, Elodie."

"It wasn't your fault," Elodie replied. "Anyway, forget about him. He's not important."

"If I thought you believed that . . ."

"Vicerin will get what's coming to him soon enough. Right now we have more important things to worry about." Samial and Lady Darrand listened attentively, waiting for her command. "First we need reinforcements so we can take down these Helkrags quickly. And then we're going to find Cedric and Sylva."

Leaving Lady Darrand to round up the other ghosts, Elodie crept to the shadows near the stable gate. The smoke was thicker here, and provided excellent cover. She watched with her heart in her mouth as Lady Darrand returned leading a line of phantom soldiers through the fighting toward her. At once the Helkrags left off attacking what was left of the crowd and turned to face them.

Within moments, the ghosts were gathered around Elodie, their faces drawn with whatever passed for fatigue in their phantom plane of existence. The Helkrags were prowling to and fro, but seemed reluctant to attack this strange new enemy without provocation.

"What is your plan, Your Highness?" Lord Winterborne asked gravely.

"We're going back to the swamp," Elodie answered.

Lady Darrand's eyes grew wide. "Does this mean what I think it does?"

Elodie wiped the mud from her face.

"Yes," she said. "Let's go and raise an army."

CHAPTER 13

Theeta swooped in from the ice-blue sky. Beneath her, the bright sun made a thorrod-shaped shadow that rippled over the snow toward Tarlan. Her wings shone.

Tarlan shrugged off the heavy furs that Captain Leom had given him. He didn't need them anymore. His battered old cloak was more than enough. Besides, seeing his oldest friend filled him with a warmth that even the bitterest wind couldn't chill.

As Theeta drew near, he was surprised to see she was carrying two riders. Could one of them be Melchior? Tarlan couldn't imagine her allowing anyone other than the wizard to ride on her back.

Theeta landed in a flurry of snow. She dipped her head and tilted her wing, allowing her passengers to climb down. Tarlan looked on dumbfounded as a skinny boy about his age sprang nimbly to the ground before helping down his companion: a woman whose face was scarred on one side by a terrible burn.

Tarlan stared at the newcomers.

They stared back.

A sudden gust of wind sent the woman's long hair streaming out in a red-gold pennant. Tarlan's hair did the same. The boy's hair was shorter, but flashed that same familiar color as it was ruffled by the breeze.

"Gulph," said Tarlan. It was little more than a whisper.

The boy, whose back was oddly twisted, gave him a tentative smile.

"Tarlan," he answered. Like his brother, all he could manage was a croak.

"I saw you," Tarlan went on, his voice gathering strength. "In Idilliam. In the battle. But when I looked for you again, my father was—"

"Our father."

"Our father." Tarlan shook his head, struggling to comprehend it. "You're here. You're alive."

He didn't trust himself to say any more. A pressure was building inside him, as if his whole beating heart were trying to climb into his mouth. The woman was gazing at him through the veil of red-gold hair that was dancing in front of her face. Her eyes were wet with tears.

I've never seen you before, Tarlan thought.

Yet, somehow, he knew exactly who she was.

"Mother," he said.

Saying the word released the pressure, and suddenly he was running toward them, crying out and flinging his arms wide. Gulph and Kalia came forward in their turn, and the three of them met in the snow in a knot of laughter and tears. Tarlan hugged them, and they hugged him back. Never had he felt such warmth, such acceptance, such a sure and breathtaking sense of *coming home*.

Never had he felt such love.

"You're alive!" Tarlan said again, laughing as he tousled Gulph's hair. His brother was shorter and thinner than he was, and the odd kink in his back made him shorter still. But looking at his face was almost like looking in a mirror.

"I am!" Gulph's grin was enormous.

Before Tarlan could speak again, Kalia clutched him to her.

"My boy!" she sobbed. "My dear, dear boy!"

Tarlan touched his fingers gently to the scar on her face. "What happened to you, Mother? Elodie said that Brutan had you executed, burned alive. . . ."

Kalia's tear-filled eyes widened. "Elodie? You have seen her? Spoken to her?"

"Is she all right?" Gulph demanded. "Where is she?"

"She's alive. We were together, in the Trident camp with Melchior. She was . . . we were . . ." Tarlan's tongue tangled in his mouth. There was so much to tell. Where in all of Toronia should he begin?

His mother saw his confusion. "My Elodie is alive," Kalia said. "That is all I need to know. The rest of the story can come later. For now"—she pressed her hands against Tarlan's cheeks—"it is enough that we are together."

Something hard pressed against the small of Tarlan's back: Theeta's beak. Wiping his tears aside, he turned to face his thorrod friend.

"Brother mother." Theeta arched her neck and preened, clearly pleased with herself. "Thorrod bring."

"Yes. You brought them." Tarlan touched the palm of his hand to the sharp tip of her beak, then rubbed his forehead against its cool curve. "Thank you, Theeta."

"Together now. Together right. Together strong."

"I know. That's what you were trying to tell me all along, isn't it? I'm sorry, Theeta. I was stupid. I should have listened to you."

Theeta planted her huge claws wide in the snow and glared down at him with her bright black eyes.

"Together fight."

Tarlan became aware that Kalia and Gulph were both staring at him. His mother's face was flushed with pride, but when his brother spoke, his voice was filled with pure amazement.

"You're talking to it! You're talking to the thorrod!"

"Theeta," said Tarlan. "Her name is Theeta."

"But it's . . . you mean you can . . . ?"

Tarlan grinned. "I talk to animals. It's sort of what I do. Theeta's my closest friend from my pack."

"You have a . . . pack?"

"Yes." Tarlan ran his fingers affectionately through Theeta's ruff. "But I saw what *you* can do, Gulph—turning invisible on the battlefield like that. Now, that's an impressive trick."

"It's got me out of a few scrapes."

"I'll bet."

Tarlan could hardly take his eyes off his brother. But thinking about his pack had reawoken his desire to return to Toronia.

"Come on," he said, adjusting his cloak and springing onto Theeta's back. "If we make good time, you'll meet the rest of my pack before the sun goes down. Then we can rescue Elodie."

"Rescue?" said Kalia as he helped her up.

"I don't like the sound of that," said Gulph, joining them. "Who's holding her prisoner?"

So, as Theeta's enormous wings carried them aloft, Tarlan began telling his tale, starting with his suspicion that Elodie was now a captive at Castle Vicerin and then jumping all the way back to the beginning, to that fateful moment in Yalasti when Mirith had first sent him on his quest to find Melchior.

"So Elodie can summon ghosts," mused Kalia as Tarlan

described the time he'd spent with his sister in the Trident camp.

"We all have powers," Tarlan agreed.

I don't think I've ever talked as much, he thought. *It's as if everything has been building up to this moment. Just a few days ago I thought it was all coming to an end. Now it feels like it's just beginning.*

When at last he'd finished telling his story, his mother and brother related their own adventures, which seemed even more astonishing to Tarlan than his own. Frequently during the flight he allowed his eyes to stray up to the sky, where the three prophecy stars blazed with newfound fury in the blue brightness.

We're all still alive, he thought in wonder. Soon they would all be together—and the battle for Toronia would begin.

By the time they reached Deep Poynt, the sun was sinking toward the western horizon. The forest canopy rolled beneath them like a thick green blanket. The air of Isur was warm after the cold of the Icy Wastes. Yet Tarlan felt suddenly chilled.

Anything could be hiding down there, he thought, regarding the trees uncertainly.

"So you won the battle here?" said Gulph. He was leaning forward, thin hands bunched in Theeta's ruff, eyes squinting as he peered into the growing gloom.

"Yes," Tarlan replied. "It was hard, but we beat back the

Galadronians. When I left Melchior, he was helping The Hammer rebuild the . . ."

His voice trailed away. They were flying over the hill on which Deep Poynt stood . . . or rather, had once been standing. Now all that remained of the fortress town was a mass of rubble and fallen roof beams. Smoke rose listlessly from the wreckage. There was no sign of life.

Deep Poynt had been destroyed.

"Where's Melchior?" said Tarlan.

Where's my pack?

"Kitheen here!" cawed Theeta, suddenly wheeling around to the right.

"What did she say?" said Kalia.

Tarlan scanned the sky, which was now the color of blood. Eventually he spotted a bright flash as the feathers of a second thorrod caught the dying light of the sun. The giant bird swooped down, its glossy black body a stark contrast to the vivid gold of its wingtips.

"Kitheen!" Tarlan called as the youngest of the thorrods drew into formation beside them. "What happened here?"

For a moment he wasn't sure that his winged friend would reply. It was hard enough to get Kitheen to speak at all, let alone at times of stress. To his surprise, the big black bird responded immediately.

"Tarlan go. Kitheen unhappy."

"I know. And I'm sorry. But I'm back now. Tell me what happened to Deep Poynt."

"Man flock. Kill nest."

"An army? But who's left to . . . ?" Tarlan looked around anxiously. "Where's Melchior? Where's the rest of my pack?"

"Wizard hide. Pack hide. Tree shelter."

Tarlan sighed. "All right. So they're safe. Now, tell me more about this army. Was it bigger than the first one? Bigger than the Galadronian invasion force?"

"More flock," Kitheen confirmed. "Many human. Most human. All human."

His gold wingtips flicked in agitation. Tarlan could only guess at what he was trying to say.

More humans than you've ever seen before? Is that it?

The thought sent a chill down his spine.

"What's he saying?" said Gulph, tugging at Tarlan's cloak.

Tarlan translated as best he could.

"Can you lead us to Melchior?" he asked Kitheen.

The thorrod dived toward the trees, clearly more comfortable with action than words. Tarlan jabbed his heels into Theeta's flanks, urging her to follow. The two birds landed simultaneously at the forest's edge.

"Filos!" Tarlan called, leaping to the ground. "Greythorn! Brock!"

For a moment nothing happened. Then the trees began to shake. A bear emerged, then another, followed by a flood of creatures small and large, from foxes and snakes to horses and deer. The ground shook as they made their way out of the shadows, a vast army of animals whose eager eyes gleamed in the fading light of the sun.

"Is this your pack?" said Gulph. "It's so . . . big."

Tarlan sank to his knees before the assembled animals.

"I abandoned you, and I'm sorry . . . ," he began, but that was all he said before a blur of blue-and-white fur knocked him sideways.

"Filos!" Tarlan laughed, fussing at the tigron's striped mane. "Do you forgive me?"

"There's nothing to forgive," Filos replied.

Close behind her came Greythorn and Brock, both of whom treated Tarlan to a series of slobbery licks.

"I am glad you came back," said the wolf.

"Can Brock fight again now?" growled the bear.

"Soon," Tarlan promised. "But before that, I want you to meet the two newest members of our pack."

The eyes of his friends—and of every animal present—turned to Gulph and Kalia, both of whom were watching apprehensively from their perch on Theeta's back.

Tarlan spread out his arms.

"This is Gulph, my brother. And Kalia, my mother. I want you to give them your warmest welcome."

"Welcome!" roared Filos.

The rest of the animals joined in, filling the evening air with a deafening chorus of growls, grunts, shrieks, squeals, hisses, and howls. Looking dumbfounded, Gulph lowered himself from Theeta's back. Kalia followed, her eyes shining with pride.

When the noise had died away, Gulph took a nervous step forward.

"It's, er, good to meet you all," he said. He whispered to Tarlan, "Can they understand me?"

Tarlan laughed. "Not really. But I think they know what you're trying to say."

He glanced round to see Kalia inspecting the coarse meadow grass. She scooped up something and sprinkled it into his hand.

"Sand?" He stared in puzzlement at the tiny yellow grains.

"It is everywhere," Kalia replied, dusting her palms together. "I know much about sand. Its presence here concerns me."

Tarlan frowned. During the flight, he and Gulph had talked about their powers. Tarlan had been fascinated to discover that, for both of them, their magic was somehow bound up with the idea of a desert. Kalia had listened with interest, but so far she had offered no thoughts of her own on the subject.

"Theeta and I flew through a sandstorm on our way to the

mountains," Tarlan said. "It blew out of nowhere, and vanished just as quickly. It was really odd."

Kalia's eyebrows shot up. "A sandstorm? In the snow? I think—"

She was cut off by the howls of a group of wolves at the edge of the pack. Tarlan whirled round.

Warning cries!

Soldiers were running down the hill toward them. They wore colorful robes and carried vicious-looking curved swords. Their battle cries were nearly loud enough to drown out the baying of the wolves.

"Big flock!" squawked Kitheen, taking to the air.

"Galadronians!" Tarlan shouted.

They were hiding in the ruins!

Already the Galadronians were upon them. Swords slashed into a pack of foxes, sending small bodies flying through the air. Horses reared, whinnying in alarm. Even in the chaos, however, Tarlan was relieved to see the enemy numbered no more than thirty.

"They're just stragglers!" he roared. "Spread out! Draw them in!"

Pulling his sword from its scabbard, he led Filos, Greythorn, and Brock on a long, curving run that took them around the enemy's rear flank. Gulph and Kalia followed, drawing the strange crystal blades Gulph had spoken of.

The Galadronians continued to drive their way deeper into

Tarlan's pack, hacking on all sides with their cruel blades. Obeying Tarlan's command, the animals spread apart, creating an open space into which their attackers poured.

By now Tarlan's small band was directly behind the Galadronians.

"Stop!" Tarlan bellowed.

The huge pack of animals obeyed instantly. The Galadronians faltered, suddenly realizing they were surrounded by an impenetrable wall of fur, feather, and scale. Giving them no time to recover, Tarlan drove his small band into the one gap that had been left in the wall of bodies.

"Bring them down!" he yelled.

With Tarlan leading, the rest of the pack plunged into the fray, striking out with blade and claw alike. The Galadronians fought back with guts and determination, and for a while Tarlan was afraid the enemy was too strong. But Brock was stronger still—the bear dispatched a quarter of the Galadronians just on his own—while the teeth of Filos and Greythorn proved more than a match for the Galadronian armor.

Tarlan fought hard, and was pleased to see his mother match him blow for blow.

I am my mother's son, he thought with pride.

Kalia moved fast, her crystal sword a constant blur. On the rare occasions her blade wasn't fast enough, her hand slipped inside her cloak and tossed out a spray of colored powder, which flashed into flame, lighting up the dusk and throwing the enemy into confusion.

As the number of enemy soldiers dwindled, Tarlan spotted Gulph standing away from the center of the fighting. His sword arm hung limp at his side. On his face was an expression of curious intensity.

In front of Gulph stood a Galadronian soldier—a short man in a cloak of orange and green stripes. His own expression was slack, as if he were half-asleep.

Before Tarlan could wonder what was going on, something silver shot toward him. He ducked, and the throwing knife flashed past him to land with a thud in the trunk of a nearby tree. At the same instant, Greythorn's jaws locked round the throat of the Galadronian who'd thrown it. The wolf bit down; the man's purple cloak turned red and he dropped lifeless to the ground.

"Theeta!" yelled Tarlan. "Go to Gulph! He's . . ."

Theeta was just taking to the air when Gulph came to his senses and rushed at the Galadronian soldier. Their blades met with a hollow clang. After a brief exchange of blows, Gulph's crystal sword struck home and the man fell at his feet.

Satisfied that his brother was safe, Tarlan pivoted on his heels, ready for the next attacker.

But there were no more. The man Gulph had killed was the last. The enemy was defeated.

"Are you all right, my son?" said Kalia, crossing the blood-soaked battlefield to where Tarlan was standing.

My son.

The words sounded good.

"I'm fine." He called to his brother, "Gulph—what were you doing back there?"

Frowning slightly, Gulph picked his way through the litter of bodies to join them.

"I was inside his mind," he said.

Tarlan gaped. "Inside his . . . ?"

"Mind." Gulph swallowed hard. "It's something else I can do."

Tarlan exchanged a glance with Kalia, who was staring at Gulph with openmouthed amazement.

"Do you want to know what he was thinking?" Gulph went on.

Tarlan wasn't entirely sure that he did.

"Tell us," said Kalia.

A little shudder ran through Gulph's twisted shoulders. "Sorry—it's still a little weird for me. The black thorrod—your friend—was right. The Galadronian army is big. *Really* big. Perhaps ten thousand soldiers, all armed to the teeth."

"You saw that?" said Tarlan, still struggling to comprehend Gulph's remarkable powers. "But how?"

"The soldier had seen it. That's why I was able to see it. At least, I think that's how it works."

"What else?" said Kalia. "There is more—I see it in your eyes."

"I've seen their leader."

"And?" Tarlan demanded. "What's he like?"

"She." Gulph shook his head. "I saw her. She was . . . oh, I can't describe it."

The skin on the back of Tarlan's neck was prickling. "Tell us, Gulph. We need to know."

But Gulph could only look at him with haunted eyes.

"If you cannot tell us," said Kalia gently, "perhaps you can show us."

"Show you?" Gulph replied. "What do you mean?"

Kalia pulled a small leather pouch from beneath her robe. Loosening its drawstring, she poured a handful of black sand onto the ground, then sat down cross-legged before it.

"You have mind-sight," she said. "An ancient form of magic, and one that can be shared, given the right circumstances. Gulph, will you let me in?"

Gulph sat down hesitantly. Tarlan knelt beside him, eyeing the little mound of sand suspiciously.

"You can see inside minds too?" he said. "Inside Gulph's?"

Kalia shook her head. "No. But I can draw out what Gulph saw. I can make it real enough for us all to see."

"Do it! We need to see what we're up against."

"Gulph?" Kalia took her son's hand. "May I?"

Gulph nodded.

Tarlan watched as Kalia gently pressed Gulph's hand into the sand. Black grains spilled over his fingers, seeming to move of their own accord. She touched her finger first to her lips, then to his.

"I don't see what . . . ," Tarlan began.

The air over the sand began to ripple. Heat rose, baking Tarlan's face. A bubble appeared, floating just above Gulph's half-buried hand. Inside the bubble, Tarlan saw an army.

"That's it," Gulph whispered. "That's what I saw."

Fascinated, Tarlan peered into the bubble.

He was looking down on a desert. The viewpoint was high, as if he were perched on the back of a thorrod. Below, stretched across the sand, was a line of soldiers holding long lances that gleamed in the sun.

"They're just men," Tarlan said. "We defeated the Galadronians. We can take care of . . ."

The viewpoint shifted. Now he was looking at a two-wheeled chariot drawn by a single horse. It was twice the height of a normal horse, its gold body seeming to shift strangely in the sunlight. Almost as if it were . . .

"It's made of sand," Tarlan breathed.

Riding on the chariot was a woman. She was very tall, and wore white armor that clung to her like a second skin. Her helmet was etched with strange runes. In her right hand she carried a spear.

"The Witch-Empress Hypiro," said Kalia. Her voice was trembling. "And she carries the Sandspear."

"Sandspear?" replied Tarlan. "What's that?"

"Wait," Gulph said. "Watch."

Hypiro pointed her spear toward the ground. At once, the desert around her began to shake. Bodies rose up from it, forming from the sand like sculptures taking shape. Within just a few breaths, the sand was gone.

In its place, spanning the entire visible world from horizon to horizon, was an army of giants.

"Make it go away," said Gulph. His face was pale. "As bad as it looks, it feels even worse."

Kalia touched his lips again, then blew the sand away. The bubble, and the images it contained, vanished with a faint popping sound, leaving Tarlan to ponder what he'd seen.

The stuff of the world made into an army.

"So she can make things with it," he said. "The Sandspear. I'm right, aren't I?"

Kalia ran a trembling hand down the burn scar on her face. "Yes, Tarlan. Whoever wields the Sandspear has the power to create anything they want out of sand."

"When you say anything . . ."

"I mean anything. Swords, castles, creatures. Armies. Just as you saw. And as long as Hypiro wields it, that is exactly what she will do. She wants the world. And she will raise whatever army she needs to get it."

"And she's here in Toronia," said Gulph glumly.

Standing, Tarlan pulled his brother to his feet. "Well, so are we. We just have to work out how to get rid of her." He wished he felt as confident as he sounded.

"Hypiro must be driven from these shores if you are to stand any chance of ruling Toronia," said Kalia. "Yet there may be hope."

"Really?" said Tarlan and Gulph in unison. They shared a brief, uncertain smile.

"Yes. We have enemies on two fronts—the Galadronians and the Vicerins."

"How is that hopeful?" Gulph asked.

"There are three of you."

Tarlan gazed across the battlefield, where Greythorn was helping Filos and Brock tend to the injured animals. The sky had darkened to indigo, and the stars were already bright—none brighter than the three prophecy stars, which burned directly overhead and bathed the meadow with their cold, hard light.

I thought we'd defeated the Galadronians, he thought unhappily. *Now it seems they're more powerful than ever.*

"Two enemies," he said at last. "All right. But we still have to deal with them one at a time. What else do you know about this Sandspear, Mother?"

Kalia sighed. "It comes from Pharrah, the desert realm. My original home."

"Pharrah?" said Gulph. "I've never heard of it."

"It lies far away across the sea." She touched first Gulph's hand, then Tarlan's. "But a little of it is in you. I think you must realize that now."

"So that's where you were born?" said Tarlan.

"Yes. Hypiro was in power even then. She has a deep magic that defies age—some say she has ruled Pharrah for a thousand years. That is a long time for a land to be in the grip of a tyrant."

"Is that why you left? Because of her?"

"In a way, although I did not choose to leave. You see, Hypiro was not the only person in Pharrah capable of making magic. The people in my tribe could command sand too, but we did not need an enchanted spear to make it obey us."

"She drove you out," said Gulph. "She didn't want anyone to challenge her, so she drove you out."

Kalia nodded. "Those of us she could not kill. Some of us resisted, but she is cruel beyond belief. Do you know what happens to a man when you replace all the blood in his body with burning sand?"

Tarlan exchanged a glance with Gulph. Both brothers shuddered.

"I hope you never find out," said Kalia.

Desert realm, Tarlan thought. *Desert magic. Finally, it makes sense.*

"My own magic is small compared to Hypiro's," Kalia went on. "And indeed to yours. Sand is my strength, but it is also my limitation. Without sand, I have no power at all. But Hypiro can summon sand at will."

"Well, so can we," said Tarlan. He grinned at his brother. "Can't we, Gulph?"

Gulph nodded, but he looked very serious. "I saw more in the soldier's mind," he said.

Tarlan and Kalia both turned to him.

"More?" said Tarlan. "What do you mean?"

"I saw where Hypiro is leading her army."

"To Idilliam?" It seemed obvious enough to Tarlan. But Gulph was shaking his head.

"No, Tarlan. To Ritherlee. They've already crossed the Isurian River. They're headed straight for Castle Vicerin."

The brothers stared at each other. Then they spoke at the same time.

"Elodie!"

CHAPTER 14

E lodie stood at the top of the bank, gazing across the
Forgotten Graveyard. Clouds had swallowed the sun, and
the swamp was shrouded in a gray veil of fog. The air was
damp and still.

She stretched, glad to be free of that wretched wedding dress
at last. The lightweight armor Lord Winterborne had found for
her felt good. And she was pleased to see that the tunic she'd been
given to wear over the top wasn't the rich blue of the Vicerins.

It was green—not quite the leafy hue of Trident, but close enough.

Hanging in a scabbard at her waist was a sword.

I am a soldier again.

"Will this work?" asked Lady Darrand. Elodie wasn't sure if
her ghostly friend meant raising an army or leading it against the
Vicerin forces. She supposed it didn't matter.

"Brutan is gone, once and for all. The way to the Realm of the Dead is open. I can do this."

Lady Darrand smiled. She and the rest of the ghosts who'd gathered on the bank seemed part of the mist, their bodies swirling and re-forming with a slow, natural rhythm. Elodie glanced at Samial, who nodded encouragement.

Instinct told Elodie to lift her hands. She moved her fingers, letting the air drain between them like . . .

. . . *like sand.*

A warm breeze pushed its way through the mist. The smell of damp grass was replaced by something bitter and scorched—the scent of the desert.

"Come to me," she murmured. Her words floated out into the fog. "Answer my call."

The mist was rippling like a heat-haze over sand dunes. The breeze was growing stronger. Shadows shifted among the grassy hummocks of the swamp. Gray shapes began to rise.

"Come to me!" Elodie cried. "I need you now! Toronia needs you now!"

The shapes gradually condensed into crudely sculpted human forms. As each new figure appeared, the mist rushed toward it and began to spin. Now hundreds of tiny tornadoes were whirling toward Elodie, sucking in the mist as the phantom bodies took shape.

As the ghosts gained definition, Elodie saw that she'd summoned not just soldiers but men and women of all kinds—farmers and tradespeople, hostlers and maids, young and old alike.

Frida was right, thought Elodie, observing her empty hands. *I didn't need their belongings. All I need to do is call.*

On they came, one ghost after another, while all around them the mist dispersed. Soon the air was as clear as it had been when the day began. Standing before Elodie was a vast assembly of gray wraithlike figures, all regarding her with a patient, expectant air.

Elodie dropped her hands to her sides. "I've called you here because I need your help," she told the ghosts. "The prophecy says I am to be queen, but someone is standing between me and the throne. His name is Lord Vicerin."

At the sound of his name, an eerie sigh passed through the ghostly crowd. Then one of the ghosts—a stocky farmer with a wide-brimmed hat—called out:

"It was a Vicerin soldier put his sword through me. Why? Because I refused to hand over my land!"

"Vicerin struck me down himself," cried an angry-looking woman. "I dared to free my husband from the stocks—he'd done nothing wrong!"

More ghosts joined in with tales of violence and oppression. Elodie listened in appalled silence to the injustices Lord Vicerin had committed against them. One thing pleased her—all these risen spirits were united by one thing.

They're thirsty for revenge.

She raised a hand and silence fell.

"We have a common enemy," she cried. "If you fight with me, vengeance can be yours! What do you say?"

The ghosts raised their weapons. For every sword, Elodie saw a scythe or pickax or some other common tool. From hundreds of gray, gaping mouths came a single battle cry:

"VENGEANCE!"

Elodie slid her sword from its scabbard and lofted it high. To her left and right, Lady Darrand and Lord Winterborne did the same.

"Follow my blade!" she shouted. "And today the castle will be ours!"

Her chest swelling with pride, Elodie began marching through the copse and back down the slope toward Castle Vicerin. Samial was on one side of her, the ghosts of the murdered Ritherlee nobles on the other. Behind them came the spirits of the Forgotten Graveyard.

The sounds of battle grew steadily louder as they approached the castle. In contrast, the army of the dead moved in silence, their footsteps raising not even a whisper of sound.

Good. We'll have surprise on our side.

Fifty paces short of the main gate, she signaled to the army to halt.

"There are two sets of soldiers in there," she said, pitching her voice low. "Both are our enemies. Drive them all out!"

With an unearthly hissing sound, the ghost army surged toward the gate with their motley array of weapons drawn. Elodie followed at a run, Samial and the ghosts of the Ritherlee nobles at her side.

"Our new army can take care of the enemy," she told them, "while we find Cedric and Sylva."

They burst through the gate. The outer courtyard was full of Vicerin and Helkrag troops grappling with opponents who looked no more solid than shadows. Those of the enemy who weren't fighting were fleeing, screaming out in fear as Elodie's phantom soldiers pursued them with weapons raised.

One band of Helkrags, clearly terrified of the hundreds of ghosts, spurred their elks toward a break in one of the walls. A ghostly battalion appeared from nowhere, gliding not over the ground but up the wall itself. They dropped on the fleeing Helkrags from above and tore them apart.

"They'll be in the White Tower," said Elodie, tearing her eyes from the curiously hypnotic scene. The high keep that had once been her prison was now one of the few parts of the castle untouched by fire. "I'm sure of it."

"It is defended," Samial warned, indicating a squad of Vicerin castle guards bunched at the tower's main door.

"Not for long," said Lady Darrand. She slipped smoothly past them with a pair of phantom soldiers at her side.

The guards scattered as the ghosts approached, shouting fearful warnings to their comrades to stay back. Lady Darrand ducked inside the tower; Elodie and Samial followed her in. The other two ghosts brought up the rear, their swords held out to protect Elodie from an attack from behind.

The storerooms on the ground floor were empty, just as Elodie had expected.

"If they're here, they'll be on one of the upper levels," she whispered. "Samial, can you . . . ?"

He put a finger to his mouth. Elodie and the noble ghosts ducked into the shadows at the foot of the great stone stairs that spiraled up through the center of the tower.

Peering carefully around the banister, she saw four castle guards march across the landing at the top of the first flight of steps. A moment later, the familiar figure of Lord Vicerin appeared. He'd exchanged his crown for a silver helmet with a crest of blue feathers. The visor was raised, showing his furious face.

"Follow me!" he barked. "Those children of mine are more trouble than they're worth!"

His metal boots clanging on the stone floor, Vicerin led the guards at high speed down a nearby corridor.

Elodie and the ghosts crept out of cover.

"That passage leads to the Star Chamber," said Elodie. "It must be where he's keeping Sylva and Cedric."

"It will be dangerous," Lady Darrand warned.

Elodie nodded grimly. "I'm a long way past worrying about danger."

She tiptoed up the stairs, wishing she could move as quietly as the ghosts. Heart thudding in her chest, she led the way along the corridor, wondering what they would find at the other end.

The door to the Star Chamber was open. Crouching low, Elodie peeked round it into a circular room lit by a series of tall, slitted windows. The walls, floor, and ceiling were painted dark blue and studded with thousands of glass beads. The sun cutting through the windows reflected off the beads, creating countless dazzling pinpoints of light.

In the middle of the Star Chamber stood a large, round table. Here, Elodie knew, the affairs of Ritherlee deemed too secret for the regular council chamber were discussed. Now the table had been turned into a kind of platform on which seven or eight Helkrags stood. All were clad in the familiar tooth-lined elk-hunter hoods— except one: a man who strode among them dispensing gruff orders. Elodie guessed he was the leader. His helmet was fashioned from a skull with huge eye sockets and a glossy, hooked beak.

A thorrod skull, Elodie realized with a shudder.

Lying on their backs in the middle of the table, gagged and

squirming against thick ropes, were Sylva and Cedric.

Lord Vicerin waved an arm toward them. "What is the meaning of this?" he cried in a high, nasal voice. His guards were clustered around him, swords drawn. "How dare you take what is mine? Release them to my custody at once!"

The Helkrag leader loped across the huge table. Adjusting his gruesome helmet, he glared down at Vicerin.

"These childs are prisoner!" he growled. His voice came from deep in his chest, and his accent was so thick that Elodie struggled to make out the words. "These childs are Helkrag to die!"

"Prisoners, yes. But they are *my* prisoners." Lord Vicerin spoke slowly, as if to an infant. "You will return them at once!"

The Helkrag leader drew a long, serrated knife from beneath his leather armor. His companions laughed. "You promise childs. You not deliver. We need childs to make spirits happy and make Helkrag strongest. So we take these childs and we give them to spirits."

"'Give them to spirits'?" Vicerin repeated. The muscles in his cheeks were twitching. "What are you talking about?"

Elodie could feel the blood leaving her face. She had a horrible feeling she knew.

The Helkrag leader grinned, displaying a forest of black teeth. Holding the blade of his knife close to his throat, he drew it sharply sideways. At the same time he made a sharp hissing sound.

"The Helkrags are going to sacrifice them," Elodie whispered. Her heart was racing.

Lord Vicerin put a hand to his chin. "I care little who you choose to kill. But every death comes with a price."

"You not pay price," the Helkrag snapped back.

"So you said. However, the situation is more complicated than you realize. We now have a mutual enemy. A phantom army that seeks to destroy us both. If we stand together, perhaps we can defeat it."

"Helkrags strong!" The leader thumped his chest. His comrades copied him, the impacts making the teeth in their hoods rattle.

"So if I allow this execution, you will swear me your loyalty once again?"

His words chilled Elodie to the core. On the table, Cedric struggled frantically. Elodie could hear Sylva's muffled sobs through the gag tied around her mouth.

"Helkrag make oath! Helkrag make fight!"

Vicerin sighed as if the whole affair had become suddenly tiresome. He dabbed the corner of his mouth with a blue silk sash.

"Then make your sacrifice," he said. "Kill them both."

"NO!" Releasing all her pent-up energy, Elodie burst into the Star Chamber at a run. Close beside her were the ghosts.

As they raced toward the enormous table, Elodie was grimly pleased to see the looks of surprise on the faces of the Helkrags. Even more satisfying was the expression of utter shock that had transformed Lord Vicerin's features into a pantomime mask.

"LET THEM GO!" Elodie screamed.

At the same time, she was calculating furiously. Helkrags and Vicerins combined numbered twenty. She was outnumbered, but she also had ghosts on her side.

We can take them!

Red mist clouded the edges of her vision. All thoughts ceased. Abandoning words, she let her scream become an animal cry of fury. She sprang up onto the table, bringing her sword round with all her strength. Its razor-sharp tip sliced through the bellies of two gawping Helkrags. Blood blossomed on their furs, and they rolled off the table like eight-pins.

To her left, Lord Winterborne had engaged two more Helkrags. He held his phantom sword in his right hand, thrusting and parrying with sharp, economical movements. His left hand was raised behind his head, the fingers delicately curled. The Helkrags tried to fight back, but they were slow and clumsy compared to the old but agile ghost. Within a few breaths they were lying dead on the table with their throats cut.

The three Helkrags who ran forward to avenge them died even more quickly than their comrades. Lord Winterborne, it seemed, was getting a taste for this.

As Elodie fought two more of the Helkrags, Lady Darrand cut her way through the enemy ranks to where Sylva and Cedric lay. Samial went with her, matching her swordplay blow for blow. When he reached the captives, he cut through their ropes with a single stroke.

"Run!" Lady Darrand told them. Without looking, she stabbed her sword backward and skewered a Helkrag who'd been rushing toward her. With his one hand, Cedric grabbed his sister and pulled her off the table and away from the fighting.

Something shrieked—a spine-chilling sound that came from directly overhead. Startled, the Helkrags looked up. Two of the noble ghosts were clinging to the ceiling like spiders. Their thin robes wafted around them like gossamer webs.

Still shrieking, the ghosts fell upon the enemy.

Elodie lowered her sword, panting for breath, and watched as her ghostly companions cut down the remaining Helkrags.

"Stop him!" shouted Lady Darrand. Elodie spun round to see the Helkrag leader making a run for the door.

"Here!" Lord Winterborne snatched up a fallen sword and tossed it to Cedric, who stood directly in the path of the fleeing elk-hunter.

Cedric caught the weapon—one-handed, naturally. Displaying remarkable calm, he waited until the Helkrag was almost upon him, then made a neat sidestep and plunged the sword into the enemy's side. The big man fell, twitched once, then lay still in a steadily growing pool of blood.

"A fine stroke, my young lord," cried the ghost, bowing his head.

Elodie leaped down from the table and pulled Cedric and Sylva into a fierce hug.

"I thought I'd lost you," she said, her words coming out choked.

Elodie wished she could keep hugging them forever. But there was work to be done. She whirled around, her vision still stained with the red of battle fury. Her sword twitched in her hand.

Apart from herself, Sylva, Cedric, and the ghosts, the Star Chamber was empty.

Lord Vicerin and his guards had disappeared.

"Where did he go?" she asked furiously.

"Nobody left through the main door," Lord Winterborne replied. "I kept careful watch."

"But that's the only exit."

"No," said Cedric. "Look."

He pointed to a tiny oblong of shadow on the far side of the circular chamber.

"A secret door!" breathed Sylva.

Elodie sprinted across the star-studded floor toward it.

"This way!" she shouted as she ran. "Let's stop Vicerin once and for all!"

CHAPTER 15

Beyond the tiny doorway was a dark, cramped passage. Elodie led the way along it with her sword thrust forward and her free hand running along the clammy wall. The tunnel twisted several times before delivering them onto a narrow wooden walkway at the top of one of the castle's exterior walls.

"We're on the western battlements," said Cedric, blinking as he emerged into the sunlight.

From this high vantage point they had a clear view across Castle Vicerin to the open farmland beyond. Many of the fires that had been raging in the castle were now out. The air, though still stained with smoke, was beginning to clear. Most of the inner courtyards were empty, and where Elodie could see Vicerin and Helkrag soldiers, they weren't fighting.

They were running.

"The ghosts have done it," she said. "We've won!"

But Lady Darrand shook her head. "I fear you speak too soon."

She gestured to one of the nearby fields where a line of horsemen were gathering. Their blue sashes, though torn and muddied, marked them as Vicerins. Cantering up and down the front of the formation was a rider whose ceremonial silver armor flashed like a beacon in the midday sun. The visor on his blue-plumed helmet was down, ready for battle. But although his face was hidden, there was no mistaking him.

Elodie's stomach plummeted. "So that's where Lord Vicerin went," she said. "He's going to try to retake the castle!"

Sylva was shaking her head in disbelief. "How did he get out there so quickly?"

"He is slippery," said Lady Darrand. Her voice was uncharacteristically flat. "He always has been. That is why he always wins."

"Not this time!" Elodie said fiercely. "Castle Vicerin is ours now and he's not getting it back. Come on!"

She ran along the battlements toward a set of wooden stairs. Leaping down them two at a time, she planted her fingers in her mouth and whistled. All the ghosts within earshot looked up.

"Follow me!" she shouted as she reached ground level. "Bring horses!"

As Elodie raced toward the nearest gatehouse, Sylva and Cedric fell into step beside her. They arrived just ahead of a tidal wave of ghosts—all the spirits Elodie had summoned from the Forgotten Graveyard. Rank upon rank of phantom warriors were before her. The ghosts of the murdered nobles took their place among them. They knelt, and the army of ghosts followed suit. The sight made Elodie catch her breath.

"What is your command?" Lady Darrand asked.

"My command is simple," Elodie replied. Her voice rang out, clear and strong. "Lord Vicerin is not yet vanquished. Lord Vicerin—the man who kept me prisoner. The man who stole children and used them as bait for a barbarian horde. The man who burned farmsteads and ravaged an entire realm." She looked toward Sylva and Cedric. "Who murdered his wife and sold his own children into sacrifice."

Cedric's jaw was set. Sylva blinked back tears but held her gaze.

Elodie turned back toward the ghosts. "That man out there, who thinks he can take back this castle, put each and every one of you to death!" Her words cut through the air like a sword. "But all that ends here. Now. This is our chance, come at last. If we can defeat him on the battlefield today, it will all be over."

She thrust her sword toward the sky. "Ride out with me now and justice will be done. Victory will be ours!"

A sound like rushing water passed through the assembly of ghosts. It wasn't quite a roar, but a phantom version of one. It carried a strength that gave Elodie hope. This wasn't an army of trained knights, like those she'd led against Brutan's forces during the Battle of the Bridge. Mingled with the resurrected spirits of soldiers were those of farmers and tradespeople. Yet they were many and they'd already proved themselves in battle.

They'll do it again!

Hooves clattered on the mud-slimed flagstones. The ghosts parted to reveal Samial bringing with him three magnificent horses. Elodie took the reins of the leading horse—a black mare with a long, shaggy mane—and sprang onto her back. She remembered seeing the mare in the Vicerin stables, her name painted on her stall: Valor.

"I can't ride and fight like this," said Cedric, holding up his one hand in disgust. "I'll be better on foot."

"I'll ride for both of us," said Sylva. She picked up a short sword from where it lay beside a fallen Vicerin guard and mounted a gray stallion.

"You don't have to," said Elodie, catching her hand. It was shaking, but Sylva's gaze was steady.

"Yes," Sylva replied at once. "I do."

A great cry rose up from the field beyond the gatehouse. A moment later, it was joined by a rumbling noise that swelled like approaching thunder.

"Vicerin is charging!" Elodie cried. She raised her sword. "Follow me! To battle!"

She kicked her heels into the mare's flanks and galloped beneath the stone archway and out onto the grass beyond. With an angry sighing sound, the ghost army swarmed out ahead of her.

At once, a sense of color overwhelmed her. Inside the castle, everything had been gray. Even the red stone of the walls had been dulled by the soot and smoke. As Valor carried her onto the field, her eyes were assailed by the vivid green of the grass, the yellow glare of the noon sun, the bright blue of the Vicerin sashes.

"Onward!" she yelled. "We fight for justice! We fight for Toronia!"

The Vicerin cavalry was already in full charge. But Elodie was surprised to see they were riding not toward the castle, but toward the fields in the north. Was the enemy trying to outflank them?

No sooner had she thought this than Vicerin—clearly identifiable in his shining armor—raised his arm and barked out a command. At once, the cavalry wheeled around and started charging straight at the leading ranks of the ghost army. Gathering speed, the swarm of ghosts plowed into the enemy. Gray figures flowed like liquid, toppling the horses and rolling over the top of the fallen riders in living waves.

Lord Vicerin held back, leaving his horsemen to engage Elodie's troops. His white stallion was standing on a low, grassy mound, giving him a sweeping view of the battlefield.

"Let's get him," said Sylva. "You and me, together."

"Hie!" Elodie urged her horse. She rode straight toward the line of fallen Vicerins, whose bodies made a seemingly impenetrable wall between her and her target. Sylva, riding close behind, echoed her cry.

Tightening her legs around the saddle, Elodie snapped the reins and urged yet more speed out of Valor. The wall of dead Vicerins approached at dizzying speed. At the last moment, the black mare leaped, seeming to fly over the bodies of the fallen before landing at a full gallop on the other side.

Now Elodie was bearing down on the cavalry's second wave. She drew back her sword, but was forced to swerve sideways as Sylva cut across her path.

"Keep going!" Sylva shouted. She'd lost her sword, but the years she'd spent competing in the Ritherlee Horse Trials were clearly paying off as she kept her stallion weaving backward and forward through the Vicerin ranks, guiding him through intricate dodges and changes of course.

"Ride, Elodie!" she called. "I'll keep them busy."

Be careful, Sylva! Oh, be careful!

The red mist closed over Elodie's vision. At the same time, the white horse on the grassy mound reared up. The decorative panels of his silver armor shimmered in the bright sunlight. The blue-plumed helmet turned, and suddenly Lord Vicerin was staring straight at her, his eyes glinting behind the visor that obscured his face.

As Vicerin's sword came up, so Elodie's came down. Hauling on the reins, she converted her horse's forward motion into a fast turn, slashing her blade against her enemy's suddenly exposed flank. But he was quick, and her sword met only thin air. As her horse came round, she lashed out again and made brief contact with his left elbow, a glancing blow that left him unhurt.

Now the two horses were dancing around each other while their riders struck and parried, each seeking a weakness in the other's armor. Elodie could feel her body moving with a kind of animal certainty. She blocked every blow Vicerin made, and each time her own sword hit home, she felt a sense of growing excitement.

You taught me well, Palenie!

Yet, despite the accuracy of her blows, the cold metal of the Vicerin armor succeeded in repelling them all. Although the impacts must have been bruising, Lord Vicerin was holding up against the onslaught much better than he had any right to. Was there no way through that glossy metal shell?

"You were built for banquets!" she snarled as her blade struck sparks off the edge of his sword. "You're no warrior!"

Vicerin said nothing, merely glared at her through the tiny slit of his visor.

Determined to get a reaction out of him, Elodie reined in her horse briefly before spurring her straight at Lord Vicerin's. "How does it feel to be fighting your precious puppet? To be beaten by her? Because I will beat you!"

Valor's shoulder slammed into the stallion's hindquarters. The white horse reared, throwing its rider backward off the saddle. Valor's front hooves slipped on the grass and suddenly Elodie was flying over the mare's head. She landed on her chest, the hard curves of her breastplate digging painfully into her ribs.

Air shrieking from her crushed lungs, Elodie staggered to her feet just in time to fend off a fresh blow from Vicerin, who was already on his feet. Knocked backward, she parried two more blows before noticing that his own breastplate had shifted sideways. Each time he took a step, the metal parted to reveal a pale blue undershirt.

A chink in his armor!

Remembering one of the earliest lessons Palenie had taught her, Elodie raised her sword high, clearly signaling an attempt to strike down on top of her opponent's head. As he reacted, she shifted her body weight and reversed her hold on the hilt of her weapon. Now, instead of driving it down, she was thrusting it forward—aiming it at the crack in his armor, right over his heart.

The tip of her blade was a hand's width from the gap when Vicerin's sword swung down to block it. Unbalanced, still gasping for breath, Elodie sank to her knees, her sword flying from her hands. As she fell, Vicerin kicked the fallen weapon out of reach, then drove his foot into her ribs. Badly winded, Elodie instinctively rolled sideways—once, twice, hurling herself off the mound just as

Vicerin's sword impaled the spot where she'd been lying.

"Elodie . . ."

The voice was drowned by the clank of metal armor as Lord Vicerin strode down the mound toward her. He moved with a swagger she'd never seen in him before. Panicking, she scrabbled for her lost sword, but it was nowhere to be seen.

"You haven't won yet!" she cried, staggering to her feet. Weaponless, she bunched her fists and held them up. Her knuckles were bloodied. Her ribs throbbed.

"Elodie . . ."

Samial?

He was running across the battlefield toward her. His hands were cupped around his ghostly mouth. He was shouting, but she could barely hear him over the sounds of battle.

"The arrowhead!" he was yelling. ". . . only chance . . ."

Lord Vicerin was five paces away. Four. He closed both hands on the hilt of his sword and drew back the blade.

"The arrowhead!" Samial yelled again. Then he brought his hand to his chest with a stabbing motion.

Without a sound, Lord Vicerin brought his blade around, aiming it squarely at Elodie's neck. She let out a wordless scream and ducked. The sword cut through the topmost strands of her hair.

At last she knew what Samial meant.

Plunging her hand into her tunic, she closed her fingers on what she carried there. What she'd been carrying almost all the time she'd known Samial.

My arm is the arrow, she thought deliriously, *and I am the bow.*

With all her strength, she drove the arrowhead into the gap in Lord Vicerin's armor. It sank deep. Hot blood gushed out over Elodie's fingers.

A shudder ran through Lord Vicerin's body. He dropped his sword. Like lightning, Elodie snatched it up and drove it in after the arrowhead.

Lord Vicerin inhaled labored breaths through the tiny holes in his visor, but the scream of agony Elodie had expected never came. Instead, his arms and legs stiffened and he fell forward onto the ground.

Elodie watched, every muscle tense, waiting for his next breath to come.

But he didn't move again.

Lord Vicerin was dead.

"Now you truly will be queen."

Samial's voice was faint. Finally believing Lord Vicerin was dead, Elodie looked round to see her friend floating in midair between the two riderless horses. He was so faint she could barely see him.

Her heart gave a wrench.

The arrowhead had saved her—and cost Elodie her closest friend.

"No!" she cried. "Samial, you can't leave! I'll find it, I'll find it and you can stay. . . ."

She reached over Vicerin's armored body, determined to extract the arrowhead from his chest, however gruesome the task might be.

How long have I got? she thought frantically. *How long before he passes into the Realm of the Dead?*

Samial's hands folded over hers.

She couldn't feel his touch—could barely even see his fingers—but the gesture stopped her all the same.

"It is too late," Samial said gently. "My time has come at last. I cannot stay in Toronia."

Elodie was ready to collapse. Her enemy lay dead before her, and it should have left her feeling triumphant. Instead, she felt only weak and empty. All the strength she'd carried into battle had departed. Now here was Samial, her truest friend, saying good-bye.

"You're the first ghost I ever spoke to," she said, fighting back tears. "If it wasn't for you, I'd never have known what I can do. I'd never have . . ."

"You would." Samial smiled, now just a faint trace in the air. "But I am glad it was me."

"I'm glad too."

"You set me free, Elodie, that day you found me in the woods. Thanks to you, I can go to my rest." Now Samial was no more than a shadow in the air. A breeze blew, lifting him up like a pennant of sheerest silk. "And go I must, while I still have the strength to enter the Realm of the Dead."

Elodie smiled at him through her tears. "It's very beautiful there."

"I am ready."

"I know," Elodie whispered.

"I am glad to leave you as my queen."

The breeze carried him away, and he was gone.

Elodie buried her face in her hands. Sobs racked her body. Utterly spent from grief and the battle, she sank to the ground and let the darkness swallow her up.

Elodie woke with tears dried on her face. She sat up, pressing her hand to the dull ache in her ribs. How long ago had she fainted?

Above her loomed the red stone wall of one of the castle's outer turrets.

How did I get here?

The battlefield was littered with Vicerin bodies. More Vicerin troops were fleeing from the castle, a few straggling groups of Helkrags among them. The field was thronged with ghosts, and more ghosts lined the battlements of the castle. The enemy was in retreat. The battle was over.

Elodie stumbled to her feet. "We won," she breathed.

"Elodie!"

She spun round to see Sylva pulling a water pouch from the saddle pack of a nearby horse. At the sound of his sister's voice, Cedric came running from the other side of the turret.

"You've woken up!" he cried. "Are you all right?"'

"I'm fine. What happened?"

"We found you and carried you back here," said Sylva, hurrying over with the water. "There was so much blood—we thought it was yours."

"I'm all right," Elodie reassured her. "Just a bit bruised. Is it true? Did we . . ."

"Win?" Cedric grinned. "Yes, Elodie. We did."

Elodie could feel something growing inside her. A sense of triumph at last? But before it could blossom fully, Sylva started sobbing.

"Oh, Sylva, Cedric, I'm sorry . . . your father . . ."

"It's all right, Elodie," said Cedric. "We saw it all."

"I'm not crying because he's dead," said Sylva. "I'm crying because of all the awful things he did when he was alive."

"But now we've got a chance to make things better." Cedric bowed low before Elodie. "Isn't that right, my queen?"

"Yes," Elodie replied firmly. "Yes, it is."

"And it can start right here!" Sylva proclaimed. She wiped her cheeks. "Ritherlee is yours, Elodie. The realm belongs to you!"

"It does. I can hardly believe it."

One realm conquered. One step closer to the throne. Oh, I wish Tarlan and Gulph were here!

Cedric was grinning. "From now on, you can ... Elodie, where are you going?"

She had begun hurrying across the battlefield. Her hand was pressed to her throat. "To get the jewels!" she called back. "From your father. My brothers and I will need them."

I can't wait to see the look on Tarlan's face when I ...

Elodie stopped.

The ground was shaking.

"Elodie?" Sylva's voice quavered. "I don't like this."

Elodie lifted her hand to shield her eyes from the sun. There was movement on the crest of a distant hill. Figures were descending its slope toward the castle, many thousands of them. Following close behind came strange war machines rolling on great metal wheels.

Not Vicerins, she thought, observing the brilliant, multicolored costumes of these newcomers. *Not Helkrags. Then who?*

Now the rumble of marching feet was joined by the piercing sound of horns, and the thumping of drums.

A sea of curved swords flashed in the afternoon sun.

"Galadronians!" cried Cedric.

Elodie's hand remained frozen at her neck, but she was no longer thinking about the jewels. She was remembering the Galadronian assassin who'd tried to strangle her.

"They've come for Toronia," she said.

She felt cold with horror.

"So this is why Vicerin wasn't charging toward the castle," she said.

"He knew the invasion was coming," said Cedric. His eyes were wide as he stared out at the vast ranks of Galadronian troops.

Elodie remembered the messenger fetching Vicerin from the battle after she'd woken on the pyre. It must have been to tell him what was coming. Had he even struck his terrible deal with the Helkrags to fight the Galadronians, not her ghosts as she'd assumed?

"I should have known something wasn't right," she said bitterly.

Sylva took her hand. "It's not your fault. None of us realized."

Elodie looked back at the castle. Many of its walls were breached. Its armories were badly damaged by fire. Its entire complement of guards had fled, leaving only Elodie and her army of ghosts to defend it.

But how can we defend it, when we're so few?

"I thought we'd won a great victory today," she said. "But we've just stepped straight into the jaws of defeat." She ran her hand through her short hair and let out a long, despairing sigh.

"What do we do now?" asked Cedric.

Elodie felt hollowed out.

"I don't know," she said.

CHAPTER 16

ulph clung to the thick feathers of the thorrod's ruff, feeling the steady pulse of its great flight muscles thrumming through his legs. He'd heard tell of these giant birds, but hadn't realized how powerful they were. Now, having traveled all the way from the Icy Wastes to the farmlands of Ritherlee in what felt like the blink of an eye, he understood that thorrods could fly very fast, and travel very far indeed.

"I can see Castle Vicerin." Tarlan stabbed his finger toward a collection of towers and battlements thrusting out of the rolling landscape. "There—straight ahead."

Gulph, seated behind his brother on Theeta's broad back, watched intently as they drew near to the castle. Its red stonework was blackened by fire. Ribbons of smoke drifted lazily among its spires. There was no movement within its broken walls.

"There's been a battle," Gulph said.

"There's more to come," said Tarlan grimly.

Gulph turned his eyes to the hills north of the castle. Instead of green lettuce or yellow corn, the fields looked as if they'd been sown with crops of all colors . . . except they weren't crops.

They were people.

"The Galadronians," said Tarlan. "I thought the first invasion was big, but this . . ."

His voice faltered, leaving only the whisper of Theeta's giant wings to fill the silence as they watched the enormous Galadronian army first surround the castle, then pour into it.

"We can't possibly take them on," said Gulph. "We've got to think about this."

"What is there to think about?" Tarlan retorted. "Elodie's down there—if they haven't killed her already."

"Gulph is right," called Kalia. She was flying level with them, perched on Kitheen's back. "It is too dangerous."

Elodie dead? The thought of it turned Gulph's spine to ice. "They might just have taken her prisoner."

"All the more reason to get down there!" snapped Tarlan. "Down, Theeta, and fast!"

"Tarlan! No!"

But Theeta was already diving toward the castle. Gulph tightened his grip around Tarlan's waist as the rushing air threatened to blast them both off the thorrod's back.

"Make her stop!"

Ignoring him, Tarlan steered Theeta toward the flat roof of the castle's central keep. As she prepared to land, a line of archers raced out onto the battlements. Colorful robes billowing in the wind, they raised their bows and fired a volley of arrows at the oncoming thorrod.

"Down!" cried Tarlan.

He flattened himself against Theeta's feathery back; Gulph did the same. At the same moment, Theeta spread her wings wide. Gulph clung on, expecting the giant bird to begin climbing. Instead, Theeta started dropping even faster than she had before. Whipping his head round, Gulph saw why.

Those aren't ordinary arrows!

The Galadronian arrows flew high—much higher than they had any right to. If Theeta had done the obvious thing and tried to climb to safety, she'd have flown straight into their path.

And there was something else.

The arrows were trailing something behind them. At first, Gulph thought it was smoke—he'd seen burning arrows before, but smoke was usually black or gray. What the arrows were leaving behind was . . .

. . . gold?

Theeta made an abrupt turn. Gulph's stomach lurched into his throat, but he didn't take his eyes off those lines of gold being drawn across the sky. As he watched, the trails broke apart into clouds of dust. When Theeta eventually began to climb, her flight path took her directly through one of these clouds. Gulph snatched at the dust-speckled air as they sped through it. When he opened his hand, he saw that it wasn't dust at all.

It's sand!

By now, Theeta had reached the clear air through which Kitheen was still circling with Kalia on his back.

"We're all right," Gulph called. Their mother smiled with relief.

The two thorrods began cawing to each other. Gulph was about to ask Tarlan what they were saying when a third thorrod flew down. This one was a little bigger than Kitheen, with breast feathers as white as his were black.

"Nasheen!" shouted Tarlan. "Come with us!"

Below, the castle continued to fill up with Galadronian troops. The sight filled Gulph with despair.

If Elodie really is down there, I don't see how we can ever get her out.

Theeta's muscles flexed beneath his legs. He realized with a start that their giant steed had turned away from the castle and was now flying over the open fields to the southeast.

"What's going on?" he demanded. "What were the thorrods saying?"

"Melchior's here," Tarlan replied. "He's at a place called Castle

Darrand. The people of Deep Poynt are with him."

"Darrand?" The flight here had given Tarlan ample time to tell his story, but Gulph didn't recall the name coming up before. "Is that a place or a person?"

"Both. Castle Darrand is the home of Lady Darrand. I've met her before. She's quite a warrior, and no friend of the Vicerins." Tarlan flicked his head around and exposed his teeth in a feral grin.

Leaving Castle Vicerin behind, the thorrods picked up the meandering course of a small river winding through the Ritherlee farmland. The fields below them looked torn up and muddy, and all the villages they passed were burned. Gulph felt sad at the sight of such destruction. He'd heard so much about the green pastures of Ritherlee, and had been looking forward to seeing them. But he hadn't reckoned on the war.

A war that now looked unwinnable.

This Lady Darrand might be a warrior, but can she really help us take on the Galadronians?

A flock of eagles flew up from a nearby thicket. At once they started screeching to Tarlan.

"We fly southeast. Tell everyone to follow us," Tarlan told the eagles.

With answering screeches, the eagles dived for the ground.

"They're from the pack," Tarlan explained to Gulph over his

shoulder. "Poor old Greythorn. The eagles said he's had a hard time keeping them all running fast enough. Thorrods fly fast."

"I'd noticed. Is Greythorn the leader? When you're not around, I mean."

"Sort of. He's just a bit smarter than the rest. But he's really part of a team. Greythorn, Filos, and Brock—they're sort of like my generals."

Whenever Tarlan spoke about his pack, his eyes grew bright. Gulph loved to see it. He envied Tarlan his ability to command the animals—it seemed so much more interesting than Gulph's own magical powers.

Beyond the trees, the land descended to meet a wide, rutted road.

"It isn't far now," said Tarlan. "We should be there well before nightfall."

Theeta changed course to begin following the road. As she turned, Gulph glanced back at the thicket . . . and was surprised to observe a sea of faces staring up at them.

"Wait!" he cried. "Go back!"

"What is it?"

"There are people down there. Soldiers."

Theeta's shadow slipped over the crowd of people huddled under the trees. Their silver armor was worn and dirty; blue sashes hung limp from their shoulders.

"Vicerins!" Tarlan's lip curled. "They must have run away from the fighting, and now they're holed up here. Don't they know they're sitting targets?"

"They don't look dangerous."

It was true. The faces of the soldiers were gaunt with fatigue, and their eyes were dull. A few were listlessly trying to build shelters or start fires, but most sat slumped against the tree trunks. They looked utterly defeated.

"Tarlan—how big an army does this Lady Darrand have?"

"I don't think it's really an army. More a band. But they're strong."

"A band," Gulph repeated. "So, Melchior has brought people from Deep Poynt, you have your pack, and Lady Darrand has a band." He seized his brother's shoulder. "Do you really think that's enough to take on the Galadronians?"

Tarlan's muscles tensed. Gulph softened his grip and waited.

"No," Tarlan said at last. Gulph could hear the effort it took him to admit it. "Not by a long way. They're too many." He swiveled round to face Gulph. "What are you thinking, brother?"

"I was thinking about the Celestians—how I sort of, well, won them over. I just thought maybe I could—"

"Win over the Vicerins? Are you mad? They're the enemy!"

"But look at them! They're suspicious of us, yes. But they don't exactly look hostile."

"As if you can tell all that just from their faces," said Tarlan dismissively. "Anyway, like I said, they're the enemy."

"No—Lord Vicerin is the enemy. Just like Lady Redina was the enemy in Celestis. Now that they're away from the castle, away from *him*, these people have a choice."

"And I suppose you're going to help them make it?"

"Why not?"

Tarlan's face had turned red. Gulph hated to see him angry, but he couldn't let this go.

"Tarlan, we have to talk to them. They might even know what happened to Elodie. If I'm wrong, we'll just fly away. You and Theeta are more than a match for them anyway."

He didn't think his brother would respond to the flattery. But the red flush faded from Tarlan's cheeks and he cupped his hands around his mouth.

"Can you fly on to Castle Darrand?" he called to Kalia. "Just keep to the road—you can't miss it."

"I can," Kalia replied with a reluctant nod. "What are you going to do?"

"Not me," said Tarlan, grinning. "Gulph's going to do a little recruiting."

As Gulph had anticipated, the Vicerin soldiers received them with caution. Once Theeta had landed, they surrounded the thorrod, albeit at a considerable distance. Tarlan seemed pleased about this—it would give them plenty of room to take off in a hurry if things went bad.

"Let me do the talking," said Gulph as they jumped to the ground.

"With pleasure." Tarlan folded his arms and glared at the crowd of onlookers. "Just don't take too long."

Gulph raised his hands, palms out.

"We don't want any trouble," he announced. "We just want to talk."

What he really wanted to do was ask about his sister. But mentioning Elodie's name might not be the best way to open the conversation.

"We've just come from the castle," he said instead. "Was it bad there?"

"Bad?" said a soldier whose bloodied arm was supported in a sling. "Oh, it was bad, all right."

"What's it to you?" called a woman. She wore battle-scarred armor and an expression of profound mistrust. "Who are you anyway?"

Gulph ignored the question. "Who set all the fires in the castle?"

"Helkrags!"

The man who said this stood a little away from the rest. He was short and wore heavy armor but no helmet.

"Helkrags? What are they?"

"Elk-hunters," growled Tarlan. His cheeks flushed red. "They're killers, all of them. What are they doing so far from Yalasti?"

"The great Lord Vicerin hired them." The man spat to the side. "Some allies they turned out to be."

"They were supposed to help you, these Yalasti soldiers?" asked Gulph.

"They're not soldiers! Would a soldier murder innocent civilians? Would a soldier turn on his comrades? Helkrags are murderers and barbarians!"

Gulph noted the straight line of the man's back, the proud angle of his neck. He also observed how the other Vicerin troops remained silent and respectful as he spoke.

"What's your name?" he asked.

The man pressed his fist against his chest—some kind of salute, Gulph supposed. "Captain Ariston of the Seventh Vicerin Battalion. And yours?"

"Let's come to that in a minute. Where's Lord Vicerin?"

Captain Ariston frowned, and for a moment Gulph thought he'd run out of luck. Then the officer replied, "Our great lord has not been seen for some time."

Hearing Ariston's mocking tone, Gulph understood immediately that this officer did not think his commander in chief was "great" at all.

"We might be onto something here," he whispered to his brother.

Tarlan looked doubtful. "They're loyal to Vicerin. Why would they help us?"

"Wait and see," Gulph told him. He turned back to the crowd. "But Lord Vicerin is probably safe somewhere, right?"

"Too right!" growled the soldier with the broken arm.

"Slippery as an eel, that one," said another.

"Always looks after himself does the great lord," added a third.

They hate him!

"What about his family?" Gulph asked Captain Ariston. "His children?"

"Do you mean the Lady Sylva? And the young Lord Cedric?"

The names meant nothing to Gulph. "I mean Elodie."

"That evil witch?" hissed the woman in the battered armor. "Don't even mention her name!"

"Witch?" Gulph was confused, and a little disturbed. "I don't understand."

"She died."

Tarlan flinched. Gulph's heart dropped to the pit of his stomach.

"Died?" he croaked.

"Died and rose again, only now she's with all her dead friends."

"That's why we're here," added the man. "Elodie and her army of the dead—they drove us out of our own castle."

Gulph's mind was racing.

Maybe she's not dead at all!

Tarlan had already told him about the ghost army their sister had led against Brutan—perhaps she'd managed to raise another.

Good! Maybe they'll be our allies against the Galadronians too!

"Gulph!" Tarlan was by Theeta's side with his sword drawn. "If Elodie's there, we have to find her. We have to go. Now!"

"Wait!" Gulph shot back. "Just a moment longer."

"Time's wasting!"

"Your thorrod's fast. We'll catch up to them."

This seemed to mollify Tarlan. He sat down on the grass, looking grumpy. But at least he put his sword away.

Gulph turned back to Captain Ariston, who'd watched the exchange with interest.

"I know you," the Vicerin officer said slowly. It took Gulph a moment to realize he was talking to Tarlan. "You were a prisoner. Our great lord held you in the White Tower." The corner of his mouth twitched. "You escaped."

"Yes, I did," said Tarlan with casual pride.

"That's right," said Gulph. "And Elodie was a prisoner there her whole life." He took a deep breath. "If you think about it, you were all prisoners. That's how Lord Vicerin works. He makes sure everyone does exactly what he says. There's a word for that—tyrant!"

"Our great lord is no longer in charge of his affairs." Captain Ariston's face betrayed no emotion at all.

"Maybe not. But a new tyrant has come to Toronia—the Witch-Empress Hypiro. She's come all the way from Galadron, and from what I've heard, she's ten times as bad as Lord Vicerin."

Gulph had seen enough in the mind of the Galadronian soldier, and heard enough from Kalia, to know this was true. He remembered the strange trails of sand left by the enemy's arrows, and shuddered.

"If Hypiro wins, we'll *all* be prisoners! You, me, every last person in Toronia! Is that what you want?"

Captain Ariston rubbed his hand down his face. He'd looked tired from the start. Now he looked utterly spent. He opened his mouth, but before he could speak, the angry woman shouted out:

"Why should we listen to any of this? You're just a couple of no-good ragamuffins with a great big bird for company. You won't even tell us your names."

"My name is Gulph." His words silenced the woman and carried right to the back of the crowd. "This is my brother, Tarlan. Elodie is our sister. We are the prophecy three, the triplets destined to kill the cursed king and take up the crown of Toronia."

Gulph felt his voice growing stronger. Above him, the three prophecy stars burned bright, refusing to surrender to the brilliant afternoon sun.

"Toronia has been torn apart by war. You know this better than

anyone. What we bring is a battle not for war, but for peace. *That
is what the prophecy promises: a crown of three, and a new era of
peace for all of Toronia!"*

He broke off, breathing hard, hoping his words had struck home.
To his dismay, a ripple of laughter ran through the crowd.

"Peace?" scoffed the man with his arm in a sling. "We'll never
see peace again. Not here, not anywhere."

The angry woman had drawn her sword. None of her neighbors
displayed her open hostility, but Gulph could sense the crowd as
a whole growing listless and disinterested. Clearly wishing to pro-
voke something, the woman began pushing her way toward him.
No sooner had she begun moving than Gulph heard a rustle as
Tarlan sprang to his feet, and the swish of his brother's blade being
drawn from its scabbard.

I won't let it end like this! I won't!

Fixing his gaze on Captain Ariston, Gulph clenched his fists
and sent his mind flying across the gap between them. There was a
brief sensation of flight—*hot sand beneath me, hot sun above, hot desert
wind carrying me between*—and then he was . . .

*. . . surrounded by wrestling limbs and clashing swords, a thousand
voices united in a single, monumental battle cry. All around on the
bloody field the dead lie in sorrowful heaps, and with every passing
breath the piles of bodies grow bigger and bigger until they blot out first
the sun, and then the sky, and then the world, until at last . . .*

. . . Gulph expanded his mind through the rest of the crowd, entering their shared experiences of battle and death, chaos and war, and understanding that for a long time this was all these people had known, and that they were tired, and that . . .

. . . somewhere far away, a flame is burning. It flickers in the far distant darkness of their lives, rising into view like the mast of a ship just visible on the horizon. The flame is tiny, almost nothing at all, yet inside the fire is contained a whole new world in which fresh seeds are being sown, and crops are being raised, and hearths are warm and homes are filled with children and laughter, and everything is bright because that is the single most wonderful thing that peace can bring to a person's life: light. And the name of that tiny flame is . . .

"Hope."

Gulph spoke the word so quietly he didn't think anyone had heard it. Yet the woman stopped in her tracks, and Tarlan lowered his sword, and Captain Ariston's hand fell to his side and his tired eyes grew wide.

"Hope," Gulph repeated. "That's what you want, all of you, I know it. Warm homes where hope can grow. The hope you feel for the future when you see your children play. Hope that all will be well. The hope of peace. That's what I'm offering. It's really all I'm offering, I suppose. But I think it might be enough."

He shrugged his pack from his shoulders. Delving into it, he drew out the crown. As he held it up, the onlookers gasped.

"This is the crown of Toronia. I've been carrying it for a long time, but that doesn't mean my legs aren't shaking as I stand here before you. Most of my life I've been poor, scratching a living with a band of wandering players. I've been locked up—yes, I've been a prisoner too. I've seen my friends badly treated. Seen them killed. I was in Idilliam when Brutan was king. He was bad enough, but Nynus was even worse. I've lived thirteen hard years at the end of a thousand years of fighting, and do you know what? It's enough. Enough war. Enough hardship. Enough bad times. I want the good times to begin. Don't you?"

The faces looking at him were still lined with fatigue. But there was something else in them too. Surprise? Expectation?

Hope?

"One last battle," Gulph said, stowing the crown carefully back in his pack. "If we all fight together, one last time, we can end the bad times forever. The past is over. It's time for the future to begin. Time for a new Toronia. A peaceful Toronia. That's my hope. Isn't it yours?"

The woman's sword fell to the ground with a dull *thunk*.

Captain Ariston pressed his fist to his chest, then dropped smartly to one knee and bowed his head. A moment later, the rest of the soldiers were kneeling too.

Gulph took in a deep, shuddering breath and turned to his brother. Tarlan was grinning.

"I thought animals could be hard work," he said, "but these humans take some convincing, don't they?"

"So are you glad we stopped to talk to them?"

"I suppose it hasn't done any harm."

"Am I allowed to say 'I told you so'?"

Tarlan wrapped an arm affectionately round Gulph's neck and rapped him gently on the top of his head.

"Don't even think about it," Tarlan said, laughing.

They didn't have far to fly before Castle Darrand appeared over the brow of a low hill, glowing bright in the light of the setting sun. To Gulph's dismay, what had clearly once been a grand building was now little more than a ruin.

"Will the Vicerins find their way here all right?" Gulph asked, glancing anxiously behind them.

"They know this realm better than we do," Tarlan replied. "If Captain Ariston said they'd follow us here, they'll do it."

Dusk collected around them as Theeta swooped down toward the ruined hall. The surrounding trees were thick with shadows, and more than once Gulph thought he saw figures scurrying among them. They came and went, were there and then gone. Gulph's tongue dried up in his mouth; his heart pounded.

Are they ghosts?

If they were . . .

Elodie? Are you here? Is it possible?

Theeta swooped past the caved-in roof of Castle Darrand and over a wide, battle-scarred lawn. Here, the last rays of the dying sun sliced low through the trees, making the ragged grass seem to glow.

Just as Theeta touched down, a black horse trotted into view at the far end of the lawn. On its back rode a small, slender figure dressed in silver armor. A girl. Like the grass, she glowed. Behind her horse, rippling like smoke on a breeze, came an army of phantom soldiers.

"On, Theeta," Tarlan whispered.

The thorrod took off immediately, and began skimming fast and low toward the horse and its rider with her claws brushing against the grass. The wind blew Gulph's hair back from his face.

Theeta landed again in the middle of the lawn. The girl rode up and reined in her horse. Gulph watched in a daze as she took off her helmet. A short mane of red-gold hair tousled up from beneath it. Her black eyes reflected the sunset. Gulph stared into them. She stared back. She turned her gaze to Tarlan. She laughed.

"Elodie!" Gulph had no idea if he'd said her name aloud or not. His mouth felt numb.

"Gulph." Her voice sounded like one he'd known his whole life. "And Tarlan."

No sooner had Gulph thought this than Elodie extracted her feet from her stirrups and hurled herself across the gap between horse and thorrod. Gulph and Tarlan dived to catch her, tumbling off Theeta's back and onto the soft grass, where they whirled around and around, laughing and crying and laughing again. Then, they tripped over their feet and landed in an untidy sprawl, out of breath.

"You're here!" Elodie gasped. "You're both here!"

"We're here!" Tarlan agreed.

"Together at last!" Gulph laughed.

In some strange way it seems like we were never apart.

As they lay there, laughing, the dusk crept over the lawn and swallowed up what was left of Castle Darrand. Yet here on the battlefield a single sun's ray still lingered, enclosing the two brothers and their sister in its rich golden light.

"Is it really happening?" Gulph stretched out his hand. Elodie placed her hand on top, interlacing her fingers with his. Tarlan did the same. Their touch was warm, solid, true. "Are we really going to rule Toronia?"

Just as he asked this question, the sun finally set. Even without its light, their hands continued to glow. They looked up at the three prophecy stars, burning in the darkness high above them.

Gulph didn't know what came next. But whatever it was, he was ready for it. He sent a silent thought up to the stars.

Are you really watching us? I hope you are. Oh, I hope you are! Because we're about to do something nobody's seen before!

CHAPTER 17

Crossing the lawn to the big front porch of Castle Darrand, Elodie felt as if she was floating on air. The thoughts in her head and the feelings in her heart were soaring together like birds wheeling in the sky. The only thing keeping her steady was having her hands clasped tightly around those of her brothers—Gulph on her left, Tarlan on her right. She felt that if she let go, she would fly up into the night and never be seen again.

The hall was a mess of fractured walls and fallen rafters. However, the porch—a high stone arch enclosing a wide set of steps—was largely undamaged. Elodie was overjoyed to see who was waiting for her in its shadows.

"Sylva! Cedric!"

The phantom army had straggled somewhat during the march from Castle Vicerin, and they'd become separated. Delighted to see them again, Elodie ran the last few paces to where they stood waiting on the bottom step.

"We've only just got here. We were about to explore . . ." Belatedly Cedric registered the presence of Tarlan and Gulph, and closed his mouth with a snap.

"Look!" Elodie was breathless, partly from running, partly because her heart wouldn't stop turning somersaults. "They're here!" She held up her brothers' hands. "My brothers!"

Cedric shuffled his feet. "I . . . uh, it's a pleasure to meet you." Then he clapped his hand against his forehead and broke into a grin. "What am I saying? It's *wonderful* to meet you!"

"Hello, Tarlan," said Sylva, and Elodie wondered if there was a hint of shyness in her voice. "It's good to see you again."

"I always knew you were on our side!" Tarlan said to her.

Gulph was standing a little apart in his lopsided way. Sensing his awkwardness, Elodie pulled him forward. "This is Gulph."

"Hello." Sylva smiled. "So you're the only triplet who hasn't been locked in our castle."

"I suppose I am. I feel left out!" Gulph wasn't as dashing as Tarlan, nor as tall, but when he grinned, his whole face became suddenly handsome.

Black eyes. Red-gold hair. Being with my brothers is like standing between two mirrors.

At the top of the porch stairs, the once-grand doors leading into the hall hung in splinters. Now a group of gray figures, their bodies wispy like smoke, drifted through them into the starlight.

"Lady Darrand!" Tarlan started to run up the steps. Halfway up he stopped. "You . . . you're a ghost. I'm so sorry."

"You know Lady Darrand?" said Elodie, joining him.

"We met when I first came out of Yalasti." Tarlan looked distraught, but Lady Darrand was staring at him in wonder.

"This is your brother, Elodie?" she said. "Tarlan saved the life of my daughter, Sorelle. I swore to help him in return one day. Now I will repay the debt, and gladly."

Spreading the wispy yellow robe she wore over her armor, she knelt. Beside her, Lord Winterborne and the rest of the Ritherlee nobles did the same.

"Hail the prophecy," said Lady Darrand softly. The others took up her words in a kind of murmuring chant. Elodie felt her skin break out into gooseflesh.

As the chanting died away, Lady Darrand descended the steps to meet them.

"My hall is yours," she said. "You will find friends and allies waiting for you inside. Oh, do not look so surprised—Castle Darrand is not quite the ruin it looks from the outside." She faltered, then went on. "Sorelle is with them. Thanks to you, she is safe and well. But . . . I do not wish my daughter to see me this way. As long as I remain visible, she might . . . she might . . ."

"It's all right," said Elodie quickly. "I understand. I can make it like it was before. I'll be the only one able to see you. That's what you're asking, isn't it?"

Relief washed over Lady Darrand's phantom face. "Thank you, my queen. Now, if you will excuse me, we must set up camp. And you should go inside. They are waiting."

The rest of the nobles followed her down the steps. As they joined the ghost army assembled on the lawn, Elodie imagined a flurry of sand blowing across them all. The night air rippled, like the air that hangs over desert dunes, then settled.

"Where did they go?" said Tarlan.

"Nowhere," Elodie replied, gazing at the army that now only she could see. "They're still there."

"It's sort of funny seeing invisibility from the other side," mused Gulph.

"Well, are we going in?" said Tarlan. He exchanged a mischievous grin with his brother.

Elodie poked his ribs. "What are you two laughing at?"

"Nothing. It's just that there's someone waiting to see you," Tarlan said.

"Who? How do you know that?"

"You'll find out," Gulph teased.

"You're insufferable!"

It was gloomy inside the hall. The high ceiling was full of jagged cracks and gashes, but all they could see through the holes were the smashed rafters of what had once been the roof. Thick rugs squelched under their feet, and the wooden floor beneath them creaked. The whole place stank of smoke.

"There's light ahead," said Tarlan.

Sure enough, through a doorway at the end of a short corridor sprang a flicker of orange firelight. Elodie, remembering the layout of the castle from her last visit here, decided it must be coming from the banqueting hall.

"Is it safe?" said Gulph.

"Lady Darrand said it was," Elodie replied.

"Then what are we waiting for?" put in Tarlan.

As soon as they entered the banqueting hall, Elodie's nostrils were assaulted by the delicious aroma of roasting meat. Her eyes found its source immediately: A wild boar had been skewered on a spit and was turning slowly in the room's enormous stone hearth.

A handful of people were busy tending to the boar, while dozens more sat in the many chairs that were scattered around the hall. Some were eating and drinking; others were repairing weapons or mending clothes; all were talking. The hubbub was overwhelming.

As soon as the triplets entered, the banqueting hall fell silent but for the crackle of the flames. A giant-sized man with thick red hair turned to face the newcomers. A massive hammer swung from his heavy leather belt.

"These are the people of Deep Poynt," Tarlan said. He was about to say more when the big man stepped aside, revealing a wizened figure in a tattered yellow robe. Elodie recognized him at once.

"Melchior!"

She hurried across the floor to greet him, scarcely able to believe it was him. She wanted to shout for joy, but she contented herself with simply getting to him as quickly as she could.

A few paces short of where the wizard stood, Elodie halted and stared into his watery old eyes. She hadn't seen Melchior since he'd set out with Tarlan on his quest to regain his magic. So much had happened since then. She hadn't even had a chance to ask her brother if the quest had succeeded.

Should you hug a wizard? she wondered, feeling small and insignificant beneath his ancient, inscrutable gaze. Deciding it didn't matter, she hugged him anyway.

"Hello, Elodie," said Melchior, returning her embrace. Looking past her, he added, "Hello, Tarlan. And you must be Gulph."

Elodie stood back, but still couldn't tear her eyes away from the wizard. Nor, it seemed, could he stop looking at her and her brothers.

"This day," he said. "This day . . . I have waited for it, oh, for the longest time. For long years my faith faded and I believed it would never come. But here it is, and here you are. The three of you, together again. The stars still shine. The prophecy still holds."

Was he crying? Or were his eyes just twinkling in the light of the fire?

"Melchior . . . ," Elodie began. The wizard silenced her with an upraised finger and a twitch of his mouth that may or may not have been a smile.

"I am not really the one you wish to see."

"You're not?" Elodie wiped her cheek and found it wet.

Melchior moved aside. Behind him stood a slender woman with red-gold hair. One side of her face was twisted by an old burn scar. Despite it—even partly because of it—she was very beautiful.

If Elodie had thought about it, she'd have said all the surprises were done with. Her brothers. Then Melchior. And now . . .

Mother! My mother! That's my mother!

Kalia's arms wrapped themselves around her. Elodie had no idea how she'd reached them. Perhaps she'd floated into their embrace. She couldn't speak for sobbing, couldn't think past the soaring, roaring thunder in her head.

Our mother!

"Elodie! Elodie! Oh, Elodie!" When she wasn't speaking her name, Kalia was smothering her face with kisses. "Oh, here you are, my beautiful daughter! Here you are at last!"

Touching her was like coming home.

"Thank you," Kalia was saying, speaking now to the watching wizard. "Thank you, Melchior, for saving my babies. For saving me. Thank you for watching over us all. We owe you everything. Everything."

Elodie had no idea if he replied. She was only aware of her mother, her brothers. She was lost in her family, and found at last.

A little while later, Elodie was seated at a table near the fire, with Gulph and Kalia to her left, Tarlan and Melchior to her right. Cedric and Sylva sat opposite. In the middle of the table was a mountain of steaming boar meat, which the Deep Poynt giant—whom Melchior had introduced as The Hammer—was serving onto a set of fine china plates.

"We found them in one of the pantries," The Hammer explained, handing round the plates in his ham-sized fist with surprising delicacy. "Everything smashed but these."

"I'm sure Lady Darrand wouldn't mind us using them," said Elodie.

From the corner of her eye, she spotted the little girl Tarlan had already identified as Lady Darrand's daughter, Sorelle. She was playing in the corner of the banqueting hall with a gang of scruffy-looking Deep Poynt children.

Poor thing, Elodie thought as Sorelle giggled at some joke one of the other girls had made. *I know what it's like not to have a mother.*

"So is it true?" Tarlan was asking Gulph. "This lost realm—whatever it's called—has been buried for a thousand years?"

Elodie watched, amused, as Tarlan stuffed a huge wedge of meat into his mouth. There was no doubting which of the three of them had been raised in the wild.

"It's called Celestis, and yes, it's true." Gulph had just finished relating the story of his adventures in the underground realm but seemed happy to give his brother a summary. "It's made of crystal—an amazing place. Dark, but very beautiful."

Melchior was shaking his head. "It is incredible. Celestis did indeed vanish one thousand years ago, when King Warryck murdered Gryndor and two of his companion wizards. The magical forces unleashed by their deaths opened up a chasm beneath the crystal city, and Celestis fell into the earth. Everyone thought it had been buried forever. Yet now the lost realm has been found."

"What about its people?" Elodie asked.

"They're on our side," said Gulph firmly. "They're waiting for me in Idilliam. They'll help us when the time comes."

"It is help we need, no mistake about that," rumbled The Hammer, filling his mouth with a handful of meat that made Tarlan's portion look tiny. "Those Galadronians with their burning arrows and their war machines—if they take the rest of Toronia the way they took Deep Poynt . . ." He shook his shaggy head.

"Nor must we forget Lord Vicerin's army," Melchior pointed out. "It would not do to ignore his—"

"Lord Vicerin is dead," said Elodie. "I killed him."

A hush descended on the banqueting hall. The people at the surrounding tables stopped eating and listened with avid interest as Elodie explained how she'd raised her army of ghosts from the swamp and driven back the last of the Vicerin forces.

"I lost my sword, but I had another weapon. An arrowhead. I stuck it into his . . ." She caught sight of Sylva's anguished face. "He's dead."

Her mother's hand stole across the tabletop and gripped hers.

"You were brave, my dear," Kalia said. "You did what you had to do."

The Hammer thumped the table.

"It is very well!" he boomed. "Vicerin dead? His army scattered? Now there is nothing to stop us from taking his castle. There is no better fortress in Ritherlee. Once we have established our base there, we can—"

"No," Gulph interrupted. "We can't do that. The Galadronians are already there."

The Hammer's face fell. "Do you mean . . . ?"

"They're occupying the castle. And their army is bigger than any of us thought. They have strange weapons."

"He's right," Tarlan agreed.

"No army is unbeatable," said The Hammer, but his voice was full of doubt.

"This one might be," said Gulph glumly.

The silence dragged out. At last, able to stand it no longer, Elodie turned to the wizard.

"Tell us, Melchior," she said. "What must we do?"

The wizard's brow furrowed. He ran his hand through his beard and looked at Kalia. Kalia nodded.

"It is your battle." Melchior's gaze took in first Elodie, then Tarlan, then Gulph. His voice sounded very old. "You must decide."

I knew you were going to say that.

No longer hungry, Elodie threw herself back in her chair and folded her arms. She was fascinated to see Tarlan and Gulph do exactly the same thing, at exactly the same time.

Think, Elodie! Think!

She stared into the fire, but the flames were distracting. Closing her eyes, she let her mind drift. *It's time to go to war. But how can we stand against an enemy like this?* She thought about the battles she'd been in, beginning with her very first taste of fighting, when a group of Isurians had blocked the path of the Trident army as they marched through their village.

That wasn't really a fight, more like a standoff. The Battle of the Bridge—now that was a fight.

She shivered as she remembered the titanic clash on the

Idilliam Bridge, the soldiers of Trident beaten back by Brutan's undead warriors. It was only the intervention of Sir Jaken and her first ghost army that had saved the day.

My first real battle, she thought, and a trace of the red mist crept into the darkness behind her closed eyelids.

After the battle, Trident had retreated into the Isurian forest. But the period of rest had been short-lived, thanks to the Vicerins.

Thanks to Stown's treachery.

Thanks to . . .

". . . the ambush."

"What, Elodie? What did you say?" Gulph asked.

"Huh?" Elodie opened her eyes. She wasn't aware she'd spoken aloud.

"What did you say?" Gulph repeated. He and Tarlan were looking earnestly at her.

"After the Battle of the Bridge, we were ambushed," she said slowly. "The Vicerins took us completely by surprise."

"Go on," said Melchior.

Elodie frowned. "Surprise. That's the key. When you're outnumbered, it's the only advantage you've got."

"But if the Galadronian army is as big as you say . . ." The Hammer began.

"That's just it. It's not about how many soldiers they've got. It's about what they're expecting."

"What do you believe they are expecting, Elodie?" said Kalia.

"Just what any invading force would expect: resistance."

"I don't understand," said Sylva. Seated beside her, Cedric shared her puzzled expression.

"Think about it." Elodie was sitting upright now, talking fast. "We have to assume that Hypiro wants to rule Toronia. To do that she has to take Idilliam. But instead of making her way straight there, she's sent her army to Ritherlee. Why?"

"It's one of the three realms of Toronia," said Tarlan. "If she wants to rule the whole kingdom, she'll have to take Ritherlee sooner or later."

"Four realms," put in Gulph. "Don't forget Celestis."

"Never mind how many realms there are," said Elodie with a wave of her hand. "Think about what the Galadronians are *doing*."

Tarlan was nodding and smiling. "They're building a nest."

"Exactly! Before marching on Idilliam, they want to establish a base. Why? Because they know the Toronians are going to put up a fight!"

The Hammer grunted. "You spoke of surprising the enemy, yet you tell us they already expect attack by a Toronian army. You have returned the argument to where it began."

"No, I haven't!" Elodie stood. "We're not going to send an army against them! We're going to send three!"

259

Under Elodie's direction, the mountain of meat was cleared away. Grabbing a brass candlestick from the shelf over the hearth, she planted it in the middle of the now-empty table.

"Castle Vicerin," she said.

She brought a basket of fruit from one of the other tables and arranged several dozen grapes in a wedge-shape, the sharp end pointing directly at the candlestick.

"Our human soldiers," she explained. "That's you and your people, Hammer. Also the Vicerins you met up with along the way, Gulph. And the people from the hall here. Anyone and everyone who can carry a weapon and is ready to fight."

"The people of Deep Poynt will not let you down." The Hammer's eyes glinted with excitement. "Just give me your orders."

"Gulph will do that. He'll be in charge of this main force." She raised a silent eyebrow at her brother and was pleased to see him nod agreement.

"That's one army," said Tarlan. "What about the others?"

Elodie scooped up a handful of dried dates from the basket. These she scattered to the right of the candlestick.

"My ghosts. I'll be waiting with them in the swamp. We'll hold back until Gulph's army has engaged the enemy. Then we'll attack. That's surprise number one."

"What's the second surprise?" The grin on Tarlan's face told Elodie that he already knew the answer. By way of reply, she laid out a carpet of red berries to the left of the candlestick.

"You, Tarlan. Your pack, and all the animals you can rouse between now and the time we attack. You'll come out of the woods to the west. It's the last thing they'll be expecting."

She stood back, satisfied. The candlestick representing Castle Vicerin was surrounded. Slowly, deliberately, she reached out and tipped it on its side. It hit the tabletop with a loud clang.

"This might work," said The Hammer with slow deliberation.

"It *will* work," Tarlan corrected him.

"Of course it will," Gulph agreed. "Elodie thought of it."

Kalia rose from her chair and circled the table, appraising her daughter's strategy. "It is a good plan," she said. "But we cannot afford to underestimate Hypiro's powers."

"Kalia is right," said Melchior gravely. "The Sandspear is a fearsome weapon—one of the greatest relics from the ancient world. Every time we bring down one of her warriors, the Witch-Empress will cause another to rise up. We will not just be fighting one army. We will be fighting a hundred."

"If that's true"—Cedric briefly touched the fallen candlestick—"attacking their soldiers will only buy us time."

"You speak the truth," Kalia said, nodding. "The only way to defeat Hypiro is to destroy the Sandspear."

The Hammer thumped the table. The candlestick bounced off the table, rolled across the floor, and landed in the fire. A ragged cheer rose up as the flames licked around its metal curves.

"Then destroy it we will!" roared The Hammer. "Together we will grind these Galadronians into this good Toronian soil! Then, when we have wiped them from our boots, the triplets will have the crown!"

More cheers. Fists pumped the air. The children who'd been playing leaped up and down, adding their small voices to the din. Elodie felt elated but also fearful. There was so much at stake . . . and so little room for error. She saw her warring emotions reflected in the faces of her brothers, and was glad they shared her feelings.

Now it was Melchior's turn to stand. Raising his arms, he calmed the uproar.

"The Sandspear is not our only problem."

"It isn't?" said Elodie uncertainly.

"Alas, no. Have you forgotten about your jewels?"

Elodie clutched instinctively at her throat. Beside her, Tarlan and Gulph did the same.

"Lord Vicerin! Mine and Tarlan's are still hanging round his neck. Gulph, have you . . . ?"

His face solemn, Gulph parted the collar of his tunic to reveal a gold chain. Hanging on the chain was a bright green gem.

At least one of them is safe, thought Elodie in relief.

"The jewels are important," Melchior said, "although I know

not why. Gryndor wrote of them. He gave me his scrolls for safe-keeping, shortly before the crystal city was buried. It was Gryndor who wrote the words of the prophecy, yet even he was not clear about what purpose the three jewels serve."

"There's a room," said Gulph. "A sort of throne room. It's in Celestis, out on the lake. Its walls are covered with jewels just like this one."

"Then it's obvious," said Tarlan. "That's where we have to take our jewels."

"Well, we can't do that until we've got them all back," said Elodie, rising to her feet once more.

Kalia clasped her wrist. "Elodie—you cannot go back to find Lord Vicerin's body. The castle will be swarming with Galadronians. It will not be safe."

"I know. But I've got the perfect person for the job."

Elodie awoke to the sound of whinnying horses and clashing metal. She yawned and stretched—after all the excitement of the previous night she hadn't expected to sleep at all. Rousing herself from the bed she'd made in the corner of the banqueting hall, she made her way to Castle Darrand's main entrance.

Dawn light was streaming through the open archway. The lawn outside was thronged with people, all of them busily preparing weapons and armor for the coming battle.

Elodie grabbed a handful of food from a long trestle table on which a breakfast of bread and fruit had been laid out, then crossed the grass to where Cedric and Sylva were saddling up Valor and two other horses.

"So you decided to join us, sleepyhead?" Cedric laughed.

"You should have woken me up."

"We didn't want to disturb you," said Sylva. "It's going to be a big day, and we thought you could use the sleep."

"You were probably right. Is my horse ready?"

Cedric finished tightening Valor's girth strap. "Everything's ready, Elodie. We're just awaiting your command."

On the far side of the lawn, Gulph was talking to a group of Deep Poynt men. As Elodie watched, several Vicerin soldiers—their blue sashes unmistakable—cautiously joined them. Gulph said something to one of them, who laughed. Then they were all laughing.

"They like him," said Sylva, following Elodie's gaze.

"They'll follow him," added Cedric.

That's my brother, thought Elodie with a tingle of pride.

Nearby, The Hammer was inspecting a battalion from Gulph's combined army. Behind them, Elodie could see the invisible battalions of her ghosts assembling in the trees.

On the other side of the lawn, a huge pack of animals had

gathered. Tarlan was addressing them from the remains of what had once been an ornamental fountain. Beside him stood the wolf and the tigron Elodie remembered from the time they'd spent together with Trident. Tarlan also seemed to have added an enormous bear to his high command since she'd seen him last.

Overhead, the three thorrods circled endlessly, their feathers blazing in the morning sun.

We're ready. I actually think we're ready.

Elodie was about to go over to Gulph when Melchior's voice rang out.

"Elodie! Tarlan! Gulph! Children of the prophecy, kings and queen of Toronia—will you come to me now?"

All heads turned toward the wizard. He was standing on the steps of Castle Darrand with Kalia at his side. Between them they carried three sets of armor.

A shiver ran down Elodie's spine.

Feeling the eyes of the three armies on her, she made her way to the bottom of the steps. Gulph and Tarlan met her there.

"No going back now," said Tarlan.

"Never," Gulph agreed.

Elodie took their hands. Together they mounted the steps.

"This is yours, Elodie," said Kalia, handing over the silver armor she'd worn during the battle at Castle Vicerin. "And here is armor for you, Gulph, and you, Tarlan. I recovered it from the strong room inside the hall. It will fit you well."

Elodie was first to dress, flexing her arms and making sure the edges of the breastplate didn't rub against them. Tarlan watched her closely, then clumsily donned his own segmented suit of polished bronze. He completed his ensemble by tying his tattered black cloak around his neck.

Gulph's awkward posture made it hard for him to wear regular armor, so Kalia had picked out a set of gold chainmail and a light helmet, which kept falling down over his face. Elodie adjusted the chinstrap, then helped him settle his pack on his shoulders.

"This is heavy," she said. "What's inside it?"

To her surprise, Gulph whirled round, gaping at her.

"I'm such an idiot! I never showed you!"

Elodie exchanged a glance with Tarlan, who looked as bemused as she felt. "What didn't you show us?"

Gulph took a deep breath. "It's the crown! The crown of Toronia! I've been carrying it for so long I just forgot. . . . I can't believe I didn't tell you!"

Elodie put her hand to Gulph's pack. She could feel the hard, cold metal beneath the fabric. A thrill ran through her.

"Do you want to see it?" said Gulph.

Reluctantly, Elodie pulled her hand away. "No," she said. "Not yet."

"Elodie's right," said Tarlan. "Let's wait until the battle's won."

They stood for a moment, contemplating the contents of Gulph's pack. Then Kalia said, "I see a stretcher floating through the trees. Either the world is stranger than we thought, or our spies have returned."

They emerged from the woods—Lady Darrand, Lord Winterborne, and the two Ritherlee nobles who'd fought so bravely in the Star Chamber of Castle Vicerin.

Lying on the stretcher was the corpse of Lord Vicerin.

Elodie hurried down the steps to meet them. "You found him without any trouble?"

The ghosts laid the stretcher down at her feet.

"His body had not been disturbed," Lady Darrand replied. "We were not seen."

Lord Vicerin's corpse was still clad in the same silver armor. The same ornate helmet, complete with its elaborate blue plume, still obscured the face. The same trail of blood—dried now and dark—stained the left side of its breastplate.

Elodie was dimly aware of Sylva and Cedric watching her. Everyone was watching her—Melchior and Kalia, her brothers, the assembled armies.

Just do it, she told herself, ignoring them all, ignoring the clamor of her heart as it tried to climb its way out of her chest. *It's only a dead body. Take the jewels and you won't ever have to see him again.*

Hands shaking, she tugged at the top of his breastplate. It didn't move. The body was sickeningly heavy. There was no gap between the top of the breastplate and the bottom of his helmet.

She was going to have to lift up the visor.

The last thing Elodie wanted to do was see Lord Vicerin's face again. But she had no choice.

What if he isn't really dead? What if I pull back the visor and his eyes open?

If that happened, she wouldn't even be able to scream. She'd probably just drop dead on the spot.

Don't be so stupid. He's dead. You know he is. Just do it!

Elodie slipped her fingers under the bottom of the visor and slid it up.

Her heart stopped. Her hands flew up like startled birds. She decided she was going to scream after all. But when she tried, she found she had no breath.

She was unable to believe her eyes.

The man inside the suit of armor—the man she'd killed—was not Lord Vicerin.

It was Stown.

CHAPTER 18

E lodie's scream split the air. Gulph rushed immediately
to his sister's side. Tarlan, bigger and stronger than him,
pushed past them both and tore the dead man's silver
breastplate loose. Beneath the armor was a tunic stained almost
black with blood.

"No jewels!" Tarlan roared, flinging the breastplate across the
grass. He stared at the face of the corpse. "It's not Vicerin!"

"Who is he, Elodie?" said Gulph, gently holding her trembling shoulders.

"Stown!" she said. Her hand was clamped to her mouth, muf-
fling her words. "He betrayed Trident and ended up fighting for
the Vicerins. He's . . . he's the one who executed Fessan!"

Gulph stared at her, unable to speak. Executed? Fessan was

Ossilius's son, and Gulph's heart wrenched for his friend. He didn't want to believe it.

"I don't understand!" Tarlan's hands curled over the dead man's exposed throat, as if he wanted to strangle him.

"A decoy," said Gulph, recovering his composure. "This fancy armor—it's Lord Vicerin's?"

"Y-yes," said Elodie.

"They must have switched places," said Gulph. "You thought you were fighting Lord Vicerin, but it was really this Stown."

"Vicerin was always a coward," Elodie replied. "I should have known he'd never put himself in real danger."

Gulph thought back to his encounter with Captain Ariston and the Vicerin soldiers the previous night. What was it they'd said?

"He's probably safe somewhere. Slippery as an eel."

He helped Elodie up. Tarlan, still crouching over Stown's body, glared up at them.

"Vicerin is still alive," said Gulph. "And he still has both your jewels."

Sylva, watching from where she stood near the horses, began to wail. Cedric embraced her as best he could with his one arm. Gulph could only imagine their confusion. Should they be happy that their father wasn't dead after all, or distraught that their enemy was still at large?

At the top of the stairs, Melchior and Kalia looked down with matching expressions of concern.

"I thought I'd defeated him," Elodie said in a flat, low voice. "How could I have been so wrong?"

"He tricked us!" growled Tarlan. He rose to his feet, red-faced, his fists clenching and unclenching.

Someone needs to stay calm here, thought Gulph.

"This doesn't change anything," he said, pitching his voice so that everyone on the lawn would hear. "If Lord Vicerin marched in here right now, nobody would join him. His soldiers are our soldiers now. Their loyalty lies with Toronia."

"I don't think I can—" Elodie began.

"You can," said Gulph firmly. "Our first concern is the Galadronians. We have to drive them out of the castle. Drive them back where they came from."

"If I see Vicerin again, I'll kill him with my bare hands!" said Tarlan.

"And you may get that chance." Gulph frowned, thinking hard. "He might still be at the castle. If he's as treacherous as you say, he might even have struck a deal with the Galadronians."

Elodie nodded slowly. "Yes . . . yes, Gulph, you could be right. I wouldn't put it past him."

Gulph watched as she gathered herself, straightening her

back and standing tall in her armor. Beside her, Tarlan bowed his head and dropped his hands to his sides, visibly bringing his anger under control.

"Are you ready to do this?" he said to them both.

"Yes," said Elodie, brushing a lock of red-gold hair away from her face. She'd told Gulph how she'd cut it short while she'd been with Trident; now it was beginning to grow back. "I'll go and tell the ghosts that we're ready to march out."

"All right. And you, Tarlan?"

"I'm fine," said Tarlan. "I just need to finish talking to my pack."

They left without another look at Stown. Gulph considered detailing some of his soldiers to carry the body away, then decided he had more important things to do.

Let the crows have you. For killing Fessan, it's all you deserve.

Seeking out The Hammer, Gulph found the big man deep in conversation with Captain Ariston. Between them, they'd arranged into formal ranks the people of Deep Poynt, the Vicerin troops, and those who'd survived the assault on Castle Darrand.

There are hundreds here, Gulph realized with growing anticipation. *This is actually beginning to look like an army.*

Three horses had been prepared for them; The Hammer's was a huge war-mount with shaggy white hooves and legs like tree trunks. Both Gulph and Ariston had been given sleek Vicerin chargers.

Unused to riding, Gulph took several moments to settle

himself in the saddle. When he was finally comfortable, he noted with surprise that all his troops were staring at him.

Looks like there's something else to be done before we fight, he thought.

Placing his hand on the hilt of his sword, he said to the watching soldiers, "I want us all to remember why we're here."

"To kill the enemy!" called a Deep Poynt man carrying a scythe.

There was some laughter at this, and a few cheers. But many people, Gulph noted, looked apprehensive or even fearful.

"That's true." His voice gained volume as he spoke. "But this isn't about killing. It isn't even about fighting. Those are just the things we have to do if we want to bring this war to an end. *That's* why we're here. If the battle is won today, tomorrow you won't have to fight anymore. You can go home to your families and start rebuilding what the enemy has destroyed. You're not waging a war. You're fighting so that the war will end. You're fighting so that peace can begin! Fighting to survive. That's what you are: my Army of Survivors!"

This time the cheers were louder. Some faces remained fearful, but most of the soldiers now stood erect and resolute, with their weapons held high.

Elodie's voice floated out from the nearby woods. Gulph couldn't make out her words, but he could tell from her tone that she was delivering her own speech to her invisible army. Then Elodie shouted something and the whole line of trees shimmered. Figures appeared, seeming to form themselves out of the dust-filled dawn air: men and women, some armored, some not, as varied in costume and countenance as Gulph's own army, yet at the same time as transparent as smoke.

Cries of alarm broke out among the ranks of Gulph's human army. Captain Ariston and The Hammer rode up and down the lines, keeping order. Gulph waved his sword.

"Don't be afraid! They are our friends, our allies. Just like you, they're fighting for what they believe in. The only difference is that their homes lie in the realm beyond. Will you stand with them?"

For a moment, he feared the sight of Elodie's ghost army had been too much of a shock. Then Lady Darrand appeared at the front of the line of ghosts. She raised her arms, then lowered them. As one, the ghosts bowed to their human counterparts.

After the briefest of pauses, the Army of Survivors returned the bow.

A Vicerin woman started clapping her hands. Soon everyone was applauding. The ghosts straightened up and lifted their thin, wavering voices into the morning air. From the other side of the lawn came a cacophony of animal shrieks and howls as Tarlan's enormous pack joined the strange dawn chorus.

Elodie rode to the front of her phantom army on her fine black mare. Tarlan leaped onto the back of the golden thorrod, Theeta. Gulph caught the eye first of his sister, then his brother.

The rising sun turned their red-gold hair into flaming beacons.

Together, they raised their swords above their heads, shielding their eyes as the blades burned bright with the light of the prophecy stars.

So, this is it, Gulph thought in wonder. *We're finally going to war.*

By the time they'd left Castle Darrand behind, the sun had already risen above the trees. Cresting the brow of a low hill, Gulph reined in his horse and looked back into the morning glare.

The three armies streamed out behind him. His own Army of Survivors were finding it hard to march in time, and it was as much as The Hammer and Captain Ariston could do to keep them together. But they looked bold and confident.

And more than ready for a fight.

To Gulph's right, Elodie seemed to be having an easier time with her Army of Ghosts. Sylva and Cedric rode with her at the head of a gray river of phantom figures, which flowed effortlessly across the landscape. At Elodie's side, her long hair flying in the breeze, rode Kalia.

To Gulph's left ran the pack—Tarlan's formidable following of beasts and birds. Gulph had lost count of the number of animals whose loyalty Tarlan commanded. There were foxes and wolves, horses and deer, boar and bears, eagles and snakes . . . a dizzying array. Leading the pack was Tarlan himself, riding on Theeta's back.

Nasheen flew with them, carrying Melchior the wizard. Tarlan's other close friends—the wolf, the tigron, the giant bear, and the black-breasted thorrod called Kitheen—seemed to be acting as his lieutenants, keeping the animals on course and in formation.

Oh, Pip, Gulph thought, *I hope I get to see you again, so I can tell you all about this.*

The sky remained cloudless throughout the day, the prophecy stars clearly visible except at noon, when the midday sun overwhelmed them. They reappeared as the sun began its descent into the west, one red, one gold, one green.

One for each of us.

Tarlan had told Gulph and Elodie how he'd seen one of the stars dim and believed it was because Gulph had died in the fires at Idilliam. The triplets now thought its light had faded while Elodie made her extraordinary journey to the Realm of the Dead.

I hope the stars never go out.

The afternoon shadows were lengthening behind them when they reached the thin arm of woodland shielding the eastern side of Castle Vicerin. Here Gulph raised his arm and brought his army to a temporary halt. No sooner had he done this than Theeta swooped down to circle low over his head.

"It's time for us to part!" Tarlan called down. "Good luck, brother!"

"And to you!"

Gulph watched with a mixture of admiration and fear as Tarlan and Melchior led the pack west and south to where the woods grew thick, to lie in wait there until the time was right to launch their surprise attack.

"Gulph!" called Elodie. "Are you ready?"

"I've been ready all day!" he shouted back. "Stay safe, Elodie!"

"See you on the battlefield!"

Spurring their horses, Elodie and Kalia rode north toward the swamp she'd called the Forgotten Graveyard. Behind her went Sylva and Cedric, and the immense rolling tide that was the Army of Ghosts.

"That just leaves us, lad!" boomed The Hammer. Jostling his enormous horse close, he gave Gulph a backslap so powerful it almost catapulted him from his saddle. "Forward ho!"

Branches clawed at Gulph's face as his horse picked its way through the narrow belt of trees. He spent a few moments brushing them aside, and then they were through and into a wide, flat field. Gulph continued to ride forward, allowing his soldiers to fan out behind him.

In the middle of the field he stopped and stared at what Castle Vicerin had become. The sight took his breath away.

When Gulph had last seen the castle—only the day before—it had been halfway to becoming a ruin. Several of the towers had collapsed, and fires had still burned in its many courtyards, blackening the crumbling walls with soot.

Now it was transformed.

Every breach in the castle's red stone walls had been repaired with smooth patches of gold. In place of every fallen tower stood two new towers, also of gold. A new moat had been excavated; it seemed to be filled with a liquid that rippled with a life of its own. Like the new defenses that overlooked it, this liquid was the color of gold.

Not gold . . . sand.

The battlements of the resurrected castle were lined with soldiers. They wore flowing robes of many colors, some plain, some patterned. Some had pale skin, others dark, and some were the color of the gleaming sand.

Gulph's horse stirred restlessly. He patted its neck. Behind him, the Army of Survivors was silent.

Sudden movement caught his attention. Soldiers edging round the castle's northern tower? When he looked that way, he saw nothing, but the tower seemed strangely taller.

Hypiro must be using the Sandspear, he thought. He remembered his mother's words: Whoever wields the Sandspear has the power to create anything they want out of sand.

"I do not like this," murmured a voice in his ear. Gulph jumped, but it was only Captain Ariston. The Vicerin officer looked troubled. "Shall we advance?"

Gulph gripped the reins, trying to think clearly over the thunder of his own heartbeat.

"No," he said. "Let them get a good look at us. The more we can hold their attention, the more time Tarlan and Elodie have to get into position."

"You speak sense, Your Highness," rumbled The Hammer, riding up to join them. "Yet I care for this quiet no more than our Vicerin friend here."

"I am no Vicerin," Ariston snapped. Gulph looked at him in surprise. Ariston shrugged. "I am a Toronian."

Time dragged on. The sun, sinking slowly into the west, fired its rays straight into their faces, glaring between the castle's turrets and making the enemy soldiers crowding its battlements hard to see. All was still, and yet Gulph couldn't help feeling there was movement happening everywhere, always just out of sight.

The Army of Survivors began to grow restless. Muttered conversations broke out. Neatly formed columns started to break up. Metal blades clattered nervously.

Still the Galadronians didn't respond.

"Does our army look so feeble to them?" growled The Hammer. "Do they think us beneath them? I say let them come! Let them see what we are made of!"

"I don't think that's it," said Gulph. "I think they're trying to intimidate us. Make us feel uneasy."

"It seems to be working," remarked Ariston, regarding the concerned faces of the soldiers.

"Well, I won't let it." Gulph took up his reins. "Very well, then. If they won't come to us—I will take the fight to them."

Digging in his heels, he spurred his horse forward.

"No, lad!" roared The Hammer. "There is great danger here!"

"Of course there is! That's why we came!"

"Then at least let me come with you!"

"No!" Gulph called over his shoulder. "Stay here! Hold the line and wait for my signal! I have to do this alone!"

"I will come with you!"

Gulph wheeled his horse around. Much as he admired the big man's bravery, he knew what he had to do. "I am your king," he told The Hammer, "and I say you will not!"

The Hammer stared at Gulph with his jaw gaping wide. He seemed about to protest, then thought better of it.

"Yes, Your Highness. As you command."

Gulph spurred his horse into a gallop. Warm air smacked his face.

I must be crazy!

He stopped on the bank of the newly created moat. As he'd suspected, the liquid that filled the trench wasn't liquid at all—it was a churning, spitting cauldron of sand. From the top of the looming castle wall stared down the faces of the Galadronians. At least half of them possessed the strange golden sheen he'd seen from a distance, and he wondered if Hypiro had conjured them like she had sections of the castle.

Gulph scanned the rows of soldiers. "I come in the name of Toronia!" he shouted. "I wish to speak with your leader, the Witch-Empress Hypiro!"

Something whistled through the air barely an arm's length from his head. There was a loud *thunk* behind him. He glanced back to see a metal bolt from a side bow buried in the grass. His nerves screamed, his heart pounded. He had to muster all his courage just to stay in the saddle.

I won't let them see how afraid I am.

An odd-looking shadow was descending the castle wall. Gulph blinked—had someone dropped something from the battlements? Then he saw it wasn't a shadow at all. It was a doorway.

The doorway—a vertical black oblong—continued to slide down the wall until it was at the height of a second-floor window. There it stopped. Around the edges of the slot, the sand from which this part of the wall was made flexed for a moment, then became solid.

Gulph held his breath.

Something emerged from the wall immediately below the doorway: a finger of sand that seemed to grow out of nothing. It extended halfway across the moat before stopping. The end swelled and flattened, became a circular platform. All the while this was happening, a dusting of sand rained down from the underside of the structure to be greedily sucked down by golden tendrils reaching up from the moat.

A woman walked out of the doorway and crossed the curious half bridge. Hairless, she was almost a giant—to Gulph's eyes, she looked at least a head taller than The Hammer. Her face was broad, smooth, and deeply tanned. It was impossible to tell how old she was. Her flexible white armor seemed to follow her every movement.

On her right arm she carried a round shield emblazoned with a symbol that might have been a lightning bolt, or perhaps a striking snake.

In her left hand she carried a long golden javelin that blazed as if it were filled with fire.

The Sandspear!

"This is Hypiro!" she called. Her voice was deep and melodic. "She who is named the Scourge of the Desert. She who is named the Light of Galadron. She who is named Witch-Empress. Who dares to come to her door? Who dares to call her name? Speak!"

It was the very same woman he'd seen in his vision, and then in Kalia's bubble of magic. Yet seeing her in the flesh was entirely different.

It was terrifying.

Gulph tried in vain to sit up straight, acutely aware of how bent his skinny body must look under the weight of his armor. Then he scolded himself for thinking that way.

I don't need to be scared. I have more right to be here than she does!

"My name is Gulph!" he shouted. "If it's fancy names you like, I suppose you could call me One of Three, or King of the Prophecy, or Child of the Stars. But all that really matters is the message I bring."

"Speak your message."

"Toronia is not yours to take!"

He'd expected Hypiro to sneer at this, perhaps even laugh. But the giant warrior-woman showed no sign of emotion.

"What you say is of no consequence. Hypiro has taken the realm of Ritherlee. Her army is rested. Her defenses are reinforced. The remaining realms of Toronia will fall in their turn. It is inevitable."

Hypiro turned smoothly away and set off back toward the doorway she'd somehow conjured in the castle's sand-built wall.

"You're sure of that, are you?" Gulph yelled at her retreating back. "You're sure that every village in Ritherlee is under your control? Every tree in Isur? And you haven't even been near Idilliam yet."

The Witch-Empress waved a dismissive hand. "Hypiro will take Toronia. This is what she will do. This is how it will be."

"Not as long as we're alive!"

Hypiro had reached the doorway. Here she paused.

"*We?*" she said.

"My brother, my sister, and me! We are the Prophecy Triplets, and this is our kingdom. If you want to take Toronia, you'll have to take us first."

Still Hypiro's expression didn't change. Gulph thumped the horn of his saddle in frustration. Was there nothing he could say to draw out the Galadronian army?

"The prophecy you speak of is a children's tale," the Witch-Empress said. "That Toronia's citizens cling to it is a sign of how barbaric this kingdom has become. Hypiro will be glad to rid Toronia of this superstition."

Again she turned away. Desperate now, Gulph did the only thing he could think of.

Bunching his fists, he thrust his thoughts across the moat on a wave of dry, pulsing heat. Even before his physical body had time to blink, his disembodied consciousness had plunged into the retreating mind of the Witch-Empress Hypiro. At once, he was swallowed by . . .

. . . the roar of the triumphant crowds, the riot of bright flags and banners as the Galadronian army sweeps into Idilliam, everywhere a sea of color and chaotic rejoicing. Riding high on a golden platform, overseeing the victory, is Hypiro herself, directing her troops to cut down the last defensive line of the pitiful Toronian army. And there, on three wooden scaffolds, hang the bloodied bodies of three children with red-gold hair, hunted down and murdered by Hypiro's own assassins before being displayed for all to

see. Even now, her slaves are stacking firewood beneath their mutilated corpses, ready to burn . . .

. . . silencing a scream, Gulph reminded himself that none of this had happened yet. He also remembered that he couldn't control Hypiro's actions.

But maybe I can change what she thinks. Better still, what she fears.

No sooner had he thought this than he was . . .

. . . rising up from the wreckage of Idilliam, an army of brave and powerful warriors with the strength to drive back the invaders. Shrunken in defeat, the once-mighty Witch-Empress turns on her heels and flees back to her ships, back to Galadron, defeated at last and resigned to the knowledge that there, in the heart of Toronia, the triplets sit in triumph on their three thrones . . .

. . . and as Gulph broke free and returned to his own body, the triumph came with him, filling him up from the heels of his boots to the crown of his head. At the same instant, Hypiro's tanned face darkened with the unmistakable shadow of pure rage. Waving the Sandspear furiously above her head, she vanished into the doorway, which immediately collapsed as sand from the surrounding wall poured into the space where it had been and froze in place.

It worked—I made her angry! thought Gulph in satisfaction as he galloped back to where The Hammer and Ariston were waiting. *Now let's see what she does.*

Just as Gulph reached the front line of his army, horns began sounding from the towers of what had once been Castle Vicerin. All along the battlements the Galadronian soldiers were swarming like ants.

It's the whole castle that's swarming!

Gulph watched, stupefied, as the sand-covered walls of the castle peeled apart. This time it wasn't just doorways that were appearing—it was gateways. Three, four, five enormous mouths opened up, spitting out tongues of sand that extended all the way across the moat to meet the field beyond. Pouring out of the newly formed gates, racing across the waiting drawbridges, came hundreds of enemy warriors.

There was no time to think.

"Attack!" roared Gulph. "Attack!"

At once The Hammer drove his horse along the front line, breaking several battalions away in an effort to flank the Galadronians even as they made their first charge. At the same time, Captain Ariston directed another smaller force to come round at them from the opposite direction.

Gulph led the main body of the army out to meet the enemy head-on, urging his horse on as the gap closed between them and the oncoming Galadronians. At the last moment, he pulled up short and shouted the command he'd been drilling into his soldiers all the way here:

"Lances!"

Responding immediately, the front line of the Army of Survivors dropped to their knees and planted the blunt ends of their spears into the ground, creating a row of lethal points angled upward to meet the enemy advance. It was a simple strategy—one that should have seen at least half the Galadronians taken by surprise and impaled.

Instead, it was Gulph who was surprised.

The instant the Galadronians made contact with the spears, their bodies turned to sand. Gold mist exploded through the ranks of Gulph's army. On every side, men and women fell to the ground choking and clawing at their eyes. Many flailed uselessly with their swords, and Gulph could only look on in horror as several of his troops fell under the blows of their own comrades.

"Second line!" he yelled. "Second line!"

But the next row of soldiers was already in disarray. Out of the swirling cloud of sand came squads of regular Galadronian troops, swinging their curved swords with cruel accuracy.

One Galadronian—a sand-colored man dressed all in purple— made straight for Gulph. Gulph parried his first two blows, feeling the impacts judder all the way up his arm. As the man struck out for the third time, Gulph slipped his feet from the stirrups and jumped nimbly up to stand on the saddle. The enemy's weapon came round; Gulph jumped over the blade and stabbed his own sword down into the Galadronian's chest. Even before the man had hit the ground, Gulph was back in the saddle and riding into the heart of the action.

Two more Galadronians came at him. Fighting fiercely, he beat them both back. All around him the battle raged, the sight and sounds of it filling up his senses: the thunder of horses' hooves; the bellows and screams of the soldiers; the rising dust and swirling sand. Cutting through the chaos was the sharp orange light of the setting sun.

"Onward!" roared The Hammer, wielding his hammer like a club and smashing his way through the Galadronian ranks. The pincer movement had found little success, so now that the two armies had met, there was nothing left but to slug it out, hand to hand. And, as they'd always known they would be, the Army of Survivors were hopelessly outnumbered.

Gulph brought his sword down on another Galadronian head. As the enemy soldier collapsed to the ground, three more gateways opened in the castle walls, spilling yet more soldiers onto the battle-field. Many of them were riding on wheeled machines that looked as if they were built entirely from spinning blades and spitting fire. Gulph had never seen anything like them.

We won't last long like this! He raised his sword against another attack. *Tarlan, Elodie—where are you?*

CHAPTER 19

C urse these trees! We'll never reach them in time!"

Tarlan thumped the air in frustration. From his vantage point high in the sky, he could only watch helplessly as the Galadronians surrounded Gulph's pitifully small army. The mixed troops of Vicerins, Darrands, and Deep Poynters fought bravely, but little by little they were drowning in the rising tide of the enemy forces.

Theeta circled back over the woodland. Looking straight down through the canopy of trees, Tarlan could just make out his pack as they struggled in vain to push their way through the unusually thorny undergrowth. Brock led the charge, swiping whole trees aside with his massive paws.

"I thought we'd get through more quickly," groaned Tarlan. "Well done, Brock—we're relying on you."

"Fire claws!" cawed Theeta suddenly.

Puzzled, Tarlan looked at the battlefield again. Rolling through the middle of the Galadronian ranks were war machines similar to those he'd seen at the fishing village where the invaders had first made landfall. These machines were bigger, and moved so fast that all he saw was a frenzy of spinning blades, most of which seemed to be covered in flames—the "fire claws" Theeta had done her best to describe.

Wherever the machines drove into the ranks of Gulph's army, soldiers fell instantly and began to burn.

"Tarlan!"

It was Melchior, shouting up from the woodland below. Tarlan guided Theeta down to the tiny clearing where the wizard was waiting beside a large earthy mound.

"How is Gulph doing?" the wizard demanded as the thor-rod landed.

"Badly. Melchior, we've got to—"

"Theeta! A feather, if you please."

She looked round at Tarlan and blinked.

"Do it, Theeta! Whatever he says!"

Lowering her huge head, Theeta allowed Melchior to pluck a single golden feather from the ruff around her neck. Tarlan watched bemused as the wizard held the feather up before his eyes and ran the end of his staff along its length.

"What are you doing?"

"I am counting the strands."

"What good will that . . . ?"

A large tree exploded into splinters and Brock burst into the clearing, followed closely by Greythorn and Filos. Behind them, Tarlan could just make out the enormous shadowy mass of the rest of his pack, slowly forcing their way through the thorn trees.

From the opposite direction, he could hear the shouts and screams from the battlefield. *So close*, thought Tarlan, *but so far. Hold on, Gulph! Just hold on!*

"Melchior! We have to keep moving!"

"Seven hundred and thirty-eight!" the wizard announced. He planted the feather in the top of the mound of earth. "Tarlan—I need ants!"

"What? I don't understand!"

"One strand for every ant. One ant for every tree. Do you see?"

Tarlan suddenly realized the mound was an anthill. But why . . . ?

Don't argue! Just do it!

Pushing back the sounds of the battle, ignoring the struggles of his pack to force their way through the trees, he thrust his thoughts deep inside the mound.

The ants' nest was full of tiny, buzzing minds—tens of thousands of them. Tarlan squirmed his way to the middle of the seething mass of insects and roared out a pure, simple thought:

One ant! One strand!

He flew backward out of the nest and watched in amazement as hundreds of black insects boiled from the top of the anthill. It looked like a volcanic eruption. They swarmed up the thorrod feather and began snipping through the individual golden strands.

In the forest before them, trees began to topple.

They fell so quickly that Tarlan barely had time to register what was happening. Every time an ant cut through a strand and carried it away, another thorn tree collapsed sideways. As each tree fell, a fresh beam of sunset light pierced the woodland. Soon there was only a single line of trees standing between them and the battlefield. As the ants stripped away the last few strands, this final barrier disappeared and the way ahead was clear.

"The magic of numbers!" Melchior cried. "It has never let me down yet!"

I hope it never does.

"Attack!" Tarlan bellowed. "Take them by surprise! Attack now! Attack now!"

Theeta took off, flying straight between the few trees that were still standing. Arrow-fast, she emerged low over the battlefield and shrieked an earsplitting thorrod war cry. Matching screams sounded to Tarlan's left and right and suddenly there was Nasheen with Melchior riding once more on her back. Beside her flew Kitheen, his huge golden beak agape, his enormous talons skimming the grass.

Close behind came the rest of Tarlan's pack. The ground trembled beneath them, and the air resounded with their howls and roars. The Galadronians pulled up short, turning and gaping at the oncoming army. Tarlan could only imagine what a terrifying sight his pack must be as they surged out of the forest, a tidal wave of teeth and claws.

This is what happens when you challenge the prophecy three! This is how we fight back!

Even as the feeling of triumph surged through him, more Galadronian troops started pouring out of the curiously reshaped Castle Vicerin.

Elodie! We need you now!

And there she was—a rider galloping out of the low swampy land to the northeast of the castle, her armor burning in the fierce red light of the setting sun. Following her was what looked like a wall of gray mist. As it drew near, the mist condensed into the forms of individual soldiers. Elodie's army of ghosts.

Theeta struck the Galadronian army's flank like a boulder rolled from the slope of a Yalasti mountain. The impact knocked a dozen or more men to the ground instantly. As she plowed deeper into their ranks, the thorrod began to rake the enemy with her claws and stab down with her beak. At the same time, Tarlan was hacking and slashing with his sword. By the time they'd completed their first pass, he guessed they'd felled at least thirty enemy soldiers.

Nasheen and Kitheen both struck with similar force. Surprised and confused, their orderly lines torn apart, the Galadronians had no time to regroup before the rest of Tarlan's pack crashed into them.

At the same instant, Elodie's ghosts hit them from the north.

"There's Gulph!" Tarlan shouted in Theeta's ear. "Get as close as you can!"

The thorrod sped to where Gulph was fending off a trio of Galadronian foot soldiers. As Gulph's sword pierced the chest of the nearest one, Theeta's claws tore out the throat of the second. Tarlan dispatched the third with a single blow of his sword.

"Thanks, brother!" Gulph screamed, wheeling his horse around.

"Where's Hypiro?" Tarlan yelled.

"Still in the castle! Never mind her! We've got enough to deal with here!"

Gulph charged into a fresh wave of enemy soldiers. Close behind him rode The Hammer and Captain Ariston. Satisfied that his brother could handle himself, Tarlan urged Theeta back to where his pack was in the thick of the fighting.

What he saw gave him hope. The ordinary Galadronian soldiers were no match for his animal warriors. When they came up against the biggest beasts—bears and horses and big-antlered stags—they were ripped apart or crushed. The larger carnivores, under the leadership of Filos and Greythorn, tore through anything that got in their way. And the smaller creatures were everywhere, bringing down the enemy by sheer weight of numbers.

And yet . . .

Something's wrong here.

Climbing skyward after yet another attack run, Tarlan noticed that every time a Galadronian fell, another seemed to take his place. The newly risen warriors all shared the same curious yellow-ish color—it was in their clothes, their armor, their skin . . .

Sand-warriors! We knew this would happen! But we're doing nothing about it!

Tarlan hustled Theeta to where Nasheen was circling over a cluster of Galadronian war machines. Melchior was standing on the thorrod's back, his staff pointed down toward the ground.

Tarlan watched with astonished eyes as Nasheen appeared to split first into two, then into four. An eye blink later, there were eight white-breasted thorrods spinning over the enemy machines.

Sixteen! Thirty-two!

At the same time, the whirling scythes of the war machines began to tangle together. Instead of hundreds of blades there were now only dozens, now just a handful.

Four blades! Two! One!

The machines had been spitting out tongues of fire. Now a single giant candle flame rose from the center of a juddering tangle of machinery.

Looking at it made Tarlan's eyes hurt. He remembered when

the Galadronians had attacked them on the Isle of Stars. Melchior
had used his magic to collapse the entire army into the body of a
single soldier, whom Tarlan had then killed.

One sword stroke, and they all fell.

This was the same. But it was also different. While Melchior's
magic somehow kept all the Galadronian war machines folded into
one place, the same spell had turned Nasheen into an entire flock
of thorrods. The cluster of gigantic birds plunged down onto the
machine, shredding it with their countless claws, tearing into it with
their innumerable beaks. Tarlan wiped his aching eyes, and by the
time he brought his hand down from his face, the Galadronians' fleet
of war machines had been reduced to a pile of smoking splinters.

But even as he pumped the air with his fist, an entire regiment of
sand-warriors marched out of the smoke.

"The Sandspear!" called Melchior from the back of Nasheen—
who was now single and whole once more. The wizard looked
exhausted. "You have to stop her!"

*He's right. It doesn't matter how hard we fight here. As long as Hypiro
has the Sandspear, it's hopeless.*

"Theeta!" Tarlan cried. "To the castle!"

The thorrod obeyed at once, carrying Tarlan straight into the
full glare of the setting sun. Their course took them directly over
Elodie, who had leaped from her horse and was fighting back-to-
back with Kalia. Cedric and Sylva were battling nearby, while

all around them thronged the misty gray bodies of Elodie's loyal ghost soldiers.

"Tarlan!" Elodie screamed as Theeta swooped past her head. "What are you doing?"

Tarlan didn't want to stop. *But she has to know what I'm doing. Just in case . . .*

Pulling Theeta into a screaming turn, he yelled down:

"Hypiro! I'm going to stop her!"

"What? You can't do it alone! We have to—"

"If I don't come back, it's up to you and Gulph!"

"Tarlan! Don't . . ."

But she was already far behind him.

Theeta made straight for the castle. Hunching low, Tarlan bared his teeth against the blast of the wind. Below them, hundreds of sand-warriors were appearing out of the ground. Still more were pouring over the golden bridges that spanned the new moat.

"That wasn't there before," Tarlan remarked as Theeta sped over the sand-filled trench.

"Woman giant," Theeta cawed. She turned sharply toward a spindly tower projecting from the eastern battlements. Standing on a balcony near the top of the tower was a huge female form clad in some kind of skintight armor. She was bald and carried a shield slung over her back. Both her hands were clamped on something long and sharp, which she was swinging around like a quarterstaff.

"It's her!" cried Tarlan. "And that must be the Sandspear!"

As Theeta arrowed toward the tower, the eyes of the Witch-Empress found them. She made a vicious swipe with the Sandspear, and the sand in the moat exploded into life. Hundreds of golden arrows shot skyward. As they crossed Theeta's path, they grew wings. Suddenly Tarlan was surrounded by flapping, shrieking birds.

Sand-eagles!

Reacting instantly, Theeta rolled onto her back. Tarlan felt his legs flying free. Burying his fingers in the thorrod's feathers, he clung on, only dimly aware of the thrashing motion Theeta's claws were making as they tore through the enemy flock. Sand blew past him, stinging his eyes and filling up his mouth. He spat it out, horrified by the thought of what Hypiro's enchanted sand might do if it got inside him.

Completing her roll, Theeta resumed her plunge toward the tower. The flock of sand-eagles had been reduced to a cloud of golden powder. In the light of the sunset it seemed to glow from within. As Theeta flew through it, the sand knitted itself together, becoming not hundreds of birds but one.

A sand-thorrod.

It was three times the size of Theeta. Its wings were wider than a warship's sails. When it opened its hooked beak, the cavern of its throat looked big enough to swallow Tarlan whole.

"Kitheen come!" screamed Theeta.

Her wings pumped the air, propelling her toward the titanic sand-thorrod. Tarlan had no idea if the other thorrods were close enough to hear.

It's too big! he thought, holding tight and drawing his sword. *Hypiro is too powerful!*

The sand-thorrod filled the sky. Its enormous wings were barbed along their whole length with claws. As Theeta powered toward it, the monstrous bird brought up its talons. Each one was as long as Tarlan was tall. Despite being made of sand, they looked ice-sharp.

At the last moment Theeta slipped sideways. Lashing out her claws, she drew six parallel gashes across the exposed breast of the sand-thorrod. At the same time, Tarlan thrust his blade into its throat. An exultant cry rose up inside him, but evaporated into nothing when he saw streams of sand close easily over the wounds. By the time Theeta circled round again, all signs of injury had vanished.

"We'll never get past it!"

Theeta began another attack. "Kitheen come!"

As she screamed out her companion's name, Theeta swooped in and raked her claws once more across the breast of the sand-thorrod. As she did so, another set of claws erupted through the beast's throat. Kitheen's claws.

"Kitheen come!" Theeta repeated triumphantly.

Instead of veering away, she dived straight into the body of the sand-thorrod. Meanwhile, Kitheen was a blur. His black breast flashed in and out of Tarlan's vision as he looped over and around Theeta's speeding form, slicing in all directions with beak and claw as if he were trying to tear open the sky itself. Within a couple of breaths, the sand-thorrod had completely disintegrated.

"Tower close!"

The balcony rushed toward them. Tarlan sheathed his sword and made ready to jump. His eyes and nose were clogged with sand. The wind tore at his cloak, finally ripping it free from where it had been tied to his armor. An air current sucked the cloak away, a ragged black pennant vanishing into the sunset.

"Theeta blind!"

Tarlan tried to wipe the sand from her face. But it was too late. They hit the tower and he was thrown into the air. Theeta's body lurched beneath him, then spun over his head, her huge wings flailing out of control before slamming into the side of the tower still in the light of the setting sun. For an instant Tarlan was weightless, and then his body crashed down onto a gritty surface, hit some kind of wall, and stopped.

Thud. Thud. Thud.

The sounds grew louder, relentless in their ceaseless rhythm.

Someone walking toward me!

Dazed and gasping for breath, Tarlan clawed sand from his eyes.

The red of the sunset poured in, almost blinding him. He peered through his tears, saw that he was lying on some kind of platform of sand.

The balcony!

A shadow fell over him. The footsteps stopped. His head clearing, Tarlan looked up to see the gargantuan figure of the Witch-Empress Hypiro looming over him. She was holding the Sandspear over her head. Its tip was pointing straight at Tarlan's chest.

A golden bird's wing suddenly rose up between them. For a moment, Tarlan was confused. Had the Witch-Empress conjured another sand-thorrod? Then he saw the sheen on the feathers, the way they reflected the sunset.

Theeta!

Tarlan scrambled to his feet, but his relief was short-lived as Theeta's protective wing was dashed aside by a single blow from the Sandspear. His thorrod friend, clearly still recovering from her crash landing, shrieked in pain.

Tarlan reached for his sword, only to discover that it was gone.

Hypiro was walking slowly toward him. Tarlan backed away. Behind the Witch-Empress, Theeta was trying desperately to clamber up onto the balcony parapet. Her right wing moved stiffly, and it was clear to Tarlan she was hurting.

"You resemble the other one," said Hypiro silkily. "A brother of this so-called prophecy, perhaps? Once Hypiro has killed you, only two will remain."

"That's two more than you can handle!" Tarlan retorted.

"Hypiro thinks not."

Kitheen flew out from behind the tower's roof. He dived at the Witch-Empress's head, forcing her to duck. As the black-breasted thorrod swept past Tarlan, a voice rang out:

"Tarlan! You have done all you can! Leave her to me! Now jump!"

Tarlan whirled and found himself staring straight into the face of Melchior, standing on Nasheen's back and brandishing his gnarled wooden staff in the same way the Witch-Empress Hypiro was holding the Sandspear.

"Melchior! I don't—"

"Jump, I tell you!"

The Witch-Empress struck at Tarlan's legs with the Sandspear. Tarlan sprang up onto the parapet. He looked around for Theeta, but his thorrod friend had gone.

At least one of us managed to get clear.

"Jump, Tarlan!"

Hypiro was preparing to strike at him again. There was nowhere to go. If he jumped, he would fall straight down into the moat and its hungry ocean of sand.

"Melchior—I can't . . ."

Melchior's voice softened, speaking clear and close, as if

the wizard were whispering directly into Tarlan's ear.

"Trust me, Tarlan. Trust Theeta. Now JUMP!"

Tarlan jumped. The Sandspear sliced through the air in the very place where he'd been standing. He tumbled as he fell. Then, for the second time, all his breath was knocked out of him as he landed in a mass of golden feathers.

"Theeta catch!" cried the thorrod in triumph.

"Yes, Theeta did," Tarlan panted, clutching gratefully at her feathers. "Thank you!"

"Wizard danger!"

What does she mean? Is Melchior in danger? Or is danger what he's brought?

"Up, Theeta! Up! Now!"

Pumping her wings hard despite her injuries, Theeta climbed back up toward the tower. There they found Melchior and Hypiro facing each other—the Witch-Empress poised on the parapet, the wizard balanced on the back of the hovering Nasheen. Both staff and Sandspear were outstretched, tied together by a writhing river of sand. Hypiro's flexible armor rippled as her muscles bulged beneath it. Melchior's wrinkled face was contorted in agony.

"Melchior!" Tarlan yelled.

The wizard's mouth was moving. Clearly he was chanting some kind of spell. Tarlan could feel something pulsing through the air— the wizard's magic?

With each pulse, the sand-colored bricks from which the tower was built seemed to tremble. Then, gradually, the bricks began to fold into each other, each one absorbing its neighbor.

Two bricks become one. Four bricks become one. Eight bricks become one.

Suddenly Tarlan knew what Melchior was trying to do.

"He's collapsing the castle! Without the castle, she's got nowhere to defend! Nowhere to hide!"

By now Melchior's magic of numbers was familiar to Tarlan. But this was the first time he'd seen someone resisting it. As the tower shrank around her, Hypiro conjured more sand out of the moat and into the end of the Sandspear. Soon both she and Melchior were surrounded by an ever-growing whirlwind of sand.

"Bad sky!" screamed Theeta, retreating before the spinning sandstorm could suck them in.

"Melchior!" Tarlan shouted again.

By now he could barely see the wizard, so thick had the swirling cloud of sand become. It became increasingly hard for Theeta to remain airborne, and she squawked in pain with each beat of her injured wing.

"Down, Theeta!" said Tarlan reluctantly. "There's nothing more we can do. And it isn't safe to stay."

Like a falling leaf, Theeta fluttered down to a clumsy landing on the field beside the moat. After checking she was all right, Tarlan slipped from her back and stared up at the castle.

Castle Vicerin was shrinking. The collapse was slow and strangely orderly, as each row of bricks folded into the next, and the next, and the next. Towers contracted. Roofs curled up like forgotten flowers. Little by little, the ancient fortress in which Tarlan had once been held prisoner, where Elodie had grown up not knowing her brothers even existed, was being counted out of existence.

The ground thundered with the sound of approaching horses. A moment later, Tarlan was looking into the faces of his brother and sister. Both Gulph and Elodie looked blood-spattered and exhausted.

"We've figured out how to kill the sand-warriors!" said Gulph. "We're forcing them into the swamp! Tarlan, I think we're turning the tide!"

"Is that Melchior up there?" said Elodie. "What's he doing?"

"He's counting her away!" said Tarlan. "He's counting it all away!"

Now the walls and sloping ramparts were down to head height. Where once Castle Vicerin had stood, now the vast bowl of the sky was visible. The sun appeared, angry and red on the horizon. Only a single tower remained standing—a slender needle surrounded by a spinning gyre of sand.

The last few bricks condensed into a single block of stone, which dissolved to nothing.

The sandstorm spun itself into a blur.

The tower exploded.

The blast knocked Tarlan off his feet. Slowly he picked himself up and tottered toward the place where the tower—and the castle—had once stood.

"Gone," said Elodie in dazed wonder. She was coated in sand from head to toe. "My old home . . . it's gone!"

Gulph was staggering to his feet. He too was covered in sand. "Where's Melchior?"

Where the sandstorm had been, nothing now remained. Tarlan blinked into the glare of the sunset.

"There he is!" he shouted, pointing at a winged shape just emerging from a last lingering patch of airborne sand. "Nasheen! Down here!"

He ran to meet the descending thorrod. Gulph and Elodie were close behind him. As soon as Nasheen landed, Tarlan leaped onto her back and helped Melchior down into the arms of his brother and sister. Like them, the wizard wore a coat of sand; it had buried itself in his wrinkled skin, making him look ten thousand years old.

The instant his feet touched the ground, Melchior grunted and stumbled, barely catching himself with his staff. He brushed the sand from his face, revealing a complexion so pale it was almost transparent. He looked impossibly ancient, impossibly frail.

"Is . . . she . . . gone?" the wizard asked. His voice was a mere ghost of what it had once been. Hearing its weakness sent a shiver down Tarlan's spine.

"Yes," he replied. "At least, I think so."

Melchior nodded.

"That . . . is . . . well."

"What about you, Melchior?" said Elodie. "Are you . . ."

To Tarlan's dismay, the wizard was shaking his head.

"The magic I used . . . to destroy her powers . . . it was . . . unnatural."

"Unnatural?" said Gulph.

"Yes. I have used . . . such magic . . . before."

"Yes, Melchior," came Kalia's voice. "When you saved my life."

Tarlan, Elodie, and Gulph turned to see their mother climbing down from her horse. She ran lightly over the sand-clogged grass to where they were standing.

"Forbidden magic." Melchior stroked Kalia's burned face with a trembling hand. "There is always . . . a price."

Kalia fumbled in her robe and brought out a small potion bottle. There were tears in her eyes.

"Prices can be paid," she said. "I have magic too."

She was about to pull the stopper from the bottle when Melchior's hands closed over hers.

"I am beyond . . . even your potions . . . Kalia."

The wizard's head sagged. His breath caught in his throat.

"There must be something we can do," said Tarlan. "If Hypiro is dead, surely we can . . ."

Something long and golden slammed suddenly into the trampled grass directly between Tarlan and Melchior. Where it struck, tiny manlike figures made of sand seemed to spring briefly into life before sinking back into the ground again.

The Sandspear! Where did that come from?

Shocked, heart hammering against his ribs, Tarlan made a grab for it. The Sandspear flew backward before he could make contact, landing neatly in the hand of the tall, broad-shouldered woman who was striding over the battlefield toward them.

"Hypiro!" Tarlan cried. "You're supposed to be dead!"

"Evidently Hypiro is alive," the Witch-Empress replied.

As she spoke, Hypiro whirled the Sandspear around her hairless head, clearly preparing to throw it again.

Tarlan reached for his sword and discovered all over again that he'd lost it.

"Here!" Kalia seized a large broadsword from where it was strapped to the saddle of her horse and tossed it to him. "Take this!"

Tarlan caught the broadsword by the hilt. As he held it up, Elodie and Gulph came to his side. Kalia joined them. All three had their own swords raised.

"Three of the prophecy and one of the sand," said Hypiro, eyeing Kalia intently. "The witch at least will know the power of the

Sandspear to repel all magic, even that of the old world."

She threw the Sandspear again. It landed quivering beside Tarlan's foot. The ground quaked. Sand spilled upward, clutched briefly at his ankles, then subsided. Again the Sandspear hurled itself back into Hypiro's waiting fingers.

Now she was only ten strides away.

"Her powers are coming back," Kalia warned. "The next time she throws it—"

Before she could finish, the Sandspear was lancing through the air, aimed straight at Tarlan's throat.

Someone darted in front of him.

"No!" he yelled, horrified at the idea that one of his siblings—or his mother—had sacrificed themselves for him.

It wasn't them.

It was Melchior.

The Sandspear struck the wizard in the shoulder, knocking him to the ground. As he fell, Hypiro sprinted straight at Tarlan, dark lips peeled back from white teeth, white armor ablaze in the light of the bloodred sun. Her hand was outstretched, beckoning. But the Sandspear, lodged in Melchior's shoulder, wouldn't obey her command.

"That's the trouble with sand," said Tarlan, bringing up the broadsword. "It just slips through your fingers."

He brought the huge blade around. Its keen edge struck the neck of the Witch-Empress Hypiro, cutting her head clean off her body with a single stroke. The body ran on clumsily for three more steps before crumpling to the ground. The head rolled into the moat, and was gone.

Tarlan dropped the sword. Hands shaking, he turned to see Kalia tugging the Sandspear out of Melchior's shoulder. When she'd freed it, she tossed it aside, her face twisted with disgust.

"Oh, Melchior," she said. "I'm so sorry. After all we have been through, that I should have lived only to see you die."

"Die?" The word pierced Tarlan like an arrow. He ran to Melchior's side and dropped to his knees. "What do you mean? He can't die. It's just his shoulder. Look—it's hardly bleeding."

"Death comes . . . to us all," Melchior gasped.

"But . . . but you're a wizard. You can survive anything."

"Remember . . . the Isle of Stars, Tarlan."

"I *do* remember. That's what I'm talking about! The Isle of Stars—that's where you went under the water and got your powers back. Your magic! Your immortality! Everything!"

The wizard was shaking his head. "Not . . . everything."

The stones in the walls. When they were all lit up, that meant his powers were restored.

Tarlan's stomach lurched.

"There was one stone that didn't light up." The words were like splinters in his throat.

"One stone," Melchior agreed. "The Stone of Immortality."

"No! No!" Tarlan felt tears filling his eyes. He felt Elodie's hand on his left shoulder, Gulph's on his right. He felt sick. "I woke you too soon! I'm to blame!"

Now Melchior's hand was there too, gripping his.

"You did nothing wrong, Tarlan. Everything happens . . . for a reason."

The wizard coughed. Blood sprayed from his mouth, staining the white of his beard. His eyes clouded, then cleared.

"Gulph," he said, his voice thin but a little stronger. "Bring out the crown."

The weight of Gulph's hand left Tarlan's shoulder. Tarlan continued to stare into Melchior's watery eyes. Three points of light were reflected in each one. The prophecy stars.

Don't die, Melchior. Please don't die.

Something else was moving inside the wizard's eyes. Another reflection.

Something gold.

Now Gulph was kneeling beside Tarlan, handing something over to the wizard.

The crown of Toronia!

Tarlan's breath caught in his throat as he saw it for the first time.

The crown was very beautiful, smoothly curved and intricately etched with runes.

"My . . . staff," Melchior whispered.

Elodie picked up the ancient wooden stick, which the wizard had dropped when the Sandspear had impaled him. Then she too sank to her knees.

Melchior took the staff from her in one shaking hand, and the crown from Gulph in the other. He touched them together.

"A simple spell . . . to end with," he said. "One . . . two . . . three . . ."

He dropped the staff and handed the crown back to Gulph.

Tarlan gasped.

Even though Gulph had taken the crown, a second crown remained in Melchior's hand. It was identical to the first. The wizard gave it to Elodie.

They all stared in wonder.

Melchior was holding a third crown.

He held it out to Tarlan. Tarlan took it. It was very heavy. The metal was cold against his skin.

The wizard spread his palms. "That . . . is all . . . I have . . . ," he said. Then his head sank back onto the grass, and his eyes closed.

Melchior was dead.

Dropping the crown, Tarlan buried his face in his hands and began to weep.

CHAPTER 20

Gulph gaped at Melchior's body in disbelief. He'd known the wizard for such a short time. How could he be gone? It wasn't fair.

Seeming to work on their own, his hands carefully stowed the golden crown back into his pack.

Not just one crown now. One of three.

Beside him, Tarlan was still sobbing into his hands. He and Melchior had been through so much together.

He must be heartbroken.

It hurt Gulph's heart also, to see his brother so upset.

"Tarlan," he said, gently taking his brother's arm. "I think we should—"

A huge tremble threw him to the ground. Kalia tumbled past him, her arms flailing wildly as the ground heaved beneath her.

Gulph rolled instinctively, regaining his feet while Tarlan and Elodie were still sprawled in a tangle of limbs. A rumbling filled the air. Sand blew past in a storm. Gulph couldn't see, could barely hear.

"Get up!" he yelled, yanking his siblings to their feet.

Abruptly the air cleared. The howling wind reversed direction, sucking Kalia and the triplets toward the spot where Melchior lay. Gulph dug in his heels and held on to his family for dear life.

A single beam of yellow light erupted from Melchior's body. Gulph watched in awe as it punched its way skyward. It was aimed directly at the prophecy stars. He could feel its heat baking his face. At the same time it felt ice-cold.

The light split in two, then in two again. The individual beams continued to separate until there were thousands of intertwining strands all shooting upward in a spinning, screaming gale.

The ground continued to shake.

"This is what happens when a wizard dies!" Gulph shouted, remembering the awful moment when Limmoni had been executed in Idilliam.

Her magic went into Brutan's corpse and rose him from the dead.

"Melchior's magic is leaving the world," cried Kalia. "I fear this means he must have been the last."

"The last?" Elodie shouted.

"She means the last wizard," Gulph replied with sudden understanding.

The ground split apart right at Gulph's feet. Rocks burst forth spraying black soil. Gulph grabbed Elodie's hand and together they ran, vaulting over the large cracks that were opening up beneath them.

"Where's Tarlan?" Elodie cried as they cleared yet another gaping chasm.

Gulph shot a glance back over his shoulder just in time to see a black-cloaked figure snatch up the Sandspear from where it lay near Melchior's body and vanish into the turbulent air.

"Tarlan's all right! He's got the Sandspear! Where's Mother?"

"I saw her running the other way," Elodie replied. "I think she's safe."

As they continued to flee the earthquake, an alarming thought came to Gulph.

We're heading straight back into the battle!

But when they finally reached stable ground, he saw that everyone still on the battlefield was scattering too. Tarlan's pack of animals was fleeing back into the woods, yipping and screeching in panic, while The Hammer and Captain Ariston were directing the Army of Survivors out of danger in a remarkably orderly fashion. Elodie's ghosts seemed to have vanished altogether, while the Galadronians . . .

They're running away!

And so they were. Everywhere Gulph looked, he saw a rainbow of colorful cloaks in full retreat. Even over the rumble of the earthquake he could hear their shouts and screams:

"She's dead! Hypiro is dead!"

"Toronia is cursed!"

As for the sand-warriors . . .

With Hypiro dead, they must have just disintegrated.

Elodie tugged at his hand. "Gulph—slow down! We're safe!"

He slowed to a trot, then stopped altogether. Chest heaving, he stared back across the battlefield. The land was crisscrossed with tremendous cracks all centered on a single spot: the place where Melchior had fallen. A single figure knelt there, head bowed. Nearby, a woman in a gray robe was picking herself up.

"Tarlan and Mother!" breathed Elodie. "They're all right!"

She started forward, but Gulph held her back. "Give them a moment."

The air rippled and Elodie's ghost army appeared with Lady Darrand leading the way.

"The enemy is vanquished," Lady Darrand announced, her pale face seeming to glow. "What are your orders, my queen?"

Elodie looked down at the golden crown in her hand. She'd been clutching it the whole time they'd been fleeing the earthquake. Now it seemed she was seeing it for the first time.

"Follow them," she said firmly. "Make sure they reach their ships. Make sure they leave Toronia."

"Would you have me give them a message to take to their homeland?"

Gulph saw a smile at the corner of Lady Darrand's mouth.

"Yes," Elodie replied. "Tell them never to return."

Leaving Elodie to finish sending her ghost army on their way, Gulph crossed the battlefield to where his troops were resting. He moved among them, congratulating those who were still standing, assuring the tired and injured that help was on its way. Halfway round he came across Cedric and Sylva tending to the wounded.

"Thank you," he told them. "I'm glad you're all right."

Whenever he came across someone who was crying—and there were many of these—he told them how sorry he was for their loss.

Toward the end of Gulph's circuit, The Hammer caught up with him and draped one enormous arm around his shoulders.

"Victory is ours!" the big man boomed. "You have won the battle, King Gulph! You have won the day!"

"We have won the field," Gulph said. "But not the war."

The Hammer frowned. "How so?"

"Lord Vicerin is still at large. This won't be over until he's been found, and made to answer for his crimes."

The Hammer looked uncertainly at the exhausted men and women sprawled before them. "Your soldiers are loyal, to be sure. But after such a fight . . ."

Gulph rubbed his eyes. He felt even more tired than when he'd climbed the chasm out of Celestis. His head ached. His whole body ached.

Suddenly he wished Captain Ossilius were here to guide him.

"I await your orders, Your Highness," said The Hammer.

And Gulph discovered that he knew what to do after all.

"You're right. Our soldiers have done enough for today. Take them back to Castle Darrand. Give them food. Tend their wounds. Let them rest." He hesitated, wondering what Ossilius would say. Then he had it. "We'll do this one step at a time."

Leaving The Hammer and Captain Ariston to rouse the Army of Survivors, Gulph picked his way back through the maze of cracks to where Tarlan was kneeling. Elodie was already there. As Gulph arrived, she was bending down to pluck something from the ground. Curious, Gulph leaned in for a better look.

Where Melchior had lain, a small patch of wild yellow flowers had sprung up. They glowed in the sunset light. Elodie tucked the single bloom she'd picked into her hair. They remained there in silence for a while, the three of them together, as the sun sank slowly below the western horizon.

At last Tarlan stood. Tears had cut through the dirt on his face. Gulph stared at him, feeling suddenly uneasy.

Something's wrong here.

Gulph shook off the thought. "You can't blame yourself, Tarlan," he said. "Melchior told us this was meant to be."

"Gulph's right." Elodie put her hand on Tarlan's arm. Then her face dropped. "Where's Mother?"

Tarlan looked around. "I don't know. I saw her here before, but . . ."

His heart sinking, Gulph scanned the battlefield. Kalia was nowhere to be seen.

Tarlan's grief seemed to shift as this new worry made him spring into action.

"Theeta!" he yelled. "Nasheen! Kitheen!"

Within a few moments the three thorrods were there. Tarlan gave them instructions, and the gigantic birds flew off in separate directions, skimming low over the torn-up battlefield in search of Kalia.

Gulph's eyes returned to his brother.

Something's wrong.

"Tarlan! Where's the Sandspear?"

"What?" Tarlan looked confused. "How would I know?"

A figure in a black cloak, snatching it up . . .

"Where's your cloak?"

Tarlan's hand brushed the shoulder of his breastplate. "I lost it. Somewhere by the castle, I think."

"Then who . . . ?"

A terrible roar echoed across the battlefield. Something enormous lumbered out of the twilight.

One of the thorrods coming back? Gulph wondered. *It's big enough . . . but it doesn't sound right.*

The immense creature plodding toward them wasn't a thorrod

but a giant cat with a rust-colored mane. When it shrugged its shoulders, a pair of enormous batlike wings unfurled from its back. Another shrug, and a huge scorpion's tail reared up over its back. The tail was tipped by a vicious-looking hook dripping clear liquid.

"It's a manticore!" Elodie gasped. "I've only ever seen them in books. But it's made of . . ." Her voice faltered.

The manticore was made of red sand. The same red as the stones from which Castle Vicerin had been built.

Riding on the winged monster was a tall man wearing a tattered black cloak. Tarlan's cloak. He was carrying the Sandspear.

The man was Lord Vicerin.

"No," Elodie moaned. "No, no, no!"

The jaws of the manticore parted to reveal two rows of wicked fangs. Gulph tried to tell himself they were only made of sand.

It doesn't matter. They'll go through you like a newly sharpened sword.

Vicerin had revealed his own tombstone teeth in a wild grin. He loosened Tarlan's cloak from where it was tied around his neck and tossed it into the wind, revealing Tarlan and Elodie's jewels hanging against his chest. The movement also revealed someone sitting behind Vicerin on the manticore's back: a slender woman with red-gold hair. She was completely encircled by sand-colored chains.

"Mother!" Gulph shouted, running forward. "Let her go!"

"No, Gulph!" Kalia screamed. "Get back!"

Lord Vicerin jabbed the Sandspear in Gulph's direction. The

weapon stretched out, growing longer. Before Gulph could react, it struck him in the chest, knocking him to the ground.

"Gulph!" Tarlan sprang toward him.

The end of the spear burst open, growing dozens of tentacles that proceeded to crawl up Gulph's chest. He cried out in revulsion and tried to bat them away. The tentacles settled on his throat, tightened, then retreated at blinding speed. The elongated Sandspear shrank back into itself until it was balanced once more in Lord Vicerin's hands.

Dangling from its end was Gulph's green jewel.

"Three jewels for three realms!" Vicerin crowed.

He plucked the jewel from the Sandspear and added it to the others hanging around his neck.

"Three realms," he repeated, with an expression that was as much a snarl as it was a smile. "But only one king."

Tarlan lifted Gulph to his feet, then drew his sword.

"Come on, brother!" he hissed. "If we rush him together . . ."

But Vicerin had turned the Sandspear on Kalia. The manticore swayed beneath them, its bat-wings flapping idly, the tip of its undoubtedly poisonous tail twitching in the twilight.

"If you want your mother to live, I suggest you stay where you are, boys," Vicerin crooned. "You too, my dear Elodie."

"If you do anything to hurt her, I'll kill you!" Elodie shouted.

"Well, yes, but you tried to do that once before, did you not?"

"What do you want?" Gulph cast a frantic eye east across the darkening battlefield, but The Hammer had already led his army out of sight. Elodie's ghosts had vanished on their mission to escort the Galadronians out of Toronia. And Tarlan's pack had retreated to the sanctuary of the woods.

We're on our own.

"I want answers," said Vicerin in answer to Gulph's question. With his free hand, he fingered the three jewels. "Possessing these trinkets is one thing. Knowing what to do with them is quite another. They have power—mmm, yes, oh I can feel it throbbing through them. But power must be directed, yes?"

"You won't get anything from us!" shouted Tarlan furiously.

"Even if we did know, we wouldn't tell you," added Elodie.

Vicerin's face grew stiff. More tentacles sprouted from the end of the Sandspear. They clamped themselves onto Kalia's head, smothering her face completely. Her body squirmed against the chains, and her head tossed from side to side.

"If you want your beloved mother to breathe again, you will tell me now," Lord Vicerin intoned.

"But we don't know what—" Elodie began.

"The old throne room," Gulph blurted. "Underneath Idilliam, there's a kind of cave. That's where the thrones are."

Vicerin's eyes were barely visible in the gathering dusk, but Gulph could see that they'd narrowed. "And the jewels?"

"All over the walls. Green gems, just like those. I think . . . I think that's where they're supposed to go."

"You *think*? You don't *know*?"

Behind Vicerin, Kalia's heels were drumming weakly against the manticore's back. Her face was completely covered by the sand tentacles.

"You heard him!" Tarlan yelled. Gulph could feel his brother's body quivering with rage. "That's all we know! Now let our mother go!"

A loose lock of hair had fallen across Vicerin's brow. Delicately he patted it back into place, then smoothed his hand over the top of his head. After a moment's pause, he gave the Sandspear a slight twist. The tentacles detached themselves from Kalia's face with a dreadful sucking sound and retracted back into the magical weapon.

Kalia fell forward, gasping for breath.

"Mother!" cried Elodie.

"It's all right," said Gulph, putting his arm round her. "She's all right."

"Your mother is alive," Vicerin agreed. "I believe I will keep her that way, for a while at least. She may prove useful. As for you three brats"—he lifted the Sandspear over his head—"now that the prophecy is dead, it is only fitting that you should die too. How nice that you will have a chance to do so together."

Laughing, Lord Vicerin stabbed the Sandspear at the ground

and swept it in a wide circle. The fractured soil began to heave.

Another earthquake! Gulph thought frantically.

But it wasn't an earthquake. Wherever the Sandspear pointed, golden figures began to rear up out of the ground. Sand-warriors. Each one was twice the height of a man.

Leaving his newly summoned army to claw its way into the twilight, Lord Vicerin tugged at the mane of the manticore, turning it north and urging it on with an excited shout. The great sand-beast galloped across the battlefield and into the darkness, carrying with it Kalia, the three green jewels, and the last shred of Gulph's hope.

"If it's a fight you want . . . ," Tarlan began, drawing his sword as the army of sand-giants surrounded them.

". . . it's a fight you'll get!" cried Elodie, completing her brother's words and brandishing her own blade.

But Gulph could only mourn.

We won the battle but lost the war, he thought in despair. *Which means we've lost everything.*

The circle of sand-giants closed in. The triplets stood with their backs together, swords at the ready. Above them, a purple blanket of cloud rolled across the heavens, extinguishing even the prophecy stars.

Darkness fell.

ACT THREE

CHAPTER 21

"Watch your left!"

Elodie whirled at the sound of Tarlan's voice and slashed her sword into the darkness. She felt the blade quiver as it sliced through the body of a sand-giant. The creature rocked backward, barely visible in the gloom.

"Get back!" shouted Gulph, stabbing blindly at the oncoming enemy horde.

Elodie could feel every movement her brothers made, so closely were their backs pressed together. She felt Gulph's shoulders flex as he thrust out his blade. She sensed Tarlan's legs stretching as he swept his sword upward in a high arc. Every time one of them struck a blow, the air filled with spraying sand.

The night seemed to thicken around them. Elodie fought on, willing the battle rage to fill her vision with the familiar red mist. But there was no mist, only darkness.

Footsteps on my right! She swung her sword and more sand flew.

Something whistling—there! She ducked beneath a hissing blade and cut the legs from beneath her invisible foe.

A rattle of stones! She parried a heavy blow from a sand sword, somehow managing to turn her body and deflecting the enemy back away into the night.

The clouds parted, spilling starlight across the battlefield and revealing the towering figures of the sand-giants looming all around them. The sand they were made from was red—the same red as the stones of Castle Vicerin. Their faces had mouths but no eyes. Each of them had two pairs of arms.

At the sight of such formidable foes, Elodie wished the darkness would return.

"Theeta!" Tarlan roared, pushing back yet another of the huge rust-colored warriors. "Bring Brock! Bring Greythorn! Bring them all!"

Vicerin's sand-warriors recoiled a little at the sound of his voice, and a spark of hope kindled in Elodie's heart. Gold feathers flashed in the starlight as Theeta led Nasheen and Kitheen into view, their beating wings just visible over the heads of the enemy.

Elodie's excitement died as a flock of sand-eagles swooped down to surround the thorrods.

"Fight through!" Tarlan commanded.

The beaks of the thorrods snapped, and their huge talons clawed, ripping the sand-eagles apart. But for every bird they brought down, two more took its place. Wings of sand swarmed around the thorrods, dragging them down toward the ground.

"Theeta!" Tarlan wailed.

How long can the sand creature keep re-forming now that Vicerin's gone? Elodie wondered.

Long enough for them all to die?

She glimpsed sudden movement in the corner of her eye.

"Tarlan!" she shouted. "Behind you!"

Distracted by the thorrods, Tarlan hadn't seen a sand-warrior driving a spear down toward his chest. He jumped aside, and the barbed weapon thudded harmlessly into the ground. Yet, in saving himself, he'd left Gulph's back exposed.

Elodie brought up her sword just in time to block a sand ax aimed at Gulph's neck. Gulph tripped, but managed to turn his stumble into a forward flip that carried him over the slashing blade of yet another of the four-armed enemy. Recovering, he rejoined his brother and sister, and the clouds closed in once more.

Blind again, thought Elodie in despair, listening to the hideous, voiceless crackling sounds of millions of grains of sand grinding against one another. *Any moment now we'll be dead too. Just three more bodies lying on this . . .*

She froze.

"What is it?" snapped Tarlan. "Elodie! Are you—"

"Bodies!" she cried. "Of course!"

"What are you talking about?" Gulph grunted as he parried two colossal blows in rapid succession.

No time to explain!

All around Elodie, the air was full of sand. Sand like tiny insects. Sand like grains of light, shining even in the dark.

Elodie let herself ride on the sand. Its heat carried her out over the battlefield, the blood-soaked grassy plain where hundreds now lay dead. Perhaps thousands. Except . . .

I am not going to them. I am bringing them to me!

The sand came from the desert. The desert brought heat. The heat flowed into her, drawing with it all the sleeping power of the dead, gathering it up, waking it up.

"Wake up!" Elodie yelled. "Wake up and rise! We need your help! Rise up and fight!"

Wind gusted, not merely parting the clouds but driving them back. A wave of starlight crashed over the battlefield. As the light came down, phantoms began to rise like shadows in the mist.

As the ghost soldiers closed in around the enemy, five enormous creatures reared up nearby. The ghosts of bears. Standing on their hind legs, the enormous phantom animals were even taller than the sand-giants.

Tarlan gasped. "They were in my pack!"

The ghost soldiers fell upon the sand-warriors, their wailing battle cries sending a chill down Elodie's spine. The roars of the bears were even eerier—thick and watery, as if their throats were clogged with the mud in which their bodies had been lying.

"Come to me!" she yelled, opening her arms and using all the force she could muster to draw the dead toward her. "Come to us!"

More ghost soldiers surged out of the night. More animal spirits heaved themselves up from the ground—foxes, wolves, big cats, and a pair of huge, hissing snakes. Ghostly claws and phantom swords ripped into the bodies of the sand-giants, reducing them to clouds of red dust swirling in the night air. Every time a cloud tried to re-form into a soldier, another ghost was there to tear it apart.

Something screamed across the sky. Elodie glanced up to see a flock of ghost hawks racing to the aid of the thorrods. The sand-eagles were no match for their scything claws, and within a few breaths the entire enemy flock was nothing more than a rain of red sand scattering over the ground.

The wind gusted, stronger now. It gathered up the fallen sand and blew it high into the sky. The sand spread, thinned, disappeared. The clouds vanished too. The stars shone down, three blazing brightest of all.

Elodie doubled over, suddenly exhausted. She gasped in one breath after another. The night air tasted cool and clear.

"Are you all right?" said Gulph. She nodded, unable to speak.

"That was incredible!" cried Tarlan. "Theeta! Are you all okay?"

The thorrod squawked something in return. Then she turned to Elodie and cawed again. Elodie had no idea what the bird had said, but she fancied it might have been "Thank you."

"I'm okay," she said, straightening up. "But we're not."

"What do you mean?" said Tarlan.

"I mean that for every breath we waste here, Lord Vicerin gets another step closer to Idilliam."

"More like twenty steps," Tarlan suggested, "given how fast that manticore was going."

"Twenty more steps between us and our mother," Gulph pointed out.

"If he hurts her . . . !" snarled Tarlan.

"We've got to catch him," said Elodie. "There's no time to waste."

"Then we'll fly!" Tarlan pursed his lips and whistled.

At once, the three thorrods swooped down. They landed in a line, shaking the last few grains of sand from their feathers. Elodie's new ghost army pressed close behind them, grim-faced soldiers and panting beasts all eyeing the triplets with keen interest.

"Follow us," Elodie told a man dressed in the uniform of a Vicerin guard. Death had turned the blue of his sash to a watery gray. "All of you, follow us as fast as you can. Bring the ghost animals too, if they will come."

The phantom soldier nodded. Around him, a sea of ghost faces mouthed agreement, their combined voices the faintest whisper on the night air.

Elodie ran to Nasheen. The white-breasted thorrod had already dipped her neck to receive her. As she grabbed the giant bird's ruff, Elodie saw Gulph springing lightly onto Kitheen's back. Tarlan and Theeta had already taken to the air.

"Move fast!" she shouted to her ghost army as Nasheen carried her into the sky. "We cannot afford to delay!"

The thorrods flew low over the battlefield, heading for the woods to the northeast. A corridor of broken trees clearly marked the route taken by Lord Vicerin as he had carried Kalia toward Idilliam on the back of his lion-headed steed.

As the group approached the forest, a huge pack of living beasts and birds spilled out from among the trees. Leading them were three animals she recognized at once: Greythorn, Brock, and Filos.

"Follow us!" Tarlan ordered his pack, echoing Elodie's own command to the ghosts. "Come as fast as you can and don't stop for anything!"

An unearthly chorus of roars, howls, barks, and screeches rose up from the trees. Elodie supposed Tarlan could understand everything that they were saying. The thought made her feel strong.

"Follow! Follow fast!" Now it was Gulph who was shouting, not to an army of ghosts or a pack of animals, but to a column of human soldiers trooping slowly along a forest track—the remains of his army making their way back to Castle Darrand.

"Where do you go so fast?" boomed a voice from the ground. Elodie saw a flash of red hair and realized it belonged to the man known as The Hammer.

"Idilliam!" Gulph replied. "After Vicerin. He has our mother. We'll meet you there!"

"Yes, my king!" The Hammer's mighty voice dwindled as they sped past.

The thorrods flew fast through the night. The stars revolved, and the darkness between them grew deeper. The steady rhythm of Nasheen's beating wings lulled Elodie toward sleep, but each time she felt her chin lolling against her chest, she forced herself awake. She didn't want to miss a single moment of this.

Time blurred. The landscape slid past, and before Elodie knew it, the battle-scarred fields of Ritherlee had melted into the rich green forests of Isur, while ahead . . .

. . . ahead, the sky was on fire!

"It can't be morning yet," said Gulph.

Nor was it. The three prophecy stars hung over Idilliam, their light filling the seemingly endless night with a peculiar, shifting glow. A light that was green and gold and red, all at the same time. A light of all colors, focused in a single place.

"It's beautiful," gasped Elodie. "And terrible."

"Like a storm," muttered Tarlan.

On they sped, into a sky that flashed and raged, as if it knew that the moment Toronia's fate would be decided was at hand.

CHAPTER 22

It hurt Tarlan's eyes to look at the colors in the sky. He could see that Elodie, sitting alert and upright on Nasheen's back, was entranced. Gulph too seemed gripped by the sight. But Tarlan was more interested in what was happening on the ground.

"There!" he shouted, pointing toward a smoking trail of destruction leading through the Isurian forest, which was thinning now as they neared the rocky terrain surrounding Idilliam.

He tugged at Theeta's feathers, steering the thorrod down toward the scar in the trees. There at the head of the trail, still riding on the hideous manticore, was Lord Vicerin. In his right hand he held the Sandspear. Kalia was seated behind him, her body almost completely wrapped in chains.

The manticore was moving with incredible speed, now running, now flying. Its lion's jaws tore down any trees that stood in its way. Its great bat-wings carried it up and over any obstacles too big to destroy. Its scorpion tail pointed triumphantly toward the sky.

Following Vicerin, in a long line that stretched all the way back to the dark horizon, was an army of red, four-armed sand-warriors. Each time the manticore leaped, Vicerin jabbed the Sandspear toward an outcrop of rock, which exploded into dust. As the dust settled, more warriors rose up to join his growing attack force.

"Is there no stopping him?" cried Gulph, bringing Kitheen in to fly close on Tarlan's left.

"One thing at a time," Tarlan replied through gritted teeth. "First we need to beat him to the throne room. Come on, Theeta!"

Digging in his heels, he urged her over the heads of Vicerin and his sand-borne soldiers and on toward Idilliam. Vicerin's face was turned up toward them. The flashing colors of the prophecy stars painted his pale cheeks with weird streaks of color. Vicerin's mouth opened as he shouted something, but he was too far away, and his words were lost.

As they flew over the chasm toward the ruined city, Tarlan's eyes finally began to adjust to the strange rainbow of light that was boiling over the blackened buildings. The last time he'd made a flight like this, Idilliam had been ablaze. Now that the fires were out, Tarlan thought he'd never seen a more sorry-looking place.

The shells of burned-out buildings lay slumped against each other. Splintered towers jutted like broken teeth. Even under the vivid colors of the light in the sky, all looked drab and gray.

"It's dead," said Tarlan, shocked by the extent of the devastation. "The whole city is dead."

"But Celestis isn't," Gulph replied. "And that's where the throne room is. Can your thorrods fly down into the chasm?"

Tarlan patted Theeta's neck proudly. "My friends can fly anywhere!"

"Strange wings," cawed Theeta, rearing up in distress.

"What do you see, Theeta?"

"High light. Strange wings."

She stabbed her beak toward the prophecy stars, where two shining forms were just visible, spiraling down from the glowing sky. They rode fast on enormous green wings, their crystalline bodies capturing the many colors of the storm and turning them all to a familiar, dazzling green.

"The wyverns!" Tarlan exclaimed.

"Wyverns?" said Gulph uncertainly. "What are they?"

"Creatures from before the war. I found them in the mountains. I . . . I think I woke them up."

"What are they doing here?"

"I don't know."

"Are they dangerous?"

Tarlan hesitated. "I suppose they are, in a way."

"I saw something that looked like them," said Elodie, sounding awed. "In the Realm of the Dead. It helped me when I was fighting Brutan."

"Maybe they're here to help us too," Tarlan said.

The two wyverns dropped like falling rocks toward a vast pile of blackened rubble heaped in the center of Idilliam—the pitiful remains of Castle Tor.

They told me I wasn't ready before. Does this mean I'm ready now?

But ready for what?

He kicked his heels, turning Theeta down toward the chasm, which was so deep that even the sky's brilliant light couldn't penetrate it. It wouldn't be long before Lord Vicerin got here. Time to move.

No sooner had Theeta begun to descend than a tremendous crashing sound echoed across the chasm. Looking up in alarm, Tarlan saw the two wyverns tearing into the shattered remains of Castle Tor. Screeching, they ripped up great chunks of stonework and hurled them into the chasm. They plowed huge furrows through the mass of fallen buildings, gathering up mountains of rubble and tipping them into the waiting abyss.

"What are they doing?" wailed Gulph.

"Look out!" cried Elodie as stone blocks began hailing around them.

As the thorrods weaved through the deadly rain, the triplets raised their hands over their heads to protect themselves from the smaller rocks.

"There's magic at work here!" Tarlan shouted.

He could see it was true, could *smell* it. Not only were the wyverns gathering the debris, but they were somehow gathering the light, too. Their bodies burned with it. Their green crystal wings grew extra membranes of flickering color, becoming larger and larger until each one spanned half the city. Within moments, all the buildings were gone. The wyverns had flattened the city to ground level, leaving only smoke-shrouded plain surrounded by the ever-present chasm.

Except . . .

"No!" Gulph cried.

"Higher!" barked Tarlan. "Fly higher, now!" With a growing sense of dread, he urged the three thorrods up through the rain of stones.

The chasm was gone.

As the dust settled, Tarlan saw that the wyverns had taken what had once been the city of Idilliam and packed it down into the chasm, filling it all the way to the top. They had wiped clean the land where the city had once stood.

And buried Celestis forever.

"My friends!" cried Gulph, distraught. "I told them to wait here

for me! I told them I'd come back to Celestis! And now they're . . .
they're . . ."

"Gulph," said Elodie, "maybe it's not as bad as—"

"How bad do you want it to get?" Gulph replied, tears spilling
from his eyes.

Tarlan surveyed the devastation with growing anger. Had he
really thought the wyverns were here to help?

How could I have been so stupid?

"Come to me!" he bellowed at the wyverns, both of which were
now circling nearby on wings returned to normal size. He tugged
at Theeta's ruff and she reared up. "Get over here, now! Answer
for what you've done!"

He didn't really expect them to obey. But, to his surprise,
they flexed their wings and flew over to where the three thorrods were circling.

Each of the wyverns was at least as big as Seethan, the great old
thorrod who'd been so horribly slain by the Helkrags. The draft
from their enormous wings buffeted Theeta, and Tarlan had to
cling tight to stop himself being thrown from her back. Out of the
corner of his eye, he saw Elodie and Gulph holding on for dear life
to their own thorrod steeds.

The wyverns weaved back and forth in the light-filled air. Their
golden eyes glowed. Their red claws opened and closed, over and
over again. Tarlan had the sudden, strange feeling that the many

facets of their green crystal bodies were about to unfold, revealing magic the likes of which he'd never seen.

"Why did you do that?" he demanded.

"We did what needed to be done," said one of the wyverns. It had a notch in its wing, which Tarlan remembered from their first encounter in the mountains.

"What does that mean?"

"In order to rise," said the second wyvern, "the world must fall."

"We were here then," said the first wyvern, "and we are here now."

"The world is a circle," said the second wyvern. "Now it has turned."

"Stop talking in riddles!" snapped Tarlan. "What about all the people you just killed?"

Theeta's body began to tremble beneath him. He stroked her neck to calm her, then realized that she wasn't afraid. She was shaking because *everything* was shaking—the air, the ground, even the all-surrounding light that had turned the night into an impossibly colorful day.

"What's happening?" gasped Elodie.

"Falling. Rising. Turning." The wyvern with the notched wing bowed its crystal head.

"Down there!" cried Gulph. "Look!"

Tarlan stared down past Theeta's beating wings. An immense

crack had opened in the middle of the dusty plain where Idilliam had once stood. As he watched, a second crack crisscrossed the first. The ground was vibrating, humming like a vast and faceless choir. Then it tore itself to pieces.

Something speared upward through the largest of the cracks. A tower rising up from beneath the ground. Its diamond sides shone in the flickering storm. More towers followed, one after the next, this one reflecting the air's golden glow, that one catching red bolts of lightning as they lanced out of the clouds, yet another pulsing with pure green radiance.

"It's made of crystal!" cried Elodie.

Gulph's eyes were wide. "Celestis!"

"So that's what it looks like," said Tarlan. "Maybe your friends are safe after all, Gulph."

A tremendous cracking noise echoed through the heavens as more structures broke through from underground—houses and halls, inns and armories and countless smaller buildings that might have been shops or storehouses, bakeries or barns, a castle decked with a hundred ornate turrets. Like the sky above them, the structures shone with many colors—the red of rubies, the blue of sapphires, the yellow of topaz. An entire city of crystal, climbing its way back into the light.

"Why have you done this?" said Tarlan, looking the first wyvern in the eye.

"Because now you are ready," the wyvern replied.

Tarlan shivered.

Below, the rebirth of Celestis was almost complete. Tarlan watched in wonder as the final few buildings of the newly awoken city settled into place. Then the tall central tower—the first part of the city to have emerged—rotated regally on its base. A hundred green turrets unfolded from its diamond roof, a field of emerald flowers opening their petals to the light. Something like a ripple passed through the entire city, from one side to the other. Then, finally, all was still.

"Is this it?" said Elodie. "Is this really Celestis?" Her eyes were shining and her cheeks were flushed.

Gulph nodded. "The buildings seem to have moved around a bit, but I recognize Lady Redina's house, and the big meeting square, and . . . oh!"

"What?" Tarlan asked.

Gulph pointed to a tiny crystal building near the shore of what looked like a large pond. "Our mother's cottage."

The three thorrods had been circling, as entranced by the rise of Celestis as the triplets were, but now Theeta gave a warning screech.

"Enemy!"

Tarlan looked across what had once been a chasm, and which was now filled to the brim with the rubble from the ruined city of Idilliam. Speeding toward them over the packed-down layers of smashed stones and crushed timbers was the manticore. Riding on its back—no, *standing* on its back—was Lord Vicerin. Behind him came his army of sand-warriors.

"He's coming," Tarlan called to the others. "Look!"

"There's too many of them," said Gulph. "And he's so *fast!*"

"My thorrods are fast too, Gulph," Tarlan replied. "Anyway, they'll have to slow down when they reach the city. That's when we'll strike!"

Gulph straightened his shoulders. "This is it, isn't it?"

"Time to fight for Toronia," said Elodie. Gripping Nasheen's feathers with one hand, she drew her sword with the other. "Are you ready?"

Tarlan grinned first at his sister, then his brother. "I've never been more ready for anything!"

Already Lord Vicerin had reached the arched gateway leading into Celestis. As they watched, he led his army down the wide central street, straight to the foot of the newborn citadel with the diamond tower at its center. There, as his warriors fanned out around him, he brought the manticore to a halt and raised the Sandspear above his head.

"Now!" cried Tarlan, pulling his sword from its scabbard. He pressed his knees against Theeta's flanks. "Dive, Theeta! Dive fast and fly true!"

She was moving even before the words had left his mouth.

Nasheen and Kitheen fell into formation to her left and right. Wind screamed past Tarlan's face, blowing his long hair out behind him. Light reflected up from the facets of the diamond tower, bathing him in color.

Just the three of us, he thought grimly. *If the wyverns joined us, we might stand a better chance.*

He glanced back, and saw to his surprise that the two wyverns were flying close behind Theeta's tail. It was almost as if they'd heard his thoughts.

Maybe they did!

They sped toward the vast courtyard that lay in front of the diamond tower. The courtyard was filled with tall red sand-warriors, all turned to face their master as he drove the giant manticore toward the door of the tower.

"Stop there!" Tarlan roared. "Stop and face us!"

Vicerin whirled round, one arm stretched out for balance, the other held high as he brandished the Sandspear aloft. Behind him, Kalia squirmed against her chains. The manticore snarled and lashed its scorpion tail at the oncoming thorrods. Steaming liquid squirted from the tip, and Tarlan steered Theeta in a wide circle to avoid the poisonous spray.

"There is much I would like to say to you!" Vicerin grinned, displaying his huge, horselike teeth. "But what I most want to offer you is my heartfelt thanks!"

A group of sand-warriors stabbed upward with their spears, but the thorrods were just out of reach. Tarlan led Nasheen, Kitheen, and the wyverns in a slowly tightening spiral over Vicerin's head.

"You won't thank us when we're done with you!" he shouted down.

"Oh, but I *do* thank you, my dear, dear children. By bringing those wretched wyvern creatures here, you have delivered Celestis right into my hands. It does make everything so much simpler, do you not think?"

Tarlan could sense Theeta wanting to fly lower, but he held her in check. He was all too aware of how vulnerable Kalia was, chained on the back of the manticore behind Vicerin. One false move and . . .

"I shall enjoy living here as king," Vicerin went on. "And I am so glad you arrived in time to witness my coronation. Also in time to die, of course. I shall enjoy that part most of all, I think."

"If you dare to touch my children, I will kill you myself!" shouted Kalia.

Lord Vicerin's face contorted with fury. He drew back his hand and slapped Kalia. She fell back, crying out, blood running from a cut above her eye.

Hot anger rushed up through Tarlan's body. He felt his fingers tighten in Theeta's ruff, felt his lips peel back from his teeth.

"Leave her alone!" he roared.

Together they plunged down into the courtyard. Nasheen and Kitheen followed, lashing out with their talons at the waiting sand-warriors. Gulph and Elodie swung their swords, cutting through the sea of upraised weapons. Tarlan made straight for Vicerin.

As Theeta drove her way down, the manticore's tail stabbed up toward her throat. She banked to the side, narrowly avoiding its venomous tip. At the same time, Vicerin brought the Sandspear down on the manticore's back. A shudder ran through the beast's rust-red body, and then suddenly its wings were flying free, each with a life of its own.

"Again, Theeta!" cried Tarlan, guiding her round for another pass.

As she circled back, the disembodied wings grew teeth and claws and wrapped themselves around the two wyverns, which were busy carving their way through the ranks of the sand-warriors. The crystal beasts broke off their attack, fighting furiously to disentangle themselves from the embrace of these strange new foes.

"Tarlan!" shouted Kalia. "Don't try to—"

Vicerin struck her across the mouth. Tarlan howled with rage and spurred Theeta forward once more. Again they came close, and again the manticore's lashing tail drove them back. Vicerin spun the Sandspear in his hand, causing a wormlike creature to sprout from the place on the manticore's back where its wings had been. It lashed its coils around Theeta's claws, dragging her down.

"Theeta fall!" she screamed.

Without thinking, Tarlan scrambled out onto her wing, rolled over its trailing edge, and grabbed the thick feathers underneath. Now he was hanging directly under her wing while she flapped furiously in her efforts to stay airborne. Each flap brought him close to Theeta's dangling claws, and the worm-thing that had enfolded them. Each flap also threatened to wrench his arm from its socket.

Ignoring the agony in his shoulder, Tarlan waited for the next low point of the wing's arc, whereupon he slashed out and down with his sword. The first time he missed. The second time his blade sliced clean through the neck of the worm, and sending a spray of sand directly into Vicerin's face.

"Up!" he cried, crawling painfully up Theeta's flank and onto her back.

Theeta didn't need telling twice. With her claws released, she quickly gained enough height to clear the manticore's tail, then came round for yet another attack.

Fighting for breath, Tarlan hastily scanned the courtyard for the other thorrods. He spotted them both engaged in furious combat with a squad of sand-warriors near the door to the tower. Both Gulph and Elodie were reaching far out from the backs of their flying steeds, beating the enemy with their swords. Both looked exhausted.

"Wait, Theeta," said Tarlan, reining her in. Anger throbbed at his temples, but he forced himself to ignore it. Forced himself to stop and think.

Gulph cut down a pair of sand-warriors. Vicerin pointed the Sandspear and two more took their place.

Between them, Elodie and Nasheen bowled over a whole column of enemy soldiers. It took just one gesture from Vicerin to bring them back to life.

The worm growing from the manticore's back had already grown two new heads.

"What does it take to bring him down?" cried Tarlan in frustration.

"Shining wings," said Theeta.

"What?"

"Crush city. Crush human."

Of course. The wyverns. If they're powerful enough to flatten Idilliam, Lord Vicerin should be no trouble.

With all his heart, Tarlan wished the wyverns would attack.

"But how do I know they'll obey me?"

No sooner had he said this to Theeta than something green flashed in front of him. It was the wyverns, disentangled from the manticore's free-flying wings and diving in perfect formation toward Lord Vicerin.

Attack!

Obey!

Tarlan realized he was hearing the wyverns' thoughts. Then he realized that they echoed his own. They had heard his command.

But it wasn't a command. I just thought it.

The first wyvern hit the manticore's lion head. The second hit its scorpion tail. Lord Vicerin and Kalia flew high into the air, and were immediately enveloped by a cloud of red sand. The diamond tower trembled from bottom to top. The door at its base broke into three great shards of crystal, which fell and smashed. Clouds of dust billowed out.

The wyverns immediately climbed back into the air, leaving Tarlan to rub sand from his eyes. Gradually the cloud thinned. Vicerin was nowhere to be seen.

Tarlan faltered. The glimmer of hope that had risen in his breast died away to nothing. It wasn't just Vicerin who had disappeared.

Kalia was gone too.

CHAPTER 23

When the wyverns crashed down on top of the manticore, they sent a huge cloud of sand rolling over Gulph. As Kitheen blundered blindly into it, Gulph tried desperately to hold on. But the black-breasted thorrod swerved, and his fingers slipped through the giant bird's feathers. Losing his grip, he fell.

He hit the ground hard, instinctively rolling to absorb the impact. Regaining his feet, he immediately checked that his pack was still strapped securely to his back. To his relief, he could still feel the curved metal edges of the three crowns through the rough material.

They're safe! But am I?

He peered into the slowly clearing dust. His first concern was Kalia. He'd seen her thrown clear from the manticore's back when the wyverns had struck. Now she'd vanished.

I'm losing everyone. First Ossilius and Pip. Now my mother!

Something huge slammed into his shoulders, sending him flying. He turned his tumble into a somersault, spinning over the head of a nearby sand-warrior and landing nimbly on his feet. He whirled, only to see the enemy soldier smashed to dust by the very thing that had struck him.

The manticore!

It didn't look much like a manticore anymore. Wingless, and lacking a head and tail, it was little more than a slablike body on legs. Yet the double-headed worm jutting from its back was probing the air with obvious eagerness. It sniffed at Gulph and a pair of tooth-lined jaws gaped wide, releasing a burning stench.

Gulph brandished his sword.

"Come on, if you dare!" he yelled.

The monster lunged toward the sound of his voice, twin mouths snapping and spitting. Gulph held his ground, waiting until the last moment before leaping aside. He slashed its flank as it bounded past. Slow to react, the manticore barreled into a line of sand-warriors.

Gulph ducked behind a chunk of diamond. The monster might be crippled, but he feared it would soon get the better of him.

Air whooshed as a thorrod flew low over his head. It was Theeta, carrying Tarlan toward one of the peculiar flying wings that had detached itself from the manticore's body. Tarlan's sword sliced through the huge flapping membrane, breaking it into tiny pieces.

Each fragment instantly transformed into a sand-bat. Swarming, they fell snapping onto Theeta's wings.

Gulph leaped on top of the crystal shard he'd been hiding behind, the sharp edges scratching his legs. He no longer cared if he was seen—Tarlan was in trouble! He picked up a handful of diamond shards and began hurling them at the bats.

"Leave my brother alone!" he shouted.

Some of his missiles hit their targets, exploding the unlucky bats into powder. The rest disrupted the swarm, allowing Theeta to pull herself free and gain valuable altitude. As she did so, one of the wyverns swooped down and used its great red claws to tear into the confused enemy flock.

"Thanks, Gulph!" Tarlan shouted, clinging to Theeta's back and swinging his sword through the few remaining sand-bats.

Gulph turned his attention back to the ground, and almost immediately spotted Elodie. She was surrounded by sand-warriors. Yelling as he ran, he cut his way through the enemy ranks to join her. Back-to-back, they parried the blows raining down from the towering soldiers.

"Here we are again!" gasped Elodie, driving her sword into the belly of a sand-warrior.

"Did you see what happened to Mother?" Gulph yelled, beating back another.

"No! You?"

"No!"

They circled around each other, valiantly fending off their attackers. But with each blow he struck, Gulph felt his hopes draining away. They'd survived one battle only to be swallowed up by another.

Outnumbered again. Only this time there really is no chance of escape.

A warrior appeared from nowhere and hefted its sword over Gulph's head. It was standing close enough for Gulph to see every tiny grain of sand in its body. Muscles of sand bulged. Tiny beetles popped clear of the soldier's coarse red skin, then buried themselves again.

Gulph began to raise his own sword in defense. The sand-warrior's massive fist closed around its blade. A mouth gaped in its eyeless head, ready to swallow him.

As the hilt of the sword slipped through his fingers, Gulph found himself staring death in the face.

"FOR CELESTIS!"

The cry seemed to come from far, far away, as if in a dream.

Hearing it, the sand-warrior faltered, its sword hanging in midswing. Its mouth closed and its fist opened, releasing Gulph's sword, which Gulph caught deftly.

The sand-warrior turned toward the sound of the voice. The soldiers around it turned too, their blank faces creasing with puzzlement, or fear, or both.

The voice rang out again, louder now.

"FOR IDILLIAM!"

Gulph could hear the sound of running feet. Boots thudded on the hard ground, crunched in the splinters of broken crystal. More voices took up the cry.

"FOR TORONIA! FOR THE PROPHECY!"

The line of sand-warriors parted down the middle, half the enemy troops circling back to the main gate and the rest taking up defensive positions in the middle of the courtyard. Through the gap that had opened up, Gulph saw a wave of human soldiers rushing up a ramp from some lower level of the citadel. They wore a motley mix of bronze and leather armor, and carried crystal swords and shields.

Leading them was a tall, gray-haired man he knew all too well.

"Ossilius!" Gulph yelled, leaping joyfully into the air.

"No quarter!" Ossilius roared. "Kill them all!"

He cut down three sand-warriors with a single blow. As he brought his sword round for another strike, a small figure lunged past him and felled another. It was Pip.

"Pip!" Gulph's heart had stopped in his chest. Now it seemed to swell like a hot, happy sun. "Pip! I'm here!"

Behind his oldest friend, racing to battle along with the combined forces of Celestis and Idilliam, were the rest of the Tangletree Players.

Gulph's heart started up again, not just beating now but positively thundering at the sight of his friends, alive after all.

He turned to Elodie. She grinned back at him. He grabbed her hand.

"Come on!" he said.

They sprinted between the lines of sand-warriors, hacking them down as they went. By the time they reached Ossilius, the grizzled old Captain of the Guard had brought down a dozen more of the enemy. With short, sharp commands, he instructed the newly arrived army to spread out and drive back the hordes of sand-warriors. Slowly but surely, the tide of the battle was turning.

Gulph skidded to a halt in a loose pile of sand. He licked his lips and raised his sword, ready for the red grains to re-form, for more sand-warriors to rise up around him.

But the sand just lay there.

"Vicerin's been gone too long," said Elodie. "He's not bringing them back to life."

"Your mother's magic is helping too!" said Ossilius, holding up his crystal blade in triumph. A magical aura surrounded its blade. "It seems Kalia's potion is good for more than just the undead! All our blades are soaked in it!"

Gulph grasped his old friend's arm. "I thought you were dead."

Ossilius wiped sweat from his face and smiled down at him.

"Do you think I would allow myself to die before seeing you on the throne, Gulph?"

Gulph laughed. "There's really no stopping you, is there?"

"We all have to stop sometime, Gulph. But I plan to keep going for a long time yet to come!"

Before Gulph could respond to that, Pip threw her arms around his neck.

"I knew you'd come back!" She laughed. "I knew it!"

"Let me guess," said Elodie. "You must be Pip."

Pip flushed. "And you must be Princess Elodie." She gave an uncertain little bob of a curtsy.

Gulph hugged Pip back joyfully. "When the wyverns tore down the city, I thought you'd all been crushed. How did you survive?"

Pip pried herself loose. Her face was pink with excitement. "After you left, Ossilius took us deep underground, all the way back to Celestis. We've been training there ever since. Then, when the city rose again—"

A sand-warrior broke through the front line and rushed at them. Ossilius ducked calmly beneath its swinging battle-ax and chopped it in half. The enemy soldier collapsed in an instant, the sand cascading over the ground as if emptied from a giant hourglass.

"I knew you would come here," Ossilius said. "The throne room calls you."

"Yes," said Elodie. "We've got to get there, right away."

"I am proud to open the way to it!" Ossilius bowed low, then held up his shield. Gulph saw a familiar symbol etched into the crystal: the three-pronged crest of Trident. "And I am proud to take up the fight that my son, Fessan, began!"

Gulph exchanged a glance with Elodie. His sister's face had turned pale. Feeling suddenly sick, he remembered what she'd told him about Fessan's execution. How could he possibly break such dreadful news? Yet Ossilius had to be told.

"About your son," Gulph said hesitantly. "He's . . ."

"Fessan will join us soon!" Ossilius's cheeks were flushed and his eyes were bright. "The prophecy will bring us together again—I am sure of it!"

With that, Ossilius plunged back into battle. *It will have to wait*, thought Gulph, watching in awe as he led one group of Celestians against a column of sand-warriors, then leaped onto a crystal outcrop to shout directions to another. A man dressed in the uniform of the Idilliam army ran up to consult him, and then Ossilius was off again, racing through the battle to direct yet another assault.

"He might be an old man," Gulph said to Elodie, "but on the battlefield he's unbeatable."

"Now I know where Fessan got it from," his sister replied sadly.

Theeta flew in low over their heads, knocking aside a line of sand-warriors that had been creeping toward them.

"Thanks, Theeta!" called Gulph.

"Your friends came just in time!" Tarlan called down from the thorrod's back. "I'm glad they're safe. And I'm glad they're good with their swords!"

His teeth flashed in a grin. Then, as quickly as it had appeared, his smile faded. He cocked his head as if he were listening.

"What is it?" said Gulph, suddenly alarmed.

Tarlan was staring into the distance. His look of shock deepened with every breath. His eyes grew wide.

"Tarlan!" The tremor in Elodie's voice betrayed her concern. "What's wrong?"

Gradually Tarlan's smile returned.

Unable to bear the suspense, Gulph leaped on top of a block of crystal. Elodie followed him. Looking out over the heads of the battling soldiers, Gulph saw a fresh wave of people pouring in through the main gate.

Reinforcements! But from where?

The new arrivals were dressed in winter furs. Leading them was a thickset, bearded man wearing a heavy bearskin. His broadsword glinted in the multicolored light of the aerial storm.

"Captain Leom!" Tarlan and Elodie shouted his name at the same time, grinning widely. Gulph thought his brother and sister had never looked more alike than in that moment.

"Tarlan—are these your friends from the mountains?" he asked.

"Leom is a friend to us all," Elodie replied. Her hands were clasped tight to her chest.

Theeta bucked in the air as a wayward sand lance flew past her head. Tarlan calmed her, then shouted to the man in the bearskin, "You came!"

"We set out from the fortress days ago," Leom roared back. "And now that the chasm is filled in, it is easy to get across."

The fur-clad soldier led his army across the courtyard toward them, hacking at sand-warriors as he came. "We were at the Toronian border when we saw the crystal city rise out of the ground. We knew the final battle must be at hand. So, here we are!"

"And you are most welcome!" That was Ossilius. Like Gulph and Elodie, he'd found a high spot from which he could look over the whole battle. "Quickly now—I need two squads in the south quarter, and three beneath the tower!"

"It is already done!" Leom barked back, relaying the orders to his troops. Clusters of sand-warriors fell as the mountain folk pushed forward, driving the enemy within range of Ossilius's waiting army, whose crystal swords brought them down one after the other.

"Now they're the ones who are outnumbered!" Elodie held up a crystal sword. It glowed just like the one Ossilius had been carrying.

"Where did you get that?" he said with a grin.

"Ossilius, of course!" she answered. "As long as we've got these, they don't stand a—"

"Gulph! Help me!"

He recognized Pip's voice instantly. But where was she? He spun round, frantically scanning the courtyard, but all he could see were soldiers sparring amid blocks of crystal and heaps of sand.

"Where are you?" Gulph was starting to panic.

"There!" cried Elodie, pointing toward the base of the tower.

The horribly mutated manticore was there, crouched over something on the ground. The two-headed worm on its back reared up, ready to strike.

Trapped beneath one of the manticore's paws, struggling in vain to free herself, was Pip.

"Leave her alone!" Gulph raced over the sand-covered ground. The way was littered with sharp chunks of crystal. Some of these he hurdled, others he used like ramps, running up them and turning his momentum into flips and somersaults that carried him high over the heads of the remaining sand-warriors.

He reached the manticore just as the worm struck at Pip. With difficulty, she fended it off with her upraised arms. Without slowing, he ran his sword into one of its hind legs. Screeching in pain, the manticore whipped round, yanking Gulph's sword from his hand.

It was useless anyway, Gulph thought. *If only I had one of Mother's blades!*

The manticore's damaged leg was already starting to rebuild itself. Turning its attention from Pip, the worm struck out at Gulph.

Diving beneath the monster's legs, he rolled through a prickly carpet of crystal splinters, stopping only when his shoulder fetched up against the tower wall.

"Pip!" he shouted, scrambling to his feet. "Grab your sword!"

Still trapped beneath the manticore's foot, his friend clawed uselessly at the sand. Her crystal sword lay in the shadows, glowing faintly, far out of reach. Gulph lunged for it. The worm came round again, its twin sets of teeth gnashing in Gulph's face, driving him back. One of the sets of jaws gaped around his head. There was nowhere to run. He raised his arms, knowing they wouldn't protect him.

"Leave my brother alone!"

Elodie's voice rang out clear and true. Her glowing crystal sword came down, chopping straight through one of the writhing necks of the worm and sending the head tumbling across the ground. The second head struck at her like a snake. She ducked just in time to avoid being decapitated.

"Get her!" Elodie yelled, waving her free hand toward Pip. "Before it can . . ."

But the fallen head of the worm had already re-formed itself. Like a hideous tumor, it wrapped itself around one of the manticore's feet, then swarmed up its body and reattached itself to the waving neck.

Gulph stared at Elodie's crystal blade in dismay.

Even Kalia's magic isn't strong enough against this monster!

"Two heads!" Elodie shouted, waving her sword in the air as she circled the re-formed manticore. She flashed a determined glance at Gulph, fixing him with her gaze. "Two blades!"

Gulph thought he understood. But he had no sword.

"Gulph! I can't . . . breathe . . . !" The manticore's paw was planted heavily on Pip's chest, crushing her beneath its weight. Her fingers clawed weakly at the sand.

The manticore's legs weaved back and forth in front of Gulph, a set of constantly shifting barriers between him and Pip's crystal sword. Gulph jumped forward, only to be knocked bodily aside by one of the manticore's massive legs.

There's no way through!

"Gulph . . ." Pip's eyelids fluttered closed.

"Hurry, Gulph!" screamed Elodie.

The manticore's legs weaved back and forth, back and forth.

Like a dance.

And so it was. A dance. A performance. And like any performance, it was all about rhythm, all about timing.

It's just one more show of acrobatics for the crowd. Only this time I'm not doing it for applause. I'm doing it to save my friend's life.

The manticore shifted its weight, tracking Elodie as she continued to circle it. Left foreleg, rear hind leg, left hind leg, all the while keeping the bulk of its weight pressed down on poor Pip.

Left foreleg . . . rear hind leg . . .

And there between them . . .

A gap!

Gulph threw himself into the narrow space between the manticore's enormous legs. One huge paw lifted, allowing Gulph to roll beneath its tangle of twisted claws. Now he tumbled to the side, landing on the balls of his feet and immediately flipping forward as the next gap opened up. One set of claws slashed the air to his left, another to his right. Gulph found the sweet, still space between the two and shot through it like an arrow.

For a single, short breath, he was flying directly over Pip. Her eyes flickered open, gazing up at him as his body made an arc above her, his arms and legs bunched, his entire body turning about its perfectly balanced center.

Looking down into Pip's face, he saw her silently mouth his name.

He hit the ground on his shoulder, rolled for the final time, and came up in a crouch. He threw out his right hand. It came to rest exactly where he'd known it would—on the hilt of Pip's sword.

Gulph's fingers closed. He stood up. He felt tall. His back felt straight. The manticore spun before him like a monstrous carousel. Elodie appeared from behind it, sprinting toward Gulph with her own sword outstretched. She dug in her heels, sliding through the sand to come to a halt directly beside him. Gulph brandished his sword. His sister brandished hers. They were like reflections in a mirror.

The worm's two heads came down. Two swords came up, their crystal blades slicing clean through the manticore's paired necks.

The heads burst apart, showering Gulph and Elodie with sand. A wave rolled down the worm and into the manticore's body. Sand exploded, and a pulse of sound rolled across the courtyard. In all directions, sand-warriors froze in their tracks, then disintegrated. For an instant, the entire courtyard turned the color of blood.

"Pip!" Sliding the crystal sword into his scabbard, Gulph rushed to kneel by his friend. He brushed sand from her face and lifted her up. She coughed up more sand, then opened her eyes, stared at Gulph, and hugged him.

"That was quite a show," she croaked.

"Worthy of the Tangletree Players?"

"The crowd would be on their feet!"

As he helped Pip up, Gulph realized the courtyard was almost silent. With his best friend on one side, and his sister on the other, he made his way cautiously through the drifts of sand. More sand rained down around them in a glittering shower.

Gradually the air cleared. Not a single sand-warrior remained standing. Glancing up, Gulph saw only the huge arrow-shapes of the thorrods and wyverns as they patrolled the light-filled sky. Of the sand-bats and eagles there was no sign.

Presently, Theeta separated herself from the rest of the flock and flew down to land before them. Tarlan climbed down from her back. He looked exhausted.

"We did it!" he said, embracing Elodie roughly. He clapped Gulph on his shoulder. "No stopping us once we get together!"

"It isn't over," Gulph warned.

"No," said Elodie, touching his arm. "But with Vicerin gone, we're safe from the Sandspear. For now."

The fur-clad figure of Captain Leom strode up. He bowed, first to Tarlan, then Elodie. Letting go of Gulph's hand, Elodie grinned and hugged him.

"You're a good man," she said. "I always knew you were."

Leom gave her a grave smile, then offered a third bow, this time to Gulph.

"It is my honor to serve you all," he said, sinking to one knee.

"And mine," said Captain Ossilius, emerging from a line of Celestian soldiers. He took Gulph's hands and squeezed them. He shifted his glance first to Tarlan, then to Elodie. "This is a great day for me, to see the three of you reunited at last. And it is a great day for Toronia."

Gulph felt a swell of pride, and was amused to see Tarlan shifting his feet awkwardly. He wondered if his brother would ever be truly comfortable among people.

"Who's this?" Tarlan said gruffly, waving his hand at Pip.

"My friend," Gulph replied. As he introduced her, the rest of the Tangletree Players gathered around him. He was about to start introducing them all, when a dreadful thought made his stomach contract. He suddenly knew why Tarlan wasn't smiling.

Mother! Where has he taken you?

"So this is your family," Pip was saying. She sounded a little awe-struck. "I'm . . . I'm pleased to meet you all."

Gulph gave her a brief hug. "You're all my family," he said. "And there will be plenty of time later for everyone to meet properly. But now . . ."

"Now we have work to do," said Tarlan. His brow furrowed and his lips pressed together.

"We have to rescue Mother," Elodie asserted. "He must have taken her to the throne room."

Gulph nodded. "If he survived the wyverns' attack, that's where he'll have gone."

"Oh, he survived all right!" snarled Tarlan. "I was stupid to think he wouldn't."

"No, you weren't," said Gulph. "You separated him from his army. If you hadn't done that . . ."

"None of that matters now," said Elodie. She grabbed Tarlan's hand. Tarlan seized Gulph's. "Are you ready?"

"Let's get him!" Gulph answered.

CHAPTER 24

Elodie's glowing crystal sword bounced against her hip as she ran. With the three of them carrying similar magical weapons, surely nothing could stand in their way. Nevertheless, they couldn't afford to waste time.

Everything's at stake now, she thought. *The kingdom, the crown, our mother.*

Our destiny.

Together, Elodie, Tarlan, and Gulph passed through the gaping doorway of the diamond tower and into the citadel beyond. Close behind them came Ossilius, Leom, and the Tangletree Players.

Inside the citadel, a forest of crystal columns opened out into a vast chamber. Diamond windows captured the dazzling colors raging in the sky above and splashed them over the walls and floor. It was like running through a rainbow.

"Here!" cried Gulph, leading them toward a low bridge spanning a dry channel of gleaming sapphire. "We can take the river!"

"What river?" said Tarlan. "Where's the water?"

"It drained away when Celestis rose up," gasped Pip, who was running behind Elodie. "Lots of things moved around."

"Some of it looks different," Gulph agreed, halting in the middle of the bridge. "But I recognize enough of it to know where we're going."

"So where *are* we going?" Tarlan demanded impatiently.

"Over the side!" Gulph leaped from the bridge, landing lightly in the empty channel below.

Elodie vaulted over the rail and landed next to him on the blue crystal riverbed. A breath later, Tarlan joined them.

"We're nearly there, aren't we?" Elodie said. Her blood was fizzing through her body, as if all the colors in the air had soaked into her skin and were filling up her veins.

"Look, it slopes down." Gulph pointed ahead to where the dry channel became a rapidly descending ramp. "If I've worked this out right, it should take us straight to the throne room."

"Will we be able to stop when we get there?" Tarlan eyed the slippery-looking slope uncertainly.

"I'm not even going to think about stopping!" said Elodie. "Not until this is finished, one way or another." She grabbed Tarlan's hand, then Gulph's. "Who's going first?"

Tarlan grinned. "We all are!"

As one, they raced forward. Elodie's feet first slid on the smooth crystal, then slipped from beneath her. Gulph fell at the same instant, and between them they dragged Tarlan down with them. Now they were on their backsides, slithering helplessly down the rapidly steepening slope of the sapphire riverbed.

"I hope . . . ," Tarlan began, and then they were plunging into the mouth of a yawning tunnel. The light winked out, leaving them in total darkness. Elodie tightened her grip on her brothers' hands, and clenched her teeth against the jolts as they plummeted down the twisting channel. Afraid as she was, she couldn't help letting out a whoop of exhilaration.

The riverbed steepened into a chute. Elodie's stomach lurched into her throat. For a moment, they were falling like stones.

When we land, we'll break every bone in our bodies!

They flew along the ridge, which gradually flattened out, slowing their descent until they were slipping along at little more than a walking pace.

Green light bloomed around them. The ridge spilled them onto a wide, open floor. Still hand in hand, they continued to slide, stopping only when they reached the foot of a towering set of diamond steps.

Breathless, Elodie clambered to her feet.

"Is this it?" she gasped. "Are we here?"

Beside her, Tarlan was helping Gulph to his feet.

"It's the throne room," said Gulph. "It was just a cave before, but"—he shuddered—"this is where I killed it."

Eyes wide, Elodie looked round. The mountain of steps rose before them. Draped across one of its slopes was the skeleton of some monstrous creature that looked part-snake, part-bird.

"The bakaliss?" she whispered.

"Lady Redina." Gulph's face was white.

Walls of blue-green jade soared overhead, curving inward to meet in an immense vaulted ceiling. Walls and ceiling were studded with dazzling green emeralds. Spiral pillars rose like twisted fingers, not so much supporting the structure as caressing it.

On top of the steps, at the mountain's peak, stood three thrones. One was made of green emerald, the next of red ruby. The third was made of gold.

"Elodie!" cried a familiar voice. "Tarlan! Gulph!"

Tied to one of the pillars near the thrones was Kalia. She squirmed against the ropes, the gag hanging loose around her chin. Her eyes blazed with joy.

"So," snarled Vicerin, down at Elodie, "*you* are the reason!"

"The reason for what?" Elodie replied. She started forward, eager to race up the stairs and free her mother. But Gulph's hand closed round her arm, holding her back.

"The reason it isn't working," Gulph called up to Vicerin. He was smiling fiercely. "You worked so hard to get those jewels. You came all this way. But it's all been for nothing, hasn't it?"

Baring his horselike teeth, Vicerin held up his fist. From it dangled the three jewels he'd stolen from them.

"No games!" he shouted, still fixated on Elodie. "Tell me what I must do with these wretched trinkets. Tell me, or your mother dies."

"Don't listen to him!" shouted Kalia.

"The jewels won't work for you," said Gulph simply.

"That's because they don't belong to you," Elodie added. "Those jewels are ours. The magic is ours. And the crown"—she cocked her head to the side—"that's ours as well."

There was a great commotion behind them as Ossilius, Pip, and a seemingly endless stream of battle-worn soldiers poured down the channel and into the throne room. On the opposite side of the chamber, Theeta flew in through a low archway, closely followed by her fellow thorrods and the two wyverns.

Elodie's heart soared as her friends and allies gathered around her and her brothers. Their voices murmured threateningly. Their armor clanked. Their crystal weapons glowed.

"You're beaten, Vicerin!" she cried, mounting the first step. Tarlan and Gulph followed her. "You might want the crown, but the crown doesn't want you!"

Vicerin's expression changed slowly from anger to what looked like triumph. Elodie hesitated.

"Do you think you are the only ones with magic at your

command?" Vicerin held up the Sandspear.

"Quickly!" shouted Elodie. "Don't let him get the advantage!"

Drawing her sword, she started running up the steps. Her brothers followed close on her heels. The air above Vicerin's head was boiling. A cloud of sand appeared from nowhere, billowing outward and transforming into an army of bloodred warriors. Their bodies were rough, like unfinished sculptures. As they flew through the air, their blank faces sharpened, and their stubby limbs became flailing arms and legs. By the time they hit the ground, they were fully formed.

Elodie found herself running straight toward a pair of freshly made sand-warriors. Before they could react, she sliced her sword through them both. The crystal blade tore through them, its magic unbinding their bodies. Sand exploded around Elodie. She ran on, climbing ever higher.

More shapes formed out of the swelling cloud of sand—giant bats, and strange six-legged beasts with heads like shovels and teeth like plowshares. Elodie ducked as one of the bat-things flew low enough for its claws to tangle briefly in her hair. She shook it loose and it flew on, headed straight for the thorrods.

Meanwhile, Tarlan was engaged in frantic swordplay with a knot of sand-warriors. Cutting one down, he threw back his head and called for the thorrods. At once, Theeta forced her way through the swarm of bats toward him. Tarlan knocked aside another enemy soldier, then leaped onto Theeta's back as she swooped down to meet him. Together, they flew over the battle and began to hack their way through the flocks of flying creatures that had been summoned by the Sandspear's magic.

Reassured that Tarlan was safe for now, Elodie looked round for Gulph. She spotted him nearby, using his sword to drive a herd of crablike creatures toward the skeleton of the bakaliss. Pip was with him, and as Elodie watched, they were joined by the rest of the Tangletree Players. The blows of their swords and the snapping of the crabs' claws were steadily reducing the giant bones to dust.

Shouts rose up from below. Spinning round, Elodie saw Ossilius forming his troops into battle lines just in time to meet the first wave of Vicerin's new army. The immensity of the battle—and its suddenness—was too much to take in.

We've just defeated one sand army. Are we really supposed to face another?

A sword hissed. Elodie threw up her own blade instinctively. It clashed with the enemy's weapon barely a hand's width from her face. With a scream, she pushed her attacker away, prepared to thrust . . . then stopped.

"Sylva?" she stammered, staring straight into the face of the girl she'd known all her life. "What are you doing?"

Sylva said nothing, simply hacked at Elodie with her sword once more. Elodie knocked the blow aside. Sylva came on, forcing Elodie back down the steps. Elodie parried blow after blow, unwilling to strike out at her.

"How did you get here?" she cried. "What are you doing?"

Elodie stumbled off the bottom step and into the chaos of the ground battle. The next instant, Sylva was gone, lost inside the press of bodies. Before Elodie could react, Cedric was there.

"Cedric!" she said. "Did you see . . . ?"

Just like Sylva, he remained silent. He raised his one hand. In it was a mace, its bulbous end studded with cruel spikes. He swung it toward Elodie's head.

Ducking, she backed away in confusion. This didn't make any sense.

"Don't!" she cried. "I don't want to hurt you!"

Then Cedric too was swallowed in the confusion.

Forcing her way through the throng, Elodie regained the steps. Gulph was still struggling amid the remains of the bakaliss, only it wasn't the crabs he was fighting anymore.

He was fighting Pip, his face a mask of horror.

"Gulph?" Elodie murmured.

The air hummed as Theeta swooped past. Tarlan was leaning out from her back, thrusting his sword again and again at a man who was clinging on to the thorrod's dangling claws and trying to stab at the giant bird's breast.

The man was Captain Leom.

Elodie staggered backward until her shoulder fetched up against something hard. It was the skull of the bakaliss. The monster's empty eye sockets seemed to glare at her. Her head felt ready to burst.

She glanced up the steps to where Vicerin was prowling from one throne to the next, waving the Sandspear around like a madman.

Our friends! she thought desperately. *Somehow he's turned our friends against us.*

"How are you doing this?" she yelled.

Tarlan had managed to knock Captain Leom to the ground. But a horde of sand-warriors had taken the man's place. They clutched at Theeta's claws, trying to drag her down.

As the thorrod fought to break free, an old woman emerged from the enemy ranks. She wore furs and carried a hunting spear. Elodie watched aghast as the woman drew back her arm. She was aiming the spear right at Tarlan.

Mirith?

It was the same old woman she'd met in the Realm of the Dead—the frost witch who'd raised Tarlan. But Mirith was dead. And the woman trying to kill Tarlan was no ghost.

"You're not Mirith!" Elodie shouted, sprinting up the steps and striking the woman down with her sword.

"Mirith!" Tarlan howled in anguish. He turned to Elodie, eyes blazing. "What have you done?"

"It's not her!" Elodie replied as the old woman's body collapsed into a heap of sand. "It's just a trick! Don't believe your eyes!"

Understanding dawned on Tarlan's face. Hearing her words, Gulph steeled himself and ran his sword through Pip's stomach. For an instant Elodie's heart stopped.

I've made him kill his best friend!

Then Pip's body burst open and red sand rained down around Gulph's feet. A moment later, the real Pip emerged from behind a jumble of giant bones and embraced him.

Filled with new fire, Elodie began to fight her way back up the steps.

"You think your magic's real?" she shouted, cutting a sand-warrior down. Hearing her voice, Lord Vicerin paused to glare down at her. "Well, it isn't. It's all a fake. Just like you're a fake!"

"Is this real enough for you?" Vicerin retorted. He turned the Sandspear on Kalia, who was still struggling to free herself from the ropes tying her to the pillar.

Six crimson snakes rose up around Kalia. She screamed. The snakes drew back their heads and bared their fangs. Just as the serpents were about to strike, one of the wyverns slashed at them with its ruby claws, reducing them to sand.

"I can summon people too!" Elodie cried. "Only my friends aren't illusions!"

Now she was halfway up the steps. From the corner of her eye, she saw Gulph running to catch up to her. Tarlan was circling above her head. Her brothers' eyes were ablaze.

She drew in her breath.

"My friends are real!"

Red mist gathered at the edges of her vision. Desert wind moved through her. Her mouth filled with sand.

Good sand! she thought wildly. *My desert!*

"Rise up!" she shouted. "Rise up from the Realm of the Dead! Come to me now!"

The wind howled, blowing in from far, far away. But the distance no longer mattered.

Once I needed their graves, she thought in triumph. *Not anymore. Now I can bring them from anywhere! Anyone I choose! Here and now!*

"Rise, Lady Vicerin!" Elodie cried. "Have your revenge!"

Hearing his dead wife's name, Lord Vicerin recoiled.

The air rippled, and a ghost appeared at Elodie's side.

At the sight of her, Vicerin fell to his knees.

Lady Vicerin was tall, just as Elodie remembered her. Even in death, she carried herself with haughty pride. Her body shimmered, gray like smoke.

The dagger she carried looked as sharp as the glint in her eye.

"Shall I kill him for you?" Lady Vicerin's voice rustled like a breeze through river reeds.

"Do what you want with him," Elodie replied.

Lady Vicerin smiled.

As the ghost of Lady Vicerin began to ascend the stairs, Elodie opened herself to the desert wind once more, and sent out a fresh summons.

You whose crystal wings I freed. Come and join the ones you left behind.

A sigh floated through the throne room. Something that was both green and gray appeared, seeming to condense out of the empty air. The third wyvern.

Its wings were like shadows, and its eyes were like stars, and when it met its brothers, it opened its throat and screeched in sadness and joy.

Elodie closed her eyes. What was the name of the thorrod Tarlan had told her about? The one who'd been killed in Yalasti, and whose skull had been worn as a trophy by the leader of the Helkrags? For a moment she couldn't remember. Then it came to her.

Seethan! Your friends are waiting for you. Come now!

He appeared suddenly, like a storm, scattering the enemy before him, a giant bird almost twice as big as Theeta, his feathers drifting like gray snow, his cries somehow faint and piercing, both at the same time. Seeing him, the other thorrods threw their wings high and bent their heads low, like servants greeting a king.

On the platform, Lord Vicerin cringed, looking small.

On Theeta's back, Elodie saw, Tarlan was smiling with joy.

Now, Trident, she thought, and the desert wind blew hotter than a furnace. *All of you who fell. All of you that I love. Palenie, come. Fessan, come. Come all of you, come now!*

They came, a crop of shadows that formed itself instantly into an army and began carving its way through the enemy ranks. Once, their flags and tunics had been green. Now they were gray. And yet, somehow, nothing had changed.

"Elodie?"

It was just a whisper, but one that sent a tingle down Elodie's spine. She turned, and there was Palenie, the girl who had once been mistaken for her, and died as a result. Palenie smiled. Elodie smiled back.

"The Realm of the Dead is a happy place now," said Palenie. "Thanks to you, Elodie."

"But we will always be happy to leave it too." The second voice belonged to Fessan. Even in death, the scar on his face remained. Yet, even in death, he was handsome. "As long as it means serving you."

"Yes," Palenie agreed. "So, is there something we can do?"

Elodie drew in a deep, shuddering breath.

"There is," she said. "Please, save my mother."

Their bodies flowing like silk, Fessan and Palenie glided smoothly up the steps toward Kalia, joining Lady Vicerin as she advanced toward her promised revenge.

Spotting the oncoming ghosts, Lord Vicerin circled in front of
Kalia. His eyes were wild and scared. He jabbed the Sandspear at
Fessan. Arrows of sand flew from the end of the magical weapon.
Fessan brushed them aside with his sword.

"You have no power over me now, Vicerin," he said, laughing.

Meanwhile, Palenie had vanished, only to materialize behind the
pillar to which Kalia was tied. She slashed at the ropes, freeing her
in an instant. Hand in hand, they sprinted down the stairs to where
Elodie was waiting, leaving Vicerin to battle with the ghosts of all
the people he'd wronged.

"You've done well, my dear daughter," said Kalia, holding Elodie
close. "But you must not underestimate Vicerin. The Sandspear—
he has barely scratched the surface of its power."

"Well," said Elodie, "a scratch is all he's going to manage. As
soon as Fessan gets hold of him . . ."

She trailed off. Kalia was shaking her head.

"Your ghosts will stem the tide," she said, "but they cannot turn
it. As long as Vicerin has the Sandspear, there is no army in the
world that can stand against him."

By now, Gulph had joined them. He reached out and squeezed
Kalia's hand. He was smiling, but his eyes looked tired and his body
was tense.

"Then what can we do?" Elodie blurted. She looked in despair
over the battle. The ghosts she'd summoned were indeed pushing

the enemy back, and the presence of Seethan and the lost wyvern had shifted the balance of power in the air. Yet already Vicerin had conjured a whole new regiment of warriors to surround the thrones and protect him from Fessan and the other ghosts.

"You know what to do," said Kalia.

"We do?" said Gulph.

Elodie glanced up to see Tarlan guiding Theeta down to the steps. He hopped lightly to the ground, leaving the thorrod back to continue the battle in the air. He gave their mother a brief, hard squeeze.

"You say we know what to do," he said. "Well, what is it?"

"The Sandspear comes from Pharrah," Kalia went on. She fixed her eyes first on Tarlan, then on Gulph. Finally her gaze settled on Elodie. "I come from Pharrah. And you . . ."

"Yes?" said Elodie.

"You came from me."

Elodie rolled her tongue around her mouth. It felt hot, gritty.

"Desert magic," Gulph murmured. "We have it in our blood. All of us. It's ours to control, every time we use our powers."

"That's right." Elodie stared at Gulph, at Tarlan, at Kalia. "It isn't his magic—it's ours!"

Elodie grabbed Gulph's hand. He grabbed Tarlan's. The triplets stood united on the steps, as the battle raged above them and below.

"There's only one of him," she said. "But the crown is for three!"

CHAPTER 25

Gulph felt heat bubbling from Elodie's fingers. Tarlan's hand was burning hot. It was as if his brother and sister had turned to fire. The flames were inside him, too.

Gulph started to climb, and the others followed.

When they were halfway up the steps, Lord Vicerin suddenly spun the Sandspear around, forcing back the ghosts who'd surrounded him with a single, mighty stroke. The magical weapon hummed and blurred. A tornado of sand grew around it. It spun madly, hissing like a nest of snakes, scattering the ghosts altogether.

As the whirlwind began to rotate more quickly, it spat out gobbets of sand. They flew down toward the ascending triplets, transforming rapidly into winged creatures with pincers for mouths. Some reached out with clawed arms; others trailed probing tentacles. The air around them glowed and fizzed.

"Tear those brats apart!" bellowed Vicerin.

The heat swelled inside Gulph. With it came something entirely unexpected.

Calm.

"They can't hurt us," he said. "We don't have to be afraid."

"I hope you're right!" Elodie flinched as the swarm of flying monsters bore down toward them. Steam boiled in their wake, and Gulph understood that the creatures were burning up inside. Just like they were.

An idea came to him. A crazy idea. But a good one.

Slowly, deliberately, Gulph slipped his sword into its scabbard and unclipped his belt. The weapon clattered to the ground.

Gulph! What are you doing? The voice rang out clear and loud. It was Tarlan's. It took Gulph a moment to realize that his brother hadn't even moved his lips.

We're not here to fight, he thought back. *We're here to end the war.*

Tarlan's eyes widened. Then he too unbuckled his scabbard and let his sword fall. Beside him, Elodie did the same.

The sand creatures don't belong to him, Gulph thought.

No. Tarlan's response was instant. *They belong to us.*

Will they obey us? That was Elodie.

They have no choice, Gulph answered. *Are you ready?*

Yes. Elodie's response was as bright as a flame.

Yes. Tarlan's thought cut through it, a furious snarl.

Then yes, Gulph agreed. Hesitating, he added: *We can hear each other's thoughts.*

Yes.

Yes.

Gulph smiled.

Yes!

United as they never had been before, the triplets raised their hands. The avalanche of flying creatures broke over them like a wave. The impact rocked Gulph backward, but he stood his ground. Sand scoured his face. He pushed back against the torrent. He felt Tarlan and Elodie doing the same. Thousands of bodies battered them. Millions of grains of sand.

They're all just dust on the wind, thought Gulph.

Immediately heat blasted through him. Just like when he turned invisible. Only this was stronger. Bigger. He knew that Tarlan and Elodie felt it too. He could feel their minds opening like flowers, welcoming the desert magic.

Working as one, they gathered up the heat and threw it back at their attackers. The creatures instantly began to glow white-hot. Gulph watched in amazement as the individual grains of sand fused together. The creatures merged, their bodies melting into a shining ring of light that started to circle the heads of the triplets.

Not one ring! Three!

The glowing rings rippled like molten glass. One gold, one

green, one red. Beads of light sprayed from them.

They looked like crowns.

Looking down at the battlefield, Gulph sent out a fresh thought with all his strength, and all his will. *This stops here! This stops now!*

He spotted Captain Ossilius amid the mass of bodies. His friend had frozen in the act of striking down a sand-warrior. Gulph repeated his silent command, and watched with relief as Ossilius lowered his sword and took a step back. All around him, his soldiers did the same.

The enemy warrior Ossilius had been about to strike stood motionless for an instant. Then its body began to melt. What had once been a man-shaped column of sand became a shining stream of light that spun briefly on the spot, then rippled through the air to join the three shining crowns spinning above the triplets.

All across the battlefield, weapons went down, and sand-warriors turned to lines of liquid glass. Shouts of alarm became cries of relief as the enemy was sucked into the crowns.

Of all the faces Gulph saw, only one showed no sign of surprise. Kalia, her red-gold hair blowing as if in a desert wind, wore a smile of infinite pride.

I think we're ready, came Tarlan's thought.

I think so too, agreed Elodie.

Gulph made a final scan of the battlefield. Not a single

sand-warrior remained. The air was clear too—the only creatures flying inside the cavernous throne room were the thorrods and the wyverns.

The three rings of energy spun above them, an entire enemy army fused together and burning as bright as the desert sun.

Vicerin teetered on the topmost step, still twirling the Sandspear over his head. The tornado of sand had disappeared. His entire army had disappeared. He looked very small.

Lord Vicerin! Gulph launched the thought like a javelin. *We're coming for you!*

Vicerin trembled as if Gulph had struck him a physical blow. He mouthed something Gulph couldn't hear, and held out the Sandspear as if to ward them off.

Gulph raced up the stairs. Tarlan and Elodie matched him stride for stride. As they neared the platform at the top, the crowns of light expanded. Vicerin shrank, stumbled, fell. He raised his arms, his face a mask of terror. The crowns encircled him, spinning his body in a frenzy.

The heat gushed out of Gulph. He could feel it leaving him— the fire, the light, the dizzying sense of being in touch not just with the roots of magic, but the roots of the world itself.

It's going, he thought, and while a small part of him felt sad, another part felt relieved.

Elodie's thought chimed against his. *Don't worry, Gulph. The magic isn't going away. It's just going to sleep. It will be there whenever we want it. It's in us forever.*

The crowns shrank into a blinding knot of light. It was so bright that Gulph couldn't bear to look at it. He could no longer see Vicerin at all.

If he's not dead after this, thought Tarlan, *he never will be.*

Now they were just ten steps from the platform at the top of the stairs. Eight steps. Seven. Gulph thought of Melchior, who had worked his magic through the power of numbers. Gulph's own magic—and that of his siblings—was different, but no less strong. Nevertheless, his feet felt heavy. Every movement was an ordeal. Beside him, both Tarlan and Elodie were gasping with the effort.

Five steps. Three, two, one . . .

By now, the glowing crowns had shrunk almost to nothing. They blazed briefly, then abruptly winked out of sight. In their place was a cloud of white smoke. The wind that had been howling through Gulph's head died to nothing. He felt suddenly cold, and completely exhausted. Elodie staggered, and Tarlan had to catch her before she could fall.

The smoke cleared.

"No," croaked Elodie. "It can't be. . . ."

Standing before them, his face slashed and bloodied, his once-shining armor now blackened and buckled, was Lord Vicerin. He was moving stiffly. He was grinning like a madman.

He was still holding the Sandspear.

"It protected him," growled Tarlan. "Just like it protected Hypiro."

The Sandspear vibrated in Vicerin's trembling hand. Light crackled at its tip, like a tiny thunderstorm. Now Gulph understood where all the power they'd unleashed had ended up.

What do we have to do to defeat him? he thought hopelessly.

"Do you still believe in the power of the prophecy?" Vicerin growled. "You would do better to believe in the power of me!" He circled behind the nearest of the three thrones, lips curled to reveal his enormous teeth.

"Put that thing down!" said Elodie. "It's over, can't you see that?"

Vicerin's delicately plucked eyebrows climbed up his forehead. "I think not, my dear. You see, this lovely spear is doing something rather special for me."

"It's making you even crazier than you were before," snapped Tarlan.

"It is making me invincible!" Vicerin retorted.

Gulph heard footsteps. Glancing round, he saw Captain Ossilius leading Kalia, Pip, and what looked like the entire army up the stairs toward them. Gulph had never been more pleased to see his old friend.

Vicerin's eyes flicked to Ossilius, then settled on Gulph.

"You can keep your thrones," he said, pressing his hand to his throat, where the three green jewels still dangled. "I may even let you have these pretty things—for the short time you have left to live. All I really need is what is in your bag—yes, you, the deformed one, I am talking to you!"

Gulph shifted his pack on his shoulders. He could feel the round shapes of the three crowns pressing through the cloth, as if eager to escape.

"Never," said Gulph. "You'll never have them."

"I disagree," Vicerin replied.

With a triumphant yell, he thrust the Sandspear toward Gulph. Gulph sprang backward, but not fast enough to dodge the beams of energy that shot from the end of the weapon. They encircled his body like hands made of burning glass. Hot tentacles tightened around his legs and neck. Fingers probed under his arms, stealing into his pack. Vicerin jerked the Sandspear like a fisherman reeling in his catch, and Gulph flew through the air toward him.

"Gulph!" shouted Tarlan, clutching at his brother.

Gulph landed heavily, and immediately started to wriggle. But the tentacles were knotted so tightly he could hardly even breathe. Vicerin loomed over him, preparing to stab the Sandspear down into his chest. Tarlan and Elodie raised their swords and prepared to rush to Gulph's aid.

Someone pushed past them and threw himself between Gulph and Vicerin. It was Ossilius.

"Let the boy go," snapped the former Captain of the Guard. His voice shook with fury, but the hand that was holding his sword to Vicerin's throat was as steady as a rock.

"The Sandspear will kill you before you can kill me," Vicerin crooned. "And the boy will not be saved."

"Take the crowns!" Ossilius growled. "Take whatever you want. Just let Gulph go!"

"Ossilius!" Gulph cried. "No!"

Vicerin looked suspicious, then pleased. "Are we to call this a surrender?"

"No," Ossilius answered. "More a distraction."

Without further warning, he struck an almighty blow with his sword—not at Vicerin, but at the flickering lines of light connecting Gulph's body to the end of the Sandspear. The glowing crystal blade made a hideous sucking sound as it sheared straight through them.

The tentacles of light that had bound Gulph grew slack and melted away. At once Tarlan and Elodie were there, pulling him to his feet.

Suddenly unbalanced, Vicerin staggered backward. He stabbed the Sandspear at Ossilius, shrieking in anger. A jagged bolt of light slammed into the captain's stomach, hurling him back between two of the thrones.

"No!" shouted Gulph. Shaking off his brother and sister, he rushed to where Ossilius lay in a pool of blood.

"Leave me," Ossilius croaked. "Don't let him . . ."

Something yanked at Gulph's pack. Already weakened, the straps snapped. Gulph lunged, but he was too late. Vicerin was running toward the rear of the platform, the pack clutched to his chest. Gulph clearly saw a flash of gold from one of the three crowns of Toronia poking out of the top. Nearby, more steps led down to a distant exit.

"Stop him!" Tarlan roared.

A green blur sped down from the cavern heights and smashed into the steps, right in front of Vicerin. The entire cavern trembled. The wyvern lifted its head from the crystal stairs, which were now crazed with cracks, and roared.

Vicerin darted sideways. One hand was clenched tight on Gulph's pack and its precious cargo; the other held the Sandspear. The chains around his neck snapped, and the three green jewels scattered.

Smash! A second wyvern dived down, crash-landing on the edge of the platform and forcing Vicerin to backtrack completely. Crystal showered down from above. Vicerin raced behind the thrones toward the thickest of the pillars supporting the ceiling.

Gulph saw there was a door set into the pillar.

"Tarlan!" he cried, unwilling to leave the badly wounded Ossilius. "Elodie! Block his escape route!"

Elodie ran to the pillar and took up station in the doorway. Meanwhile, Tarlan had set off to intercept Vicerin.

"Tarlan!" shouted Gulph. "Be careful! He's still got the—"

Glassy fire flashed from the end of the Sandspear, aimed right at Tarlan's head. Dropping beneath the sizzling light, Tarlan threw himself headlong across the smooth crystal, sliding clean over the platform's edge and tumbling out of view down the steps.

Now there was nothing between Vicerin and Elodie.

Slam! The third wyvern crashed into the pillar, just above Elodie's head. With a scream of surprise, Elodie leaped aside. The doorway folded in on itself. Broken chunks of crystal showered down, creating a mountain of rubble between her and Vicerin. The huge impact shook the cavern from top to bottom, knocking half the surrounding army off their feet.

Vicerin tripped and went sprawling, his arms thrown wide. Gulph's pack split down the middle, spilling the three crowns across the platform.

Vicerin's fingers flew open. The Sandspear flew through the air and landed on the seat of the gold throne.

For a moment, all was still.

Ossilius twitched in Gulph's arms. "You know . . . what he will choose," the captain croaked. "Make sure . . . you get there . . . first."

Gulph stared at Vicerin, poised on the far side of the platform. Their eyes locked. Between them stood the three thrones of Toronia.

Crowns. Jewels. Weapon.

Which would Vicerin go after?

All he's ever wanted is power, Gulph thought.

That told him everything he needed to know.

"I will kill you all!" screamed Vicerin. Ignoring the crowns, ignoring the jewels, he lunged toward the Sandspear.

Gulph set off at the same instant.

As long as he's got that weapon in his hands, nothing else matters to him, not even the prophecy.

Vicerin was six steps away from the Sandspear.

Gulph ran straight toward the first throne, leaping at the last moment and spinning through the air over its emerald back. He landed on his hands, bending his arms to cushion the impact, rolling and springing upright to continue his sprint.

Vicerin now had just four steps to go.

His breath burning in his throat, Gulph ran at the middle throne, the one made of ruby. He was about to jump again when he realized with horror that he was already too late. Acrobatics were all very well, but tumbling took up precious time.

What am I supposed to do? Run straight through the throne?

The thought came and went in a flash. Accompanying it was a sudden blast of hot air. Gulph's whole body began to tingle, telling him what it wanted to do.

But invisibility won't help me here!

There was no time to think. No time to doubt. He opened his body to the strange magic of his ancient desert roots. He felt the familiar liquid rush in his bones as he pushed his body into transparency, then cried out in astonishment as he realized he could . . .

. . . *just keep pushing!*

Running hard, ignoring the solid crystal bulk of the throne that was rearing up in his vision, Gulph allowed the desert heat to pump deeper than it had ever gone before. His body became light, like smoke, then thin like the air itself. He became invisible, then went beyond. He was there, and not there.

Gulph ran straight through the ruby throne as if it didn't even exist.

Continuing his headlong rush toward the gold throne, he extended his invisible, intangible hand. For the briefest second, he made his fingers solid enough to grab the Sandspear as he flashed right through the middle of that final obstacle. Having snatched up the weapon, he skidded to a halt and spun to face Lord Vicerin, who was still two paces short of where his prize had been.

With a shudder, Gulph shook off the magic he'd allowed to envelop him. He wondered how he must look to Lord Vicerin—a sweat-soaked boy materializing from nowhere, right before his eyes.

"Give that to me!" Vicerin growled.

Gulph brandished the Sandspear and was pleased to see his enemy shrink back.

"The prophecy holds!" he proclaimed. "Get back, you

cowardly, slimy thing! Do you hear me? You are nothing, and the prophecy holds!"

A sliver of crystal broke away from the cracked ceiling and tumbled through the air. The thorrods, who had been circling overhead, screeched warnings to the crowd below. The soldiers scattered just in time, leaving the sharp-edged fragment to crash down onto the foot of the steps.

Rainbow light poured through the hole in the ceiling, flooding the throne chamber with dazzling colors.

If victory looks like anything, thought Gulph in triumph, *it looks exactly like this!*

Gulph advanced, forcing Vicerin back against the gold throne. The light surrounded him, gave him strength. Vicerin cowered, his hands bunched against his chest, his face a mask of hatred.

"Kill me now, boy!" he spat. "You might as well!"

"That's exactly what he *isn't* going to do," said Elodie, clambering over the piles of shattered crystal.

"She's right," agreed Tarlan, appearing at the top of the steps. "Though if I still had my sword, I'd be happy to run you through myself."

"It's what you deserve," said Gulph. "But killing is no way for a king to start his reign. Or a queen."

"We will show you the mercy you denied to others," added Elodie.

"Mercy?" Vicerin looked suddenly hopeful.

"Behind bars," said Tarlan. "For the rest of your life."

"Prison?" Vicerin's lips pulled back from his teeth. "For one of such noble birth as I? You cannot possibly—"

"Be quiet!" snapped Elodie. "Toronia has heard enough from you!"

"But I must—"

SILENCE!!!

The chamber trembled again. Vicerin flew backward against the throne, his eyes flown wide. The crowd gasped.

Gulph exchanged an awed glance with his brother and sister.

Did we say that out loud? he asked.

Or did we just think it? asked Elodie.

Whatever we did, put in Tarlan, *it certainly shut him up.*

A groan rose up from the other side of the platform.

"Ossilius!" Gulph half turned, then hesitated. He stared at Tarlan. "I have to go to him!"

"Go," Tarlan replied. "We'll keep an eye on this maggot. Elodie?"

Elodie nodded. As she did so, a regiment of ghosts surrounded Vicerin. Leading them were two women wearing matching expressions of disgust. The first was Lady Darrand. The second was Lady Vicerin.

At the sight of the two women he'd killed, Vicerin crumpled.

Gulph thrust the Sandspear into Tarlan's hands and raced to where Ossilius lay. One of the ghosts followed him. They reached the wounded man at the same time and fell to their knees together before him.

The wound in Ossilius's chest was terrible, and the pool of blood he lay in was deep. Yet his old, lined face looked peaceful. He smiled at Gulph. Then he glanced at the phantom figure kneeling beside him. His smile widened to one of surprise and joy . . . then collapsed into dismay.

"Fessan," he croaked. He raised a trembling hand toward his son's scarred face. "You're here. But . . . but you're . . ."

"I am here, Father," Fessan replied. Gently he took his father's shaking fingers. "That is all that matters."

Ossilius's eyes turned back to Gulph. "My son," he said. "This is . . ."

"I know," Gulph replied. His eyes had filled with tears.

"Both of you," Ossilius whispered, reaching his other hand up to Gulph, who took it. "Both of you . . . here with me. My two sons . . . together . . ."

"Hush," said Gulph. "Don't try to speak." He could barely speak himself.

A small hand came to rest on his shoulder. He knew without turning that it was Pip.

"I brought your mother," his friend said. "I thought maybe . . ."

Now Kalia was kneeling beside them. She touched the palm of her hand to Ossilius's brow.

"Is there anything you can do?" Gulph asked.

Kalia shook her head, and Gulph's heart balled up in pain. "He is beyond my healing," she said. "I am sorry."

"No need . . . for sorrow," Ossilius murmured. His eyelids fluttered. "My work is done. You have it, Gulph. The crown . . . of Toronia. You have it. And I . . ."

He grunted. His eyes closed, pinched with pain. When they opened again, they were locked on Fessan.

"I have you," he said, the words flowing from him in a single, soft gasp. "My son . . . will you take me . . . with you?"

Fessan nodded. He was beginning to fade away.

"I am ready, Father," he said. "Let us go together."

At the same moment Fessan disappeared, Ossilius's face grew still. He looked happy. Gulph wished him happiness forever.

"I'm sorry," said Tarlan.

Gulph looked up to see his brother standing over him. The dancing light pouring through the hole in the ceiling splashed colors across his red-gold hair. Tarlan draped his tattered black cloak over Gulph's shoulders. Then he lifted Ossilius's sword and placed it in Gulph's lap.

Overcome with grief, Gulph broke down into helpless sobs.

Pip's arms enfolded him, then Kalia's. Gulph hunched over, filled with sorrow at the loss of the man who had befriended him in the dreadful prison known as the Vault of Heaven, what felt like so long ago.

Now it will be Vicerin who's locked up.

The thought broke through his sadness with unexpected urgency.

Out of nowhere, dread grabbed him.

Something is wrong!

He leaped to his feet. Wiping away his tears, he saw Lord Vicerin still surrounded by ghosts. Elodie stood before him, but she was turning away, clearly about to make her way over to her brothers. Vicerin was folded up like a flower.

"What's wrong?" said Tarlan, lifting the Sandspear.

"I don't know," Gulph replied. "I just suddenly thought . . ."

Vicerin brought his hands from beneath his cloak. In them he held a jeweled dagger. Even from this distance, Gulph could see it was a beautiful, ornate thing.

A deadly thing.

Taking the ghosts completely by surprise, Vicerin sprang to his feet. He raised the dagger. The tip of its blade was aimed at the center of Elodie's back.

"Elodie!" screamed Tarlan.

"No!" yelled Gulph at the same instant.

Elodie's eyes widened, but it was far too late for her to react. Already the blade was plunging down.

A streak of gold flashed down from above. A blur of wings enfolded the throne. A piercing squawk rang out through the chamber. A lethal beak snapped shut.

Theeta!

Lord Vicerin's body tightened, then relaxed. The dagger fell from his hand. For a moment, he dangled from Theeta's beak like a broken puppet. Then the beak opened, and he fell to the crystal floor, dead.

Theeta threw back her head and shrieked. At once, Nasheen and Kitheen flew down to join her, letting out harsh cries of triumph.

Shocked into silence, Gulph grabbed Tarlan's hand and rushed across the platform to where Elodie was standing, dazed. They hugged her tight. Rainbow light bathed them. They sobbed, and laughed, and sobbed again.

At last they broke apart. Joining hands, they made a circle.

"It's over," said Gulph.

"Yes," Elodie agreed. Like Gulph's, her cheeks were flushed and wet with tears. "It's all over at last."

Tarlan grinned. "Not quite."

CHAPTER 26

Tarlan stepped away from Gulph and Elodie. They seemed happy to wait in the silence that lingered after the death of Lord Vicerin, but he was ready for more. Not more fighting—Gulph was right, the war was over—but ready to take whatever action was needed to round off this long, strange day.

Is it day? he thought, gazing up through the ragged hole in the crystal ceiling. *Or is it night?*

The magical storm of light that had been hanging over the citadel was still raging, sending its shafts of color down into the throne room. What lay beyond it? The night sky? The midday sun? Tarlan had no idea.

Striding between the thrones, Tarlan bent and scooped up the three jewels from where they lay on the crystal floor. When he turned them over in his hands, their facets caught the rainbow light and turned it green.

He returned to the others in time to see Gulph handing the Sandspear to Kalia. Their mother cradled the weapon uncertainly.

"It's right that it should pass to you," Gulph reassured her. "It's from Pharrah, like you. We know you'll use it only for good."

"I will," Kalia replied. Reaching back over her head, she slipped the magical weapon through the strap of her robe, securing it on her back. "I swear it."

Bowing, she crossed the platform to where the three crowns were lying. She picked them up, one at a time, then went to stand near the ghosts, who had retreated to a respectful distance. Many of them—Lady Darrand and Lady Vicerin especially—were regarding the body of Lord Vicerin with a hatred so intense that even Tarlan couldn't miss it.

"The Realm of the Dead is too good for the likes of him," said Tarlan.

"It's where he's headed all the same," Gulph replied. Then his eyes widened. "Oh, but Ossilius and Fessan are there. What will Vicerin do to them when he . . . ?"

He broke off and gaped at Elodie. When Tarlan saw what she was doing, he gaped too.

Their sister was waving her hands slowly back and forth over Vicerin's body. Her eyes were half-closed, and her lips were moving, although Tarlan couldn't hear any words.

"What are you . . . ?" Gulph began.

"Wait, Gulph," said Tarlan. "Look."

A mist was rising from Vicerin's battle-damaged armor. As they watched, it condensed into the shape of a man—Lord Vicerin's ghost, floating an arm's length above his corpse.

The ghost's head swiveled to look first at Tarlan, then at Gulph, finally at Elodie. The ghost's arms reached out to the girl Vicerin had once called daughter.

The ghost was pleading with her.

Elodie bunched her hands into fists, then jerked them apart.

Vicerin's ghost disintegrated. Shreds of vapor flew apart like strands of rotted fabric, then vanished. Tarlan heard a long, soft sigh—and then silence fell.

"Is he . . . ?" Gulph began.

"Gone," said Elodie. Her shoulders slumped.

"Where?" Tarlan asked.

"Nowhere," Elodie replied. "He's *gone*."

"Well," said Tarlan. "Good riddance."

Elodie rubbed her palms slowly together, then dropped her hands to her side. "Yes. Good riddance."

Tarlan remembered the jewels. "Here," he said, holding them out.

Eagerly Gulph and Elodie each took the jewel that belonged

to them. Tarlan supposed that most people would think they looked identical. But they weren't, not quite.

Just like us, he thought.

"What are we supposed to do with them?" said Elodie, holding up the gold chain and letting her jewel swing to and fro in the rainbow light. "Do we just wear them?"

"I don't think so." Tarlan eyed the walls of the chamber, which were studded with jewels similar to theirs. "This place—it's just like the Isle of Stars. Only there it wasn't jewels—it was stones. Melchior told me to study them while I was waiting for him to get his magic back. He told me to remember what I saw."

"And did you?" asked Gulph.

"Yes." Tarlan tipped his head back and scanned the domed ceiling. "The stones looked like stars, and the patterns they made were the constellations." He waved his hand. "The patterns here are just the same."

"One jewel for each star," Elodie went on. She looked up at the ceiling. "There must be a place for them here."

"Three blank spaces, waiting to be filled," said Gulph.

"There!" said Tarlan. He pointed straight up, to the patch of ceiling directly above their heads. In the center of a triangular diamond slab were three tiny holes.

"Theeta!" Tarlan shouted.

She flew out of the light, her wings beating in silent, majestic rhythm, her golden feathers seeming to glow from within. Tarlan bounded onto the emerald throne, then leaped from it onto the thorrod's back. Throwing his jewel's chain around his neck, he bunched his fists into her ruff and bared his teeth into the wind.

"Nasheen!" he cried. "Kitheen!"

The other two thorrods swooped down from where they'd been circling, gathered up Gulph and Elodie, and launched themselves after Theeta.

As they climbed, Tarlan glanced down at the huge crowd gathered in the chamber below them. There were thousands of them—men and women, ghosts and animals. All of them together had helped to bring him and his siblings to this place, and this time.

Am I really in charge of all these humans now? he thought in wonder. *Oh, Mirith, if you could see me now.*

Theeta veered past one of the twisting diamond columns and pumped her wings hard, climbing faster and faster. The ceiling rushed toward them as if they might crash into it, but Tarlan laughed, knowing Theeta was in complete control.

When she reached the hanging slab of diamond, Theeta slowed to a hover. The three holes gaped, a perfect triangle waiting to be filled.

Tarlan unclipped the jewel from its chain and held it up.

He had just enough time to wonder if it mattered which hole he used, when something tugged at his hand. The jewel popped free of his fingers, hung suspended for a moment, then rose upward. Locating itself in the nearest hole, it settled into place with the tiniest of clicks.

Green light bloomed inside the jewel, more dazzling than the sun.

Throwing his hand across his face, laughing aloud, Tarlan steered Theeta away from the slab, allowing Nasheen to slip into place behind them. He watched, awestruck, as Elodie repeated his actions.

When her jewel was in place, it began to glow brilliant red.

Finally it was Gulph's turn. Standing upright on Kitheen's back, he thrust his jewel toward the one remaining hole. It leaped from his hand and thudded into position. In the depths of the gem, golden light flared.

Tarlan pursed his lips and whistled. Nasheen and Kitheen responded instantly, falling into formation on either side of Theeta.

The trio of thorrods landed together, their golden feathers reflecting the colorful light still flooding through the hole in the ceiling. As the triplets dismounted, and the giant birds folded their wings, the light began to fade.

"Look!" gasped Elodie. "The jewels!"

Tarlan tipped back his head and looked upward. One by one, the countless green gems set into the chamber walls were lighting up. A web of light raced up toward the ceiling, converging at the slab of diamond where the triplets' jewels were burning bright.

"It's beautiful!" cried Gulph.

As the jewels sprang into life in the walls, so the rainbow storm that had hung over the citadel died away completely. Blackness replaced it, and Tarlan had the answer to the question he'd pondered over earlier.

It's night. All the stars are coming out.

He clutched his arms around his chest, marveling at the patterns of the constellations. They reminded him achingly of the Isle of Stars.

They reminded him of Melchior.

"Are you all right, Tarlan?" Elodie asked, gently touching his arm.

He nodded, not trusting himself to speak.

The jewels blazed brighter still, then suddenly shrank to tiny pricks of white light. Warm wind blew past them. The ground shook. The walls of the throne room shimmered, then disappeared. The slab of diamond vanished too. But the three jewels—green, red, and gold—remained. Except they were no longer jewels.

They were stars.

Tarlan turned a slow circle. No longer contained by the towering walls, the platform now looked out across the city of Celestis. Crystal towers glistened beneath the starlight. Beyond them, Tarlan could see the darkness of the Isurian forest, the distant surge of the mountains to the north, the promise of Ritherlee to the south.

Listening hard, he even thought he could hear the snow-filled song of Yalasti.

A crowd of people surged up the steps toward them. Two figures rushed up to Elodie and spun her around—Sylva and Cedric, their faces splashed with mud and bright with happiness. Behind them came ranks of ghosts, led by Lady Vicerin and Lady Darrand, avenged at last.

A huge man with red hair forced his way through a line of soldiers. A gigantic hammer dangled at his belt. Clasping his enormous hands around Gulph's waist, the Defender of Deep Poynt raised Tarlan's brother aloft. His army cheered.

A wolf's howl rose from the far side of the platform. Mingled with it was a feline snarl and a triumphant, rumbling roar. It sounded like music to Tarlan. Grinning, he opened his arms wide to welcome Greythorn, Filos, and Brock, bounding in a row toward him. Following them was a tide of animals—horses and deer, foxes and flying eagles. The ground thundered beneath them.

"You are here!" yowled Filos, bowling him over. Tarlan hugged the tigron, burying his fingers in the blue-and-white stripes of her fur. Her warm tongue rasped across his face.

"Yes, I'm here!" He laughed. "We're all here!"

"And the battle is over," added Greythorn. He pressed his muzzle against Tarlan's cheek and winked his one good eye. "It is time to rest."

"Yes." Tarlan scratched the soft place between the wolf's ears. "I'm ready to rest."

"Another battle soon?" inquired Brock, gently shouldering Filos and Greythorn aside. Wrapping his muscular forelegs completely around Tarlan, the enormous bear squeezed him tight. "Brock will be ready for *that.*"

"I'm sure you will," Tarlan replied, laughing again as he gasped for breath. "Oh, it's good to see you all! I can't believe we're all together again! I can't believe we've done it!"

"*You* have done it," said Greythorn gravely. The wolf flicked his tail toward Elodie and Gulph. Hand in hand, laughing together, Tarlan's brother and sister were making their way toward them through the happy crowd. "You and your pack."

"You're all my pack," Tarlan replied.

Prying himself free from Brock's affectionate bear hug, he joined his siblings.

"We made it!" said Gulph, grabbing Tarlan's hand.

Gulph's green eyes shone; so did Elodie's. Tarlan knew that his must be shining too. He felt light on his feet, ready to fly.

I'm here, Mirith! I'm here, Melchior! And you're here with me. I'm sure of it.

Did the stars above him twinkle in reply? Or was it just the tears in his eyes?

"Are you ready, my dear children?" said a familiar voice.

Kalia was standing before the three thrones. Her gray robe hung from her slender body. Her red-gold hair wafted in the breeze. Her scarred face shone with happiness.

She was holding a round crystal tray.

On it were the three crowns of Toronia.

"Yes, we're ready," said Tarlan, regarding the crowns uncertainly. "Only . . . I don't think we know quite what to do."

Kalia smiled. "It is very simple. In fact, as a good friend might have told you, it is as easy as one, two, three."

Theeta nudged Tarlan with her large beak. "Take perches," she advised. "Ancients come. Ancients show."

Tarlan was about to ask who she meant by "ancients" when the three wyverns plunged down from the night sky. They took up position over the three thrones, two with wings of green crystal, the third with wings that seemed made of smoke. Then, slowly, they descended until their claws gripped the backs of the great crystal chairs.

The instant that happened, all three of the ancient creatures turned to stone.

"Well," said Tarlan. "Come on."

He led his brother and sister to the thrones. None of them asked which seat belonged to whom. Without a word, Elodie took the central ruby throne. Gulph took the gold throne to her right, and Tarlan the emerald one to her left.

The crystal seat wasn't hard and cold as Tarlan had anticipated, but soft and warm. Some kind of magic, he supposed. He looked up at the frozen wyvern poised like a statue above him.

"Thank you," he whispered. "Will you come again if I call?"

It would. He knew it. They all would. Wyverns and thorrods,

wolves and tigrons and bears. His whole pack. Their loyalty to him was beyond question.

But would he ever *need* to call on them again? *That* was the question.

As they all settled into their seats, a sigh passed from one side of the crowd to the other. A sea of faces gazed up at them, yet for a brief moment only the three of them seemed to exist. Alive. Together. Victorious at last.

Kalia walked up to Gulph. Her face was solemn now. The crowd hushed. She held up the first of the three crowns. Its golden contours gleamed in the starlight.

"King Agulphus," she proclaimed, and lowered the crown onto his head.

She moved along the line to where her daughter was waiting. They looked so alike, Tarlan thought.

"Queen Elodie." Kalia held the second crown high, then nestled it into the waves of Elodie's red-gold hair.

Now she was approaching Tarlan. He saw his own face reflected in the gold of the crown, and in his mother's eyes. He felt hot and cold.

"King Tarlan."

He closed his eyes. Something touched his head, embraced it. The crown was both light as a feather, and heavy as the world. It was a perfect fit.

The crowd roared. The ground shuddered as ten thousand feet stamped against it.

Opening his eyes, Tarlan grinned at his mother. Then, without thinking, he stood up. Beside him, Gulph and Elodie did the same. The crowd bellowed loud approval.

Glancing at Gulph, Tarlan shrugged, planted one foot on the seat of his throne and hoisted himself up to stand on it. Laughing, his siblings followed suit.

I never planned this, Tarlan thought in wonder as he gazed out across the jubilant throng. *I even tried to run away from it. But I ended up here all the same.*

Now that he was here, he couldn't imagine being anywhere else.

Tarlan held up his hands. The crowd fell silent. Gulph and Elodie regarded him with amusement.

"A speech?" Elodie smiled. "From you?"

"You think you two are the only ones who can make speeches?" Tarlan grinned.

The sky was growing lighter now, and the stars were beginning to dim. All except the three burning jewels that were the prophecy stars.

"Dawn is coming!" Tarlan cried. He pointed toward the orange glow that was building on the distant horizon. "A new day! The last day of the Thousand Year War is over. The first day of the new age is here. The Age of Peace!"

The crowd erupted again. Tarlan waited for the uproar to die down, then went on.

"We stand before you today—me, my brother, my sister. We

also stand *with* you, just as we will on all the days that are to come. We will serve you. We will protect you. All the people who live in Toronia, all the animals who share their world, and all those who walk in the Realm of the Dead."

As he said this, Tarlan fancied he heard an old, croaking voice floating past him on the wind. A wizard's voice.

One . . . two . . . three, the voice whispered. *A simple spell . . . to end with.*

"Everyone used to think the three realms meant Idilliam, Isur, and Ritherlee. But they don't." Tarlan looked at Elodie. He looked at Gulph. His brother and sister nodded.

Go on. That was Elodie's voice in his head.

Yes, go on. That was Gulph.

"The first realm is the realm of men and women," Tarlan continued. "The second is the realm of the beasts. The third is the realm of the dead. *These* are the three realms of Toronia."

The cheers of the crowd were deafening now. Tarlan could feel the noise vibrating through his body, though the ground. It was as though Toronia itself was rejoicing.

"Three realms united in peace at last!"

The sun rose. The prophecy stars burned brighter than ever.

"United by the Crown of Three!"

The new day began.

EPILOGUE

— Ten Years Later —

Theeta shifted her weight in the nest. The knot of branches and moss had been growing harder of late. But then, the nest was old. Just like Theeta.

Craning her neck, she peered over the low wall surrounding the top of the tower. Below, the crystal buildings of the human city sparkled in the sunlight. Theeta did not understand why humans chose to spend so much time living under cover. But there was a lot about humans that she didn't understand.

Still, the city did look beautiful.

She moved again, but still she could not get comfortable. Her back ached. No matter. It was just her old body reminding her that there was something she must do.

Reminding her that the time had come.

Wincing a little, Theeta buried her beak in her right wing and plucked out one of the long flight feathers. She turned it in the sun, so that it sent beams of golden light out into the day.

It did not take long for the others to come. Nasheen arrived first, her pale breast flashing bright. She landed on the wall and croaked her greeting. A moment later, Kitheen arrived. Were those the first signs of gray in his black feathers? Theeta thought so.

"Death feather," Theeta said. "Thorrod take."

She held out the feather.

"Theeta live," Nasheen protested. "Theeta stay."

Kitheen cocked his head in surprise. But, in his usual fashion, he said nothing.

"Theeta go," said Theeta. "Theeta old. Theeta die."

They sat for a while in silence, the three thorrods, as the sun rose slowly toward noon. Theeta remained patient and still, giving her old friends the time they needed to accept this new, hard truth.

At last, Nasheen bent toward her. Theeta did not move. Nasheen closed her beak gently around the long golden feather. Her black eyes were wet pools. She lodged Theeta's feather carefully between the feathers of her own wing, then settled back onto her perch.

"Give Tarlan," Theeta instructed. "Tarlan take. Tarlan know."

"Tarlan human," Nasheen replied uncertainly.

"Tarlan know," Theeta reassured her.

Stretching her wings painfully, Theeta stood. Old, dry branches broke beneath her wrinkled claws. No matter. She would not be needing them again.

"Not go," blurted Nasheen.

"Time now," Theeta replied. "Remember Theeta."

"Never forget!" snapped Kitheen. He looked around, as if startled by the sound of his own voice. Quietly—almost too quietly to hear—he added, "Kitheen love."

"Love Kitheen," echoed Theeta, touching the tip of her beak to the tip of his. She did the same with Nasheen. "Love Nasheen."

Spreading her wings, she heaved herself slowly into the air. The weight of the world fell away, and, as she always did when she was flying, Theeta felt free.

"Where go?" Thorrods rarely asked questions, but Nasheen clearly could not help herself.

"Fly home," answered Theeta. "Ice home. Mountain waits."

Her two friends gazed up at her, wings twitching, clearly wanting to join her. Theeta's feather shone from its temporary home in Nasheen's wing. Soon Tarlan would have it. He would know what it meant.

"Stay now," Theeta soothed. "Stay well. Theeta happy."

Cupping her wings around a billow of wind, she rose high, then dived down past the top of the tower, gathering speed as she went. Gradually the aches left her body. She swooped beneath a curving arch of crystal and made a long, banking turn to the south.

The streets below were filled with humans. Some tilted their heads up and waved as Theeta sped past. But most were more interested in the celebrations going on in the main city square. Scanning the crowd with her keen eyes, Theeta picked out the young man Gulph had become. His back was still twisted, but he had grown tall, almost as tall as his siblings. Gazing into his gentle face was a curly-haired woman whose name, she knew, was Pip. Today they had joined their hands and joined their lives. Theeta, who had never had a life-mate of her own, wished them all the joy of the world.

As Theeta passed over the happy couple, she saw Gulph shaking the hand of a bearded man in a bright purple robe.

Otherland human, she thought, remembering the strange ships that had come in from the sea, and the terrible army they had spilled across the land. Now Gulph had made peace between Galadron and Toronia, and old enemies had become new friends. It was a sort of magic.

Melchior would have approved.

After clapping the Galadronian on his back, Gulph gathered up Pip in his arms and spun her away through the mass of dancing, singing humans. They whirled so fast that their feet hardly seemed to touch the ground. Almost as if they were flying.

Reaching the edge of the crowd, Theeta spotted Elodie, tall and beautiful in her golden armor. Her long hair framed sharp, intelligent features, and her hand rested on the sword she always wore at her side. Theeta sensed that someone equally elegant was walking beside her, although there was nobody to be seen.

Gone human, she told herself. *Spirit soul.*

Elodie made her way through the knots of humans around her, continually speaking and pointing and nodding, clearly giving out instructions, clearly in control. Theeta guessed it was Elodie who was in charge of the wedding celebration, just as she was in charge of Toronia's peacekeeping army, which kept human affairs running smoothly across the kingdom.

Human affairs. Such complicated things. Theeta supposed she would miss them. But Yalasti beckoned.

Soaring over the outskirts of the city, Theeta scanned the park-lands until she spotted a familiar figure crossing one of the neatly trimmed lawns. He was the tallest of the three, broad and muscu-lar, his red-gold hair cropped short. Yet Theeta still saw a boy with lanky limbs, a tangle of hair, and the wilderness in his soul. Her heart swelled in her chest, and her wings faltered. Should she fly down to meet him? But, if she did, he would plead with her to stay.

Yet Theeta knew she had to go.

Nasheen would give Tarlan the feather, and Tarlan would know everything he needed to know. The feather contained Theeta's wish that he should live a long and happy life. It was her final gift to the only human she had ever truly loved.

It was her good-bye.

She steered a course behind the trees, so that Tarlan would not know she was there. In any case, his attention was on something else: the lame wolf cub he had rescued on his latest tour of the kingdom. They called him the Protector, and Theeta thought that was only right. Tarlan was strong. In his sure, human hands, Toronia would stay safe for a long, long time.

Tarlan whistled and pulled some meat from his pocket—scraps from the wedding feast. The wolf cub limped eagerly over and took the food from his master's hands. Tarlan knelt and fussed the little creature. Across the distance between them, Theeta felt the warmth of his love.

A gray-bearded human emerged from the trees and trotted over the grass. It was Captain Leom, beckoning Tarlan to come back to the celebrations.

"Join him," Theeta croaked under her breath. "Together stay."

Tarlan shouted a greeting to his old friend. To Theeta's ears, his cries sounded little different from the cries of the baby she had discovered in the Yalasti snow, all those years ago. It was Captain Leom who had placed the infant Tarlan down, and it was Theeta who had picked him up.

Now it was time to give him back.

Theeta flew on, past the statue of Captain Ossilius that stood in the south corner of the park, then out over the forests of Isur. The sun crept past the high point of noon. By the time it began to sink into the afternoon, Theeta had reached the big river, and Ritherlee beyond.

Air streamed past. The day flowed with it. Fields filled with crops. Animal herds. Running streams and rolling hills. There a castle of strong red stone, newly built in the place where Castle Vicerin had once stood. Humans filled its courtyards, and when Theeta flew past, they smiled and waved. Peace. Everywhere peace.

The sun sank into the west. The air chilled and the land rose. Hills became mountains. Grass gave way to snow.

Theeta climbed higher. The aches were back, deep in her bones. But it did not matter. Her wings moved smoothly, easily. When she finally landed, she would not need to move them again.

The mountains slipped by. Ice enveloped the world. The sky turned first orange, then red. Theeta was gold inside the light of the setting sun. Behind her, just visible to her sharp thorrod eyes as a distant, shimmering glow, twinkled the crystalline light of the human city she had left behind.

Three more wing beats, and that light would disappear from her vision.

Two wing beats.

One.

The far-off light melted into the sunset and was gone. Theeta flew on. She was old. She was tired. But, like Toronia, she was at peace.

She was nearly home.

Don't miss the new series
from #1 *New York Times* bestselling
author Brandon Mull.

DRAGONWATCH

EBOOK EDITION ALSO AVAILABLE

Aladdin
simonandschuster.com/kids

Looking for another great book?
Find it
IN THE MIDDLE.

Fun, fantastic books for kids
in the in-beTWEEN age.

IntheMiddleBooks.com

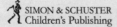 SIMON & SCHUSTER
Children's Publishing   f /SimonKids   🐦 @SimonKids